"What is going on, Ben?"

"First you, then Rita. You're both acting so strange," Jill said.

Ben's palms began to sweat. Could Rita know?

Oh, God, did everyone already know?

"Ben?" Jill moved her hand up to his cheek.

He touched her fingers and drew them to his mouth. He kissed them. "I love you," he said.

She didn't move. He knew that she knew there was more, that he was holding on to something.

He cleared his throat.

"Something's happened."

Off Season

Jean Stone

BANTAM BOOKS

NEW YORK   TORONTO   LONDON   SYDNEY   AUCKLAND

In memory
of my parents—
who would be pretty amazed.

This is a work of fiction. Names, places, characters, and incidents
are either the product of the author's imagination or are
used fictitiously. Any resemblance to actual persons,
living or dead, or locales is entirely coincidental.

Off Season

A Bantam Book / January 2001

ISBN 0-553-58086-8

Published simultaneously in the United States and Canada

Bantam Books are published by Bantam Books, a division of Random
House, Inc. Its trademark, consisting of the words "Bantam Books"
and the portrayal of a rooster, is Registered in U.S. Patent and
Trademark Office and in other countries. Marca Registrada.
Bantam Books, 1540 Broadway, New York, New York 10036.

PRINTED IN THE UNITED STATES OF AMERICA

OPM   10   9   8   7   6   5   4   3   2   1

Acknowledgments

Thanks to Sgt. Flora Bergeron of the West Springfield, Mass., Police Department; Lydia Kapell, M.D.; Meg Mastriana, L.I.C.S.W., Crisis Program Director at the Psychiatric Crisis Center, Springfield, Mass.; and special thanks to Cindy Smith, M.S., Learning Solutions Partner, Motorola University, Boynton Beach, Fla.
Also thanks to Dana and Marilyn of Bickerton & Ripley Books, Edgartown, Mass., for their on-going support!

Chapter 1

Mindy Ashenbach sat in the middle of her quilt-covered bed, yanking red yarn from her Raggedy Ann's head.

"Bastard," she muttered with each pull, feeling bittersweet satisfaction in using a swear word that would have made her grandfather mad. She tugged another clump, then squeezed her eyes shut. "Rotten bastard."

She sat quiet a moment, half-holding her breath, half-waiting for punishment. But the room was silent—the whole house was silent, the same way it was after school every day when she came home from helping at Menemsha House.

What made her think today would be different?

What made her think that even if anyone knew what had happened, they would have cared?

She flung the now hairless doll across the small room. It bounced off the windowsill and landed with a thud beneath the slant-roof dormer. It wasn't as if she needed the dumb doll anymore. She was ten, after all. Too old to believe that I-love-you-heart crap.

She sucked in her lower lip and folded her arms. Then somewhere inside her a tremble began, like the rumblings of a volcano she'd seen on TV. It started in her belly, the place where it ached sometimes when she was scared. It started in her belly and stuttered its way up her chest to her throat. Then she opened her mouth, and out it came: one big wailing cry.

"Bastard!" she cried out. "Bastard! bastard!" She wondered if this was what it felt like when you died, if your insides ended up coming out, if all of your hurt ended up on the floor, facedown and alone like Raggedy Ann.

Suddenly, the door opened.

"Mindy? What the hell are you doing?" It was her grandfather.

She clutched her aching belly and tried to lick the wet places that were on her cheeks.

"You were supposed to make meat loaf for dinner," he snarled. That's when she smelled his familiar sea-scent, the warning that he'd been fishing today and he would be tired. "The last time I checked," he continued, "meat loaf takes more than an hour. Now quit your day-dreaming and get downstairs." He started to close the door, then stopped, as if sensing something was not right. "What's the matter with you, girl? You hear from your mother again?"

Anytime Mindy was upset, Grandpa figured it was because her ne'er-do-well mother, as he called her (his ne'er-do-well daughter-in-law, reckless widow of his ne'er-do-well son, Mindy's father), had phoned or sent a post-card from an exotic port-of-call like Exuma or Caracas or wherever the yacht she was captaining that week or that month or that year had taken her now.

But no, it was not her mother who had upset Mindy.

It was that bastard. Who hadn't ended up caring about her any more than anyone else.

Grandpa stood at the half-open door, waiting for an answer. If Mindy said yes, Mom had called, she knew it would end the conversation: Grandpa would groan his grumbly, cigar-smoked-up groan, and go away. All she would have to do was lie. Then everything would be back to normal.

But her belly ached.

And throat had closed up.

And her doll no longer had hair.

"Ben . . . ," she said quietly.

Grandpa sighed and stepped inside the room. "I can't hear you, girl."

She sniffed. God, she hated that she'd sniffed like Lisa Pendergast, the crybaby of the fourth grade. She closed her eyes. "Ben Niles," she managed to say.

He grabbed her shoulders. Her eyes flew open. Grandpa's face was all of a sudden in her own. "What about Niles?" he barked.

It was no secret to Mindy or half the damn world that Grandpa and Ben were not friends. But the way Grandpa's steely eyes bored into her now was as scary as the night she'd come face to face with a big ugly possum.

She wondered if Grandpa was going to have a heart attack like he did last year after the bluefins stopped running.

He shook her a little. "What about Niles?"

She tried to swallow. She wanted him to let go. "Nothing," she whispered.

His grip grew tighter. "What about him?" he shouted. "Did he hurt you?"

Mindy lowered her eyes, thinking that, yes, Ben had hurt her. Not the way Grandpa was hurting her now, but he'd hurt her. Her eyes were filling with tears again. She blinked. The tears fell on her jersey.

Grandpa began to pant. "Did he touch you?" he hissed. "Did that son of a bitch touch you?"

And then she realized why he was so upset. She'd seen those movies at school, the ones about sex. The ones that warned you not to let yourself be *vulnerable,* and what to do if some man (or woman) touched you *there.* She looked at her grandfather but did not respond.

The hissing grew silent. Then Grandpa said, "Where, girl? Where did he touch you?"

She looked up at Grandpa. He didn't look like his heart was going to attack. Instead, he looked almost as if, like her, he was going to cry, like he was sad and worried and afraid all at once. All for her. For half a second Mindy thought he was going to hug her. The only one who'd ever done that was Ben. And he hated her now.

"You can tell me," Grandpa said. His voice was softer now, his grip less intense. "Please, Mindy. Just tell me. Goddammit. Where did he touch you?"

She looked across the room to hapless, hopeless Raggedy Ann, then back to her grandfather, who still waited for an answer. And in that instant she decided that even though Ben hated her now, maybe Grandpa did not. Maybe somebody loved her, after all—her grandfather, her own flesh and blood.

Mindy slowly put her hands on her chest, on top of her red-and-white-striped jersey, right where her nipples were trying to grow breasts. "Here," she said quietly. "He touched me here."

Chapter 2

 Ben Niles sat on the floor of his Menemsha House museum and stared at the pile of cedar and oak wood sticks that he would craft into an old-fashioned lobster trap as soon as he figured out how.

He raised his Red Sox baseball cap, ran his hand through his thinning hair, and laughed. This was, he reminded himself, his dream. No longer the premier restoration guru of old Yankee houses, Ben now played with sea-weathered sticks instead of smooth-polished black walnut, collected two-buck admission fees instead of five-figure paychecks, and savored eager smiles of elementary school kids instead of kowtowing to arrogant rich folks who wanted their million-dollar houses upgraded to two.

Since he'd met his wife, Jill, he'd given it "all" up. The same way she'd given up her high-profile television career to be with him on Martha's Vineyard. And now, thanks to Jill, Ben had found passion in both his life and his work, which included finding new ways to teach kids the crafts of their ancestors. The latest was the damn lobster trap, which he was staring at hopelessly when the telephone rang with blessed distraction.

It was his wife, calling from the mainland—Vermont, to be exact.

"I miss my new husband and I love him and I can't wait to come home," Jill said, her voice as soft as the silk of her nightgowns that he loved to feel brush his skin in their bed, that he loved to slide off her to make room for him. He looked down at his jeans, grateful that fifty-three was not too old for the enormous erection his wife could unwittingly produce. His glamorous, second-chance, *seven-years-younger* wife, his friends had teased. Ben had smiled at their envy, but silently was often stumped that a city-savvy, classy lady like her saw anything at all in a common rogue like him.

"I miss you and I love you and I can't wait for you, too," he said, and realized that he'd never have talked to his beloved Louise that way, but then, they'd been the same age and had grown more sedate than romantic in the years before her death. He cleared his throat. "Do you know how to build lobster traps?" he asked his new, city-savvy wife. *Her* forefathers, after all, were native islanders. He was merely a transplant from Baltimore, though he'd now lived on the Vineyard more than half of his life.

· "I watched my father make them." The softness in her voice now sounded even softer, a little depressed maybe, a little bit blue.

Lonely, he figured. *Like him.*

"I thought he owned the great 1802 Tavern," he said, trying to lift her mood, trying to pretend that talking on the phone was as good as sitting next to each other, sharing the same air.

"He owned the tavern, and he sold the traps to the tourists. To use as coffee tables."

Yes, her voice was definitely depressed.

A pretend laugh came from Ben's throat. "No! Not lobster trap coffee tables! Did he paint on velvet as well?" He unlaced his boots and took them off.

The laugh she returned was too late and out of sync, a laugh with an edge not just of loneliness, but of something . . . else. He wanted to ask what was wrong, but she said, "You'll thank me when I show you how the kids can use different colors and patterns to customize their lobster trap 'trademarks.' And you'll be glad when I show you how to load them with bricks so they won't sink in the water. The traps, not the kids. Oh, and you might want to call them lobster *pots*. It's more—authentic."

"Like your father's?" He pushed aside the pile of sticks with his wool-socked foot. Maybe she was just tired.

"If I didn't love you," she said with a feeble attempt at nonchalance, "I would hang up now."

"Please do," he replied. "Hang up and come home. I miss the hell out of you."

Her tender, small moan said more than a million words could have.

"Honey?" he asked. "Is everything okay?"

She paused a moment, then said, "Sure. I've lined up the last two interviews for tomorrow. I'll be home the day after that."

He nodded as if she were there in the room. He was proud that Jill was an independent producer now, even though it meant she was away too often, putting together "video features," she called them, then trying to sell them, if not to the networks then to feeder services that passed them on to television stations to use in their news slots. He was proud, yet frustrated for her, because the work was slow going and success had not yet kicked in.

Sort of like with Menemsha House, a dream in the making.

"How was your day?" she asked.

"Good," he said. "Great." He did not tell her that a busload of paying autumn tourists had canceled their trip to the museum today; he did not tell her that he and Mindy Ashenbach had had a misunderstanding and that she'd run home in tears; he did not tell her that he'd spent the last two hours reviewing the museum's pitiful books. He did not tell her these things because he did not want her to worry any more than she already did.

She paused another minute, and Ben was not sure if she was thinking of him or of that something "else" again. Then she asked, "Anything on Sea Grove?"

Sea Grove. He'd almost forgotten. "Shit," he said, "this is the first of October. I have to try and get another building permit this week." Sea Grove was a proposed development of exclusive waterfront homes whose construction could generate local jobs and boost the island economy, including his own. But the town was meagerly doling out the permits, eight per month, on the first Tuesday of each month, first come, first serve. So much for overbuilding on the island. "Hey," he said, hoping humor would help, "I have an idea. Maybe I should put a lobster trap coffee table in every living room."

"Get out of that place and go home," Jill said, her voice once more forcing cheer. "Maybe my daughter has made you a gourmet dinner."

"Ha!" he responded, knowing that eighteen-year-old Amy was less capable of cooking than Ben was of making lobster traps. Pots. Whatever they were.

"I love you," they told each other before hanging up. Ben returned to his work. For their dreams to come true, one of them had to have a good grip on life, and he guessed that right now, that one needed to be him.

It would have been easier to have told him, right then on the phone before she went home from Vermont. It would have been easier, but then he would have worried and there might be no need for that, not now or not ever.

There might be no need because she could simply say no.

Then again, Jill thought, moving from the small round

table to the hard hotel bed, saying no to Addie Becker was tantamount to not feeding a pack of hungry lions: you'd have to learn quickly how to get out of the way.

She turned back toward the phone, deciding to listen to the message again.

It had come only thirty minutes ago to Ben's house in Oak Bluffs, the place he'd converted, in part, to a studio for Jill, a postproduction facility in honor of her new career.

She dialed the number, then the code to retrieve saved messages.

"Jill, it's Addie. I need a favor."

Her tone was not acerbic, not like the last time they'd spoken, three years ago, when Jill had been struggling to surgically extricate herself from the agent's acrylic-fingernailed clutches. At a huge financial expense, she'd finally succeeded.

"The network wants to reformat. Maurice Fischer—remember him?—has asked if you'd consider a temporary slot in February, as a fill-in for Lizette. February," she repeated. *"Sweeps, darling. Remember them?"*

Addie paused, and Jill braced herself for what she knew was coming next.

"Before you say no, Jill, think about your flagging career. Then call me. Pronto."

Addie's voice stopped, and the machine beeped three times to signify that there were no more messages, no eager requests from networks or feeder services for packages of Jill's own production, no other offers of fame or fortune.

Once, of course, she could have had it all. But it had been her choice to walk out on *Good Night, USA,* the network "good news" television newsmagazine that had been conceived by her, but had gone on to Emmy-award-winning acclaim without her.

It had been her choice to have Lizette French replace

her as the on-air TV co-anchor to Christopher Edwards—
the man dubbed by the media as "the sexiest man alive"
and, by Ben, "Mr. Celebrity."

It had been her choice to bail out on her partnership
with Christopher off-air, too, trading in his huge pear-
shaped diamond and international renown for Ben's
plain gold band and life on an island.

They were choices she had not once regretted.

Soon after she left the show, Jill spent two years heal-
ing, coming to terms with the loss of both of her parents,
and helping Ben restore her legacy, the white sea captain's house in Edgartown that had been in her family for
generations. She and Ben turned the widow's walk into a
spectacular Jacuzzi room and added a long back porch
for red geraniums and Adirondack chairs and a great
view of the harbor. She'd even brought her mother's gardens back to life, and now blue hydrangea and pale yellow beach roses and tall wonderful wildflowers gently
swayed in the breeze that drifted in off the water.

Last summer she'd married Ben, the man she'd probably fallen in love with the first time she'd seen him more
than three years ago, when she'd opened the door wearing no makeup and sporting just-rolled-out-of-bed hair.
The fact that the bed she'd just rolled out of she'd been
sharing with Christopher had not mattered much at the
time.

But it had become a huge part of why she had to say
no now.

Still, Addie was right. Alone, on her own, Jill was having a difficult time reshaping her career. Even getting
good freelancers, shooters and editors, was tough. The
one she was using here in Vermont she'd begged out of
Boston with a steep one-shot fee.

There was a time she never had to ask if someone
wanted in on a job, because success indeed bred success,
and everyone wanted to be associated with winners.

But right now she couldn't get a nibble from a network, let alone a commitment from one story to the next, not from a feeder service, not from someone to shoot it.

Blackballed, Ben had said. He blamed Addie, of course, saying that the barracuda of an agent must have had more power than they'd once thought.

Life in the limelight, for all its glamour and glitz, was vicious and fleeting and all a big game.

Yet for reasons she did not understand, Jill did not pick up the phone now, return Addie's call, and simply say "Thanks, but no thanks."

After hanging up the phone, Ben had attacked the lobster trap with gusto. Some rope webbing for the "door," some slats for the sides, and suddenly it looked like the picture in the book he'd found at the library, a picture similar to the one Mindy said she'd downloaded from the Internet but that he was too damn stubborn to follow because he didn't like computers and didn't trust that dot-com stuff.

So now the coveted trap was complete, and it looked damn fine, and it was only eight-thirty—too early to go home to the empty house in Edgartown: empty, of course, except for Amy. Unlike Jill's son, Jeff, Amy had not fled for college in England as soon as their mother and Ben announced marriage plans.

He could go to his own daughter's over in Tisbury. With a husband and two kids, Carol Ann had become a good old-fashioned cook. Maybe she could rustle up some leftovers for her old man.

He supposed what he should do was work on the plans for Sea Grove. Or at least try and determine where he was going to find room for the kids to build these damn lobster traps now that he'd "mastered" the craft.

Maybe some coffee would help.

He stood up and stretched, then headed to the tiny galley kitchen he'd installed for emergencies like this. As he scooped coffee into the old aluminum pot, he thought he heard voices. And leaves rustling outside.

"Hello?" he called out. No answer. He shrugged and put the pot on the two-burner stove, when he heard voices again. "What the hell?" he muttered. He set down the pot and walked to the window.

He peered out the window into the darkness. It was, of course, impossible to see anything because on the Vineyard darkness was darkness, especially once summer had rolled into fall. He snapped off the inside light and hit the switch for the floodlights.

In the small parking lot, parked behind his prized '47 black Buick, was a police car. One man had already emerged and was leaning against the car, looking toward the museum. Then the driver's door opened, and a man Ben recognized as Hugh Talbot got out.

Ben squinted, as if squinting would tell him what the hell Hugh, the sheriff of Gay Head, was doing there. If Ben had been home at Edgartown and not at Menemsha, his first thought would have been that the museum had burned down. Again. The mere thought spun his memory back to that ache of a day when he had looked across the ridge of dunes and seen Menemsha House enveloped in red-orange flames, when fire had brought pain and anguish and death to the island.

Instinctively, he backed from the window. Then he noticed another man cut across the lawn and march toward the police car. Even in the darkness, the heavy gait and untrimmed beard made the man recognizable: it was Dave Ashenbach, Ben's unpleasant museum neighbor, Mindy's grandfather, the man who had finally stopped grumbling about "trespassing," or so Ben had thought.

He watched Hugh and Ashenbach exchange what appeared to be sharp, angry words. Then Ben sighed and

walked toward the door. Whatever was going on, he figured it was no coincidence that this small crowd had
gathered in his parking lot. Opening the door, he adjusted his Red Sox cap and stepped onto the front steps
without his boots, with only his heavy gray socks on his
feet.

"Gentlemen," he called, "what brings you here on this
fair night?"

The men stopped talking and looked in his direction.
No one said anything.

Scowling, he stepped down and padded toward the
men.

Hugh raised a hand, gesturing him to stop. Automatically, Ben did.

Hugh turned to Ashenbach. "Don't move a fucking
muscle," he said, "or we'll cuff you, too." Then the sheriff started toward Ben.

"Ben," he said slowly, as he approached, "how're you
doin' tonight?"

Something about Hugh's words or his walk or the way
his face was masked in the shadow from the floodlight
sent a sharp surge of warning up Ben's spine. "I'll be better once you've told me what the hell's going on."

Hugh turned again, as if to be certain Ashenbach had
not moved. Then he looked at Ben. "Let's go inside."

Something had definitely happened.

Jill. Quickly Ben shook off the thought. He had, after
all, just talked to his wife. But Amy? Had something happened to her?

Oh, God, he thought suddenly, a chilling numbness
slithering down his arms to his hands. Maybe it was not
about Jill's daughter, maybe it was about *his.* Maybe
something had happened to Carol Ann . . . or to one of
his grandkids. . . .

He didn't move. He couldn't move, as if someone had

poured cement into his socks. "Say what you have to say right here, Hugh."

The sheriff glanced back to the cruiser, then to Ben. "Inside," he repeated.

Somehow Ben managed to pick up his feet. Somehow he put one in front of the other in the slow-motion motion of time crawling forward to that unwanted destination known as Bad News.

Hugh followed him inside. He pulled Ben's hands behind him and clamped cold metal around his wrists. "Ben Niles," Hugh said, "you're under arrest for indecent assault and battery on a child under the age of fourteen."

Chapter 3

 Rita supposed she was having a hot flash. She supposed the reason she was standing at her window with her body half-hanging outside in the freezing autumn morning was because *that* time had finally arrived, though she was only forty-six and it seemed premature.

The bitch of it was, she knew she was right. She'd missed her period last month and the month before that, too, and the gravity-slide of departing estrogen had already begun to thicken her middle. She'd heard of those symptoms, but no one had told her she'd be nauseous as well. The only good part, Rita supposed, was that she'd no longer have to worry about getting pregnant—as if that were an issue, for the last time she'd checked, in order to get pregnant one had to have sex.

She stepped back from the window, wondering if she'd ever have sex again, and if this quasi-hot flash didn't have more to do with nerves than with her ovaries drying up.

Not that Rita Blair had anything to be nervous about.

Throwing on the long chenille robe that she still liked though she now could wear silk, she ambled downstairs to brew up some coffee, grateful with each step that she owned this old saltbox free and clear, yet still pained by the fact that it had been the life insurance that Ben Niles—Kyle's employer, Jill's husband, her friend—had taken on Kyle that had paid off her debts, that had set her financially free. The death of the son, saving the life of the mother. Though it had been over three years, Rita knew that would never be right.

As she entered the kitchen, her heart filled with Kyle, she didn't expect anyone to be at the table. She screamed, startling her mother, who screamed back in return.

"Jesus, Mother, you scared the shit out of me," Rita said once she'd regained her composure. "Do you have to creep around in the middle of the night?"

"It's not the middle of the night, it's eight in the morning," Hazel commented. "And if anyone's creeping around, it's you, not me. I've been sitting here for hours. I've had an entire pot of coffee and read *The Gazette* twice over."

Rita checked herself before saying *Bully for you*, remembering that Hazel was pushing eighty and was only up from Florida for a visit, though she'd declined to say for how long. She smiled at the woman whose hair was still as flame-colored as Rita's (L'Oréal number 4LR, because they were both worth it) and marveled that the recently widowed Hazel was in full makeup already, though there were no men around as far as Rita could tell.

"I think I've hit menopause," she announced to her mother. She did not mention that she dreaded this "passage" because she'd watched Hazel go from mere crazy to berserk between her mid-forties and fifties and was afraid she was in for the same.

"Have you missed your friend?"

Hazel had always referred to her period as her "friend," as if a monthly gush of blood accompanied by double-you-over cramps was the kind of friend every girl would want. "Yes," she replied. "Twice."

"You sure you're not pregnant?"

Rita closed the cabinet a little too firmly. "I'm forty-six years old, Mother. I'm not pregnant." She did not feel a need to announce that the last time she'd had sex was last summer. She had been with Charlie, of course, because since Kyle's death, Rita was just too damn depressed to go near anyone else. After that last time, though, she hadn't even gone near him again.

"Not because Charlie Rollins wants it that way. How many times has he proposed to you now?"

Gritting her teeth, Rita began making a fresh pot of coffee. She regretted ever confiding in her mother. "I'm not pregnant," Rita repeated. "And I'm not going to marry Charlie Rollins. I'm not going to marry anyone."

"Oh, that's right, I forgot. Little Rita is too good for any man. Well, your friend Jill isn't. She's made a nice marriage for herself. You should follow her example. Take a leap of faith."

It amazed Rita that, over forty years later, her mother was still holding her daughter up to the standards of Rita's childhood best friend. It also amazed Rita that such a mention could still send prickles up her spine.

"Sorry, Mother," she said, "but it appears that the only leap I'll be making is into menopause: hot flashes, memory lapses, and vaginal dryness."

Her mother picked up the newspaper. "Then get on the phone to Doc Hastings," Hazel said. "No sense in you becoming as nuts as I was."

As nuts as you are, Mother, Rita wanted to say, but instead she asked, "You think I should take estrogen?"

Her mother opened the paper again, perhaps to double-check the obituaries (a favorite pastime) to see if anyone she knew was there, life laid out on a page. "Just call Doc Hastings. Say it's an emergency. Or you'll end up like me and no one will have the guts to tell you."

Rita wondered if all mothers had the ability to read their daughters' minds. Then she wondered how it was that, yes, Jill had finally made a "nice marriage," while Rita could no longer even make a commitment to have sex, even with Charlie, the one man in her life she supposed she'd ever loved; Charlie Rollins, Kyle's father, though he'd known that too late.

Suddenly, the thought of coffee made her feel sick. She grabbed a bagel instead and ate it dry on her way upstairs to get dressed.

Even though the season was over, Rita had told Charlie she'd still work at the tavern. Without that she'd be bored and probably anxious as hell with Hazel around. Besides, working helped take her mind off Kyle now that the tourists had departed and distraction was tougher to find.

She still had her real estate business, such as it was, and still kept her magnetic SURFSIDE REALTY sign on her aging Toyota. But Rita had long since given up trying to compete with the big guys. Nor had she succumbed to working for them. It was a matter of principle: she was a native to the island—a thoroughbred Vineyarder, the yuppies called them—and the big business maggots were not.

Of course, there was Sea Grove now, the elegant development of big-ass houses that she and Charlie and Ben Niles were planning to build. *Imagine,* she thought as she unlocked the back door of the 1802 Tavern, *Rita Blair, a real estate mogul.* But the pleasure she might have taken in the concept was once again snuffed out by the fact it had been that damn double-indemnity policy that had provided her the funds to buy in.

Ben and Charlie had tried to talk her out of it.

"Kyle wanted your life to be easier," Ben had said not long after the funeral.

"Use the money for yourself, Rita," Charlie had added.

"Buy a new wardrobe, take a trip around the world. He would have wanted you to have some fun."

But fun was the last thing Rita had felt like having. So she'd paid off her bills, including the twenty grand she owed Charlie, and stuffed the rest in the bank, where it sat until the Sea Grove deal surfaced.

They said it was a risk, but Rita figured that so far her whole life had been nothing but risks, so what was one more? Anyway, she had to believe Kyle would be happy to think she'd invested "his" money with the two most important men in his life: his boss and his dad. It made the presence of the cash a little less painful.

The tavern was quiet when Rita closed the door behind her. She glanced around the low-ceilinged, oak-beamed kitchen. The shiny copper pots hung as they should—charmingly Old New England, visibly inviting to the peering eyes of tourists, and steering their gaze away from the beat-up aluminum pans stored under the cabinets, the pans that, in reality, they used.

Then she noticed the far end of the room, where Charlie Rollins sat, Charlie the tavernkeeper, since he'd bought the place from Jill's mother after Jill's father, George Randall, had died.

"Top of the morning to you, Charlie!" Rita exclaimed. She turned on the overhead light and inhaled the aroma of coffee. Charlie was a tea man who drank coffee only to burn off the fuzz from a morning-after linger of a scotch or two. He did not do it often. "Late night?" she asked.

His answer was a chuckle. "Careful, my dear, I might mistake your concern for jealousy."

The twinge that she felt might have been just that. Hopefully, it was only her hormones or lack thereof. She dropped her oversized nylon bag into the corner, glad that Doc Hastings had agreed to work her in this afternoon. It was always difficult to find people once winter set in—so many headed south with the Canada geese except for the diehards like Rita and Charlie and Ben Niles. "I'm hardly jealous, Charlie Rollins," she said matter-of-factly. "I'm only concerned about the health of one of my partners."

He stood up and chuckled again, then rubbed a thoughtful finger across his dirty blond mustache that, in all these years, still did little to make him look his age, which was the same as hers, give or take a few weeks. Every so often—not now, thank God—Rita saw a flash of Kyle in Charlie's brown eyes, or in his smile, or in his walk. "Don't worry about me, Rita. Worry about yourself. And worry about Halloween."

She groaned. "I thought we agreed not to do the party this year."

"Amy wants it."

Jill's daughter had worked at the tavern since her high school graduation in June. At first Jill had balked, but Amy had argued that it was her birthright, the establishment having been started by God-only-knew how many generations back of Jill's family in Edgartown. It was even believed that one or two of them still haunted the place. So now Amy wanted the party, and Amy got it, because all of them—Jill, Ben, Charlie, and Rita—treasured her so much with Kyle gone.

"Will she do it all?" Rita asked. "The decorating, the ordering, the advertising . . ."

Charlie smiled. "She can't do it all, Rita. She'll need your help. And Marge Bainey's." He took his cup to the sink and splashed in the dark contents. "Marge said she'd be glad to help Amy figure the booze."

Rita stared at Charlie's back. It did not escape her that he had not looked at her when he'd mentioned Marge, the middle-aged liquor distributor from the mainland who seemed to be spending more time lately on the island than off. "Well," she said, grabbing a pile of potatoes for today's chowder, "bully for her."

"Careful," Charlie said, "that sounds like jealousy again."

"And that sounds like the response of a typical male."

"Hey," he said, hauling a bucket of clams from the refrigerator, "cut me a little slack. I gave up on you a long time ago. Just like you wanted."

Rita picked up the shucking knife and got busy. "Good," she replied.

Child molester. Sex offender.

Ben stared out the Plexiglas, iron-barred doors—Jesus Christ, they really were *bars*—at the Dukes County jail, the goddamn *jail,* and wondered what he was supposed to do next.

The only lawyer he trusted on the island was Rick Fitzpatrick, so he'd called him at two in the morning when he'd finally realized that this was no joke, not even the sickest kind. Rick did his best, but he was a real estate attorney, for chrissake, a long way from F. Lee Bailey.

The cops had finally stopped questioning Ben at five o'clock—*cops,* his neighbors, his friends. They assured him their silence because, they said, Mindy was a minor and Ashenbach demanded it, and that guy was a loose cannon on a good day, never mind now that his granddaughter had been . . . molested.

Molested. Allegedly by Ben. The only man—maybe the only person—who had ever given the kid the time of day. He'd let her hang out at Menemsha House since he'd opened the museum, partly because she was a feisty, eager kid who was obviously lonely and neglected, partly because he thought it might help soften her grandfather, Dave Ashenbach, into not being so much of a pain in the ass about the fact that the museum property abutted his land.

He'd let her hang out at Menemsha House, and he'd shown her the ropes. He'd shared folk tales of old Yankees and legends of the Indians—just trying to let a kid know that somebody cared enough to be there. He'd even taken her to the cliffs at Gay Head a few times and told her about Noepe, his old Wampanoag friend, and showed her how to see pictures in the clouds in the sky.

He'd done all these things—and this was where it got him? With Ashenbach saying he'd molested Mindy? Or worse, according to the old blowhard, with *Mindy* saying he had?

Ben looked down at his feet that were once again in socks, because his boots and his belt and his watch and probably his goddamn mind, if he had one left, had been sealed in an envelope and stuck inside a locker.

Not that he remembered putting on his boots. It must have been some time after Hugh had followed him into the museum, but before he'd stood in the booking room, cuffed to the counter, bright lights shining on him, with a lump in his gut and no spit in his mouth.

Even now he was not sure what was happening.

There had been an arraignment this morning—closed to the public at the "judge's discretion." The judge was a woman who, thank God, Ben didn't know. Mindy was not there (the rights of a minor), so there had been no chance for Ben to meet his accuser, for him to look in her eyes and say, "Hey kid, what's going on?"

Yesterday, he'd been a bit sharp with her, and he readily admitted that. Well, hell, everyone else had left, and he'd thought she had, too. He'd gone into the office—that's when she'd squealed and jumped down at him from the transom over the door where she'd apparently been hiding. She scared him; he'd yelled.

That was the story he'd told the police, the story he'd

not had the chance to tell the judge because it was an arraignment, not a damn trial.

Not that it would have mattered. Because after he'd said what had happened, one of the cops asked, "Was that when you touched her?"

Ben's anger had flared and he shouted, *"I did not touch her!"* But then the cop said, "You grabbed her, didn't you?" and Ben admitted, "Only to break her fall."

And the cop replied, "Then you admit that you touched her." And he made some quick notes.

So Ben figured it was just as well he hadn't talked to the judge. It was bad enough when he looked in anyone's eyes. The guard who brought the "breakfast" of weak coffee and a dry croissant, the court reporter, the bailiff, and the D.A.—their eyes were all tentative, veiled by the same glare.

Child molester, the glare said.

The sad truth was, if he had been the one watching, he would have glared the same way.

The child is a child, the adult is not.

The adult must be guilty, unless proven otherwise.

Because next to murder, and oftentimes worse, it was the most heinous of imaginable crimes.

Bail had been set at one hundred thousand dollars, and Ben was cautioned not to go near the little girl—*the little girl,* the judge had kept emphasizing, as if Ben didn't know Mindy, hadn't known her for at least six or seven years, since her father had died of alcohol poisoning and her mother had dumped her with Ashenbach while she set out to do God-knew-what on her own.

So now he'd been arrested and bail had been set and he was back in this godawful cell because he told Rick he needed to do this part himself. So far, however, Ben hadn't had the courage to call anyone to raise bail.

Besides, he didn't know whom to call. Jill was still in Vermont. He supposed he could call Charlie Rollins or

Rita, but this was *child molestation,* for God's sake, not a traffic violation, not something you'd want anyone beyond family to know about.

And not even family, he thought, closing his eyes. *God, not even your wife.*

From out in the hall, Ben heard the sound of low voices. That's when he realized that the longer he stayed here, the better his chances were of being found out by a gnatty gossip like Hattie Phillips or Jesse Parker, who would spread the word all over the island before sunrise or sundown or whatever the sun would do next, Ben wasn't sure, because he had not been sure of anything but the punch in his gut and the panic in his heart since Hugh had read him his rights so many hours ago.

He considered his options, if that word even applied.

It would be better to call John than his daughter. John, his son-in-law, husband to Carol Ann, father to Ben's only grandchildren, John, Jr. who was seven, and Emily, four. Yes, he would have to call John. What Ben didn't know was what the hell he was going to say.

"I think it's best if we don't tell Carol Ann," John was saying. "God, it would kill her. And what about the kids? They might be young, but they'll learn about this kind of thing soon enough. Hopefully, it won't be when their grandfather's involved."

Ben sat mute, staring out the window of his son-in-law's minivan. It was two-thirty in the afternoon—for some reason knowing the time had become important now. There had been no clock in the holding cells, and of course, his watch had been sealed in the envelope with his other "valuables." But now he knew the time. He hung on to that bit of freedom as if were a lifeline.

Two-thirty in the afternoon. It had taken that long for John to get out of work, go to the bank, and take out the bonds that Ben had stored in the safe deposit box for his grandkids. Thank God he'd once had the brains to have John's name put on the box.

"Are you with me on this, Ben? Not to tell Carol Ann?"

Ben nodded. If he'd wanted his daughter to know he would have called her and not John.

"Well, hopefully this is just Ashenbach's way of stirring up trouble," John continued. "Hopefully he'll come to his senses and realize that this can only harm his granddaughter."

Ben wondered if John knew how many times he'd used the word *hopefully* since they'd gotten in the van. He also wondered how well John knew Dave Ashenbach, a man not easily dissuaded, a man not given to giving up. Even after the Menemsha House fire, Ashenbach, it seemed, was the lone holdout of the islanders, the only one who had not helped him rebuild. It was as if he were trying to underline the fact that he did not want Ben—or the museum—as his neighbor.

"At least this won't be in the papers," John continued. "Fitzpatrick said your name and the incident won't be released because the island protects itself from each other. Whatever that means. Anyway, he assured me there's a gag order on the proceedings because the little girl is a minor. It will be kept from the people as well as the press."

Ben wanted to ask when—and why—John had talked to his attorney, but he couldn't make his brain go past John's words:

the little girl.

He might have challenged his son-in-law's placement of sympathy if he weren't so tired. And so damn numb.

"So what happens next?" Ben's son-in-law, the concerned family member, asked.

Ben glanced over at John and tried to determine if he'd

like him if he were not the husband of his daughter, father of his grandchildren. "You take me home," he said. "I go to bed." Hugh Talbot had already agreed to hang a sign on Menemsha House saying the museum would be closed until further notice. If anyone asked, Ben could give a vague excuse about closing for the season, about wanting to spend more time with Jill.

Jill.

He asked himself for the thousandth time how he was going to tell her. And for the thousandth time, he wondered how she was going to react.

Her husband the child molester.

Her husband the sex offender.

He turned and looked out at the oak trees that lined the street. Many had already dropped their rusty red leaves on the brick sidewalk, a sure sign that winter would be early and winter would be rough.

"What about legally?" John asked, interrupting Ben's thoughts. "What happens next?"

"You talked to Fitzpatrick. Didn't he tell you?"

"Well, no. I only needed to find out where to bring your bail."

Ben sighed. He felt twenty years older than he had yesterday at this time, which was now two-thirty-six. He was in no mental shape to reason with John, or to argue. "I pleaded not guilty. Now it goes to trial," he said, repeating the few words he remembered the judge saying. Those and the part about *the little girl.*

"When?"

"We don't know yet. Not for months."

"Well, you might want to think about hiring someone other than Rick Fitzpatrick. Someone with, you know, criminal experience."

Criminal? Ben kept his eyes fixed on the trees. John was, of course, right, but hearing him say it—as if he were the goddamn lawyer—pissed Ben off. "Rick's fine for now."

They drove the rest of the way in silence. Ben suspected that John was trying to assess what other legal and/or moral judgments lay in wait. When they reached the house, John didn't even pretend to park.

"Well, keep me posted," he said.

Ben got out of the van, gave a half-hearted wave, and realized that John had not asked how Ben was doing, or if he could handle this. John had not asked, not once.

As he walked up the walk, it occurred to Ben that John did not believe he was innocent.

If his own son-in-law didn't believe him—who the hell would?

Rita had had her urine tested, her finger pricked, and her blood pressure practically squeezed from her upper arm. Now she paced the hospital waiting room, waiting for Doc Hastings's nurse to call her in for her personal-and-private consultation, as if Rita would care if the whole world learned she was in menopause.

There was a time, of course, it might have mattered. Back in the days when her ongoing goal was to impress the rich and preferably famous, she might have cared. If anyone had thought she was menopausally crazed, they might have been less likely to list their summer houses with her. It certainly would have reduced her "other" activities, which included bedding down those same rich and preferably famous for a few doggie bags left over from expensive dinners or an occasional contact name or two—anything to help her survive until next season, to help her and Kyle survive.

She strolled around the waiting room that had undergone little if any change since she'd last been here three years ago. Three years ago last Labor Day weekend, to be exact. The day, and the night, her world changed forever.

She remembered the orange vinyl chairs, the huge white clock that hung over the doorway, the table that overflowed with tourist-rumpled magazines. She remembered looking through the magazines, trying to find a recipe that she'd make when Kyle came home, if he came home. She remembered how freezing cold it had been in here.

Slowly, Rita moved across the room, trying to push away the memories, trying to push down the pain. She cleared her throat and looked around the room. It held a handful of hanging-on tourists in L.L. Bean clothes and a couple of islanders in flannel shirts and jeans. She recognized no one and wondered if the island had changed when she'd not been looking, when she'd been in the vacuum since that Labor Day weekend night.

Seeing the list of doctors' names on the wall, Rita idly glanced at them. *Warren Hastings* caught her eye, the name of the ancient gynecologist who'd delivered most natives, fifty and under, on this side of the Vineyard, Rita included. Next to his name it said *Room 103.*

She absently scanned the remaining names, then realized there was no longer a listing for *Robert Palmer, M.D.* No longer a listing for the doctor who had told her that Kyle was going to die.

"Your son has third-degree burns over sixty percent of his body." The young doctor's words were rooted in her mind, her poor, helpless mind that had never been the same. "His chances of survival are slim."

She stared at the listings now, seeing not the names but the haze of the desk and the chair and the file folders that had sat on Dr. Palmer's desk in his tiny, cramped cubicle, hearing once again those hollow-sounding words, feeling that claustrophobic perception as if someone had locked you inside the dark, airless trunk of an old, unwanted car and you wanted to run but there was nowhere to run and you were as trapped as Kyle had been in the flames as he tried in vain to save Menemsha House, hero that he was.

The doctor had wanted her to go home. *We're working on him . . . it might be a while . . . I can call you to come back.*

She had not left. She had looked down at her bony, freckled knees and known that she was not going anywhere. It did not matter if it took an hour, a day, or a month. No one was going to make Rita Blair leave her son.

In the end, it was Kyle who had left her, left all of them, as he just went to sleep, freed from his pain.

And now Dr. Palmer, like Kyle, was gone.

"Mrs. Blair?" The touch of a hand on Rita's arm pulled her up from the tunnel, back to the present. "Mrs. Blair," a young woman in white said, "Dr. Hastings can see you now."

Rita looked at the young woman's kind face and wanted to tell her that her name was not Mrs. Blair, but *Ms.* Blair. People who hadn't known her all her life or who hadn't known Hazel always made that mistake, thinking Rita was married because of Kyle. A long time ago, that was okay. Now, like most things, it no longer mattered.

He was behind his desk, busily scribbling something on a pad the way doctors did, as if it were the most important note in the realm of the universe.

"Rita," he said, standing up, without ceasing to write, without raising his eyes from the notepad. "How's your mother?"

She sighed and sat down in the wooden chair across from the desk that was even older than he was. "Fine, doc." She briefly wondered if Doc Hastings had been one of Hazel's lovers, though if he had been, Rita would probably have known. Hazel would have been proud to have a doctor share her bed, if only on alternate Tuesdays or whenever he'd been willing and available.

Finally he stopped writing. He took off his glasses and smiled. "Well, well. You're looking quite well, Rita."

She wished he would sit down. She wondered if this was some kind of menopausal ritual, respect for the woman whose youth had passed over. "Thanks, doc, but I feel like shit. My mother thinks I need estrogen."

He smiled but did not answer.

Rita sat back, then forward on the damned chair. It occurred to her that a doctor's office should have more comfortable chairs. She tried to remember what kind had been in Dr. Palmer's airless cubicle, but she could not.

"It's too soon for estrogen," Doc Hastings commented. Then at last he sat down.

Rita frowned. "But I've already skipped a couple of periods. And I feel like crap most of the time."

He smiled. "Yes. That's often expected. But estrogen can't help you, Rita."

Her annoyance rose. "What do you suggest? Tofu and soybeans?"

"Well, I do suggest vitamins. And a healthy diet. And plenty of prenatal checkups. Oh, and especially because you're over forty, we'll want to do an amniocentesis and an ultrasound at about sixteen weeks."

She started to protest, then stopped herself. "What did you say?"

His smile had not faded. "An amnio and an ultrasound. They're standard for pregnancy at your age."

Chapter 4

Ben wondered if he had suddenly developed that nervous condition, what was it called? Agoraphobia? The one where you were afraid to leave your house; when even to stick your head outside the door would make your heart race and your body sweat like all get-out, the way he was sweating now, as he stood at the window, peeking through the drapes, wondering if anyone on North Water Street had learned that Hugh Talbot had been to Menemsha and escorted him off in handcuffs.

Was it possible that he had developed agoraphobia in the few hours since his life had gone completely out of focus? Since he'd gone from Ben Niles, respected homebuilder, family man, and model citizen, to Ben Niles, child molester?

"Ben?" The voice came first, followed by the slamming of the back door.

Shit. Amy was home. He let the drape fall back into place.

She rounded the corner on energetic teenage feet, tossing her corduroy jacket onto the wingback chair that had been in the room since her great-grandfather's day.

"Guess what?" she blurted out in teenage style.

Guess what? Oh, God, did she know? His throat and chest and gut tightened up.

"Charlie's going to let me run the Halloween party at the tavern. I'm so psyched. It'll be so cool." Her dark eyes flashed—the same dark eyes that resembled her grandmother's, the beautiful woman whose photo stood on the mantel in a small oval frame, the woman who might or might not have chattered and laughed as often as Amy.

Amy would stop laughing if she learned that her new stepfather was an accused sex offender.

He tried to smile or simply to breathe. "If you're in charge, the party will be nothing less than cool."

He backed up a step to put more distance between them.

She flopped onto the chair atop her corduroy and flipped back her short now-burgundy hair, which she'd recently chopped "techno-like," as she called it. "I want the party to be totally outrageous, the latest chic." She spoke as much to the ceiling as to Ben. "I want it to be the one Halloween party that everyone will remember. Maybe I'll get a special guest. Hey! Elvira! Remember Elvira, Mistress of the Dark?" She jumped from the chair. "Maybe Mom can get her—wow! Funky! When's Mom coming back?"

Ben watched Amy's animation and marveled at the innocence of youth. Had Mindy ever been allowed such innocence, or had she been too neglected? "Tomorrow," he said more quietly than he'd intended. "She's coming home tomorrow." He lightly pressed his hand against his shirt, as if that would calm his distress.

"I'll pick her up at the airport. What time?"

"Four o'clock." If Amy picked up Jill, Ben would not have to leave the house. He would not have to face his wife until . . . later. He felt relief in that.

"Great," Amy said, heading from the room. Then she

stopped and turned. "Hey, Ben? What are you doing in here anyway? Why are you standing in the half-dark?"

She was right. The room had grown dark. He glanced at his watch. The hands pointed to nearly seven. Had he been standing there that long?

"I, ah, I just came in to look outside. I thought I heard a car door." He snapped on the tall floor lamp that stood beside the chair.

"Are you going out tonight?" she asked.

Out? As in, among people? He blinked. "No. What about you? Are you working?" His voice sounded surprisingly level, normal, as if he were the same man who had seen her yesterday.

Yesterday?

With Amy's teenage coming-and-going schedule, she must not have realized he'd not been home last night, that he'd been sitting in a jail cell instead of sleeping in his bed.

"I'm off work tonight," she chattered. "I thought I'd drive to the Costume Shack in Oak Bluffs to get some ideas for the party. There's also a place I want to look at . . ." Her voice trailed off the way it always did when there was something she wanted to ask but was too hesitant. Ben had learned a lot about Jill's daughter in three short years, almost as much as if she were his own.

Oh, God, he wondered. *Will anyone think I've molested her, too?*

He tried to loosen his collar, but the top button was already unbuttoned. "What kind of a place?"

"I'm eighteen. I want my own place. There are so many winter rentals. . . ." It was not the first time she'd mentioned flying from the nest.

"What do you think your mother will say?"

Amy groaned. "I want to grow up, Ben. But Mom will never let me."

She, of course, was right. The last time she'd hinted at

independence, Jill had responded by saying perhaps when Amy turned twenty-five. Or forty.

"It's really not fair. I have some money saved. I can pay most of my own way. If I were in college, it would cost way more."

"I think your mother was hoping you'd change your mind and do just that."

"Go to college? God. I only want a winter rental."

"Did you ever hear the saying 'You can't go home again'?"

Amy rolled her eyes. "That's dumb. Besides, Mom came home again. She came back here."

Ben did not mention that Jill had waited until both her parents were dead to return to the Vineyard.

"And anyway," Amy continued, "I think you and Mom deserve some privacy."

Privacy? Right now the thought of being alone with Jill made him uneasy, a feeling he never thought he'd feel, not about her, not about his wife.

"Nice try," he said with a laugh. "But we both want you here, Amy."

"Yeah, well, it's not like she's ever around to see either one of us, is it?"

Standing up, he rubbed his chin. "I'll tell you what, kiddo. I'll go with you to the Bluffs to look at the place. No promises. But if I think it's decent, I'll put in a good word for you with my significant other."

She grabbed her jacket and had it buttoned before Ben remembered he had planned to never leave the house again. *Nothing like the distraction of a family to save you from yourself,* he thought, putting on his denim coat and following her out the door.

Distraction, of course, only lasted so long: long enough for Ben to check out the pink and green gingerbread cottage and decide it was too drafty and would cost Amy a fortune in oil heat; long enough for him to try and convince her that his objection truly was to the heat and not to her moving out; long enough to kill a few hours before it was time for bed.

Distraction, however, had not done much to help him sleep, which was why now, at five A.M., he was sitting on the watchful cliffs of Gay Head, wishing that Noepe would be here meditating.

Noepe had been Ben's friend, his *best* friend, if men could or would admit to having such a thing, to needing such a thing. The old Indian had guided Ben through Louise's cancer; through her chemotherapy, through her death. He had been there, once again, when Kyle died, when Ben had lost his hopes, his dreams, his strength.

For years, he and Noepe had met frequently at dawn out there on the cliffs. Sometimes they conversed. Sometimes they were silent, together, yet each alone amid the gentle beauty of the morning.

It was that unassuming companionship combined with Noepe's ancient tribal wisdom that Ben had revered. And it was Noepe himself: the Wampanoag tribesman who slid with ease between his deep, ancestral heritage and his job as an accountant; who glided between the past and present on quiet moccasins.

But Noepe was dead.

He'd caught pneumonia two years ago; he'd moved on to the next life as easily as he'd traversed the one he had on earth. And Ben had been faced with yet another loss, another grief to process.

So there was no one Ben could tell. No one with whom he could share this atrocity; no one whom he trusted, who would not be judgmental, who would not be hurt. Noepe was the only one who would have been fair to Ben. For Noepe had nothing at stake.

"No one knows," Rick had tried to convince Ben while they were waiting for the arraignment.

Sure. No one but Hugh Talbot and the woman judge and a couple of other cops and the guard and the court reporter and the D.A. and John, Ben's son-in-law, and Rick, and, well, Ashenbach. And Mindy.

No one, really, only them.

He wanted to scream.

Instead, he tipped his face up to the awakening sky and listened to the air, hoping to hear Noepe's wisdom float to him on the wind.

He heard a gull or two and the surf far below. He did not hear his friend.

"Goddammit," Ben said aloud, then dropped his chin to his chest. "How the hell am I supposed to fight this? What am I supposed to do?" The morning air chilled his bones. He pulled his jacket closer against him. *And how,* he added silently, *am I supposed to tell Jill?*

But on the wind there came no answer, for even his friend Noepe could not help Ben now.

Jill couldn't wait to get home. Two and a half weeks of living out of a suitcase, of sleeping on hotel sheets and drinking restaurant coffee had definitely run its course.

Once she had enjoyed life on the road; she had found excitement in unpredictability. But that had been before she'd found a real home, a real life. That had been before Ben—the biggest reason she knew she should say "No, thanks" to Addie Becker, and "I'll continue to struggle somehow on my own."

From her seat in yet another concourse at yet another gate, this one at Logan Airport, Jill tuned out the sounds of people in motion around her. As she stared out the window, her thoughts drifted to Christopher. Over the past few years she'd deftly avoided *Good Night, USA*—except once when she was on assignment in Kennebunkport. Alone in her hotel room, she'd double-locked the door so no one would catch her, as if looking in on an old lover were a criminal offense.

She'd poised herself on the edge of the bed with the remote, then boldly selected the channel.

The first face she'd seen had been, not her ex-fiancé's, but Lizette's.

Lizette the blonde. Lizette the beautiful. And one of the few women in whose presence Jill felt immensely *less than,* an unsophisticated New England frump beside a sleek California girl-star.

She'd had to admit that Lizette looked good next to Christopher, who had apparently not skipped a career beat since Jill had left him for Ben. She doubted if he'd skipped any other beats, either.

For fifteen minutes of the half-hour show, Jill had watched and wondered about what could have been. Then she'd come to her senses and clicked the program off.

Gazing around the terminal now, past the bank of monitors that heralded comings and goings, Jill looked at the unknowing faces of unknown travelers. Many of them might have recognized her now, if she had moved up instead of out. But life was about much more than fame, and the days and the nights—at least *hers*—had been far better without Christopher than they would have been with him.

She wondered if he had been sleeping with Lizette, and how he would react to Addie's asinine idea—for surely the idea had been Addie's. Addie, after all, had set the course; she had once blazed Jill's personal trail to become the Barbara Walters of the next generation. But that was then and this was now and it was simply out of the question. Jill would make it on her own, or she would not make it at all.

Then Ben would never have to be jealous.

And she would never be lured by what might have been.

She zipped her bag and looked up at the wall clock: fifty minutes remained until her connection to the Vineyard. She decided to find a cup of coffee. It would certainly be more productive and enjoyable than sitting and thinking about . . . *them.*

Crossing the walkway to the Starbucks concession, Jill felt a light touch on her arm.

"Excuse me," an elderly woman said. "Aren't you Jill McPhearson?"

Jill felt both awkward and pleased. "Yes," she replied with a smile.

"Oh, dear, we miss you on television," the woman continued. "Is it true you're battling breast cancer? Such a hideous disease, dear, but you do look wonderful—"

Jill frowned. "No," she said, "I don't know where you heard that, but I do not have breast cancer."

The old woman grinned and patted her arm. "I understand it's something you don't talk about to strangers. But you do look wonderful, dear. Take courage in that."

"But—" Jill began to protest as the woman turned and bustled down the concourse, a canvas tote bag slapping her thick hip. "But I don't have breast cancer," Jill murmured. *I am married again,* she wanted to add. *This time to a wonderful man.*

But as the old woman merged into the crowd, Jill realized that, of course, there would have been rumors about why she had left: she could not even discount the possibility that Addie had planted them. Realistically, such rumors might have been easy to believe. After all, why else would she have walked away from all that glamour and success and happily-ever-after nonsense?

She'd walked away because it had turned out to have no more substance than an empty scallop shell on a Vineyard beach, picked clean of its heart by a scavenging seagull. It was an empty shell and nothing more.

Listening to an announcement for another departure and another arrival, Jill decided the first thing she'd do when she got home was call Addie and decline, before there was any more time wasted on *if only*s and *what if*s.

"Where's Ben?" Jill asked her daughter, who had not had burgundy-colored hair the last time Jill had seen her but definitely did now. She smiled quickly at the thought that burgundy hair and the tiny heart tattoo above her daughter's ankle once would have seemed earth-shatteringly rebellious.

"He's at the museum, I guess," Amy replied, kissing her mother's cheek and helping carry the suitcases without being asked. "I left early this morning. I told him last night that I'd pick you up."

Once Jill would have suspected that meant Amy had an agenda. Now she expected it and it didn't matter: Jill no longer lived in a constant state of being braced, waiting for that proverbial shoe—or in Amy's case, platform sandal—to drop. Since she'd found that once-elusive inner peace, things like agendas and shoes and heart tattoos no longer mattered.

Still, she thought as they went out to the car and loaded up the trunk, it would be nice to go home, take a hot bath, and maybe go through the mail, before being accosted by the crisis of the week. She smiled, reminding herself that nothing was perfect, nothing at all.

"What's so important it couldn't wait until tonight?" she asked, climbing into the passenger side, liking that sometimes it was fun for Amy to be in control, both at the wheel and in her own life.

"Mom," Amy cried with a fake whine as she started the engine, "I missed you, that's all. And I couldn't wait to tell you that we're going to have the Halloween party at the tavern and Charlie's put me in charge of the whole thing. Do you have any connections with Elvira, Mistress of the Dark?"

Jill laughed. "Afraid not. Addie might, though. But it's not quite a good enough reason for me to reconsider. Sorry."

Amy was silent a moment, as she steered the car out of the parking lot. "Addie Becker?" she asked quietly. "Wow. There's a blast from the past."

Jill looked over at her daughter. "I know. I can't believe she called me."

"God. What does she want?"

Despite the burgundy hair, Amy was no longer the same restless, out-of-control teenager she had been back when Jill supposedly could have had it all, back when Addie Becker was in charge of their lives.

"Don't worry, honey," Jill said. "I'm going to say 'Thanks, but no thanks.'"

Amy was quiet again, almost remorseful, as if she were traveling not toward Edgartown but down the dark tunnel of time, back to a place she'd rather not go. "What are you saying no to?" Her curiosity apparently won the tug-of-war with her remorse.

Jill told her of Addie's request to fill in for Lizette for a month during ratings sweeps. "My guess is that the show needs a boost. Someone decided a reunion between Christopher and me would give them just that."

Amy wrinkled her nose. "If you'd stayed on the show and we'd moved to L.A., Mom, I'd probably be dead. I probably would have gotten into drugs. And sex. Oh, God," she added with a shudder, "my experience with Kyle would probably have seemed tame."

Though Jill knew it was healthy that Amy felt free to talk of the past—and Kyle—she had never quite forgotten the long-ago shock of walking in on her fourteen-year-old daughter having sex with that boy. It was a sordid, piercing picture that the dusting of time had not yet erased.

"Well, it's not going to happen. And don't mention it to Ben, okay? He doesn't know."

"Not to worry," Amy said. "But does this mean you have no connections for the Halloween party?"

Jill smiled. As much as she wished Amy had chosen to go to college, it was good to have at least one of her children around to keep life in perspective. "Was that the real reason you picked me up? To see if I could procure the Mistress of the Dark?"

"No. I wanted to ask you if I can take a winter rental."

Jill reminded herself that a minute ago she'd been eager to get home. Before she could say a word, Amy quickly continued.

"I'm eighteen, Mom. It's time I started learning how to take care of myself. Before you say no, remember that this is an island. It's not Boston or L.A. I just want a little independence practically in your backyard. I've saved some money and can almost pay for everything myself. I wouldn't need much financial help, and the way I figure it, if I'd gone away to college, it would have cost a whole lot more."

All that said, Amy planted both hands on the wheel and fixed her eyes on the road in responsible-driver posture.

Responsible, but still young.

"Not yet, honey," Jill said firmly. She sensed Amy's grip tighten on the wheel. Then she closed her eyes and wished they'd get home where Ben would restore the peace she'd just felt slide away.

•   •   •

Jill had spent twenty-five years living off-island and had traveled around the world, but she'd come to learn that, teenagers aside, there truly was "no place like home." And there was no more comfortable place to eat a meal than at the 1802 Tavern in Edgartown, where she'd grown up waiting for her father to close up for the night.

Though George Randall had been dead many years, the familiar aromas of clam chowder and dark beer still filled the restaurant, the hand-hewn ceiling beams and whaling prints on the stucco walls still sculpted the interior, and the sounds of thick-Boston-accented voices like Rita's and Charlie's told her that she still belonged there, then, now, and forever.

She had thought Ben had understood all that, but tonight he'd said he didn't want to go out. Oddly, she'd found him home when she and Amy arrived: it was only four-thirty in the afternoon, a time when Ben would usually be at the museum.

"I wanted to be here to meet you," he'd said.

She delayed phoning Addie because he suggested they go up to the widow's walk to the Jacuzzi.

She'd thought that they'd make love, but they did not.

With uncharacteristic remoteness, he'd answered her questions about life while she'd been away: about the museum, about the Sea Grove project, about Amy. Then she told him about Addie and Christopher and *Good Night, USA*. She could not tell if he was surprised that the offer had been made, or if he was pleased with her decision to say no.

She could not tell, because he seemed so distant. Oh sure, he'd responded; he'd acknowledged her and made appropriate comments once or twice. But he was not himself, and they had not made love.

She had no idea why.

And when he'd finally acquiesced to go out, he acted like a stranger, with a familiar face but a phony smile.

"My table tonight," Rita said as she approached, pad in hand and pencil tucked in the red curls over her ear. "I wouldn't mind, but your daughter says you're a lousy tipper." It might have been funny, but Rita had said the words mechanically, as if it were a stock waitress joke. Besides, Rita looked pasty and forlorn and in not very good humor.

"Are you okay?" Jill asked her longtime best friend, who replied with a pause, then a lifeless nod. Jill fiddled with the menu. "Amy's upset with me," she continued. "She wants to move out. I say she's too young."

"Yeah," Rita managed to say. "She told me. She said, 'As usual, Mom won't let me breathe.' "

Whether it was Amy's comment or Rita's bluntness in relaying it, Jill didn't know, but something caused anger to rise up in her. Maybe it seemed misplaced that Amy had confided in Rita, Jill's best friend, not Amy's. "How did you respond?" the mother of the nonbreathing daughter asked.

Rita made small doodles on her order pad but looked neither at Jill nor at Ben. "I said she's eighteen now and can probably do just about everything legal except drink or vote."

"Rita!" Jill blurted out. "I thought you were my friend!"

She stopped doodling, tucked the pencil over her ear, and folded her arms. "I also told her that the law expects one should pay one's own way. Then I reminded her that once we close the tavern for the season, she—like most of us—will have a hard time finding work. That seemed to shut her up on the subject." She plucked her pencil, again with indifference, and poised it over the pad. "So what'll it be tonight?"

Jill looked to Ben. But he seemed lost in the menu as if he were making a monumental decision, as if he didn't know the menu by heart. "I'll have the turkey and cranberry sauce on wheat toast," he said without looking up.

Jill's eyes met Rita's, who seemed not to notice Ben's remoteness. Jill shook her head. "I'll have the same."

Rita nodded. "Two gobblers," she scribbled. "Chowder?"

"No," Jill replied, but Ben just handed Rita the menu as if he'd not heard.

"So," Rita asked, "how long are you home for this time?" The question seemed more dutiful—a "How are you" or a "Have a nice day"—than caring. Without making eye contact, Rita took their menus.

"A couple of weeks," Jill replied. "I'm going to do a story on Cranberry Day."

One of their "traditions," when Rita and Jill were young, had been to bicycle out to Gay Head on the second Tuesday of October for the annual Wampanoag festival, the celebration of Thanksgiving for a fruitful cranberry harvest. Once they had even tried to pretend they were Indians.

"My great-great-grandmother was a descendent of Chief Chippewausett," Jill had told a tribal leader when she and Rita were about eleven. To her knowledge there had never been anyone with such a name, let alone one of her ancestors. But the tribal leader was kind and invited Jill and "Little Red" (the name they gave Rita) to join them in the encampment for the storytelling around a large bonfire.

So now when Jill mentioned Cranberry Day, she expected more than a nod and a remark of "that's nice" from her faithful Indian companion, Little Red. It didn't come.

She took a sip of water. Had the whole island gone insane while she'd been away? "I'll have a glass of Chardonnay, too, Rita."

"What about tomorrow?" Rita asked suddenly. "Are you working?"

Jill frowned. "Yes. For a while. I have to do the voice-overs for the piece on Vermont I'm finishing."

"Can you do lunch?" Her voice had moved from flatly indifferent to openly needy.

Jill knew she should say no: she'd been gone so long and had too much work to do, and if she ever wanted to make it on her own, she'd have to get down to serious business. That, of course, was the workaholic Jill thinking, the one who'd struggled on her own with two small children rather than remain a trophy wife for Richard McPhearson, her first husband, the cad. But the workaholic Jill was definitely the "old" Jill. And the "new" Jill was trying to be a more complete, better-balanced woman. Part—a big part—of her new life was a commitment to be there for those she loved. Rita included.

"Sounds great," she said.

Rita nodded. "Call me here when you're ready." Then she went off toward the kitchen, the disconnected waitress, to put in the order.

Jill looked at Ben, who merely smiled that fake smile again. If there had not been so many others in the tavern, she might have run screaming from the room.

"I'm sorry," Ben said as they walked the three blocks toward North Water Street and home. "I had planned to give you a nice welcome home. A romantic dinner. A memorable evening." He linked his arm through hers, wondering how or when he would find the courage to tell her what had happened, to prepare her for what was ahead.

He hadn't thought he needed to rehearse what he would say. This was Jill, for God's sake. His wife, his second chance at a soul mate. Surely she would see the hideousness of it all, surely she would believe him. . . .

Jill put her hand on his and stopped walking. "What's

going on, Ben? First you, then Rita. You're both acting so strange."

His palms began to sweat. Could Rita know?

Oh, God, did everyone already know?

"Ben?" Jill moved her hand up to his cheek.

He touched her fingers and drew them to his mouth. He kissed them. "I love you," he said.

She didn't move. He knew that she knew there was more, that he was holding on to something.

He cleared his throat. "Something's happened." She stiffened. Quickly, he added, "Everyone's okay. Don't worry. No one is sick or anything."

She relaxed a little, but still she did not speak.

"I don't know what's wrong with Rita, but I don't think it has anything to do with me. There's no way she could know."

A few leaves stirred in the breeze. Ben looked up at the lamppost. He thought of simpler times, when lamplighters lit the town at night, when men were not . . .

"Know what, Ben?" Jill interrupted. "What is it Rita doesn't know?"

He'd rather be home, safe inside, but he had started it here. And he had to finish it now.

"Shit," he said, feeling sick. He rubbed his stomach. "While you were gone, I was arrested." His eyes dropped to the ground so he couldn't see her face or sense her anger.

But instead of being angry, Jill laughed. "You were arrested?"

He closed his hand over hers again. "Yes, I was."

In the quiet that followed, the night air grew silent.

"Ben?" Jill asked, her voice no longer laughing but disconnected and worried.

"*Ben?*" Her tone changed to firm.

He sucked in a short breath. "It's all a mistake. Ashenbach is behind it."

"What mistake, Ben." It was not a question this time, but a sentence with words that clearly needed answering.

Ben looked around to assure himself that no one was nearby. "Dave Ashenbach's granddaughter. Mindy. I've mentioned her to you."

"The little girl who helps out at the museum?"

The acid in his throat might have dissipated if she hadn't called Mindy *the little girl*. Tears—tears?—formed in his eyes. "God, Jill, I didn't do it. She said I touched her, but I didn't do it."

Jill must have heard him wrong. "She said what?"

It took a few heartbeats—hers—before Ben answered. "She said I touched her breast, Jill. The charge is 'indecent assault and battery on a child under age fourteen.' What it really means is child molestation."

She pulled her hands from his. "This is a joke, right?"

He stared at her with glazed, pained eyes that said it was no joke.

"I don't understand," she said. Suddenly her hands chilled. She put them in her pockets.

Ben put his arm around her. "Let's go home, honey. We can have some coffee and I'll explain everything."

Chapter 5

 "How much is my grandfather paying you?" Mindy asked the straight-haired woman who'd showed up on their doorstep in the morning and said her name was Dr. Laura Reynolds, and that she'd come to talk.

The woman didn't smile. "Perhaps we should sit outside on the swing. It's such a nice day," she said.

"No," Mindy replied. "I'm fine right here in my room." It was safe there upstairs, she wanted to say, but did not. From there she could see Menemsha House. She could see everyone who came and went, though she'd seen no one since the day before yesterday when Sheriff Talbot went up the hill then came back down a few minutes later.

She had seen Sheriff Talbot, but she had not seen Ben. Grandpa had said Ben was in jail where he belonged.

She picked at the edge of her bedspread and pretended not to notice that the woman made herself at home in the rocking chair beside the window.

"Your grandfather is very worried about you, Mindy. He has hired me to help you sort out what happened with Mr. Niles."

Mindy looked at the woman. She knew what she was.

She was a shrink like in the *Frasier* reruns. "So how much is he paying you?"

The woman's smile was pretty even though she wore only pink lipstick and no other makeup. Still, compared to Mindy's mother, she was plain Jane. Plain Dr. Laura Reynolds, transported from Boston by the old Volvo that sat in their dirt and clamshell driveway now and by the Woods Hole ferry that brought everything to the island, unwanted guests included.

"Does it bother you that your grandfather is paying me?"

Mindy got up and went to the windowsill where her stuffed animals sat—Bowser the dog, Marlin the whale, Iggy the iguana—all gifts from her mother sent at one time or another. Raggedy Ann, of course, was long gone to the trash. "I don't care what he does with his money." She rearranged the animals, then went back to the bed.

"Was this the first time, Mindy?" Dr. Reynolds asked. "Was this the first time that Mr. Niles—or any man— touched you inappropriately?"

Inappropriately. There was that word she'd heard so often from the health teacher and the school nurse. They said it when they talked about those movies of rape and assault and when men took out their penises and put them in *inappropriate* places.

But sometimes they used the word, like now, when it just had to do with hands for touching or lips for kissing.

Mindy knew about all this, but she wished they didn't have to talk about it. It only made her more upset that Ben must really hate her now.

"The first thing we should do is find a different lawyer," Jill said to Ben as they sat alone, pretending to have breakfast. She had made french toast—thick, golden slices dusted with lacy powdered sugar and served with a dollop of the beach plum jelly she had taught Amy to make last year. Jill had taken a few bites, Ben a few more, and the rest sat untouched, interest having been diverted elsewhere.

It had been the same way last night. After Ben told her what had happened, as best as he could remember from the time he'd been handcuffed, Jill had moved about in robotic, everything's-okay movements, brewing coffee, setting out a plate of small trifle cakes that she kept in the freezer for special occasions like coming home.

They had talked most of the night, and Ben told her his decisions.

No, he did not want to tell Carol Ann or Amy. It was bad enough John knew.

No, they should tell no one—not Charlie, not Rita. No one. This way they would not place on their family and friends a burden of feeling as if they had to believe him.

And no, he would not talk to Mindy. It would only cause more trouble.

They would wait, Ben said. They would see.

Jill had not agreed with anything except the part about waiting and seeing, because surely this would be over soon. Surely someone would come to his or her senses and end this insanity.

They had talked most of the night and the cakes, like the french toast now, had gone mostly untouched.

"If I fire Rick, who else is there?" Ben asked. "I can't exactly shop around. 'Excuse me. I've been arrested for child molestation. Can you recommend a good attorney?'"

His sarcasm must have been due to stress and anger. Sarcasm was not in Ben's nature. *None* of this was in his nature.

"What about Rick?" Jill asked, trying to be supportive without sounding like a nag. "Doesn't he know someone more . . . specialized?"

"Criminal lawyers aren't exactly in abundance here.

People come here for the low crime rate, remember? We're on an island. Nowhere to run, nowhere to hide."

"Well, Boston, then," Jill said, pushing her fork into the now-limp bread, dragging angry tracks through the white dust. "I can call one of my old producers at the station. He's been in the city a long time. Maybe he knows someone." Before she'd become famous, she'd been a struggling grunt reporter, a newly divorced single mother of two, working the streets, paying her dues. Maybe there was someone who still cared about that.

"That's just what we need," Ben said with defeat, "for the media to find out that Jill McPhearson now has a husband who . . ."

Jill stood and moved to the kitchen window. She looked past the back porch, out onto the yard. It was withered with autumn, blossoms turned brown, leaves already brittle. She rubbed her forearms, trying to make sense of it all. She knew who the girl was: she'd seen her a few times when Ben was rebuilding Menemsha House. She was a small, wiry child who was not shy but always seemed to be alone. Alone, apparently, with an overactive imagination.

"Don't you have to be at the studio soon?" Ben asked.

Jill gazed across the harbor toward Chappaquiddick on the opposite shore. She wondered how soon the press would pounce on the story.

Like the woman at Logan who'd asked about breast cancer, the rumors would be a blizzard of untruths. And where would the public sympathy gravitate? Toward their once-beloved Jill? Doubtful. She had, after all, walked out on a Cinderella story, which was how Addie had spun it.

She felt Ben's arms come from behind and slide around her waist. "We'll get through this, honey. Right now I don't know how, but I'll get it straightened out. I won't let this ruin our lives—or your career."

Her career. As if that mattered.

• • •

Jill made damn sure she was busy most of the day. She drove to the studio in Oak Bluffs, got the video feed from the freelancer in Boston, cut her audio with the help of Jimmy O'Neill, audio master and island transplant from the road tours of rock stars, and arranged for interviews at Cranberry Day next week. All she needed now was to find someone to shoot and edit, because the freelancer from Boston had said no.

Juggling her production nearly single-handedly was often just short of impossible, but today it seemed easier than returning Addie's call.

At three-fifteen she was sitting at the old Shaker desk that Ben had restored for her when the telephone rang. She hesitated, then decided not to answer it. It was probably Addie.

After four rings, the answering machine kicked on. *"Vineyard Productions,"* she heard her voice say. *"Leave a message. Thanks."*

Beep.

"What the hell time do you eat lunch, anyway?" The voice was not Addie's but Rita's.

Jill grabbed the receiver. "Rita," she said quickly. "It's me. I'm here."

"And I'm here," Rita replied, "starving to death."

"Oh, Rita, I'm so sorry. I got busy—" She could not confess that she'd not given their lunch a second thought because of . . . no, she could not tell Rita that. Ben would not let her place the "burden" on others. "Is it too late?" she asked. "I can be at the tavern by three-thirty."

"Forget lunch," Rita said. "But it's a beautiful day. Can you meet me at the lighthouse? I've got one whopper of a problem, and you're the only one who can help."

Jill hung up the phone and wondered how Rita could

have a problem bigger than her own, and what in God's name was going to happen next.

"I'm pregnant," Rita said as she plunked down beside Jill on the rocks by the pier—the special place they'd come since they'd been kids to share their innermost secrets and fears. She took a deep swig of water and handed the bottle to Jill, who at first was too stunned to absorb what Rita had said.

Then it sank in.

"You're kidding."

"No joke," Rita said. "I'm preggo, knocked up, in the single family way." She picked up a small stone and skipped it across the water. "Again."

"Oh, my God, Rita," Jill said, taking her own swig from the bottle with the kind of untamed gusto she'd had at seventeen when the illicit bottle had held rum and Coke. She looked out at a few sailboats that lazed in the autumn afternoon, as if the sunshine would not soon turn to dark, as if the water would not soon become winter-icy and snow-coated. It was not always comforting to know that change happened, even when some things in life remained exactly the same, like Rita and the harbor and the sunshine and the tides. "Well," she repeated, "this certainly is news."

Could she say this was wonderful, great news? That at least Rita wasn't being held emotional hostage by an imaginative ten-year-old with a vengeful grandfather? That compared to Jill's life right now, Rita was blessed?

No, she couldn't say that. Besides, Rita did not look blessed, not even close: her fingernails were bitten ragged and low.

"I thought it was the big, scary change," Rita said. "I thought menopause was making me fat."

"You're not fat, Rita," Jill said, because that was what best friends did for each other.

Rita laughed. "I'm only a couple of months now. But I'm so short that soon I'll pop out like the Pillsbury doughboy at Thanksgiving dinner." She paused, picked up another shell, and skipped it across the water. "At least, that's how I was with Kyle."

Her son's name hung in the air, then drifted on the salt breeze, a memory gone by.

"Rita." Jill rested a hand on her friend's arm, which was covered by the long sleeve of an oversized red-and-black-flannel shirt. "What are you going to do?"

Rita shrugged. "Well, I'm forty-six. I guess I'll have an abortion." She tucked her red curls behind her ears and did not look at Jill. "I had two, you know." She shook her head. "No, you wouldn't know. You were long gone to the big city by then." She cleared her throat. "One was in seventy-eight, one in seventy-nine. They were both summer things. With tourists, like I shouldn't have known better. Anyway, I had the abortions, and they didn't matter."

The air grew silent again as Jill listened to her best friend's confession, her best friend's pain. Then she put her arm around Rita's shoulders. "I know you, Rita, and I know that they mattered."

Rita lowered her head, and a tear slid from her eyes. "But I was smart after that," she said, with a short laugh. "I went on the Pill. Until a couple of years ago. After Kyle died, well, I guess I lost interest in most everything. Life. Living. Sex."

Listening to her best friend, Jill tried to determine if she'd known that Rita had lost interest in life, in living. She'd acted the same. But maybe *acted* was the key word. Rita had acted the way people expected her to behave. Not unlike the way Jill had been acting all day, carrying on with her business as if her husband had not been arrested for one of the sickest crimes imaginable, as if feelings, pain, or anger did not happen.

"Go ahead, say it," Rita interrupted Jill's thoughts. "Obviously I didn't lose enough interest in sex not to do it."

Jill took back her arm and drew tiny lines in the sand by her feet. "I wasn't thinking about that, Rita. Honest."

Rita sighed. "Well, I did have sex a few times. But only with Charlie."

A quiet grin formed on Jill's lips. "No kidding," she said. "So Charlie is . . ."

Rita nodded. "The father of my child. The second time around." She picked up another stone, examined it, then set it back on the ground.

"Rita," Jill said, "this is wonderful." This time she said it, because she truly felt it.

But Rita's glance said she didn't agree. "Why is it so wonderful?" she asked, her tone turning acrid. "I'm too old to have a kid. Besides, what if it turns out not right?" A note of fear had crept into her voice.

"That won't happen," Jill said quickly. "There are ways of finding out today. There are tests."

Rita shook her head. "I liked things the way they were. The way they've been."

"But the time inevitably comes for us to move on. As long as we let it." The time had come for Jill the day she'd met Ben. "I keep hoping Amy will be able to move on. I think she might have a crush on one of the young men I've hired."

"Amy is Amy. As for me, I'm too old. It's too late to start over."

"That's crap, and you know it. Look at me and Ben." Speaking his name nearly closed off her airway, nearly made her reveal the injustice that had happened at the whim of that . . . child.

"You and Ben," Rita commented before Jill changed

her mind. "My mother says you're the all-American family now. But tell me, Jill, are you pregnant, too?"

"Of course not." The words shot out too quickly before she could check them. "I mean, Ben is older than we are. We're not planning . . ."

Rita nodded. "Neither was I. Nor was I planning to get married."

"But now?"

"Well, for one thing, Charlie has stopped proposing. I think he's found someone else. Besides, why should 'now' make a difference? I've asked myself that a thousand times."

"And?"

"And nothing. I wouldn't be good at marriage, Jill. I've always known that. I'm too—I don't know. Too independent."

"Bull. What you are is too damn scared. Well, you have a right to happiness, my friend. But you have to give yourself the chance."

Rita did not respond.

Jill looked down at the waves. "Trapped on an island in the middle of the sea," she said quietly. "That's how I always felt about the Vineyard. After I came home, after I found my mother's diary, after I met Ben, well, I realized that the only place we're ever trapped is inside ourselves."

As she heard herself say the words, Jill was not thinking of Rita. And then things became clear. Rather than feeling like victims, Ben and Jill needed to act. They needed to go on the offensive. And they needed to do it fast.

She stood up. "I've got to get home, Rita. But no matter what your decision, please promise me two things."

Rita stood and brushed sand from her jeans. "That depends."

Jill took Rita's hands. "Promise me that this time

you'll consider telling Charlie. And that—no matter what you decide—you'll keep me informed."

Letting go of Jill's hands, Rita gave her a hug. "I won't promise that I'll tell Charlie, but I'll let you know what I decide. Some secrets are meant to be shared with your very best lifelong friend."

As Jill hugged her back, she squeezed her eyes shut, knowing that, sadly, some secrets were not.

Okay, so maybe she should tell Charlie, Rita thought as she slogged through the dunes from the lighthouse en route to the tavern. Maybe she should tell Charlie and they should be married and live happily-ever-fucking-after in her little red saltbox with their adorable little child.

Maybe not.

She'd have to make a decision soon. Her first trimester was almost shot. After that an abortion could get tricky. Not to mention that although she'd hung up her form-fitting miniskirts and crop sweaters long ago (not long after Kyle died), soon it would be obvious that she was plump with child.

Hopefully, she thought with a shiver, her mother would have returned to Florida by then.

Hopefully Charlie would not ask if the baby was his.

Hey! she realized, her spirits brightening, her walk quickening. Maybe that was the answer. Why would Charlie have to know the baby was his? He didn't know she hadn't been with anyone since that last night they'd slept together back in . . .

Oh shit.

It had been the night of Jill and Ben's wedding.

If Jill knew that, she'd probably see it as some kind of magical good omen. She'd probably want to run and tell Charlie herself.

Oh, shit.

She huffed a little and slogged some more, trying not to remember the night, trying to forget that it had, indeed, been magical.

Which was why she could not forget.

It had seemed so right, so natural. She'd been mellow with nostalgia, happy for Jill, feeling safe among friends, feeling close to Kyle because from the Gay Head lighthouse on the cliffs where the ceremony was, Rita could look across the dunes and the inlet and see Menemsha House, Ben's dream, which Kyle had died trying to protect.

She had felt safe and comforted as if wrapped in a blanket of Kyle's strong presence, his sweet love. She had felt all these feelings as she stood and listened to the vows and heard the soft cry of seagulls and felt the setting sun on her face.

It had been magical, and it had been the last time she'd had sex with Charlie, for afterward it had all seemed too close, too choking, too much like . . . commitment.

She stopped and pressed her hand against a gas pain in her side. "Fuck!" she wanted to shout as loud as she possibly could, so that her voice bounced off the neat windowpanes of the perfect white houses that lined North Water Street, the houses she'd been inside only to clean or to sell, rich people's houses like her friend Jill's that were made for normal, happy families, not the Rita Blairs of the world.

Then Rita smiled as she rubbed the pain. Maybe it wasn't gas. Maybe it was a miscarriage, a saving grace in progress, a miraculous event unto itself that would end this nightmare and let her return to her life.

Such as it was.

Such as it would be.

The pain subsided. No other symptoms followed.

And then her eyes were drawn up to the sky as if the answer, the solution, were there. But there was no answer. There was only a seagull, sitting atop the sign for the 1802

Tavern. Oddly, the gull seemed to stare at her, and to smile as if it knew something, as if it were not a grungy-gray bird, but a dove come in peace and in love.

It could even have been Kyle.

She laughed out loud at the thought.

Then, resuming her walk toward the back door, she admitted that maybe a baby wouldn't be so bad after all. Maybe a baby would return some life to her tired, hurting heart. Maybe a baby would restore her faith and hope in life.

She laughed out loud again.

And maybe a seagull named Kyle, she thought, *planted these weird-ass thoughts.*

But as she reached the restaurant door, she decided what the hell, she really had nothing to lose if this time she was honest. Maybe she should, as Jill suggested, give herself a chance at happiness. She could start by telling Charlie she was pregnant once again. With his child. Hopefully the seagull would not splat on her parade.

She took a deep breath and went into the kitchen with a childlike grin, like a giggling girl holding in a big secret she could hardly wait to let out.

It was not Charlie, however, who greeted Rita today. It was Amy. She was stirring chowder.

"Am I glad to see you! Charlie's hung up in Falmouth tonight, and I'm the only one here to do dinner. Grab an apron and save me, okay, Rita honey, Rita pal?"

Rita stood staring at Amy for a moment, the once-wild teenager now the person in charge. Then she grabbed an apron from the rack as she'd been instructed and refused to think about the fact that Marge Bainey lived on Cape Cod, maybe even in Falmouth for all Rita knew.

Chapter 6

The rest of the afternoon and into the evening, Jill thought about Rita and about how life had a way of shaping more twists and turns than the crocheted stitches of one of her great-grandmother's lace doilies. She straightened, then re-straightened one of those doilies now as she stood at the tall bureau in the bedroom. Ben sat across the room on the deacon's bench that had once been in the old Congregational church and had somehow ended up there after an auction to raise funds for a new steeple and a roof.

"I've changed my mind," Jill said in a low voice, in case Amy came home and overheard. "I know what we agreed to, but I really think we need to get this out in the open. The less defensive, the less secretive we are, the better. Secrets only end up causing more pain."

Ben did not respond.

"I think we should start with Addie Becker." She waited for his reaction, which did not come. She plucked at the doily again, then went across the room to him. "As much as I dislike the woman, maybe she can help us. It seems that she needs me now. What's that old saying, 'Tit for tat'?"

He did not smile at her attempt to lighten the mood. He merely looked at the floor and studied the wide boards.

But Jill's resolve was cemented since her visit with Rita, when she'd been uncomfortably reminded of those strict Yankee curses:

Do things alone.

Don't air dirty laundry.

Suffer in silence.

Jill had watched her mother and father struggle through their lives with those restrictions; that same penance had robbed Rita of unhappiness for too many years. And Jill was determined not to go down that path.

She sat next to her husband and awkwardly continued. "You can't get the right help here on the island. But there must be someone in Boston or L.A.—an expert who deals with these kinds of cases. And one thing's for sure, Addie knows everyone."

Ben leaned forward and put his hands on his knees. "So you want the media to get involved after all."

Jill rose and went to the window. She looked down at the once-plump hydrangea, now thick with blossoms burnished to a light autumn copper. "Addie's not the media, Ben. She's a talent agent. I'm sure this wouldn't be the first time she was confronted with a delicate situation. And she has connections. If I tell her I'll fill in for Lizette, she might be willing to help."

Ben folded his arms and leaned back on the bench. "So you will tell her about me—about my *delicate* situation."

She nodded. "I don't know how much I'll have to tell her. But unless we take control of this, it's going to consume us. And unless you get the best lawyer there is, you—we—could be in big trouble." Did he realize that, or did he believe that here on the island, all things worked out?

She turned back to him. "And who knows. Maybe

with the right connections, we can even turn this into something positive. Think about it, Ben. You're not the only man in the world who's been unjustly accused. We could bring to light the whole social problem. I know the judge said the case is off limits to the press, but rules can be bent if not broken. No one would have to know Mindy was the child involved, and you'd come across as the brave one, the *innocent* brave one."

Rubbing her arms briskly, she took a step forward. She wished he'd look at her. "Ben, honey, don't you see? We have to do something. Look at us, hiding in our bedroom so Amy won't hear us. And what about Carol Ann? You can't even tell your own daughter what's going on. This afternoon I wanted so much to share it with Rita. The fact that I can't makes it more difficult."

He closed his eyes a moment. When he opened them again, they had narrowed. And his face had become pink, no, almost red. He stood up.

"This is insane," he said. "Think what you want, Jill, but do both of us a favor and don't say that telling Addie Becker will make it realistic. I'm sorry this is difficult for you. I'm sorry I've asked you not to tell our children, and I'm grateful that you did not tell Rita.

"I am sorry for all the problems this is causing you now and will cause you in the future. But have you forgotten how much it cost you to get rid of Addie? And do you think it would be easy for me to turn you back over to Mr. Celebrity? When from day one, I've worried that someday you'd regret the decision you made—to give it all up, to be here with me?

"But whatever you do, Jill, don't lie to yourself. I mean, do you really want to get me an 'expert' attorney? Or do you want Addie and her 'connections' because you want to be back there with them? Where reality never strikes home, and if it does, Addie's experts can buy someone off or cover something up?"

He stalked toward the door, then turned around. "And another thing. This isn't a slant for one of your TV stories, Jill. Call me socially inept, I don't care. But if you think I'm going to stand beside you on some kind of soapbox for the unjustly accused, you're wrong.

"And what about all those accusations that aren't unjust? I'm not going to be a party to anything that would be misconstrued as mockery of the issue.

"I am a man, goddammit. I have some pride. And in this *delicate* case, Mindy Ashenbach is nothing more than a sad, misguided child. You say you wouldn't bring her into it, but how long would it be before everyone on the Vineyard figured it out? You're a mother, Jill. Can't you see that Mindy is as much of a victim as I am?"

Turning back toward the door, he didn't hesitate as he said, "Think about it, Jill. In the meantime, I'm going to bunk in with Charlie."

Ben wondered if he was losing his grip, or if he would before this was all over. If it ever was over.

He stood in Charlie's apartment above the tavern, in the room Charlie used as an office, and wondered how his life had suddenly become one big *if*.

He looked down toward Dock Street, then up toward Main. The sky was pewter—a drizzly, grizzly pewter that veiled the white Edgartown houses and shops and made even the brightest autumn colors look like crap, which certainly was in keeping with the way he felt.

He'd spent the night there on Charlie's old pull-out sofa. He wasn't sure if he'd been glad to be alone, or disappointed that his friend hadn't returned from the mainland. Charlie was apparently shacking up with some woman who would probably, at some point, like most of them, expect him to think as she did, to think like a woman.

"Never try to teach a pig to sing." He whispered the favorite old saying to the walls. "It doesn't work, and it annoys the pig."

He knew, of course, that he was being stubborn. But it was his life and his problem, and he wasn't going to let Jill or anyone else tell him how to resolve it. Especially not his son-in-law, even though both John and Jill seemed to think a killer attorney was what he needed. Ben might be stubborn, but he was not stupid: he was not going to bring in an out-of-towner, a city slicker to save his neck. The town fathers would hate that about as much as they'd hate a child molester. Maybe more.

Glancing back up the narrow Main Street, Ben's gaze fell on the tall steeple of the old whaling church, built God-only-knew-how-many decades ago by Yankee forefathers who lived a simpler life. For some reason, or no reason at all, it made him think of Louise. A wave of sadness washed over him.

She'd been dead five years now. His companion of nearly twenty-five years, the mother of his only child, Carol Ann.

He closed his eyes. Would Louise agree that their daughter shouldn't be told about this situation with Mindy? He and Louise had always believed in sharing the good and the bad with each other and with their daughter for the strength of their family. They had not wanted Carol Ann to be raised the way they both had been—in homes where no one talked about the unpleasantries of life and kids grew up believing the world was a playground, a shelter against wrong, a shield against evil.

They had wanted to teach Carol Ann the importance of family, the value of being close. They had wanted her to know so she would be capable of trust and sharing when her own partner came along.

It was, Ben knew, about emotional intimacy. The kind of intimacy that, no matter what, he could never have with Jill. It was a closeness born out of youthful struggles experienced together: making ends meet, buying their first home, having a child of their blood come into the world.

He opened his eyes and wiped the tears from his cheeks, wondering how Louise would handle this now, his rock of silent strength, his partner for nearly half of his life. Though Ben had been the man, the macho breadwinner and hunter-gatherer of their small clan, Louise had been the one who always knew what to do, the one who had believed in Ben so many times when he'd doubted himself.

"If you want to live on Martha's Vineyard, let's do it," she'd said.

"Start your business, Ben. We'll manage."

"Make plans for the museum. Your dreams are as important as your life."

He could not recall when she'd not been supportive. He'd even let himself believe that she'd have approved of his marriage to Jill: Carol Ann had even said so, the night before the wedding.

But Jill—for all her wonder and all her goodness—was not Louise.

Jill was glamorous and gregarious, where Louise had been quiet and plain. Jill was confident and clever; Louise had been steadfast, loyal, and there, always there.

Still staring out the window, Ben felt his shoulders quiver. He leaned against the glass, looking out at the town center, out where no one who walked under the red and gold leaves of those safe tree-lined streets would guess that an accused child molester was standing upstairs, looking out into a world to which he felt he no longer belonged.

Mindy looked out the window and wished her grandfather had never insisted on tracking down her mother from the "itinerary" she'd scribbled and sent them and that he'd kept in the drawer by the refrigerator as if they might ever need to know—or care—where she was. But Grandpa said this was something her mother needed to be told, and he'd found her on an island in the West Indies, wherever that was.

She called early that morning before Mindy went to school.

"Do you like Dr. Reynolds?" her mother asked now, her voice crackly through the wires.

"She's okay."

"Is she pretty?"

Mindy shifted on one foot. She hated that her mother always seemed to think that if someone was pretty, that meant they were smarter or better than those who were not.

"She's okay."

There was a long pause over the Caribbean and up the Atlantic.

"I'd be there if I could, Mindy. But the people who own the boat are very demanding. You understand, don't you, pumpkin?"

Oh, sure, of course. Mindy gripped the phone cord more tightly. "It's okay, Mom."

"Your grandfather said he's taking care of everything."

"I guess that's why he's my legal guardian," she said. *And not you,* she did not add.

The static grew stronger. "Yes. It's been a good thing that I left you with him. With your father dead and my work taking me so far away . . ."

There were so many things Mindy could ask. Starting with *why don't you get a damn job as a waitress or something?* Or *why don't you come back here and take care of me like you're supposed to?*

Outside she could see Grandpa brush the rain from his

hat and lay a fresh tarp across the bed of his pickup truck. Next he'd come in and eat the oatmeal that she'd set out last night before going to bed. Then he'd drink his coffee and take the pills for his heart and be gone for the day while she went to school. It was kind of a dumb life that they had together, but it was predictable and it didn't hurt much.

Until now.

Until Ben had done what he'd done, and she'd done what she'd done, and now, worst of all, she had to talk to her mother—*mother*? Ha, ha, that was a laugh.

"Pumpkin?" her mother asked. "Ben Niles is still rich, isn't he?"

Mindy frowned. Next to being pretty, the one thing that mattered to her mother was money, which, Mindy supposed, had to do with her being ne'er do well. "How would I know?" she replied. "His car's pretty old."

Her grandfather came in the back door then, stomping wet leaves from his boots. Then Mindy remembered he wouldn't go fishing today, because he had an appointment with the district attorney. That rumbly feeling returned to her belly: she rubbed it a little, but it didn't leave.

"I have to go," Mindy said.

"Well, be a good girl. I'll send you something from Antigua."

Don't bother, she wanted to say, but said good-bye and hung up quickly instead, wishing that her mother had died along with her father and that she could go over to Menemsha House and help Ben for a while.

But right now one dream was as impossible as the other.

"Are you planning to live in one of those big houses you and your friends are building?" Hazel Blair asked Rita as

Rita finished reading the prospectus and sales brochure just back from the printer. Until now she'd not minded having her office in her home. After Kyle died, she'd moved her files into his old bedroom so she could feel closer to him. Unfortunately, before Kyle the room had been Hazel's. Hell, the whole house—what there was of it, with two slant-roof bedrooms and the office upstairs, and the kitchen, living room, and small den down below—had been Hazel's, who apparently now felt she had the right to come and go as she pleased.

"This house is perfectly fine," Rita replied. "Besides, what would I do with four thousand square feet? Hold a ball every other Saturday night?" She had not yet told her mother that there would soon be an unexpected addition to their family—she had hoped Hazel would return to Florida before it was obvious, and then maybe Rita would never, ever have to mention it. Denial, she'd found, was often a much happier place to dwell.

"You could have a suite of rooms for your mother." Hazel pronounced *suite* like "suit" and not "sweet," which, under other circumstances, would have bugged Rita. But she was too stunned by the content of her mother's words to be bothered by the syntax.

"What do you mean?" she asked, her eyes turning halfway back to the brochure to help mask her shock.

Even with her head half-turned, Rita could see Hazel's lips curl up and her false teeth gleam a wide plastic smile. "Well, you may find this hard to believe," Hazel said, "but I'm not getting any younger. It's time for me to settle down, and I'm not talking about getting married again."

Rita suddenly felt nauseous. "You are settled, Mother," she said, without looking up. "You have a nice mobile home in Coral Gables, remember?"

"Ah!" Hazel exclaimed, flopping onto the daybed where Kyle had once slept. "Everyone in Coral Gables is an old fart. I saw more action in the dead of any winter on the Vineyard than any of them dreamed about seeing in their combined lifetimes."

"Mother," Rita said, closing the brochure, "you are too old to be getting any action. And too old to think about moving back to the island. You've always hated the snow."

"I've been thinking about it ever since Kyle died. My grandson. And I only saw him six times after he turned eighteen."

Hazel had been busy chasing—and unbelievably, catching—a husband, her first, at age sixty-eight. "Well, it's too late now, Mother. Coming back to the Vineyard isn't going to change that." She had not meant to sound sarcastic, really she hadn't. But the tight lines that set around the corners of her mother's Love That Red mouth told her she had been.

"It's not too late for me to spend time with my daughter, Rita Mae. I only gave you this house so you could pass it on to Kyle. Now that he's gone, well, I don't want to take it back, but I was hoping you'd at least let me live here."

At this stage of her life, Rita had not planned on a roommate of the maternal persuasion, especially Hazel. Then again, she also hadn't needed to consider the advantages of a built-in baby-sitter.

Hazel nodded vigorously. "Year round," she confirmed. "I want to come home, Rita Mae. I want to live with you again. We'll have a blast. Just like old times."

Thankfully, old times would not include having to rent out the house during the summer and bunk in with various neighbors for a week here and there. Hopefully, they would not include hearing her mother's lovemaking noises echo through the century-old walls. But there would be companionship, and there would be a baby. Just like old times.

Jill would give anything to go back in time, to last summer, to their wonderful wedding on the walkway that encircled the top of the Gay Head lighthouse, to the way the ribbons in her hair drifted in the breeze off the cliffs as she professed her love publicly to Ben Niles, as if anyone in attendance hadn't known about it already.

But as she looked out the widow's walk on the rooftop of her house, at the half-naked treetops and the slate-colored sky, she was quickly reminded that this was not Gay Head and this was not summer.

She leaned back in the Jacuzzi and tried to decide what to do.

She could get out of the tub, get dressed, and go find her husband.

She could stay here until she became prunelike and limp, dwelling on what might have or should have or could have been.

Or she could pick up the cell phone and dial the number she knew so well, the one that belonged to Addie Becker.

She eyed that phone, which in and of itself was a haunting reminder of Addie-the-agent: chaotic and crazy and always on.

With a deep, lonely sigh, Jill rested her head against the vinyl pillow and tried to concentrate on the warm water seeping into her pores. She loved this tub: she missed it when she was on the road. It was one more of the lovely things Ben had brought into her life.

"This would make a great hot tub room," he'd said that first day she'd met him when he came to the house. It had been Addie who'd hired Ben to renovate the house so Jill could put it on the market and get on with her life.

It had been years—twenty-five exactly—since Jill had left that house and run from the Vineyard, escaping her mother. In that time, she'd seen her only a handful of times, the last of which had been a few years before, at her father's funeral.

She once liked to think that her absence had not been completely intentional, but deep down, she had known otherwise. When her mother died, she decided to settle the estate and be done with the island once and for all.

The plan had seemed sensible. She had not counted on finding her mother's diary right there in the widow's walk; she had not counted on learning the reasons she had been so . . . unmotherly. She had not counted on finding forgiveness for her mother and for herself, and she had definitely not counted on falling in love with Ben Niles, the uncommon laborer with the penetrating gray eyes.

Ben—the man who, last night, had selfishly chosen to sleep in a room over a tavern rather than in the same bed as his wife.

He was not the first man in her life who'd turned out to be self-centered. There had, of course, been Christopher, narcissistic celebrity baseball star turned TV anchor. Before him had been Richard—Jeff and Amy's father—who had preferred a revolving audience of one, preferably a woman other than his wife. Once, she'd selected men the same way she chose dresses: quickly, hardly trying them on, just wanting to get it over with and get on with the dance.

Ben had been different.

Ben *was* different, she reminded herself. He cared about life and people and kindness and honesty. He did not do anything unless he did it well. And he did not deserve this kind of treatment, not from a ten-year-old girl he'd been trying to help, not from an idiot of a vindictive fisherman, and not from the police, who knew Ben better than that.

She could be angry with Ben, but he didn't deserve that, either.

What he did deserve was the best legal defense that could be begged, borrowed, or bought. And to buy it, one needed not only connections but very big money. The kind she could hope to amass only by working for the network.

Jill reached across the deck and picked up the phone. Before she could change her mind, she dialed the number she knew so well.

"Becker," came the voice on the other end of the line. Addie always seemed too busy to extend a pleasant hello. Apparently, some things hadn't changed.

Jill sucked in a small breath. She moved partway up from the water, exposing the tops of her breasts to the autumn-chilled air. "Addie," she said, "this is Jill."

In the silence her pulse quickened. She knew it wasn't from the heat in the tub.

"Jill," the agent replied matter-of-factly. Not "How are you?" or "What have you been doing the last three years?" or "I'm sorry I blackballed you." Simply "Jill."

"I've been thinking about your offer." Jill closed one arm across herself, shielding her naked vulnerability from the woman who had cost her so much. "Maybe it's not a bad idea. For me to fill in for Lizette."

Again silence loomed—silence, dead air, the unnerving stalled space that was one of Addie's tactics in subtle manipulation. It was a tactic Jill detested.

"Would it be for the whole month of February?"

"Plus a week in December for preshow publicity. And, yes, of course, the whole month of February."

February was prime time in the ratings wars of TV land, the critical time when midseason replacements were administered as booster shots, when season specials and heavy hitters were pulled out of the darkness in order to position each station for the almighty advertising dollar.

"When do you need a definite answer?"

Addie sighed loudly. "Well, I can't wait forever. This is network, not local."

Yes, she knew that. It was a RueCom show, produced by Maurice Fischer, the ratings wizard, and aired on those stations that had not given her stories from Vineyard Productions the time of day, night, late night, or fringe.

"If you don't want it, I need to find someone else," Addie continued in a voice that suddenly sounded close to sincere. "I was only trying to do you a favor."

A favor. Yes, Jill wanted one, too, but one that involved a link to a powerhouse attorney. She closed her eyes and swallowed a small, shallow swallow. She pictured herself on the set beside Christopher, a fake smile on her face, an ache in her stomach.

All for the sake of sweeping the sweeps. Or so they would think.

Jill McPhearson on the set with Christopher Edwards would be one hell of a way to sweep.

So they needed her.

But she needed them—maybe more.

"Send me a contract," she replied, then said a quick good-bye without second-guessing why she had done it or how long she could keep it from Ben.

Chapter 7

Thanks to Jimmy O'Neill the audio master, Jill got a shooter to work with them on Cranberry Day, a pro out of Albany with whom he'd once traveled.

She took the call in the garden shed and was grateful that it was from Jimmy: Jill had nearly forgotten the job was imminent, she'd been so immersed in chopping back hydrangea and painting the back porch and blasting her way through other physical busywork chores. Anything to try and forget about the rest of her life. Anything to try and forget that soon she was going to ask Addie about an attorney, and that she'd done something certain to make Ben more angry at her than he already was.

Anything to forget she'd be doing *Good Night, USA*, as if she were picking up her life where she'd left off, which she was most definitely not doing.

She told Jimmy she'd book the videographer—Devon Pike was his name—at the Beach Plum Bed & Breakfast. Then she hung up the phone, wiped the moisture of fine-misting rain from her brow, and sighed, just as Amy appeared at the doorway of the toolshed.

"I saw Ben at the tavern," she said. "What's going on?"

Jill leaned against the wooden workbench and pulled off her gloves. She wasn't sure if Amy meant what was going on overall, why was Ben at the tavern at ten in the morning, or why had he not slept at home last night. Most probably her daughter wasn't interested in Jill's progress disassembling the dried-up gardens of summer.

"Did I tell you I'm doing a segment on Cranberry Day? It should be unique. Maybe more cable programming will want it." She turned to the workbench and cleaned off the trowel and old hand clippers.

"That's not what I meant," Amy replied. "Ben stayed at the tavern last night. Why?"

Jill kept cleaning tools. It was easier than looking her daughter in the eye because, unlike her son, Amy adored Ben. "The coolest stepfather you could have found," she'd said to Jill the night they'd told the kids they'd decided to marry. But what would Amy think if she knew about . . . this? Would she defend her cool stepfather? Or would she look at him differently, wonder what the truth was, no longer want to be in his presence?

She wanted to tell Amy and yet . . .

Still, she could not lie. "Ben and I had an argument."

"Jesus, Mom," Amy said, an accusatory tone springing forth, a tone that reminded Jill of Amy's early teenage years when her daughter had believed that anything, everything that went wrong or merely awry, had to, in some way, have been Jill's fault.

"Don't be melodramatic," Jill responded with quick defensiveness. She dropped the tools in a peach basket and pulled off her rubber boots. "It's nothing we won't resolve." She still was not looking at her daughter. "Marriage is no easier than dating, Amy."

Immediately she was sorry she'd said that. Amy often complained that there were no decent boys on the island, which Jill suspected was simply an excuse not to date anyone seriously, something that, as beautiful and intelligent as her daughter was, Amy had not done. Ever. It was as if her experience with Kyle had left her frightened of men or of getting involved. Which seemed so out of sync for such a beautiful girl with so much style and so much, well, pizazz.

"Well, what are you going to do, Mom? You can't leave him down there."

"I did not leave Ben anywhere, Amy. He went of his own volition. In fact, it was his idea. Now if you'll excuse me, I've got to get cleaned up. I want to go over to the studio and take care of some things."

"But, Mom—"

"Did Ben say where he was going?" she asked.

Amy shrugged. "Menemsha, I guess."

The very name of the place that had once made Jill joyous about Ben's dream now curdled her insides. She turned around. "Don't worry, honey, it was nothing. Just a small argument."

"It was big enough for him to leave home."

Jill forced herself to look into her daughter's eyes. "We'll be fine, honey." She hoped she sounded more convincing than she felt. "It takes more than a lovers' quarrel to break up true love."

Rita smiled. "Mom, I'm pregnant." She stood alone before the full-length mirror in her bedroom, studying her face as she practiced breaking the news to Hazel.

The smile was not right. It was too smartass.

She frowned.

"Mother, I'm pregnant." No, too serious.

She lifted her chin. "I'm going to give you another grandchild, Hazel." No, too stupid.

Rita sighed and dropped onto the bed. This would be so much easier if she didn't feel like a scared seventeen-year-old again, or that she'd be labeled the town pump again—loosey-goosey, easy-make, slut. This would be so much easier if her mother had just stayed in Florida like most ordinary women her age.

Running her hand over the small, bump-in-the-road mound that had begun to form in her belly, Rita remembered that Hazel was, always had been, anything but ordinary. Not until her mother had left for Florida had Rita begun to appreciate her for what she'd been—a mother who, no matter what, had always found ways to support her daughter and her illegitimate grandson, ways to protect them from the gossip piranhas, and ways to help her stay just ahead of the wolves at their paint-peeling door.

The "ways" that Hazel had found may not have been conventional, but they had worked. There had been favors given and taken to and from tourists—male tourists, of course; there had been that infernal bunking with neighbors, a week at a time, enabling them to rent out their house in season for a few extra bucks. Through it all, there had been Hazel. Never-give-up, pain-in-the-butt Hazel, who had helped Rita raise Kyle with open-arms love.

Rita hadn't realized those things until Hazel was gone. Gone only to Florida, thank God, not gone as in dead like Jill's mother.

All Rita knew now was that if her mother was planning to move back, she had to be told what the future would hold, and she had to be told sooner rather than later.

Rita hauled herself from the bed and headed for the stairs, about to tell her mother, for the second time in her life, that her daughter had been dumb enough not to keep her legs crossed.

"It's Charlie's, isn't it?" Hazel asked from over the tops of her reading glasses, her eyes dancing with excitement instead of piercing with anger the way they had the last time, way back when. She dropped the book she'd been reading into the basket next to her chair. It was a collection of

Henry Beetle Bough essays. Rita wondered if Hazel was brushing up on the Vineyard past in order to make way for the future. "Rita Mae?" she demanded. "That baby has Charlie Rollins for a father, doesn't he?" She pointed at Rita's stomach.

"I do declare, Mother," Rita said, "you must be a soothsayer."

Hazel let out a loud guffaw. "Some people just have the right biological connections."

Hazel, of course, did not know that Rita had "connected," biologically speaking, with two other men besides Charlie. She briefly wondered if Hazel, too, had experienced an abortion or two back in her tourist-hopping days.

"Yes, well, whatever you call it, the connection seems to have worked."

Hazel stood up and gave her daughter a hug. "Another baby. This is wonderful, Rita Mae. And this time the baby will know its father."

Rita stiffened and stepped back from her mother. "Not yet, Hazel," she said sternly.

A frown sharpened Hazel's seventy-eight-year-old forehead. "What are you talking about?"

"I'm talking about Charlie, Mother. This is between me and him." She sucked a small breath through her teeth. "And I don't know yet what I'm going to tell him."

Hazel groaned and sat back down on the chair, the wooden frame creaking. "You're forty-six years old, Rita Mae. Haven't you learned anything all these years?"

"Yes. I've learned that I'd be no good at marriage. I've told you a thousand times that I'm not like Jill."

"And what about Jill? Does she know?"

"Yes."

"And?"

Rita huffed a small huff. "Mother, please. Jill might wish otherwise for me, but I'm sure that even she knows I'm better off on my own. As will be the baby."

Plucking at the rollers in her red-rinsed hair, Hazel pursed her matching red lips. "Well, missy, you're forgetting one thing."

Rita put a hand on her hip and waited for the next comment that was surely forming right now in her mother's quick mind—too quick for her age, too sharp for a senior.

"You're forgetting about Mr. Rollins. This is a new century, Rita Mae. Fathers have rights that they didn't have back when Kyle was born."

Florida was definitely a much better place for her mother. Maybe Rita would buy her another mobile home. One with a bigger *suit* of rooms, where she could live out the rest of her meddlesome days.

"Well, believe it or not, you don't know everything, Mother. For instance, you don't know that Mr. Rollins has himself another woman. I'm sure he is no more interested in marrying me than I am in marrying him." She spun on her heel and headed toward the kitchen.

From the living room, she heard Hazel mutter.

Rita snapped on the tap and filled a glass of water.

"I said," came her mother's raised voice, "when is the blessed event?"

Rita took a big gulp then closed her eyes. "April," she answered quietly. "The end of April."

As Jill drove along Beach Road toward Oak Bluffs, she wondered how soon they'd know when the trial would be. She needed to decide if she should tell Ben before or after they found out—before she told Addie or after they'd lined up an attorney, a John Grisham hero who would get to the bottom of this and know what to do to vindicate Ben.

Before or after. Either way, he was going to be angry.

She set her jaw squarely and fixed her eyes on the narrow road. She told herself it didn't matter how angry Ben was. They could not pretend that this was not happening.

They could not pretend that everything was fine. Pretending was the worst way to live life, Jill had long ago learned, because sooner or later it caught up with you. The pretending stopped, the game was over, and usually the pain was worse.

She wondered how long Ben would stay at the tavern.

She wondered if this was going to ruin her marriage.

Then she wondered how intense the anxiety level would be back on the anchor desk with Christopher, and how she would survive it. And if she was selling her soul to save the man she loved.

Her gaze drifted off to the right, then to the left. The afternoon sky was clear and blue and uninterrupted by the summer colors of parasails, tourist blankets, and striped beach umbrellas, and the air unpolluted by assault sounds from boom boxes, car horns, and the scrape of skateboards on pavement.

Instead, the beach was sandy white, protected by the bike trail on one side and by the small, grassy dunes on the other, and all was autumn-peaceful. Yet everything she saw and everything she felt was muted by the sorrow that veiled her heart. She blinked and fat tears rolled down her cheeks.

Ben was in his old workshop behind the house in Oak Bluffs, guiding a buzz saw through a sturdy two-by-four, determined to replace the old window frame that he'd been meaning to replace for six years.

Now was as good a time as any. He could not go to Menemsha. He could not risk running into Ashenbach or going to the museum that was too close to Mindy, too close to trust himself to not bang on their door and say, "Tell them the truth, kid. Tell them what really happened."

It did not matter that the museum was his business, his potential means of half-assed support, the real half, of course, coming from his wife, to whom he could not go, either.

He rammed the saw through another board and supposed he should be grateful that this had happened off season, after the bulk of museum visitors had oohed and ahhed and returned to the mainland and their day-to-day lives. He supposed he should be grateful. But right now gratitude wasn't an easy emotion to muster.

Part of the board broke free and dropped to the unfinished floor. As Ben bent to retrieve it, the workshop door opened. From where he was crouched, he saw a pair of feet in classy, smooth leather shoes.

"Oh, shit," he said aloud.

Then his wife stooped beside him, took his face in her hands, and wiped his tears first, then her own.

"I love you so much," she whispered there in the small, dark, sawdust-smelling room.

He put his arms around her and pulled her toward him, burying his face in her soft, silky hair, releasing himself to the warmth of her thin but strong arms. "Oh, God, Jill, I'm so sorry about all this. What are we going to do?"

Without answering, Jill pulled away from him. She unbuttoned her shirt and slipped off her bra. With her small fingers, she cupped her breasts, holding them as if they were meant just for him, as if she were offering her love in her hands.

Slowly he leaned into her. Slowly he began sucking one of her dark nipples, until it grew moist from his mouth and firm from his tongue. Gently he touched his teeth to it; she let out a soft cry.

From under the workbench he pulled out an old tarp and laid it across the floor. And there, amid canvas and sawdust, he took her as his, his lover, his love, his wife.

Chapter 8

"In a few days you're going to give a deposition," Dr. Reynolds said to Mindy.

Almost a whole week had passed since Grandpa had found Mindy in her room, since he had gone to the police and the whole world had changed, and this woman with the plain hair and pink lipstick was now here almost every day, trying to act like she was her mother, though she looked nothing like her mother, more like the school nurse.

They once again sat in her bedroom with the door closed to "insure privacy," the doctor had said.

"What's a deposition?" Mindy asked because she did not know what one was and wasn't sure if she had one to give.

Dr. Laura Reynolds smiled. "It's like being in a video. The lawyer will ask you questions about what happened with Mr. Niles. A camera will record what you say and do."

"What do I have to do? Play with dolls or something?" She remembered one of those movies in school where they used dolls to show what parts of who were okay to touch and what parts were not. She'd been about six at the time and had already figured out the parts on her own, not because of some dumb movie, but because she and Derrick Smith, who had since moved off-island, had looked at each other's "parts" quite closely on several occasions.

"You'll only have to answer questions about that afternoon. The trial is a long time from now, and they want to know everything before you forget."

Mindy looked out the window, wishing she could go outside and play, ride her bike to the beach maybe and look for lucky stones.

"Will they ask me about sex?"

"Maybe. Does that bother you?"

Mindy shrugged. "Will they ask me about Ben?"

"Yes, of course. That's what this is for. To prove what Mr. Niles did so he will never do it to any other little girl again."

"Oh," Mindy replied.

Jill said she wanted to tell Carol Ann and Amy. "You could use some family support," she had argued to Ben, then added that no matter what Amy and Carol Ann thought, it was better that they knew. Before they heard it some other island-rumor-mill way.

"I called Carol Ann," she told him now, as they sat in the music room of the old sea captain's house, the place that was home. "The only night this week she and John can make it for dinner is the night after Cranberry Day."

Ben wondered if family "support" entailed having things swirl around him and in spite of him like the way he felt he was being manipulated into telling the girls.

"The freelancer will be here then, and I'll be working with him and Jimmy," Jill continued, oblivious to his nonreaction, "so it will be a little tight, but I can work it out. Oh, and don't forget, while we're at it, we need to remind Carol Ann that she and John said we can take the kids to Sturbridge. It will be fun, Ben. You need to absorb yourself in something fun."

He looked over at the oval-framed picture of Jill's somber-faced grandmother. How much fun had she had in her short Yankee lifetime? Would she think that anything that could happen between now and the trial could be absorbing enough to be classified as fun?

The truth was, he'd almost forgotten he'd promised to go to Sturbridge with Jill for her next story—something about Thanksgiving stuff in the seventeenth-century reenactment village. But she was right about one thing: he had looked forward to taking his grandkids. He had also looked forward to getting fresh ideas like building lobster traps—ideas he could adapt for Menemsha House.

If he ever opened Menemsha House again.

He stood up from the chair and went to the window. He rubbed his lower back: he hated the way he ached sometimes these days, as if the intrusions of the world around him had violated his spine as well as his psyche.

Outside, Edgartown slept its post-tourist sleep.

"I'm still not convinced we should tell them," he said, because his voice seemed to need to give it one more try. Intellectually, of course, it made sense.

Tell them before they learn some other way.

Running from something only makes you look guilty.

These people love you. Of course they'll believe you.

Those were the "intellectual" things he'd say if this had happened to a friend, Charlie Rollins, for instance. But it hadn't happened to Charlie. It had happened to him.

"We're a family now, Ben," Jill said firmly. "Let's act like one."

The thought that she might be right finally won out.

He closed his eyes and wondered how he would survive until the day after Cranberry Day, and how he was going to tell the girls without breaking down.

Jill Randall McPhearson Niles became someone else when a camera was pointed at her face, someone Rita hardly recognized, someone like Diane Sawyer or Lesley Stahl or one of those TV women who always seemed so much smarter than she was.

It was true Jill was smart, way smarter than Rita. Hell, she'd always been, always would be. But right now, as Jill interviewed the tribal medicine man about traditions of the cranberry harvest, she also came across as the perfect, all-together woman that Rita would never be. And that had nothing to do with smarts.

Once the camera was off, Rita hoped Jill could take a few minutes for her—to congratulate her for deciding not to have an abortion and for telling Hazel the news. Then she admitted to herself that maybe what she really wanted from her famous friend Jill was some advice about Charlie, now that it was clear another woman was in his life.

Rita moseyed through the scant crowd over to the recreation of an ages-old encampment on the north side of Aquinnah. She poked around the food tents where quahogs, chowder, and venison simmered in a blend of island aromas. Then she strolled from the crowd to the edge of the cranberry bogs, their bright red now reaped, their fertile fruit passed.

She thought about how lucky she was to be having another chance, if that's what this was. She thought about Kyle . . . Would he watch over this baby, his brother or sister? Yes, he would. Of course he would.

Blinking back a mist that had come to her eyes, Rita looked back toward the festivities to see if Jill was finished. But before she saw Jill, she saw Charlie himself, wandering through the people, headed—oh, God, he was headed her way.

Rita tugged at the edges of her big flannel shirt, trying to conceal her not-quite-plump tummy.

"Hey, lovely Rita," he said, which she could have taken as a compliment, but he—and many others—had called her that ever since they were kids, after an old Beatles song.

"Hey, Charlie," she said with a nonchalant toss of her red curls that were hinting of gray, thanks to Doc Hastings, who'd told her that pregnant women were warned not to use hair dye—one of the hundred or so new terror-inducing directives that had sprung up sometime between when she'd had Kyle and now. She had not hesitated to tell the doctor that she had smoked and drank and done God-only-knew-what and Kyle had turned out just fine. But the doctor had merely shaken his head as if to say things were different today, as if she didn't know.

She leveled her gaze on the unknowing father. "Looking for some old cranberry stories to tell at the tavern?" Though she looked straight at him, she was acutely aware of the right and the left of him. He was alone.

"Actually," he said, "I was looking for you."

If her heart leaped through her shirt, she wondered if he'd notice. Or was he drunkenly in love with Marge's sweet mainland ass? "Is Amy okay?" She'd not seen Amy for a few days, having decided to back off work at the tavern until she had the courage to tell Charlie her news. Perhaps she would never work there again.

"She's fine. She's busy planning the Halloween party. Doing a great job, too." He stepped closer to her than she would have preferred. "What about you? How are you doin'? I haven't seen you for a while."

Rita shrugged. "Tourists are gone."

"Not all of them."

"Enough. Besides, I stay on the island. These days you seem to prefer land."

Charlie's laugh was gentle and warm. Kyle had had

Charlie's laugh. She touched her stomach and wondered if this baby would, too.

"I wanted to ask you a favor," he said. "I'm thinking of renting my apartment."

She blinked. "What?"

"My apartment. I'm going to take off for the winter. Florida, maybe."

She didn't allow herself even the tiniest gulp. "Florida? I thought that was for whitehairs. Are you getting old, Charlie?" There would be plenty of time for gulping much later, like all winter or the rest of her life.

"Maybe you could trade with my mother," she added. "She has a nice trailer in Coral Gables. And if she stayed in your apartment, she'd be out of my house." Her words sounded oddly as if she were happy he was going, as if there wasn't a pain growing bigger in her stomach or an ache swelling in her throat.

He put his hands in the pockets of his well-worn jeans. "It was just a thought," he said. "I'll close up the tavern for the season after Halloween as usual. But if I'm gone, I hate to think there would be no one upstairs. Watching out for the ghosts, or for vagrants or . . . whatever."

Rita remembered more than one time when "vagrants" had appeared—like when Kyle had been conceived in the secret room, or when Amy and Kyle had been caught there in a similar private act. "Do you want me to list the apartment?" she asked, putting her hands in her pockets, mimicking Charlie's action but unable to stop.

"Sure," he said. Then he looked at her sort of queerly, at her cheeks, then her nose, then her mouth. "Rita," he began, and she felt herself back away.

"Don't forget to at least let Ben know where you're at," Rita said, "in case we need help with Sea Grove this winter."

He laughed again, this time, with a small edge. "Why

would you need me? We're still short two building permits, and we can't break ground until spring."

Also in spring the baby would be born. But of course, he didn't know that.

Rita shrugged again. "Money," she said with a lighthearted tone she did not feel. "We might need more of your money."

Then she turned and walked, not toward where Jill was but back to the parking lot. Because all Rita wanted now was to get in her car, drive down to the beach, and have herself one hell of a much-needed cry.

"Why can't the guys come for dinner tomorrow? Jimmy and—what's his name?—Devon from Albany?" Amy asked her mother when Jill finally came home just after midnight.

It had been a long day of shooting, made longer by selecting the scenes she thought they might use. Amy had stopped by the studio with sandwiches and chowder—an act that might have been mistaken for benevolence had she not lingered in the edit suite, watching every move made by the editor and the audio man until Jill could not think straight and asked her to leave. Nice as the guys were, they were employees and, worse, roadies.

She slipped off her shoes, sat down on the tall kitchen stool, and rubbed her foot, knowing that no matter what she thought, her daughter would do as she pleased. She supposed she should be glad that Amy was showing an interest in men, though she was not sure which had caught her eye—Jimmy with the ponytail or Devon with the shaved head.

"They can't come because Carol Ann and John are coming," Jill said wearily. "It's a family dinner."

"Oh, Mother, that's absurd. We're hardly the Cleavers. Besides, no one does family dinners anymore."

Jill stood up, went to the cabinet, removed a large mug, and dropped in a tea bag. "Maybe it's time to reinvent that."

"But Mom, it's rude. You drag this guy to the island. You can't just ignore him."

Oh. So it was Devon, the bald one, the one she'd *dragged* from Albany.

"Jimmy is perfectly capable of entertaining Devon," she said. "Besides, they have work to do."

"Well, I still think it's rude."

Jill pressed a hand to her temple. "Amy, please. I'm tired. Tell me how your day was. How's the Halloween party coming?"

Amy averted her eyes the way she did whenever she was exasperated with her mother. "I decided to do the whole place in black light and decorate only in Gothic and glow. I hope you can manage to get there and not be out of town."

Black light, Gothic, and glow. Her daughter definitely had creativity. Not without guilt, Jill wondered if Amy's talents would go undeveloped on the island and subsequently be lost.

Ignoring the hint of sarcasm that had crept into Amy's voice, Jill said, "Ben and I will be at the party. It sounds really great."

"It's not great, Mom. But it's the best I can do here on the Vineyard."

She didn't sound as if she were complaining, but still, Jill could relate.

"You're not trapped here, Amy. You know that." She wasn't sure she was saying that to reassure herself or her daughter.

"I know, Mother. I'm here because I want to be. I don't need that other stupid world. Why won't you believe that?" She turned on her platform sneakers and clomped from the room.

Staring after her daughter, Jill wondered how it was that Amy knew herself so well, when Jill, twenty-eight years older, often didn't know herself at all. She took her tea from the microwave and wondered if her daughter would lose some of that unbending allegiance to the island once she learned what had happened to Ben, once she learned what was going to happen if her mother, Mrs. Cleaver, did not reacquaint herself with that other stupid world.

It was getting into the best scallop season, when the tiniest Nantucket Bay scallops were reaching their peak of melt-in-your-mouth sweetness. Jill hoped scallops would put the family in a wonderful mood and take the edge off the news she and Ben had to tell—and help Ben be more comfortable in telling it.

She also wondered why her middle name had not been Pollyanna.

Late that afternoon she had left Devon with a preliminary edit of the Cranberry Day story, hurried to the fish cooperative, then raced to the produce market, determined to create a magnificent dinner, even if it could not cushion the news. The important thing was that they were moving forward, telling the children, doing something that would make her feel more in control of the otherwise bleak situation.

It would be out in the open, there would be no secrets, and they could *talk* about it like normal, grown-up adults who had nothing to hide from the people they loved.

Then Jill could talk to Addie. Then she could secure a top-notch attorney who would make everything right. And then maybe some of the drawn, puttylike paleness would leave Ben's face.

She was taking homemade blueberry buckle from the

oven when the telephone rang. She glanced at the clock: five-forty-five. Only forty-five minutes until John and Carol Ann arrived. She almost let the machine answer the phone, but it could be the studio: Devon or Jimmy might have a question. Setting the hot dish on the butcher block counter, she picked up the cordless.

It was not the studio, it was John.

"I hope you haven't gone to a lot of trouble," Ben's son-in-law said, "because we can't make dinner."

Jill's gaze fell on the blueberry buckle. It looked as sumptuous as any her mother had ever created. "Oh," she replied. "Is everyone all right?"

The pause that followed could have been Jill's imagination, but she did not think so.

"Yes, well, I have some work to catch up on. And Emily has a cold. We hate to leave her with a baby-sitter."

Jill wanted to say that their family was more important than John's work, and that she didn't believe for a minute that Emily had a cold. She wanted to ask what was really going on. But John was Ben's son-in-law, not hers, and Jill still was unsure what position was expected of the stepmother to a nearly thirty-year-old woman with a family of her own.

"Well," she said, "that's too bad. Can we reschedule?"

There was that pause again.

"Let me get back to you, okay? We're so busy."

She decided this was bull. "Ben needs his family, John."

"So do I," John replied. "If he intends to tell Carol Ann, I can't stop him. But I honestly feel he should keep this to himself and not drag her—or us—into it."

Staring at the blueberry buckle, she was surprised it did not explode into flames—an incendiary response to the heat and anger that now flared inside her. "You're wrong, John. You're not being fair."

"And another thing," John added. "Don't count on the kids going with you to Sturbridge. I think they should stick close to Carol Ann and me until this mess blows over. If Carol Ann knew the truth, I'm sure she'd agree. Take care, Jill."

He hung up as unexpectedly as he'd called.

Jill sat there a moment, listening to the dial tone. Then Amy appeared in the kitchen.

"What time does the rest of the family arrive?" she asked coolly.

"They don't," Jill answered. "Carol Ann and John can't make it."

"Great," she said, her voice shifting to normal as she swooped down on the dessert. "Maybe I'll run some of this over to the studio. Is it blueberry?"

Ben was learning to kill time. He'd replaced the windows in the Oak Bluffs workshop, visited the contractor who was going to handle the house foundations at Sea Grove, gone out to the job site and walked around a few hundred times pretending to be checking things out though there was nothing yet to check and wouldn't be until they broke ground in spring.

He wondered if this was how he'd kill every day from now until the trial, then decided all he really needed was to kill this day, at least until dinner.

He still didn't want to tell the girls. But Jill was insistent, and he did not have the strength to argue, or the brains to sort it out and make a rational decision himself. He used to have brains. He used to have a quick mind that could calculate the cost of a high-ticket renovation right there on the spot, a mind that could visualize every post and every beam of a job before it was a job. But since his arrest, he often couldn't remember where he'd left his keys. And worse, he often didn't care.

When he arrived back in Edgartown, he parked the car and walked up the path to the house. Instinctively, he went to the kitchen. Jill was there, sitting silently. Amy stood at the counter shoveling something with blueberries into a refrigerator container.

Jill looked up. "They're not coming," she said.

He slouched against the doorway. "Not coming?" She must have meant Carol Ann. She must have meant John.

She shook her head.

He glanced over at Amy, who seemed happy, unaffected by the knowledge of his problems. Carol Ann was probably happy, too. Perhaps he'd been right to leave them out of this.

He turned to Jill, who looked as tired as he felt. "This isn't going to work, is it?" he asked.

"No," she replied. "I guess not."

Amy loaded the container into a paper bag. "What's not going to work?"

"Nothing," he said. He needed to ask Jill what really had happened, why dinner had been canceled, and if it was because of John. He needed to ask, but he could not ask with Amy right there.

He pulled off his baseball cap, hating this cloak-and-dagger stuff, hating that he could not even be himself in his own goddamn house even though technically the house was his wife's and not his.

"Well," he said steadily, "I guess that means all the more scallops for us."

"Not me," Amy said. "I'll be in Oak Bluffs." She picked up the bag, grabbed her jacket, and blew out the door.

He turned back to Jill.

"Let's not talk about it," she said, standing up. "I'm sick to death of talking about it, so please, not tonight."

Chapter 9

When Rita called in the morning, Jill was sitting in the bedroom, trying to decide when—how—she would tell Ben that she'd agreed to do *Good Night, USA* after all. They had not made love since that day in the workshop; despite their bond and what she'd thought was their love, the day-to-day edge was not going away. Last night's aborted dinner had not helped. Nor had matters improved later, when she'd told him that his grandchildren would not be going to Sturbridge Village. He had gone to bed quietly at a quarter to eight.

"So I haven't told Charlie yet," Rita was saying. "Now it looks as if I won't have to, if he's in Florida all winter. With that woman."

Jill tried to focus on what Rita was saying. "But it's not right," Jill said into the phone. "He should be given the choice." Though the words conveyed her true feelings about Rita's situation, Jill had an anesthetic feeling of being one person on the surface and another underneath. Friend on the surface, tormented soul beneath. Public persona versus reality. Once it had been an acceptable way of life. But then the stakes had not been as great because she had not really cared. Or loved. "Maybe Charlie's testing you," she added. "To see if you'll notice that he's gone."

"He asked me to find a winter renter for his apartment. That hardly sounds like a test. Which reminds me," she added, "what about Amy? It would be perfect for her, Jill. And it's only two blocks from you."

"No," Jill said without hesitation. "I told you, she's too young." She was beginning to feel like the "broken record" her mother had always referred to when Jill asked for "permission" to do things with Rita.

Can I go to the movies? Can I go to the dance? Can I go to Illumination Night without a chaperone this year?

No.

No.

No.

Don't ask anymore. I'm not a broken record.

Fast-forward another generation. Different sound system. Same record.

"God, Jill, I don't understand you. When you were her age, you left the island. You were totally on your own."

"Maybe I want her life to be easier than that. Maybe I want to protect her a little more. Besides, she's not as mature as I was."

"Bullshit. She's probably more mature. She's been through more."

Jill made no comment.

"She'd be happier, Jill. And Charlie would be thrilled."

And then she realized whose agenda Rita had in mind. And why. "Wait a minute," Jill said. "If Charlie's apartment is rented, he might be more inclined to leave the island for the winter. Then you could be sure of avoiding him, right?"

What followed was silence—sweet, "so there" silence.

"You say you don't understand me, Rita. Well, I can

say the same for you. You're pushing Charlie into that other woman's arms."

"Oh, for God's sake, Jill, stop overreacting. I've already told you I'm not going to marry him, so what's the difference?"

Jill closed her eyes and wondered why she was arguing with her best friend over things that really didn't matter to her. She was so tired, worn out from talking and analyzing and trying to figure out how to do what and when. "Forget it," she said. "Do what you want."

"I'm not working at the tavern now. I'm staying home to oversee my mother, who's begun knitting booties. Anyway, keeping my distance from Charlie should help."

"What about the Halloween party?"

"I told Amy I'd be there. Guess I'll go as a pumpkin."

"Rita—"

"No more advice, Jill. I know how you feel."

She paused a moment, then said, "No, Rita, I said before, whether or not you tell Charlie is your business. I just want you to remember that life, that *relationships,* are fragile. Even friendships." She felt herself grin. "But I guess we've proved that."

Suddenly Ben came into the room holding what looked like a FedEx envelope. His teeth were clenched, and his gray eyes were dark.

He stared at her a moment, then said, "Hang up the phone."

She looked at the envelope. And then she knew.

"Rita, I have to go," she said slowly, then clicked off without saying good-bye. She sat there, eyes glued to her demise, waiting for Ben to erupt as he probably would. As he probably should.

"What the hell is this?" He tossed the cardboard envelope in her lap.

She looked down at the white, orange, and purple. The tearstrip had been torn, and the contents were exposed.

"I thought it was something for me," Ben said. "Bids for Sea Grove. I thought wrong."

For the first time since she'd known Ben, Jill felt fury. And it was coming from him. "Ben, I—" she began, "I did it for us."

"For *us*?" Surprisingly, he did not shout, but his voice shook, and he had not moved, not a muscle, not a breath. "You lied to me—for us? Please explain how lying to me is going to help *us*."

"Please, Ben. We need the money."

He did not say a word, not even *go to hell* or *screw you, lady*. Instead, he just stood there a moment, then abruptly turned and went out the door.

Was he going back to the tavern? He could live there now. He could rent the apartment from Charlie and not have to come home all winter. Or ever again.

Perhaps their love had been too magical, too unrealistic, with the end of it only a day—or a FedEx envelope—away.

Through choking-back tears, she pulled out the papers and glanced at the contract. It was neatly, properly written for the month of February: February, her first network job.

Ben went to the tavern, because he had nowhere else to go. Since marrying Jill, he'd relinquished his privacy: she had taken over his old house in Oak Bluffs—his refuge—and right now it was occupied by a couple of odd-looking young men at digital controls. He could go out to the cliffs at Gay Head, but without Noepe, there was little solace there.

He could not go to his house, and he could not go to his daughter's.

So he went to the tavern in search of a friendly face, or

at least a face he did not want to scream at. Hopefully Ashenbach wouldn't be there.

Ashenbach wasn't, but neither was Charlie. Amy was alone, standing on a chair, stringing gaudy fake cobwebs from the centuries-old beams.

"I hope you're not defacing a historic monument, young lady," Ben said from the foyer.

"Hey, Ben," Amy said, turning slightly. "You're just in time to give me a hand."

Great, he thought, something constructive to kill some more time and help take his mind off—no, he wouldn't think about that.

"Is this really a historic monument?" Amy asked.

He shrugged, handing her more cobwebs. "I'm sure it was to your mother's family." He was proud of himself for not letting his voice crack when he said "your mother."

She jumped down from the table and surveyed her work. "I'm going to replace the lightbulbs with black light so that everything white and anything fluorescent will glow. Then we'll have centerpieces made from orange and green lightsticks on every table. What do you think?"

"Sounds ghoulish."

Amy laughed. "Wait until you see it! I'm glad you guys are coming."

He wondered what he'd wear for a costume and if "CM" should be embroidered on his lapel, and if it should be scarlet. He forced a smile. "We wouldn't miss it."

"Well, I'm amazed Mom won't be out of town." She tacked a few bats to a wall print of a whaling ship. "Then again, I suppose it will be a good way to check up on me."

Ben scowled as if he didn't know what Amy meant.

"Do you think she'll ever let me cut the cord, Ben? Take Charlie's apartment. He's renting it for the winter. Do you think for a minute Mom would let me have it? No-o-o-o-o. Forget it!"

No one had told him Charlie wanted to rent his apartment over the tavern. Was he moving in with that woman, the one from the mainland? Ben wanted to ask but was more concerned right now with Jill's need to control Amy's life. It wasn't a lot unlike her need to control his, too, to try and make this ordeal go away on her terms, not his. "Have you mentioned the apartment to her?"

"I had my secret assistant do it for me. Rita. Mom said no way. As expected."

To Ben, this seemed like a perfect solution. If Amy rented Charlie's apartment, she'd be out of the house, away from the opportunity of learning about Mindy. Amy was eighteen—and she was supporting herself. Well, almost. A good dose of independence might be just what Amy needed to help her realize how important family support—and furthering her education—really was. And it would sure give him and Jill more freedom to sort things out, their marriage included.

He took off his cap and rubbed his head. "Has Rita rented it yet?"

"Don't know. Hey—what about you? Not that it's any of my business, but the tension around home is so thick, you couldn't whack it with a ginzu. Maybe you should take a break. An amicable separation before it leads to marital disaster."

Ben stiffened. "Your mother and I are just fine, Amy. And you're right, it's none of your business. But when I married her, I made it my business to see that you're happy, too. And if I have anything to say about it, you'll have this apartment. If it's what you really want."

She dropped the bats, flung her arms around him, and kissed him square on the lips.

Just at that moment, Jill walked through the door.

Jill wasn't sure how to describe what she felt when she walked in and saw her husband in her daughter's arms, lips upon lips. If it hadn't been for Mindy Ashenbach, she might have thought nothing.

She watched in stunned silence as her husband untangled Amy's arms a little too quickly.

"Jill," he said, as if speaking her name would eradicate any negative insinuation the act had evoked.

"Ben," she replied, trying to push down a seed of doubt that had neatly been planted. "I was hoping I'd find you here."

She looked at Amy, who looked at Ben, who looked at Jill, then Amy, then back at Jill.

She blinked. "Rick Fitzpatrick is looking for you." She supposed she shouldn't have mentioned the lawyer in front of Amy, but right now she wasn't feeling very patronizing of her husband or his problems.

"Rick?" Ben asked, stepping away from his stepdaughter. "It must be about the land titles for Sea Grove."

She wanted to blurt it out right then and there, to tell Amy about Mindy so she could watch his face freeze in dull shock, the way hers felt frozen now. Instead, she folded her arms. "Oh, yes, I'm sure."

He put his hands on his hips as if in defense. "Amy was just thanking me because I promised to put in a good word for her. It seems Charlie wants a winter renter for his apartment. The fact that you plan to be gone so often would make the apartment ideal for Amy. No sense in turning her into a housekeeper for this old man."

Jill wanted to kill Ben for bringing up the apartment right in front of Amy, as if she had not already said no. She also wanted to kill him for hinting that Amy would be better off out from under the same roof where he lived. As if she didn't trust him. As if . . .

Ben moved closer to her. "Come on, Jill, what do you say? Let her have a try. She'll only be two blocks away."

Inside her jacket pockets, she balled her hands into fists. "Do what you want, both of you," she said. "I don't care anymore."

With a shriek of delight, Amy high-fived Ben and Jill went out the door.

Something must have happened. Rita had known Jill for over forty years, and in all that time she'd never once changed her mind, had only grown more stubborn after she'd made a decision. Well, of course, she had changed her mind and married Ben and not that celebrity asshole, but Rita never believed she'd been serious about him in the first place. After all, a big part of the reason Jill had become so successful was because she had sense.

So when Jill called Rita in the morning and told her she had changed her mind and wanted Amy to have the apartment, Rita was surprised. She wasted no time in leaving a message on Charlie's machine, in case he ever bothered to haul himself out of Marge Bainey's sack long enough to see if the rest of the world was still there.

Apparently he hauled himself out not long after lunch, because a few minutes later, he was on the phone.

"So it looks like you're off to Florida whether you like it or not," Rita said. "Or you'll be bunking at the homeless shelter in Vineyard Haven."

"Or with you and Hazel," he said with a chuckle, which Rita did not think was very funny.

"Do you want me to draw up a lease agreement? What about the rent? You never mentioned what you want."

"For Amy? Come on, Rita, she's family. Besides, the heat might be costly if it's a cold winter, but it will be better for the building if it's on. If she wants cable TV, she'll have to pay for it to be installed. Those things plus the fact she'll be watching out for the tavern should make us about even."

"That figures," Rita said. "I finally make a real estate deal, and the guy wants to cut me out of a commission."

"I'll send you a pink flamingo for the lawn."

A baby stroller might be more appropriate, she wanted to say. She felt a slow pang of sorrow that this time separation from Charlie seemed somehow permanent. A fleeting thought that maybe she should tell him about the baby, that maybe she should stop him from doing anything stupid like marrying Marge Bainey, went through her mind and did just that: fleeted. When he came home in the spring, it might be too late for them, but it wouldn't be too late for him to be a father to his child, if she decided he should be, if that was what he wanted, if he weren't so angry with her that he ignored their baby.

No, Rita thought, Charlie was like Ben Niles. Neither had a mean bone in his body.

"When are you leaving?" Rita asked. "Not that I care, but Amy might like to know when she can move in."

"Well, I hadn't made definite plans, but now it looks as if you've forced me into them. Give me a few days after the Halloween party to get organized. How about if she moves in the following weekend?"

"Good deal," Rita said, then rang off, feeling somehow elated that she'd beaten the odds and would not have to face Charlie and tell him the truth and risk him wanting to marry her and her having to say no.

Chapter 10

Mindy took her time walking home from the school bus. Part of her was hoping if she were late, she wouldn't have to go today. Tomorrow might be better. Or next week.

But she saw the doctor's old Volvo as soon as she reached the driveway. The doctor stood outside with Grandpa—oh, God, was he going, too?

He was. They were.

Grandpa hustled Mindy into the pickup truck. The doctor said she'd follow them, so she wouldn't have to come back out to Menemsha. Mindy was glad because that meant she wouldn't have another "session" today, another hour of talking about fairly stupid things and getting neither of them anywhere, wherever they were supposed to be going.

"Let's stay with this a moment," the doctor said whenever the subject of Mindy's mother came up.

"And what about your dad?" she must have asked a skillion trillion times, though Mindy barely remembered him and told her so.

Stupid questions wasting time. Wasting Grandpa's money.

She wanted to tell him that now, but when she looked over, he sat forward on the seat and said, "You be sure to tell them how Niles made you come there every day after school."

He scowled a familiar scowl and added, "You be sure to tell them how he always brought you snacks from that tavern—those homemade cookies you told me about. You be sure to tell them how he took you out to the cliffs and how he made you play that game."

"Making pictures from the clouds?"

"Yes. You be sure to tell them that."

You be sure of this and *sure of that*. Mindy pressed her face against the window and wasn't sure of anything.

It was a small room with only one window where someone had put a plant that was mostly dead. There were three chairs and a wooden table. The walls were painted the color of old celery: a painting of a lighthouse hung on one, a calendar on another. In the corner of the room, a video camera was set atop metal legs. Behind the camera stood a thin young guy who could have been a fisherman except he wore a white shirt and bow tie.

It wasn't how Mindy pictured a courthouse room would look. It didn't have a big bench or Judge Judy in a long black robe. It was just a room, and it just had . . . them.

"I guess we can sit down," Dr. Reynolds said, so the three of them sat.

A moment later, a man came in. He had gray hair and a cardigan sweater the same color. He smiled.

Grandpa stood up and shook the man's hand. "Mr. Winkman," Grandpa said, "nice to see you again."

Mindy crossed her feet under her and tried not to think about his funny name. Winkman. Winkie. Wink-wink. She wondered if he winked a lot or if he had a twitch. She bit her lip.

"This is my granddaughter, Melinda."

Sometimes she forgot that was her name.

"Hello, Melinda," Mr. Wink-wink said. "I'm Mr. Winkman, the district attorney. I'm going to ask you a few questions today. Is that all right?"

She wondered what would happen if she said no. She pointed to the camera. "You're going to tape me?"

"Yes," he replied. "This is what we call a deposition. You will answer my questions, then we'll show the video to the judge. That way you won't have to go to the trial."

"Will I be cross-examined?" She remembered that from the *Law & Order* reruns she watched late at night when she couldn't sleep and there was nothing else to do. Cross-examination was when the other guy's lawyer yelled and screamed and got the defendant to say things he didn't want to say, and to confess things like "I lied! I'm the killer!"

"You won't be cross-examined," Mr. Winkman replied. "You're a minor."

"Oh," she said, guessing that was good. She folded her hands. "Well, go ahead, then. Ask me anything."

Everyone started bustling around the room like they were playing musical chairs because there were four of them plus the camera guy and only three chairs.

"Just you and me," Mindy said. "I don't want Grandpa here. Or Dr. Reynolds."

Everybody stopped.

"I'm ten years old. I don't need baby-sitters."

"But, Mindy," Dr. Reynolds protested, "I think it would be better for me to—"

She shook her head. "You already know what happened. You, too, Grandpa. Just let me do this so we can go home."

Everyone but Mr. Winkman and the cameraman finally left the room.

Jill's marriage was falling apart.

How could her marriage be falling apart?

Two weeks ago she was more in love than she'd ever dreamed possible. She'd hated every second that she and Ben had to be in separate towns, in separate rooms, in separate beds. Now, even though her heart would not stop aching, she looked for excuses to be somewhere else, anywhere, where this darkness might not follow.

The "somewhere else" she'd chosen now was the studio, where Jimmy and Devon were finishing the edit. She sat at her desk, the FedEx envelope nagging at her elbow, the contract as yet unsigned. In case she changed her mind.

For the who-knew-how-many-eth time, she scanned the paragraphs. *On air Monday through Friday, February 1st through 28th. Availability for preview publicity photos in December—date and location TBD.* There was no mention of a longer-term commitment, no hint that signing this could be the ruin of her marriage, the end of life as she now knew it. There was, of course, the standard morals clause. But Jill hadn't been the one accused of "questionable" behavior that could reflect negatively on the show's production or its image.

She wanted to ask Rita if she should do it. But that would open up that can of troublesome, forbidden worms.

"How many dubs?" Jimmy, who now stood beside her, asked.

Quickly, she tried to cover the contract with her hand, to hide those worms. "The same as for the Vermont piece?" There was no sense pretending that anyone but the feeder services would be interested in her work. There was no sense pretending that going direct to the networks—to *20/20* or *Dateline*—would work.

Jimmy nodded and went to the refrigerator and pulled

out a case of tapes, which they often stored there, safe from the island dampness. Before he shut the door, Jill noticed the bowl of blueberry buckle, partially eaten. She stopped herself from asking if they'd enjoyed it. Then she wondered if Amy really would have been worse off in L.A., where she might at least have had the chance to meet more kids her age, all of whom could not be bad.

Would Amy be angry if she signed on the dotted line? But Jill could not ask Amy, for her daughter would not know all the details.

She could not ask Amy and she could not ask Rita. She could only listen to her own heart and know that unless Ben got a better lawyer, the risk was too damn high.

Picking up the pen, she hesitated only briefly before signing in triplicate.

"We need to talk, Ben," Jill said that night after a dinner of pot roast and carrots that they barely touched. Amy was at the tavern; now was as good a time as any.

Ben lowered his head. "I'm listening," he said without enthusiasm.

She wanted to shout that she needed him to do more than listen. She needed him to stop acting defeated, to stop behaving as if she were not completely on his side. But shouting had never been Jill's style. Nor was Ben the type of man one shouted at.

"Honey," she said quietly, "I know you're upset about the contract."

He took his napkin from his lap and set it on the table. "What I'm upset about is your deceit."

A twinge of guilt—*deserved* guilt, she knew—fluttered in her heart. "I know," she replied. "And I'm sorry. I didn't mean to deceive you." Well, perhaps a little, but with good reason, she admitted only to herself. But now was not the time to mention that, or that she fully intended to secure him a good lawyer. Nor was now the time to challenge him about which of the two of them was feeling more betrayed.

"I'm only afraid you think this is going to blow over," Jill said, "as if you'll wake up some morning and it will all be gone."

Silence hung in the kitchen amid the lingering aromas of pot roast and onions and ten or twenty thousand meals Jill's mother had cooked long before Ben sat here, long before Jill had known that she would, one day, truly fall in love.

He put his elbows on the table and looked straight into her eyes. "Don't pretend to know how I feel," he said, "because you don't have a clue. Take today, for instance. You walked into the tavern right after I told Amy that I would try and convince you to let her rent Charlie's apartment. She was so excited she gave me a hug and a kiss. Then I saw you standing there and the first thing I thought of was that you were wondering if you'd interrupted something . . . that if this man you'd married really was a . . . pervert."

A tiny pool of acid bubbled up inside her throat. "I did not think that, Ben." She lied because she felt she had to. She lied because she hated her doubt. "How can you even say that?" she asked, underscoring the lie, punctuating its existence into a greater sin.

He studied her, his wonderful gray eyes now sad and tired, not the eyes of a villain, but those of a man who'd been through too much, who was worn out from grief. "I knew what you were thinking because you are my wife. And because I've loved you long enough to be able to read the look that was on your face."

She wanted to crumble. She wanted to scold herself for not being more like her own mother, the dutiful wife who held back her own thoughts, her own needs, to keep her man the master, lord of the house.

Though Jill was not her mother, she knew when to let go and when to be supportive, even when she did not feel quite like doing it. "Perhaps what you saw was your own fear, honey. The fear that no one will believe you." She did not add that he might be right. Which was all the more reason they needed the best lawyer in the world.

"So you took the job in L.A." He did not mention Christopher this time, and for that she was grateful.

"Only to jump-start my career. To reopen doors that Addie closed. Remember when you said I'd been black-balled? Maybe this will end it once and for all. Trust me, Ben. Please."

"And what about us?" he asked. "I did trust you, Jill. Then you went behind my back. How can I trust you again?"

Her head was aching now; her heart was filled with tears that wanted to come out. She dropped her chin and began to cry. "Oh, God," she said, "I can stand most anything, Ben. What I can't stand is arguing with you. I can't stand fighting with each other. I feel like you're a victim and Mindy is a victim and so am I. I feel like my marriage is falling apart because of a spoiled kid."

Ben was quiet, then he spoke. "She's not spoiled, Jill. I told you. She's misguided."

She raised her head. "And what can we do to change that?"

"We can't. We can only take care of ourselves. One step at a time. Which I suppose means we—I—have to forget about *Good Night, USA*. The deal is done. I'm not going to let my petty insecurities get in the way of your career."

She lowered her eyes. "I am so sorry, Ben. For not telling you first."

He touched her cheek. "I'm sorry for a lot of things, honey. But I want us to get through this, and maybe we can if you leave Addie Becker and her connections out of it. Deal?"

She could not agree. But she knew that if she wanted to save what was left of her crippled marriage, she'd better act as if he were right. Then she could hope and pray that later he would come to his senses. Later, but not too late.

"Speaking of lawyers," Ben continued, as if he didn't realize she had not answered, "I called Rick back. He said they did Mindy's video deposition today. I have a right to see it. He said once we know what we're up against, we'll be better able to decide how to proceed."

She sucked in a small breath. "You can see it?"

"Ten o'clock tomorrow. At Rick's office. You're welcome to come." He ran his hand through his hair. "If you want."

She studied the edge of the tablecloth and knew there was no way she could say no, not if she wanted to salvage what might still be left of her marriage. She blinked back tears and raised her head and offered a small, well-intentioned smile. "Of course I want to go," she replied.

"I did chores almost every day all summer," Mindy said into the camera in response to a question posed by a nameless inquisitor in a gray cardigan. "I cleaned up after the kids, I swept wood shavings, I picked up litter in the yard. Soda cans, ice cream wrappers. Stuff like that."

"Did Mr. Niles pay you for these chores?"

"Oh, sure. He gave me ten dollars, twenty sometimes if I did extra work."

"That's a lot of money for a ten-year-old."

Mindy raised her chin. "I deserved it. I worked hard."

Despite the circumstances, Ben smiled. She was a feisty kid; he'd known that all along.

"Did he give you anything else?"

She was silent for a moment. "He didn't give me the money, Mr. Winkman. I earned it."

"Okay. Did you 'earn'—or did he give you—anything else?"

"He let me work on the crafts. Tying brooms, peg-boarding floors. And he brought food sometimes. Home-made cookies and cakes. One time his friend Rita brought homemade fudge. But it was for everybody, not just me."

"Did you ever meet Rita?"

"No. She's not his wife, though."

Ben glanced at Jill. He wondered if he'd ever told her Rita had sent fudge to the museum or if Jill had been out of town.

"How many times were you alone with Mr. Niles?"

She thought about it briefly. Then she shrugged. "Lots of times."

"Only at the museum?"

"Sometimes he took me out to Gay Head."

"Why?"

"To sit on the cliffs. To play the cloud game."

"The cloud game? What kind of game is that?"

She sighed a small ten-year-old sigh. "We looked up at the clouds and tried to pick out different shapes. Indian stuff, mostly. Tomahawks and teepees. And canoes. Stuff like that."

"Anything else?"

She chewed her lip. "We talked about owning our own purple souvenir shop on the cliffs. We figured the Indians made a lot of money that way."

The camera jiggled, as if the person running it had bumped it.

"And at any of those times did Mr. Niles ever make you feel . . . uncomfortable?"

She paused again. Ben wondered why the hell she was pausing.

"Well," she said, "sometimes."

He sat up straight in his chair.

"Why?"

Mindy's eyes darted to the camera, then back to the D.A. She did not reply.

Ben looked from Jill to Rick. He could not tell what they were thinking.

"What happened on the afternoon in question?"

The afternoon in question? Suddenly this seemed ridiculous. The guy who looked like Mister Rogers was playing Perry Mason. Ben might even have laughed if he weren't the one whose life was at stake, the Salem witch about to go to trial.

And then Mindy answered the question. Looking squarely into the camera again, she put her hands on her flat chest. "He touched me," she said clearly and distinctly. "He touched me here."

There was silence on the TV screen, silence in the room.

"Shit," Ben said. His body sagged as if someone had drained the blood from his veins and the energy from his muscles, every muscle.

"What did you do when he did that?" the D.A. asked.

The camera zoomed in and got a close-up of her face, the way he'd heard Jill instruct when she wanted to make sure the audience was paying attention. "I screamed," Mindy said evenly. "Then I ran home." She hung her head in a way that you couldn't tell, but would have bet, concealed a waterfall of tears.

Ben shifted in his seat.

Rick leveled the remote and clicked the picture off. "We're in trouble, Ben," he said. "She's very credible."

Yes, Ben thought. Even a fool could see that she was.

• • • •

"Maybe you should go to England," Ben said to Jill as they walked quietly through Edgartown on the way back home. "Visit Jeff. Get the hell away from this mess for a while."

"This mess will be here when I get back."

"Maybe not. Maybe the guilt fairy will come along and leave a calling card on Mindy's pillow."

They both knew that wasn't funny. Or probable.

They turned onto Pease Point Way, avoiding Main Street in an unspoken quest for privacy. Despite the gag order, Ben had begun to sense that everywhere he walked, every shop that he entered or restaurant that he passed, heads turned and eyes followed as if they somehow knew.

"If I go away, it will look like I'm not supportive," Jill said. "That maybe I don't believe you." Her high heels clicked on the sidewalk through the crunched fallen leaves. "I will not have anyone think that, not for an instant."

Ben put his hands in his pockets. "Do you honestly believe I'm innocent?"

They took two more steps, then three. "You are an honest man, Ben. A good, honest man. And I do not believe for a minute that you could do anything so vile."

Until that moment, Ben had not realized how badly he'd needed to hear her say those words. He had not realized it because he had not wanted to admit there was a chance that she might not say them.

She linked her arm through his. Her touch warmed him, calmed him. "I will go on the stand," she said. "I will tell the jury you could not have done it."

He smiled. "Even if Rick let you testify, no one would believe you."

"Of course they will. I'm Jill McPhearson, remember? Media star? *News* media star—who has to have a high believability factor to sit on the anchor desk. A trust factor."

His stomach turned sour. The same way it did whenever he thought about February and *Good Night, USA.* "No one on the Vineyard cares about that, and you know it," he said. "They won't believe you because you're my wife. But thanks for the effort."

She slipped her arm from his. He wished she'd put it back, where it helped steady his walk, where it helped him feel less alone. "Well, anyway," she said quietly, "I'm not going to desert you and go to England."

They walked a few more blocks, this time in silence. For all the tension between them these past days, Ben did not wonder what he would do without Jill, how he would handle this mess. He simply knew he would not handle it well.

He looked at the ground, at his wife's feet that kept pace beside him, her polished leather pumps right-lefting beside his scruffy work boots.

"I'm sorry," he said, eyes still focused on the brick walk. "I'm sorry I got so upset about your deal with Addie. If you want to do the shtick with your old boyfriend, that's your decision. As long as you don't tell them our business."

The sound of their footsteps click-clicked again.

"I don't *want* to do the show, Ben." She wrapped her arms around herself, around her thin gentle middle that always seemed so fragile and lost in his arms. "What I really want is to have the last three years back. I was happiest tending the gardens and renovating the house and falling in love with you a little more each day. That's what I would have wanted forever. But life changes. We can't stay in fantasyland forever."

"I thought you went back to work because you wanted to help until Menemsha House was under way."

She was silent, then raised her eyes to the setting sun. "I did, Ben. That's what I mean. Life changes. The things we want can change. They can change from day to day or from year to year."

"Or not at all," he said.

She turned to him. "What do you mean?"

"The way I feel about you hasn't changed, Jill."

She smiled. "You still want to protect me. You have to learn you can't protect me."

"Who says?" He took her hand. It was small and smooth in his.

"You want me to run away to England."

"No. I want you to take a little break. Visit your son."

"Bull. You want me to run away."

He looked down at their feet again. "Not completely," he said. "I also want you away from here so I don't feel the guilt that I have made your life so miserable that now you want to go back to the one you had before you met me, the one where it was all glitter and limousines and everything beautiful."

She stopped. She turned his face toward her. "Ben Niles," she said, her eyes locked on his, "you are such an ass."

Chapter 11

Rita was going as a witch because the dress was full and she couldn't be a pumpkin because she looked positively dreadful in orange. That last observation had not come from her but from Hazel, who was definitely going to drive Rita crazy before all was said and done.

The only thing keeping Rita sane these days was that after the Halloween party, the tavern would close for the season, and Charlie would be gone to Florida. By the time he returned in the spring, the baby would have been born.

All she had to do was get through this night unscathed, her secret undetected. The witch costume should help, though beneath it her jeans were beginning to groan. Three months pregnant, and already it was apparent.

She arrived early to help Amy set up. Unfortunately, Marge Bainey had the same idea. Rita had never had the pleasure.

They stood in the dining room amid a ghoulish tangle of fake cobwebs and black-construction-paper bats. She nodded when Amy introduced her to the woman and tried to pretend it was, indeed, as nice to meet her as she said.

"I've heard so much about you," said the mainlander from Falmouth, who was wearing an unnerving, teenage Cher outfit. Rita wondered if the long black tresses covered mousy gray hair, and if the tall svelte body in the fringed vest, jeans, and boots would become short, plump, and squat when the costume was removed. Miracles, after all, happened every day, or so she'd heard.

She smiled but did not acknowledge that she, too, had heard "so much" about her. "Where's Charlie?" Rita asked, quickly, hoping that no one thought she cared about the answer too much.

"Getting dressed," Marge/Cher replied with a cute grin that hinted she was quite familiar with the act of Charlie Rollins pulling his clothes on and off.

Rita did not mention that she, too, had been there and done that and now had a second, late-in-life pregnancy to prove it.

"I have no idea how many people will show up," Amy said, changing the subject. She was dressed as one of the Spice Girls. Rita wondered if everyone but her would arrive as a Top 40 megastar, then or now. Her eyes scanned the room.

"I've been telling Amy not to worry," Marge said, tossing back her "hair" and adjusting the beaded headband. "The 1802 Tavern is renowned for its Halloween parties."

"How would you know?" Rita asked, not caring about the edge to her voice. "You're from America."

The woman laughed. Rita tried not to notice that the lines of her rib cage protruded through her slinky black body suit. "I was here last year," she said. "It was right after I took on the Vineyard as an account.

"In fact," the woman continued, "that was when I met Charlie."

Slowly the words registered. *A year ago?* A tiny foot— or maybe it was gas—flutter-kicked Rita's belly, somewhere between the baby's big toe and her heart. Charlie had known Marge a whole year? He'd met her when Rita and he were still—well, not dating exactly, but still sleeping together on occasion? She wondered if . . . *never mind,* she told herself. *It doesn't matter.* The flutter-kick came again. She turned to Amy. "So where are we bobbing for apples?"

Amy turned and walked toward the fireplace. Rita gladly stepped out of Cher's aura and followed.

"I think the hearth will be perfect," Amy said, gesturing to a huge copper pot that sat there now. "I bought two pecks. Do you want to wash them?"

"A witch is definitely the right one to wash apples" came Charlie's voice from the stairs. The lilt in his voice told Rita he was trying to be funny, perhaps to cut the tension between his lovers, old and new, who now stood in the same space, breathing the same air.

Rita turned, determined to smile and convince him that it was okay. But then she noticed his costume: a sheepskin vest, bell-bottom jeans, and a Fu Manchu mustache. He was Sonny, to Marge Bainey's Cher.

And the beat goes on, she thought with quiet, resigned remorse.

By nine o'clock the party was in full swing, and Rita was exhausted from all the pretend-stuff—the pretend smiling and grinning and chatting—while trying to keep Charlie and/or Marge in her peripheral vision and hating herself for doing that; the pretend enthusiasm over costumes and beer swigging and silly games in which she once would have been an eager participant.

It was different now. She stepped outside the back door and stood in the alley, breathing in fresh air and shutting out the din behind her.

She wished she could talk to Jill. She wished they

could share the goings-on and the gossip of the party, as they had done in the old days.

But things were different now. It was like all those times when Jill was gone and Rita had walked past the house on North Water Street, with Kyle on his tricycle. The house had looked the same, even when the people inside were different, when the laughter was long gone.

It wasn't quite the same as that now, but it was different nonetheless.

Jill and Ben were inside the tavern, Jill and Ben, the all-American couple, the perfect pair. They had come tonight as ghosts: Jill, a glamour-ghost, in a sheet with ochre ultrasuede trim and pearl-white sequins; Ben, a worker-ghost, complete with tool belt and hard hat. They were cute, quaint, and together. Rita hated that women friends could always be friends until the one thing they each longed for—a man—got in the way. It was as if once the prize arrived, a lot of other things and people got screwed up in the change.

Change. There was that word again.

She looked up to the sky. Its autumn blackness was sharp and clear, and a sprinkle of stars punctured the canvas with radiant silver. She thought of Kyle and pictured him up there in the shape of a seagull, riding a star, watching over her.

She supposed he knew about Charlie and Marge Bainey. And that all hell might break loose in the spring when Charlie returned—married, perhaps—and discovered that in his absence Rita had had a baby that looked an awful lot like him.

She could always have the baby off-island and lie about his birth date so Charlie wouldn't know it was his. So Charlie wouldn't know it was another Kyle.

If she didn't know better, she'd have sworn she heard Kyle say, "Once was enough, Mom. Even though we did okay, don't cheat this baby out of a father."

The old back door hinge creaked. Rita blinked in the darkness. The two young men who worked for Jill—Jill had introduced them, what were their names?—stepped outside. Then they laughed and linked arms and kissed each other on the lips. On the lips? Hadn't Jill said Amy had a crush on one of them?

"Lose someone?" Rita asked.

The young men jumped. Their arms fell to their sides. The one with the ponytail smiled. "Sorry. It's so crowded inside, we were looking for a way out."

"Looks like you found it." Where was Amy? Did she know that the two men were with each other in . . . the biblical sense? Not that she cared, but Amy . . .

The ponytailed one pulled off a three-cornered hat that was supposed to make him look like a revolutionary soldier. But he looked more like the ruffle-shirted Paul Revere of the 1960s rock band the Raiders, than the one-if-by-land, two-if-by-sea Revere.

"Great party," he said. "Have you seen Amy?"

She shifted her gaze from the Minuteman to his partner, who was dressed as a clown, complete with a large flower painted atop his bald head. "The last time I saw her, she was judging the costume contest."

He laughed. "Well, if you see her again, tell her we took off and thanks for the invite."

Rita did not ask where they were "taking off" to, and what they'd take off once they got there.

"We'll catch up with her later. Okay?"

It amazed her how blasé the younger generation was about relationships. "I'm afraid I can't tell her anything because I've forgotten your names." She could simply have said "the young men who work for your mother," but she felt a stupid need to make them as uncomfortable as she could, as if being nasty would protect Amy from getting hurt.

"Jimmy and Devon," he replied.

Devon squeaked a horn that was tied to his belt.

Jimmy laughed. Then the two sauntered off.

As Rita watched them walk away, she wondered what would have happened if Kyle had lived, if he would have ended up loving Amy and if they would have married. Then Rita wrapped her arms around herself and headed back inside, because though change always was sure to come, she didn't have to like it. Not one damn bit.

"Last call of the year," Charlie announced with what Rita recognized as hope that the crowd would start to dwindle.

She removed her pointed black hat and wove her way to the bathroom, letting someone else handle the last round of drinks. In the nearly thirty years that she'd worked there, Rita had paid her dues.

Once in the ladies' lounge, she sat down on the small sofa and unpeeled her boots, grateful for the quiet and the escape from the crazy people. Holding her legs out, she wriggled her toes. As if in response, the baby seemed to wriggle his. She could not remember if Kyle had been active at three months.

Lifting her dress, she unzipped the fly of her jeans and rubbed her belly. "Slow down there, partner," she said. "After tonight we're home free."

Her stomach seemed bigger tonight than last night, bigger, even than this afternoon. Hauling herself up from the sofa, she went to the full-length mirror on the back of the door. With her dress raised to her breasts, Rita smoothed her hand over her mound, then stood sideways to examine its size.

She let out a low whistle. Yes, it was definitely a good thing that Charlie would be gone tomorrow. Because there was no way he could look at her and not see what she could see.

"Rita!"

Rita's hand froze over her belly. In the mirror she saw Amy emerging from a stall. Slowly she lowered her dress, but it was too late. Amy's eyes were stuck to Rita's baby belly, like peanut butter to marshmallow, like oatmeal to ribs.

With her best effort at nonchalance, Rita turned to Jill's daughter. "Hey, kid," she said, "I thought you were doing last call."

For the second or two during which the Spice Girl Amy did not reply, Rita ran through about a hundred scenarios in her mind.

My mother's cooking has made me fat.

Menopause, Amy. Just you wait and see.

Think I'd better sign up for the gym.

The scenarios came, and all of them stank. Besides, reality would soon be undoubtedly evident, and she couldn't lie to Amy.

She could deflect the conversation by saying she'd seen the video boys together. But that might hurt Amy, and she couldn't do that, either.

The only answer, then, was to tell the plain damn truth.

"Well," she finally said as Amy dragged her eyes from Rita's stomach up to her face, "looks like I'm caught. Red-handed, so to speak, as opposed to red-headed. Which I am, too, though not for long because Doc Hastings won't let me dye my hair again until my term is over."

The merriment from the distant bar sneaked into the silence of the bathroom. "You're pregnant," Amy said.

Rita smiled. "Sort of."

Dumbfounded was a good way to describe Amy's open-mouthed look.

"Don't worry," Rita added, "I'm not contagious."

"Does my mom know?" Amy asked.

Rita laughed. "Actually, yes, she does. She's thrilled."

She could tell that Amy did not know whether to show happiness or concern. Pregnancy was acceptable to her generation, but Rita was, after all, her *mother's* age, for God's sake. Rita put a hand on Amy's arm. "In case you're wondering, it's good news."

"But—"

"But what?"

"But who's—"

Well now, that question was more difficult to answer. Rita hadn't yet decided how to handle it, and if anything, she'd thought no one cared about those things anymore. But like Hazel and Jill, Amy apparently did.

She held a finger to her lips. "Don't ask, don't tell."

But Amy still stared. "It's Charlie's, isn't it?"

From beyond the ladies' room door, the party sounds revved again. Rita was about to say that it didn't matter who the father was, the baby was hers, hers as Kyle had been, mother and son, when Amy flinched.

"Does he know?" she asked. "What about Marge? He's going to Florida with her. Why would he if . . ."

Rita grasped Amy's hand tightly. "Charlie is not involved this time," she said firmly. "He is not involved, and it's none of his business. Okay?"

Amy scowled. "You're a really cool person, Rita," she said, "but you're a lousy liar."

Just then, an angry shout shot through the air, coming from the direction of the 1802 bar.

The punch Ben took to his jaw came from a lefty, an amazon guy who was dressed like Darth Vader, and had too much beer on his foul breath.

It hurt like hell.

He grabbed the side of his face as he faltered backward, crashed against a bookcase, and slumped onto the floor. He sat in something wet. Cider, he hoped, but it was not. It was too warm. He must have wet his pants. He squeezed his eyes shut and hoped the sheet of his ghost costume would mask his humiliation.

Then a big bear hand was on his shoulder, hauling him up again, swinging back that black-clothed, left arm—which someone else grabbed.

"Let him go!" came Charlie's shout.

Darth Vader dropped Ben to the floor again, turned, and took a punch at Charlie, too. But Charlie was smarter than Ben. Charlie ducked.

"Hold it!" came another shout.

Ben did not recognize the voice, but even from his compromised position, he knew the silver handcuffs were not part of a costume. They looked too real; they looked too familiar.

"Out of here, Ashenbach!" the voice shouted once again, and then Ben knew his savior was Hugh Talbot. He closed his eyes and waited for the ruckus to pass.

He waited and he drifted, as noisy crowd murmurs traveled through a tunnel down onto the wide-board floor.

The next thing Ben knew, Jill was kneeling by his side. "Ben? Honey, are you okay?"

He rubbed his jaw.

Behind her, Hugh appeared. Darth Vader was nowhere in sight.

"Your neighbor had a few too many," Hugh said to Ben, offering a hand to help him up. "I threw him in the cruiser. Are you okay?"

Ben looked at Hugh's hand but did not take it. He was too tired to stand up, too numb. He blinked, then noticed the semicircle of costumed creatures standing a self-protective distance behind Sheriff Hugh. It looked as if he'd stumbled onto the set of a John Carpenter film.

"Get some ice!" Jill demanded.

"We're all out," retorted Charlie.

"Great," Jill muttered.

Ben closed his eyes again and wished everyone would go away, wished the room would stop spinning around and around, wished the voices would speak more clearly and not as if from the bottom of the sea.

"I was afraid of this," Hugh was saying. "I heard about the party. I followed Ashenbach out here."

Now something cold was on his face. His eyes opened involuntarily. "Honey," Jill said, "you're okay now. Charlie put some cold water on a cloth."

The pain eased some. On the other side of Jill, Hugh squatted.

"You can press charges," he said, "if you want."

Ben looked at Jill. She kept her eyes on the cloth she was moving up and down his jaw.

"No big deal," Ben said. "He's been dying to do that for years." That would not be news to anyone.

Hugh stood up. "Right. Well, it's up to you."

There were witnesses, of course—the hundred or so people who still stood around the scene. Gawkers, neighbors, stunned, perhaps, that this could happen in their town, that one grown man would sucker punch another at a party in a bar.

Unless, of course, they knew the man's motivation.

But now Ben had a chance to win their sympathy. All he had to do was say, "Tell the son-of-a-bitch I did not touch his granddaughter." He could have said that, he supposed. He could have said that in front of all these witnesses who knew Dave Ashenbach was crazy, who had just seen it for themselves. Maybe Ben could win this battle after all.

Then he remembered this was not about a traffic violation or about trespassing on land.

So instead he said, "Forget it." He took the cloth from Jill. "Come on, honey. Help me up. Let's go home."

Jill helped him up, and so did Hugh.

Ben tugged at the wet sheet that clung to his back.

Then he headed for the door, as the crowd of gawkers parted like the Red Sea, clearing the way.

Rita had seen a lot in her day, and she supposed she'd see more still.

But Dave Ashenbach disguised as Darth Vader taking a punch at Ben Niles? In the 1802 Tavern? At a Halloween party, no less?

She wanted to take off after them and find out what the hell had happened. But Ben and Jill had slipped out so quickly, she figured they'd be better left alone.

Standing outside the ladies' room, she saw an unmistakable bewildered look on Amy's face. Rita stepped into the crowd. "Okay everybody, party's over!" she shouted. "See you in the spring!"

Over a few protesting mutters, she went over to the doorway and flipped a switch. Bright yellow light washed out the eerie, creepy green glow. Then she adjusted the folds of her witch costume and figured that sooner or later, she'd find out from Jill what that was all about. Because best friends had no secrets, no matter how old they got, no matter how many men came into their lives, and no matter how much things changed.

Chapter 12

 "I'm not paying for your opinion." Grandpa's words to Dr. Laura were so gruff this morning that they came upstairs and through the walls.

Mindy, however, could not hear the response, because Dr. Laura had a soft voice and never raised it up.

She didn't like that Grandpa yelled at the doctor. No matter that it seemed fairly dumb to waste all that time and Grandpa's money talking about nothing special, it didn't seem right that Grandpa was yelling. Dr. Laura was nice to Mindy, despite it all.

She went to her bedroom door and cracked it just a little. She strained to make out the words.

"Violence begets violence, Mr. Ashenbach. Mindy needs exposure to some emotion other than anger."

"What happened between Niles and me is between two men. Not a kid. And it's not your job to shrink *my* head. But if you intend to keep the job you have, quit sticking your nose into other people's business."

"Anything that affects Mindy is my business. She is a troubled child."

"Bullshit. She's no more troubled than you or me."

Mindy kind of liked that, the way Grandpa jumped to her defense.

"Well, a lack of positive parental attention can lead to much unhappiness," Dr. Laura said. "Addiction can be one manifestation. Your son was addicted to alcohol, if I'm not mistaken."

She wondered if Grandpa was going to slug her the way he told her he'd slugged Ben last night.

"There are other manifestations, of course. Difficulty making friends. Overachieving. Lying."

That last remark brought that lava rumble inside Mindy again. It rolled so loud, she was afraid they'd hear it down the stairs. She held her breath.

"My granddaughter does not lie." It came out like a hiss, as if Grandpa had his teeth clamped together and just pulled back on his lips.

There was silence for a few minutes. Mindy wondered what was happening. Was Grandpa squishing out a cigar? Had Dr. Laura quietly gone out the door, never to come back? And, if so, why did that made her feel a little sad?

"Would you prefer that I returned to Boston?" Dr. Laura had not left.

"What I think doesn't matter. The court wouldn't like that."

"So you'll keep me here because it looks good."

"It's the only reason you were brought here in the first place. Because my lawyer said we needed someone."

"Not because you were worried about Mindy."

"Because I was worried Niles would get off scot-free."

"Not because you were afraid your granddaughter's emotional stability was damaged."

Silence again.

"You know what I think?" Grandpa asked, the hiss back in his voice. "I think you'd better take your fancy words and your liberal ass out of here before I get pissed off and deck you, too."

"What about Mindy? Should I come and see her tomorrow?"

Something went *bang*, like Grandpa's hand against a wall. "Just get off my property and out of my sight before I do something you'll regret."

Mindy heard the back door shut. She closed her eyes and leaned against the wall, then heard Grandpa mumble "Stupid bitch," and she knew full well what that meant.

"Rita, we need to talk."

In all the years Rita Blair had known Charlie Rollins—and those years had been many—she'd never seen him quite so pissed off. Well, there had been the time Emma Johnston had tried to sue the tavern because she said it was Charlie's fault her husband was a drunk; and then, just a few weeks ago, after waiting in line since dawn, he'd not been given one of the last two building permits they needed for Sea Grove. Yes, Rita had seen Charlie pissed a few times over the years—but not like this, not as he was now, standing at her front door, his face tight as steel, his eyes sharp as daggers and directed at her.

She pulled her bathrobe protectively around herself. "I'm afraid I'm still recuperating from the party," she said, "and my mother's asleep—"

Charlie pushed past her and went into the house. Rita closed her eyes, took a deep breath, and shut the door behind him.

"Do you have something to tell me?" he asked.

Good old, get-to-the-point Charlie. She turned and faced him. "About what?" she asked, knowing that someone had told him—Amy, perhaps, or Jill. It must have been Amy. Lately Jill was too preoccupied with her own stuff, with her own life.

Charlie folded his arms and dropped his gaze to her belly.

"You're pregnant, Rita. True or false?"

She scrunched her red curls and thought about making a reference to this not being a game show. Then she thought of Kyle and knew he would advise her to keep sarcasm to herself.

She sighed. "Amy told you."

He moved his hands to his pockets and did not deny it. "When were *you* planning to? After I was married to someone else?"

So it was true—he was going to marry Cher. She wondered if they would live in one of the palatial homes at Sea Grove, one of the homes designed and built in part with Kyle's legacy money—their own son's money.

Suddenly Rita felt as pissed off as Charlie looked. "What the hell does it matter to you?"

In the silence of the house, she could hear him breathing. Hazel, she was sure, could hear it as well.

"It's my baby, isn't it? You're going to have my baby again, and you're not going to tell me. Again. Jesus, Rita." He did not finish that thought but ran his hand across the back of his neck. She hoped he wasn't going to have a stroke there in her foyer.

"It's not yours, Charlie," she said. She followed her words with a quick prayer that Hazel would not lunge from the bedroom, denounce her daughter, and expose the lie. "You can go to Florida. You can marry Miss Margie. You have no obligations here, except, of course, for your share of Sea Grove."

The look on his face changed, but she could not be sure what it had changed to.

"Are you sure, Rita? It's been a long time . . . well, the last time was the wedding, wasn't it? Ben and Jill's wedding?"

"I was already pregnant," she said before he could

continue, before he could conjure those images up once again, of the sun and the warmth and the love that was shared. "I didn't know it, but I was already pregnant."

The look may have been one of disappointment, she could not be sure.

"Then who . . ."

She shook her head. "It doesn't matter, Charlie." For a moment, they did not speak. Then Rita leaned against the door. "It's taken me a long time to get over Kyle," she said. "It's been so hard, you know? To fill in that hole. The way I figure it, it won't be another Kyle, but God's giving me another chance."

"But what about the father? Will he be in his life?"

"I don't know, probably not. But the world is different today. It won't be so hard. For me or for him." She could not believe that her words sounded so convincing. She could not believe that she could stand here and lie and practically believe the lie herself. "Thanks for the concern," she added, patting her stomach. "But we'll be fine."

He looked back to her belly, then up at her. "So you're glad, then?"

She nodded, hoping he couldn't see how hard she'd just swallowed.

"Well, if you're happy then, well . . ." He laughed. "Hell, I think I'm jealous. I was so pissed off and now I'm jealous. Kind of stupid, huh?"

No, she wanted to reply, it wasn't kind of stupid, it was really kind of nice.

"Jesus," he repeated, "Well, if you need anything, Rita . . ."

She shook her head, this time with her heart truly up in her mouth, this time with her brains truly down in her ass. Somehow she managed to stand on her toes and kiss his cheek. "Have a great time in Florida. Write if you get work."

Charlie smiled and ruffled her hair. "You're okay, kid, you know that? You're right—you'll be fine. We'll both be fine."

Rita nodded so she didn't have to speak again, for if she did, it might trigger a nonstop crying jag.

She opened the door, and he stepped past her.

"Give my best to your mother," he said. "I guess I'll see you in the spring."

"Yeah," Rita said, "have a nice life." Then she closed the door on the father of her two kids and wondered why she felt so sure it was right to let Charlie—the one man who had ever loved her—walk down the sidewalk and out of her life.

The following weekend brought moving day. Jill had once hoped that she'd be helping Amy pack her suitcases to go to college, not to leave home. Not at eighteen.

"Two blocks is practically next door," Amy had argued again this morning while loading heaps of clothes into the car. "In fact, if there was a huge roof over Water Street, it would almost be like I was only moving down the hall."

Packing CDs in an old shoebox, Jill mused that once one left home, it was often for good, or for twenty-five years as it had been for her, which was about the same. In the past, Amy had gone off to private school or visited her father in England, but until now she had not removed her belongings—*all* her belongings, from beaded shoes to linen skirts, from crop sweaters to feather earrings—from under Jill's roof.

Still, Jill worked busily, wanting to be finished, looking forward to leaving for Sturbridge tonight to return to some work, to return to normalcy. Whatever that word meant.

She sealed the box and realized that right now the best

she could hope for in the normalcy department was that the freelance shooter from Boston would show up in Sturbridge and be moderately good.

"How's it going?"

From the doorway, Ben smiled at her but without luster, his complexion having paled more since the altercation with Ashenbach. In the past week, he'd hardly left the house: if he didn't go anywhere, he said, he wouldn't risk getting punched out again. His attempt at humor was thin.

She tensed.

Thankfully the trip to Sturbridge would last a few days, maybe long enough to help Ben put things into perspective and free himself from the paranoia and the gloom in which he was now stuck. Even though Jill would be working, even though his grandkids wouldn't be with them, maybe Ben would become immersed in the old working village, in the architecture he so loved, and the era he was drawn to. She would encourage him to look for new ideas for the museum, crafts to teach the kids, Early American methods to show them.

Yes, hopefully, the trip would go well. And hopefully, his mood would mellow before she went beserk.

"The packing is fine," she said to him now. "It's difficult, though. Having my baby leave home." She tried to smile.

"It's a big, scary world out there, Jill. One doesn't have to leave home to be affected by it."

"When's Charlie coming?" she asked abruptly, as much to change the subject as to find the answer. Though Charlie was leaving the apartment "intact"—furniture, dishes, and anything else Amy wanted—because she was "family," Amy was determined to have her own four-poster canopy bed. She did not want to sleep on the old twin daybed that had once belonged to Jill's father, used for his refuge from Jill's tense, stoic mother, the poor man's wife.

She suddenly thought of Rita. Was the daybed where the soon-to-be baby had been conceived?

"Charlie said he'd be here around two. He's still putting things into storage."

Jill nodded and closed another box. She didn't know what to say next. It had been that way since the party: he'd withdrawn; she'd pulled away. Ben might as well be the one moving into Charlie's apartment, the one sleeping on the daybed now, for all the communication that they had.

"I know this is hard for you, honey," he said, "but I think if nothing else, this is working out for Amy."

She knew what he really meant was that this was working out for him. With Charlie off to Florida and Amy out of the house, the risk that two other people would learn about Mindy would be lower. She wondered how much he would have promoted Amy's move if it hadn't been for his arrest. Or if he would have thought this had "worked out" so well if it were his daughter, Carol Ann, moving out, instead of her Amy.

Ben began loading full shoeboxes into a carton. "What time do you want to leave tonight?"

She pushed a sheet of newspaper down into another shoebox, and with it her anguish. "I think we should be out on the six-thirty boat. But I reserved the eight-fifteen, too, just in case." She tossed in the remaining CDs and handed the box to Ben, who set it in the carton. "It will take almost two hours to drive from the Cape to Sturbridge. I don't want to get there too late."

He taped the carton and scanned the room as if looking for more things to do. Then he put his hands on his hips. "What about the sheets and blankets? Are those all packed?"

Why was he asking such an obvious question? The mattress lay barren, stripped of its covers. Even the lace canopy had been laundered, then neatly packed, for Amy to rehang in her new bedroom in her new home, where it would hover over herself and whomever she chose to accompany her in bed.

Jill stood and stretched her legs, wanting to shake off such thoughts. "Everything's ready, Ben. All we need is Charlie. And his truck."

Ben had a truck, too. A pickup they could have used, if it weren't for the fact it was parked at the museum, if it weren't for the fact Ben refused to go within a few hundred miles, nautical or otherwise, of Menemsha House and the Ashenbach land.

He walked to the window, his back toward his wife. "I spoke with Rick," he said. The lines of his back, his once well-muscled shoulders, were smaller now, almost bony, as if his pain were eating his body as well as his mind. He put his hands into his pockets. "The pretrial conference is coming up. That's when they'll set the date for the trial."

A sense of foreboding crept from her head to her toes. "When?"

"Tuesday afternoon."

"This Tuesday?"

"Yes."

She closed her eyes. "You didn't just learn this today, did you?"

"No. It was why he called the other day, when I was at the tavern helping Amy decorate."

The other day, Jill recalled, was when she'd walked in on her husband kissing her daughter. She cleared her throat. "Should I ask why you didn't mention it? You knew I have to be in Sturbridge a few days. I could have changed the dates."

"I need to do this myself, Jill. I just need to go to the courthouse with Rick and hear the date. Then I need to come home."

"So you don't want me with you. Fine. But we could have gone to Sturbridge next week or the week after."

"No, honey. I'd already decided I wouldn't be going with you. That I needed to stay here."

She wondered if "here" meant the island or the house, where he could hide from the world. "Are you going to stay in the house until the trial?" she asked.

He turned and faced her. "That's not what this is about, Jill."

"Really?"

He took his hands from his pockets and ran them through his hair, of which, like the rest of him, there seemed to be less. "Even if you had changed the dates, I still couldn't have gone. Rick says we can't be sure what Ashenbach would do if he learned I left the island."

She kicked a carton away from the bed. "You're not a freaking criminal, Ben! For God's sake, you're innocent until proven guilty, remember?"

He turned back to the window. "Jill, please, none of this is fair to you, I know that. But let me just do what I need to do. Once this is done, I'll go to the moon with you if you'd like. But right now . . ."

The muscles around the corners of her jaw tightened. "What if John, Jr. and Emily were still going? Would you have bailed out on them, too?"

He did not move. "That's a moot point, Jill. They're not going."

Her comment had cut deep, she knew. She supposed she should apologize, but she could not. "I thought you were looking forward to Sturbridge." The tremor in her voice warned her not to carry this too far, for surely it could quickly erupt into anger or, worse, to an out-and-out cry.

He came to her and took her hands in his. "I was, honey. But I'm consumed by this. I can't imagine myself going off and trying to have a good time."

She snapped her hands away. Her jaw muscles began working again. "That's fine, Ben, but as they say on the talk shows, this isn't just about you." She stopped short of reminding him that if she weren't bringing home the paycheck, that maybe she would have preferred to stay home, too. But even in her anger she could not hurt Ben that much. He was not, after all, Richard. He was not, after all, Christopher. Ben Niles was not like the other self-centered men that had screwed up her life.

Was he?

There were six people in the courtroom, not counting the two armed guards who stood at attention at the front and rear doors, waiting for Ben to try and make a break for it, he supposed. He looked around the dreary room, decorated only by two flags—one the Stars and Stripes, one with the state seal. He didn't think it was the same place that he'd been for his arraignment, but his memory of that was about as clear as a dense Vineyard fog.

The judge, however, was the same. He remembered her at her post behind the "bench," whose elevated step denoted authority.

In front of the bench was a sober-looking male court reporter.

At a small wooden table facing the judge sat Ben in the suit he'd worn to his wedding. It seemed bigger somehow, as if it had been stretched. The suit and the surroundings reminded him of the grammar school assembly when the whole class had been counting on him to spell *Appalachian,* so they could beat Mrs. Merritt's class and win the spelling bee.

Of course, he'd screwed up because he never could spell worth a damn.

All things being equal, he figured he'd felt about as

humiliated then as he did now. He wanted only to be out of there, only to be finished so he could go home.

Next to him was Rick Fitzpatrick in a navy suit that fit.

At a matching table beside them sat Ashenbach himself, though Ben's view of him was nicely obstructed by the assistant district attorney, who was not the Mister Rogers look-alike but a tall, beefy woman who wore more makeup than most island women, and whose name Ben could not remember. He assumed she'd been sent down from Boston, though he didn't know why he thought that.

Maybe because it was something to think about, something to keep his eyes from straining to see Ashenbach and to keep his mind off the fact that he was here at all, or that he had not spoken to his wife since she'd left two days ago.

"The accused is present?" the judge asked, jarring Ben from his trance.

Rick stood up. "Yes, your honor."

"Mr. Niles, do you understand this is a formal conference to set the date for trial in the matter of *The Commonwealth versus Benjamin Niles*?" Instead of looking up, she kept her eyes fixed on some papers that must have been more interesting.

Ben glanced at Rick, who motioned him to stand.

"Yes, your honor," Ben said in a voice that sounded like it belonged to the boy in the grade-school spelling bee. He clasped his hands together in front of him. He wished now that he'd not been so stubborn with Jill. It would have been nice to feel the warmth of her hand in his, instead of the cool dampness of his own palms.

The beefy D.A. stood up. "Your honor, due to the sensitivity of the allegation, and the fact that the frenzy of summertime here on the island does not seem appropriate to schedule such an important trial, the Commonwealth asks for expediency."

Ben wondered if he could spell *expediency*. Or if Ashenbach could.

"I agree," the judge replied. "Is the child receiving regular counseling?"

Ben was relieved that she said *child* and not *little girl*.

The D.A. turned to Dave, who whispered something to her. Then she whispered back, and they went back and forth a few times before the D.A. addressed the judge again. "Yes, your honor. The child has been seeing a therapist two or three times a week."

"See that it's three," the judge responded. She looked up briefly, then back down to her papers. "Schedule date for trial is Monday, April ninth, two thousand and one. Is this acceptable for counsel's calendars?"

It was acceptable.

The judge banged her gavel but said nothing more. Then she rose and swept from the room, one of the armed lackeys escorting her through the rear door.

Rick gathered his legal pad and file folder and snapped them into his briefcase. Ben stayed frozen in place, mute, awaiting the next word, which came not from Rick but from Ashenbach himself, who must have pushed past the D.A. and was now in Ben's face.

"You're going to hang, Niles," he seethed.

Rick raised a hand. "Bailiff!"

The D.A. grabbed Dave by the arm. "Move out, Mr. Ashenbach," she commanded. "Now."

In the split second before he moved, Ashenbach leaned over and spat at his prey. The spittle landed on the lapel of Ben's too-big suit.

With far more restraint than Ben had known he possessed, he stood still and did nothing, did not even look into his accoster's small eyes.

Then as Ashenbach moved, or was helped to move away, the son of a bitch laughed a deep, disgusting laugh.

Every muscle inside Ben hardened into rock. The only thing that stopped him from exploding was the knowledge that exploding was exactly what Ashenbach would want.

"Let's go, Ben," Rick said quietly.

Ben breathed a breath, trying to ignore the ache that had risen in his chest. "Give me a minute."

In the minute that Rick gave him, Ben made a decision. He was fed up with this bullshit. He was going to regain some control over his life. Jill was right about one thing: hiding was wrong. It was not going to accomplish anything, except maybe kill him. It was time to find some courage and attack this thing head-on.

He would start with a visit to his daughter and his wimpy son-in-law.

Chapter 13

 "Where are the kids?" Ben asked Carol Ann. He stood in her kitchen in his jeans and a flannel shirt. If he'd shown up in his suit, he'd have scared the hell out of her—she'd have thought someone died.

His daughter wiped her hands on a towel. "At the school with John. Getting John, Jr.'s costume for the Thanksgiving play."

Ben laughed because it was less painful than screaming. Or crying. "Pilgrim or Indian?" He did not mention that he had not seen the kids on Halloween, that he had not had an invitation. He did not mention they hadn't spoken in weeks, because time flew for both of them and now, with Jill in his life, he knew Carol Ann no longer worried about him. He had liked that, he'd thought.

"We're not sure yet who he'll be. It depends on what sizes are left over from last year."

In spite of his anguish, Ben smiled. "That was one of the first things you did when we came to the Vineyard. You were Priscilla Alden in the school play. Remember?"

"A little," she answered vaguely.

Ben was struck by the sad irony of how hard some

parents strive to build memories for kids too young to remember. He supposed that real memory started around
age ten, Mindy's age. Real memory. Ha—manufactured
memory was more like it. He sighed and sat down at the
table. "I'll take some coffee if you have it."

"Sure, Dad." She went to the sink and filled the carafe.
"It's been a long time since you dropped by for coffee after work."

Her comment seemed one of observation, not concern.
"I've been busy," he said. "You, too?"

"Winding down from summer."

She kept her back to him, busying herself at the sink.
Ben was always startled by his daughter's strong frame—
strong like Ben's had been until a few weeks ago. A sturdy
build was not always desirable for a female, yet Carol
Ann had never complained, at least not to him.

He looked around the small kitchen, which had not
seemed small when Carol Ann and John first bought the
Cape-style house when they got married. He must have
been living in Jill's house too long, his perspective skewed
by its large, high-ceilinged rooms. But though Carol
Ann's kitchen was cramped, it felt like home. A good
home for his grandchildren to grow up in.

He curled the edge of the woven cotton placemat.
"When's the play?"

"Tuesday before Thanksgiving. Same as always."

He folded his arms, trying to decide where to begin,
wondering what his opening line should be. His gaze
drifted to the window. This had been easier when he'd
practiced his lines in the car all the way across island.
"How's Emily's cold?"

Carol Ann scowled and poured coffee into mugs.
"She's fine, Dad. She hasn't had a cold in quite a while."

Well, he guessed he'd known that all along. "Not according to your husband," he said.

She looked bewildered but set the coffee down in front

of Ben and did not ask what he meant. He knew he was treading in dangerous waters—pitting the husband against the father. But it was time.

"I thought that was why he canceled dinner last month. Because Emily had a cold."

"No," she replied. "He said you and Jill were busy."

So John had lied to her, too.

He stared into his mug, the black coffee a shimmering mirror to everything but his heart. "Right now Jill's in Sturbridge," he said, "alone."

She pulled out a chair and sat across from him. "I know," she said. "John told me it didn't turn out to be a good idea for the kids to go." She sipped her coffee.

Ben did not answer because he could not speak, afraid he would blurt out something about John that he'd regret later on.

Stirring her coffee, Carol Ann studied her father. "Why do I sense you're angry at something? Or someone? For instance, me."

He grasped the handle and slowly brought the mug up to his mouth. Did he hate his son-in-law now? Was forgiving everyone in the world something one needed to do or risk going to hell? Noepe would probably have advised Ben to forgive John. Then again, Noepe was dead.

He blew on the hot liquid and watched a wisp of steam curl around the mug rim, then dissipate in the air. Without taking a taste, he set the mug down. "I'm not angry at you, Carol Ann." He closed his eyes and felt as awkward as if he were back inside John's truck, escorted by the reluctant family member from the courthouse, freed on bail.

He felt Carol Ann's hand on his. Opening his eyes, he looked down at her short, clipped nails. "Dad?" she asked quietly. "What's wrong?"

He patted her hand, managing a smile, then looked

into her gray eyes that were so much like his. The back door banged open.

"Papa!" little Emily shrieked. She bounded into the kitchen, scrambled onto Ben's lap, and planted a small wet kiss on his cheek before Ben had a chance to breathe again.

John, Jr. scurried in behind her. "Hey, Papa!" he shouted, "Wait till you see my cool costume." He rattled a bag close to Ben's face. "Chief Running Rain."

Ben mustered up joy, because kids should always have that. "Wow! The chief?" Beyond John, Jr. he saw the boy's father enter the doorway. He did not make eye contact. He did not want to be arrested for murder as well as child molestation.

"My teacher, Mrs. Galloway, wrote what the chief has to say in real penmanship, not printing," the boy's words rushed out. "I was the only one in the class who could read it."

"Good for you," Ben said. "You're smart, like your mother."

Emily tugged Ben's sleeve. "I'm going to be in the play, too. I'm a pill-grin baby."

"That's Pilgrim, Emily," her father corrected. Ben still did not acknowledge John, even when he stepped well inside the room, even when the son of a bitch eased Emily from Ben's lap.

"Speaking of Thanksgiving," he said boldly, "any plans this year?" They'd had it together every year. Even since he'd met Jill, they'd had holidays together.

His daughter looked to John, then back to Ben. "I thought John told you," she said. "We're going to Maine to see his folks this year."

John did not elaborate, and Ben did not ask. He stood up. "Well, maybe I'll see you at the play." It was clear the time had passed to confide in his daughter. He had tried; he had failed. "Guess I'd better be going. Work to do."

"Can't you stay for supper, Dad?" Carol Ann asked.

He did not look at his son-in-law. "Thanks, honey, but I promised Amy I'd have dinner with her." Then he moved his eyes to John in a long, steady glare, as if to say not everyone was afraid of him. "Thanks for the coffee," he said. He kissed the kids and his daughter and left, hoping she wouldn't notice that his coffee was un-touched.

Finally Jill cried. She had made it through over forty-eight hours in Sturbridge, mechanically taping her interviews, mechanically conversing with yet another videographer who thankfully had shown up but was disappointingly mediocre, mechanically taking her meals in her room so she would not break down in public once she stopped working.

She sat on the edge of the bed in the hotel room now, and finally she cried. But her tears were neither for her husband nor for a "misguided" little girl. They were for her. For Jill Randall McPhearson Niles, the intelligent, glamorous, have-it-all woman who suddenly had noth-ing, who suddenly was exhausted from trying so damn hard.

I need to do this myself, Ben had said. If she hadn't known better, she'd have bet he'd arranged the date for the pretrial conference, scheduled it for a day when she'd be out of town.

Alone.

Without him again.

It might be easier if he were dead, instead of at this place in between, this coma of will-he-or-won't-he sur-vive this ordeal. Or will-she-or-won't-she.

Through her tears, she turned to the one thing, God help her, that right now made any sense, that made her feel connected to something positive and worthwhile. The hotel television was showing *Good Night, USA*.

But it only deepened her sorrow to watch the picture-perfect hosts Christopher and Lizette, the untouchable darlings who did not have to deal with things like child molestation. Even if they did, Addie would have found a way to make it go away.

To make matters worse, Christopher's tan now made him even more attractive, his tawny hair blonder from the California sun, his straight white teeth straighter and whiter. He was not sensuous: his edges were too sharp, his image too perfect. Yet underlying his veneer of the sweet-talking gentleman was an authoritative, power-hungry persona that Jill had often found enticing and sometimes intimidating.

She wondered to whom he made power-love now.

As she turned down the volume, the "talking heads" become mouthing heads, smiling, sincere, making all America believe that what they said was true and that their lives were together.

What had been so wrong with that life: and why had Jill expected more? And more what? Love? That was, after all, why she'd relinquished the spotlight and stepped into this hellhole where she was now.

She used to try to avoid arguments. Whenever she and Richard, her ex-husband, had argued, she had simply gone to bed. The two fought frequently. Morning, afternoon, her escape had no time clock. She had hoped that upon waking, all dissension would be gone, magically disintegrated during that time between sleep and wake. Rarely had that happened.

With Ben, avoidance worked only for him. Avoidance and excuses.

Rick says we can't be sure what Ashenbach would do if he learned I left the island.

People who made excuses, she'd found, often had something to hide.

She grabbed the edge of the mattress and dug her fingernails into the covers. She squeezed her eyes and refused to let herself think that thought again, to even begin to think that. . . .

She heard a long, low cry, a moan of sorrow, a wail of hurt.

And then she realized that the noise had come from deep within her. And from the one question she'd been denying:

Was Ben really innocent?

Outside her room, the wind spun eddies of autumn leaves. The room had grown so still that Jill could hear them now, small tornadoes "dancing in the dark," Rita used to say back when they were girls and Jill was afraid to walk home alone. "Nothing will hurt you," Rita had reassured her. "The sounds are just leaves having a party, like the toys in the *Nutcracker* after everyone is asleep."

Jill had believed her because she had wanted to, and because, after all, they were only girls. Girls who maybe were . . . Mindy's age.

Nine. Or ten. The same ungrown-up, imaginative age that thought sex must be like being in the dark—exciting or frightening or a little of both.

And then she remembered the old corner store and the penny candy and the shelves in the back where she and Rita had stood and filled tiny paper bags with fireballs and root beer barrels and pink and yellow candy dots on white paper strips.

And that made her think of Mr. Blanchette.

He was as old as Jill's father but thin and white-haired, and he always wore the same blue-and-black-checked wool shirt in winter and a sleeveless undershirt in summer. He never spoke but sat behind the counter turning pages of small magazines that Rita said had pictures of naked women and sometimes of girls like them.

They nicknamed him Mr. Creepy, which well described how Jill felt when she looked in the dusty window and saw him sitting there, even though she'd never seen inside the magazines and did not know for sure if he was a pervert as Rita claimed.

Whether the accusation was true or false, just or unjust, when Mr. Blanchette was in the store, the girls did not go in.

Did Mindy and her friends now look at Ben the same way? Did they call him Mr. Creepy?

And could the first Mr. Creepy's reputation have been saved if he'd had a wife who'd pulled a few strings?

On the TV screen, the credits rolled. Behind the type, Jill watched Christopher remove his microphone, say some soundless words to Lizette, and smile for the camera that he knew was still set on him. Jill knew because she'd been there. And in a matter of weeks, she'd be there again. Away from the pressure. Where nothing bad happened.

Did Christopher know she'd signed the contract?

Was he pleased?

Then, without drawing her glance from the screen, Jill stopped wondering. If she were going to save either Ben or herself, she knew she had to take some action of the positive kind.

Slowly, deliberately, she reached for the phone. Then she dialed the number that she still remembered.

They were a motley group, or at least that was what Rita called them. Ben didn't care what label she gave them: he was glad that he'd not returned to the house to suffer in silence. He was grateful that Amy had made dinner for Rita and for him at her new apartment; even though it was ham and scalloped potatoes and was pretty well dried out.

Feeling grateful and glad, he was damned if he was going to think about *it* this evening. For just one evening he was going to set his mind free.

"Here's to the last of the Vineyard singles," Rita declared, raising a cup of too-strong coffee.

"Excuse me," Ben said, "but I believe I'm married." He'd helped himself to half a bottle of wine from Charlie's private stash and was feeling quite good for a guy whose life was in grave question.

"Oh," Rita said. "I forgot. Your wife's away so much."

"Ouch," he responded, but he didn't mind the barb. "Rita, you won't be alone for long. Before you know it, you'll be a family of three."

Amy looked at him queerly. Rita did, too.

"Someone forgot to tell you that a mother and a baby do not always make three," Rita said.

"Well, there's always your mother," he replied. "Three generations. That's a family, isn't it?"

Rita threw a packet of sugar at him.

Amy stood up and cut another slice of apple pie that Rita's mother had made just before she went to the senior center tonight.

"When are you due, anyway, Rita?" Ben asked. Since Jill had told him she was pregnant, he hadn't thought much about it, except to miss Kyle.

"April," she said. "And it can't get here fast enough."

April.

As in April the ninth.

Suddenly the wine and the ham and the apples did not agree on being in his stomach. He glanced at his watch and wondered how soon he could politely excuse himself and take his motley body home.

.   .   .

"I heard you were coming." Christopher's voice was exactly as Jill remembered, a touch softer than it was on TV, less in control, more like a man with feelings. She'd often wondered what exactly he'd done that day after she returned the ring, after she'd left the studio to start her new life.

Had he cried?

Or had he run to Maurice Fischer and told the RueCom boss it would be fine and they'd be better off with Lizette?

The tone of his voice now gave nothing away.

Jill twisted the cord. "I thought we should bury the hatchet before we meet for the publicity shots."

He paused. "What? And miss out on huge ratings we'd get by doing it on the air?" He did not say there was no hatchet to bury, or that he was grateful she'd left him because he'd met someone new. "Speaking of which," he continued, as if she called every evening, as if they spoke every day, "have you talked with Addie? The network decided to do the shots in New York."

She had been looking forward to a few days of sunshine and relaxation in L.A., not Manhattan's stark city landscape of pollution and high-rises. She had been looking forward to being on the opposite coast. "Why New York?"

"It could have something to do with the fact our old viewers were used to seeing us in the snow and cold."

"Then why not Boston?"

"Because New York is bigger? Better? Who knows." Unlike Jill, Christopher never questioned the whats and the whys of those behind the scenes. Which could also be why his career was so much further ahead. "I only know it's going to be the week after Thanksgiving. And we're booked at the Plaza."

Jill laughed. "The week after Thanksgiving? Well, maybe that explains it. Addie's from the city. She gets to be there for the holidays."

"Oh," Christopher replied without further comment.

In the silence that followed Jill tried to picture them at the Plaza—shooting public relations promos in Central Park perhaps, in a hansom cab with a white horse, decked out in red velvet and evergreen boughs. Would she be in fur, or would that upset too many animal-rights viewers? And why was she wondering these things when she was there on the phone with the man she'd once thought she loved?

"Is this okay with you, Christopher?" she asked. "Having me fill in for Lizette?"

"Jill," he said, his voice soft once again, "we're professionals, aren't we?"

She didn't know what she'd expected, but she didn't think it was that. Something more personal, perhaps. Something that said he cared. Or that he didn't.

"Besides," he added, "I've done a lot of things in my day, but chasing a married woman has never been high on my list."

A married woman. Yes, she reminded herself, that's just what she was. And despite how she felt, that would not change. At least not for the moment. At least not until she'd given it her very best shot.

Which meant getting off the phone with her ex-lover right now and returning to her senses—or what was left of them.

"Well, then I'll see you in New York," she said, and quickly rung off before he—or she—misconstrued why she'd phoned at all.

Chapter 14

 "Did you go trick-or-treating?" Laura Reynolds asked Mindy when she came back, a long time after Grandpa had yelled at her to leave. During that time she must have forgotten that Mindy was ten, not five.

Mindy used her tongue inside her mouth to search for the back molar that she'd been playing with all day. It was loose and ready to pop out. She wished the doctor would leave so she could put her fingers inside and see if she could pull it.

"No trick-or-treating?" Dr. Reynolds persisted. "Don't they have a party at your school?"

Mindy sighed. "I'm in the fifth grade. Only the little kids do that." She looked past the doctor out into the yard that was quiet and gray now that most of the leaves had fallen.

Mindy didn't like November much: with all the tourists gone, there wasn't much to do. And it meant the holidays were coming, which were a joke.

Thanksgiving was a day like any other, though last year Grandpa bought an already-roasted turkey from the supermarket, and she pretended her mother had come home from Timbuktu and cooked it.

As for Christmas, well, Mindy promised herself that this year she would positively not go to the community center party for the island kids. When she first came to live here, it made her feel special to get all those presents. But last year she realized it was mostly for the poor kids and the kids without anybody, which practically meant her.

If she didn't go this year, maybe no one would know she was poor and that she was without anybody except Grandpa, who never knew what to give her so he settled on a twenty-dollar bill. Maybe he wouldn't even do that this year. Maybe he was too upset about this problem with Ben. He sure seemed to be avoiding her lately, as if she'd done something wrong.

A lack of positive parental attention can lead to much unhappiness, Dr. Laura had said. *Difficulty making friends. Overachieving. Lying.*

Mindy rocked in the rocking chair in her room. "I thought my grandfather told you not to come back here."

The doctor smiled. "The court prefers that I do. They want me to help you handle the trauma before it has a chance to get too big."

"I don't have no—*any*—trauma."

The doctor frowned. "No? What Mr. Niles did to you must have been very upsetting."

She pushed at her tooth again. She remembered when Brianna Edson had spat one out one day in reading class. Brianna had plopped her bloody tooth onto her open book and watched it stain the page red. Mindy had written *Gross Out* on her notebook and showed Mark Goudreau, who sat next to her.

"Mindy," the doctor prodded again, as if Mindy had forgotten she was in the room, as if she possibly could. "You seem distracted today. Is it because they've set a trial date? Does that upset you?"

Mindy knew the doctor would have loved her to say it

did. She would have loved her to say that something—anything—upset her. Then the doctor would have something to do. "It's not until April," she said, because that's what Grandpa had told her. "I'll be eleven by then." She looked off toward Menemsha House, which had not been opened since that day. She wondered if it would ever open again, and if it was her fault if it didn't.

Difficulty making friends . . . Lying.

Dr. Reynolds had stopped talking. Mindy hated when she did that, as if it were up to her to fill in the blank space, the dead air that sat between them. She wiggled her tooth with her tongue again.

"Mindy," the doctor said after about two hundred minutes, which might have been more like two, "what's on your mind?"

"If you must know, I was thinking about you. Do you have a boyfriend? Do you let him touch you in 'inappropriate places'?"

The doctor hesitated a moment. Mindy sucked at her tooth.

"Adults are different from children," Dr. Laura replied. "But even when you're an adult, if someone touches you without consent, it's wrong. Do you understand that?"

Mindy opened her mouth, plucked the bloody tooth, and held it out to her. "This is my twelve-year molar. Does it mean I'm mature for my age?"

Dr. Reynolds sighed and picked up her bag. "Our time's up for today, Mindy. But I'll be back tomorrow. Maybe you'll be in a better mood."

Mindy watched her leave and felt a little sad but did not know why. Maybe it was that lack of positive parental attention showing up again.

· · ·

Ben got out of his car in the parking lot of the school. He'd come to see his grandkids in the play whether John liked it or not, whether the world liked it or not. He had, however, waited until the performance was about to start: no sense running into people he should not and did not want to see.

Walking into the long corridor where he'd not walked since Carol Ann had been a student, he noticed the construction paper turkeys that lined the walls. It was, of course, almost Thanksgiving. The time had passed so quickly, as if the days and weeks were racing toward April, hell-bent on getting to the trial.

Jill had come home from Sturbridge but soon would be gone again, this time to New York for press photos with Mr. Celebrity. But Ben figured it didn't much matter where his wife was these days; the conversations they had were more on edge than not, and he sadly felt more at peace when she was away.

Guilt, he supposed, was causing that. Guilt for putting her through this nightmare, which would soon be over one way or another if the calendar had its way.

The auditorium lights had already been dimmed. Metal folding chairs sat in neat rows from the stage to the back, about three-quarters of them occupied by parents and grandparents and siblings of all ages. Even in the darkness, Ben spotted Carol Ann and John sitting near the front. He scanned the room: he saw the editor of the newspaper, the head of the fish cooperative, and even Sheriff Talbot. But did not see a silhouette that resembled Dave Ashenbach's.

He took a seat by the door, in case he decided to go home.

From behind the stage, someone worked the pulley, and the old maroon curtain slowly jerked open. The audience hushed, as if this were a high-priced Broadway performance. It occurred to Ben that to most of the people there, it was just as important, perhaps more. Families—*children*—were the Vineyard way of life. He moved uncomfortably on the chair and remembered that that was why he'd built Menemsha House: for the children, to help their young minds work and play and grow into the best that they could be.

The teacher in charge stepped forward on the stage. Ben recognized her: Melanie Galloway, daughter of Dick Bradley, who owned the Mayfield House in Vineyard Haven. Like Ben, Bradley was a transplant from the mainland. Like Ben—hell, like most of them on the island— he'd had his share of struggles. Ben had not heard that being accused of child molestation had been one of them.

He quickly glanced around and wondered if the Galloways, the Bradleys, or anyone in the audience had heard what Mindy Ashenbach had done. If any of the parents, or any of the kids . . .

The collar of his corduroy shirt suddenly felt too tight. He opened the top two buttons and rubbed his throat.

Melanie Galloway introduced the first scene, the Indians alone without the Pilgrims, before the *Mayflower* arrived. A group of kids were crouched, sorting sheaves of corn. A small boy in a long feathered headdress marched onto the stage. One of the Indians looked up at him. "Chief Running Rain!" he exclaimed. "Look at the bountiful harvest we have this year!" *Bountiful* sounded a lot like *bound-full,* but Ben got the idea.

Chief Running Rain—Ben smiled as he realized it was John, Jr.—nodded. "It's enough for a big feast," the chief proclaimed, turning to the audience and waving his arms with overdrama. "Let's invite everyone we know to come and watch the football games." His too-large headdress slipped a little.

The audience laughed, including Ben.

"We don't have television yet," the minor Indian replied.

"We don't have football, either," the chief responded. More chuckles from the audience. "Oh, well, we'll have to eat a lot instead."

Ben smiled at the way they did things differently today, at how education was always challenged to hold kids' interest while teaching them . . . anything. It was why he'd wanted a hands-on museum, where they could participate, where they could feel like a part of history. As he thought about Menemsha, his depression washed over him again, this time like the running rain of John, Jr.'s Indian name.

The ache in his gut was not painful now but dull and worn down by the days and nights behind him and the anticipation of the days and nights ahead. Sitting in the auditorium, he no longer heard the words coming from the stage; his senses were as deadened as his pain, his hearing and his sight so numb that he nearly missed it when one figure—a little girl—moved down the aisle and went out the door by his chair.

He nearly missed it, but he did not.

He shot up from his chair. Without using any of the brains that he'd once had, he quietly slipped from the room and went out into the hall.

The little girl was at the water fountain. Ben adjusted his Red Sox cap and said a fast prayer, asking that he'd do this right.

"Mindy," he said as he approached her, not too quickly, not too close.

She stopped drinking. Her head froze in place, bent down, hair hanging.

"Mindy," he repeated, "are you all right?" Maybe this was his chance. Maybe once she saw him, she'd admit that she had lied.

Rather than admitting anything, she pushed the hair

out of her face. Then she stood up straight and looked at him. He noticed right away that she seemed as pale as he, except for the dark shadows that curved beneath her young eyes.

"I can scream, you know," she said.

Sweat formed on his brow. He did not wipe it off. "I know you can," he said. "But there's really no reason to, is there?"

She moved her eyes away and pretended to look at the construction-paper turkeys as if they were fine art.

"Mindy," he repeated, not going closer than a dozen or so feet but standing stationary, trying to let her know that she was safe, had always been safe with him. His thoughts raced as he tried to figure out what he should say. "I guess all I can do is ask you why."

She turned her head from the turkeys. Twelve feet was too far away to see if tears were in her eyes.

"Go away," she said.

"I can't," Ben replied. "I have nowhere to go. I cannot work. I can barely face my family. I am afraid to walk down the street or go into a store. My life is ruined, Mindy. Can you understand that?"

"Go away," she repeated, "or I'll have to scream."

He did not move.

She tipped her head back.

Then she screamed.

He made it to his car before the full fury of commotion blasted from the auditorium, before scurrying adults and running, excited children in various stages of costumes and street attire threw open the doors and charged into the parking lot.

He slumped behind the wheel of his '47 Buick, his heart pounding like even if there was a tomorrow, it wouldn't matter, he'd be dead.

He knew he should start the car and drive away, but he could not, his movements were impossible, his body had grown to lead.

Which was why he was so surprised that he trembled when a knock came on his window.

He looked outside. Hugh Talbot was there.

Ben unrolled the window.

"How you doin' tonight, Ben?"

He nodded because he could not speak.

"Had a little ruckus inside. Mindy Ashenbach let out a scream and damn near scared half the people on the island. Pilgrims and Indians included."

Ben nodded once again. Hugh tucked his hands into his pockets.

"Mindy says she saw a stranger carrying a gun."

Ben frowned.

"See anyone like that out here?" the sheriff asked.

He shook his head. "No. No, I didn't."

Hugh nodded and gave a quick slap to the Buick. "Well, you take care now, hear? And watch out for strangers."

Ben breathed a moment, waiting for things to quiet down, both inside and out. When the last of the people had dispersed, he turned over the ignition and began to drive away. That was when he noticed his son-in-law standing at the auditorium doors, hands on hips, eyes fixed on the old Buick and on the man inside.

"Looks like there was some action at the school last night," Amy said as she sat in Jill's studio, reading the newspaper, waiting for dubs to finish taping. Her mother taught her how to do it, so she could help earn "financial assistance" now that the tavern was locked up for the season and she was out of a job until spring.

Jill had also wanted Amy there so she could tell her

she was doing *Good Night, USA* after all, though she couldn't say the reason because even her husband didn't know.

"I thought you were looking at the want ads," Jill replied, not turning from the spreadsheet on her computer screen, pretending that Amy's comment had not just sent an emotional dagger through her heart. When Ben came home last night, he'd said there'd been a problem. With Mindy. Jill had simply asked if anyone found out, and he said he didn't think so but did not know for sure. With that she'd gone to bed in Jeff's old room, where she'd been spending her nights after she'd returned from Sturbridge. In Jeff's room she did not have to expose herself to such things as intimacy, like sleeping in the same bed, never mind sex.

Of course, last night she had not slept.

"It's the day before Thanksgiving," Amy replied. "Who's going to hire me on the day before Thanksgiving?"

Jill supposed not everyone wanted to ignore the holiday the way she did. She did not intend to celebrate: she was too tired to cook, and Ben hardly ate anyway. "So what happened at the school?" she asked, because she did not feel like answering Amy's question.

"Some girl screamed at the Thanksgiving play. Said she thought she saw a stranger with a gun, then decided it wasn't a gun, but a bunch of flowers someone had brought for the drama coach."

As Jill stared at the computer screen, relief seeped into her. Not the weight-of-the-world-has-been-lifted relief, but an easement of sorts, for the moment. "Who was the girl?"

"They don't give her name. She must have scared everyone to death."

Jill nodded, her eyes fixed on the numbers on the screen, the production estimates for the next quarter. She needed to resolve them before next week, when she'd be off to New York. The numbers would tell her if they'd survive until the *Good Night, USA* compensation started rolling in.

In the meantime, she had to tell Amy.

"Honey," Jill said, "put the paper down a second, will you?" She turned from the computer.

Amy lowered the *Gazette* and peered over the top.

"I need to tell you something, and I hope you understand. I've decided to do *Good Night, USA* in February."

Her daughter blinked. "Why?"

She couldn't tell her that they needed a good lawyer, that Ben was being foolish, and that she'd had to take control. "For my career, honey. I'm hoping it will reopen lots of doors."

"What about Addie?" She set the paper fully down. Her clear, smooth skin became pink, her eyes opened wide. She twirled the beaded bracelet around her wrist. "God, Mom, have you forgotten that she screwed you out of so much money? Besides, I thought we were more important than your career now. Ben, me, the Vineyard. I thought you were tired of that money crap."

"Of course you're more important. It's just that sometimes . . ."

"Sometimes what? Sometimes your work is more important?" She stood up and crossed the room. She played with the levels on the audio track. "Is it going to be just like before? When you were so busy or so tired from working to support Jeff and me that we were the ones who suffered?"

The truth came at Jill like a big water balloon, bursting on her, splashing its unwanted message in a way she couldn't simply brush away. "Honey—" she began.

"Like what about Thanksgiving, Mom? You know, that time of year when everyone stuffs turkeys and themselves? That 'over the river and through the woods' time of year when families eat cranberry sauce and creamed onions and, God help them, celery? Are you going to ignore it because you're too busy?"

Jill closed her eyes. She had not expected such hostility. And yes, she had planned to say she was too busy.

Amy turned from the controls. "And God, Mom, what about Ben? Isn't he jealous that you'll be with Christopher again?"

Jill turned back to her computer. "I'm not going to *be* with Christopher, Amy. I'm going to work with him. And no, Ben's not jealous. He knows me better than that." She opened the file that listed prices for raw stock. Somehow she'd have to guesstimate how much Vineyard Productions would use from January through March. If she was still in business, if Ben's secret did not come out and ruin their lives, not least for the way that they'd hidden it, even from family. *Especially* from family.

Amy circled the computer and sat down facing Jill. "Is he okay, Mom? I mean, Ben's not sick or anything, is he?"

She shook her head but could not look at her daughter. "He has a lot on his mind right now with Sea Grove. And Menemsha House. But no, he's not sick."

"Isn't he upset that Carol Ann is going to Maine for Thanksgiving?"

"Things change, Amy. Even holidays."

Leaning back, Amy put her feet up on the desk. "Well, no one asked me what I wanted," she said. "I'm too young to give up holidays."

If Jill did two features a month, not counting February, she could get away with a case of tapes for shooting, a couple more for dubs.

She entered a few arbitrary numbers, then moved them into columns. "What are your friends doing?"

"It's a family day, Mom. I can't exactly call someone up and invite myself."

She entered the numbers, then a few more.

"What about Rita and Hazel?" Amy asked. "Are they having Thanksgiving alone?"

"I haven't talked to Rita since the Halloween party."

"Geez, Mom. She's left about a thousand messages here. Probably at home, too."

"Excuse me, but I thought Charlie's apartment was now your home."

Amy swung her legs off the desk. "Well, I guess it might as well be."

That said, Amy stalked out the door.

Jill sighed. Her chin dropped, her head dropped, as if its weight had become too great a stress on her neck. Amy didn't deserve her anger, or her evasiveness. Jill feared that someday, unexpectedly, she was going to tell her what was really going on.

It was the same with Rita. The more often they were together, the greater the possibility became that Jill would unload the truth, dump out her pain. She'd been avoiding Rita and circumventing Amy simply because it could happen.

It mustn't happen. Not until they had a real lawyer and she knew that there was hope.

In the meantime, maybe there was something she could do to salvage what was left of her relationship with her daughter.

"Rita?" Jill's voice came on the line. "Remember me?"

"Hmm," Rita said, "give me a hint. Tourist or native?" For most of their lives, Jill had been the hot-and-cold enigma, here one day, gone the next. Once Rita had believed that it was her fault—that she was not good enough for Jill, her rich, glamorous, brilliant best friend. It had taken her years to realize that all along, *she'd* been the stable one, Jill the emotional mess. It didn't make Jill's on-and-off predictability any less distressing, but at least she understood it wasn't about her.

"Oh, I'm a native all right. And I'm on the hunt for some turkey. What are you doing tomorrow?"

"Tomorrow is Thanksgiving."

"I love you, Rita. You're always so clever."

The edge to Jill's tone said she was trying to be humorous. Rita knew that edge, and that it was actually a thin wall of protection that was preventing her from crying. Rita frowned. "What's up?"

"Nothing, really. Time for something different. Carol Ann and John are away. Jeff's gone. You know. Things change."

Was that enough to cry about? Unlike Kyle, Carol Ann and Jeff would return someday. But Rita didn't say it and would never say it. Especially when Jill sounded so glum; even though she hadn't called in almost four freaking weeks. "Well, I'd love to say I'm clever enough to cook a fat turkey," Rita said, "but the truth is, I'm too tired. And too sick to be bothered."

Her friend paused. "Oh, God, Rita, I'm sorry. I haven't been in touch. How are you feeling? Do you have morning sickness?"

"I feel like crap, and I don't have morning sickness—I have all-day sickness. The only time I feel good is when I'm asleep, and I guess that doesn't count because I can't remember it."

"Oh, dear."

"Yeah, well, this dear is counting the days until April."

There was silence a second, then Jill cleared her throat. "Are you going to eat tomorrow? What about your mother?"

"Well, yes, we are going to eat. Actually we're going to serve, then eat. The church puts on the dinner every year for those who are alone. Hazel and I are going to help out."

"Oh," Jill said again. "You did that last year, didn't you?"

"I've done it every year for the past forty or so." Perhaps Jill had been too absorbed in her own traditions, her own family, to realize that sometimes, some people were left alone.

"Do you think they need more help? Now that I'm an islander again, maybe I should get involved."

Rita shrugged. "Whatever. I'm sure they can always use an extra pair of hands. Or two, if Ben's coming along."

There was that pause again, that pause of distress. "Actually, there will be two pairs of hands, but it will be Amy and me. Ben has some kind of a flu bug, so he'll probably stay home in bed."

If she hadn't sounded so matter-of-fact, Rita might have believed her. But the flu? Ben? Well, hopefully, that's all it was and not something worse, like, hell, cancer. She shook her head and wondered why these things seemed to come to mind more often once one passed forty. Or fifty, in Ben's case. "Well, give him my best, and in the meantime, be at the church by nine o'clock. There's a lot to do before the birds come out of the ovens."

Rita hung up the phone and looked across the living room at her mother, who was sitting in the chair, making the third pair of booties for the baby yet to be born. "Don't ask me how I know what I know, but something's wrong with Jill. And it's something big, or she'd tell me what."

Mindy had no idea why she'd done it, why she'd screamed.

"I don't know," she said to Dr. Laura when the woman arrived with an apple pie to go with Thanksgiving dinner as if they would have one.

"Were you afraid he would touch you again?"

She looked at the pie that sat on the counter. It was all puffed up and golden and must have been baked at the Black Dog Bakery or at the Mayfield House, where Dr. Reynolds was living. She wanted to ask if Laura was spending Thanksgiving with her boyfriend if she had one, or if she, too, would be alone. Instead she said, "I was surprised he was there."

"And afraid?" the doctor asked again.

Mindy shrugged, because although she supposed yes would have been the right answer, it no longer felt good to say bad things about Ben. He'd looked so sad last night. And she knew that it was her fault.

Ben slept until ten, because sleeping late had become easier than getting up to do nothing. He opened his eyes and listened to the hollowness of the house.

Lying on the huge four-poster bed that had belonged to Jill's grandparents, he stared up at the canopy, the "lace ceiling," he called it, with silliness that always made Jill laugh, back when she still cared, back when she had been there on her side of the bed.

The hollowness seemed worse because it was Thanksgiving, because this wonderful old house should be filled with the aromas of turkey and pumpkin pie and laughter today, not only with air breathed in and out by a solitary man.

Maybe he should get drunk. There might be enough single-malt scotch in the cabinet downstairs. No one would know. Everyone on the island would be busy with their own families today, their own friends, or, in his wife's case, with whomever they could find.

Then again, he admitted, when she'd said she was going to the church with Amy, he had agreed. She'd asked him to go, then seemed relieved he'd said no. He told her that if he felt like giving thanks this year, he wouldn't be certain for what.

She responded by saying he might be grateful there had been no fallout from him trying to confront Mindy, right there in public.

He rolled onto his side and stared out the window. It was not a pretty day. The wind had kicked up and the branches of that oak he'd meant to prune were brushing against the window, scratching at the glass like a dog trying to get in.

If they had a dog, he wouldn't be alone today.

He was trying to decide whether to get out of bed now or ever again—when the telephone rang out in the hall. If they had a cordless phone upstairs, he wouldn't have to get out of bed. But they didn't have a cordless any more than they had a dog.

The answering machine didn't kick in: Jill must have disconnected it in her quest for privacy. He lay there for a second, thinking it could be Jill checking to see that he was okay; or Carol Ann wanting to say Happy Thanksgiving. Whoever was calling let it ring the full seven rings it took Ben to haul himself from the bed and go out to the hall.

The whoever was not Jill, and it was not Carol Ann. It was a voice he recognized from TV years ago.

"Niles?" the caller asked. "This is Christopher. Edwards." He said his name in two parts, as if the first part wouldn't mean anything without the second. As if Ben would know anyone else named Christopher with a polished, celebrity voice.

"My wife isn't home," Ben replied.

There was a loud, guffawing chuckle that Ben might have thought was caused by nerves if it had come from anyone else. "I wanted to let her know her accommodations are set for a week from Sunday."

Ben wanted to ask if he'd become one of Addie

Becker's lackeys or if there was some other reason he and not Addie was calling. And it was Thanksgiving, for God's sake, not the middle of a workday in the middle of the week. He might have challenged the jerk's motives, but he was really too tired now and didn't much give a shit. "Anything else?" he asked.

"Well, no," Edwards concluded. "I just wanted to wish you all a happy Thanksgiving. Amy and Jeff included."

Mind your own damn business, Ben wanted to shout. Instead, he said, "Yeah, sure, you too."

He did not remember saying good-bye, but he did remember that he hung up, then removed the receiver from the hook, in case anyone else decided to call. Then went back to bed without the single-malt scotch because it was downstairs and that was too far to walk.

Chapter 15

Jill went to Manhattan on Friday and spent three days shopping because her wardrobe needed updating and most of the good shops on the Vineyard were closed for the season. That was, of course, the excuse she'd given Ben. The greater reason was that she wanted to escape his depression, his deepening dark mood.

Maybe all that would change once she'd secured a good lawyer. As long as he didn't divorce her for doing it behind his back.

By Sunday evening, she was exhausted from walking and thinking and spending too much money, as if she still had it to spend.

She stepped from the shower and wrapped herself in the thick white terry robe with the Plaza logo on the pocket. Towel-drying her hair, she went into the bedroom of the suite just as there was a knock on the door—room service, no doubt, with the light supper she'd ordered.

It was not room service. It was Christopher.

She sucked in a small breath and clutched her robe tightly closed.

He smiled that tawny, tanned, straight-white-teeth smile. "You came early," he said.

"To shop," she replied.

"Did you find any bargains?"

"No. But I bought some nice things."

"Christmas gifts?"

"Not yet."

He nodded. "Are you going to make me stand in the doorway?"

"Oh," she said, and quickly stepped back as he moved into the living room, as he walked past her with his full six feet of height and his former athlete's firm body dressed in a buttersuede jacket and sleek light wool pants, not the jeans and flannel shirt of Vineyard men. For a moment, his aura enveloped her; for a moment, she became light-headed.

Ben, she forced herself to remember.

"Addie's not arriving until tomorrow," he said, walking to the window and looking down on Fifth Avenue. "In the meantime, how about dinner uptown?"

It was as if he had stepped not only into the room but back into her life, right where he'd left off, right back in control.

"I'm sorry, but I've ordered room service."

He turned back to her and smiled. "Cancel it. The truth is, I wanted you here a day early so we could spend some time alone. There are things we need to discuss."

Jill felt a little bit duped and a little bit angry, because she could not imagine that Christopher had anything to "discuss" that necessitated her being here a day before Addie, anything that required them to spend "some time alone." But he'd been insistent, and he was, well, difficult to turn down.

So she'd shooed him away and canceled her supper.

Then she'd called Ben to tell him good night, to say she was going out to meet Addie for dinner, hoping that the lie would not catch up with her.

Then she dressed, first in an outfit she'd brought from home, a three-year-old St. John knit. But when she'd stood in the mirror, she looked too much like the old Jill, so she'd discarded it for a new dress she'd bought yesterday at Escada: a beige cashmere sheath that stopped just above her ankles and had a slit on one side clear up past her knee. New Bally heels and a long tiger pin made her feel like New York, made her feel like today.

Maybe she'd gone a little too far, she thought now, as she sat across from Christopher at a small linen-covered table in a tiny French restaurant on the Upper East Side, and was uncomfortably aware that he could not stop staring at her—the woman who'd once been his fiancée.

"I guess I thought you'd look different," he said over a balloon-shaped wine goblet. He had on a pale blue sweater, the color of his eyes, and a navy blazer from Armani or someone equally chic.

"How?" she asked. "Old? Dowdy?"

He laughed. "Maybe with no makeup and soil beneath your fingernails and wearing a yellow slicker that smelled a little like low tide."

She laughed. "Sorry to disappoint you."

He sipped his cabernet sauvignon, then set down the glass. "Remember that day we trucked Maurice Fischer all over the island in the pouring rain? God, he loved it. He even loved those yellow slickers. We were bored stiff."

Jill had been bored—he was right about that. But that was before . . . "Well," she said, "yellow never was your color." She did not add that today she would not have been bored, because, until recently, she'd begun to see the island in a whole different light, a whole loving light. She raised her own glass to help ward off the guilt she now felt for having dressed up purposefully to look good for Christopher.

"We need to talk about the future," he said so abruptly it took Jill off guard.

"February," she replied.

"And more if you like."

She took a deep drink. A waiter arrived with their pâté de canard.

"Lizette is leaving the show," he said after the waiter was out of earshot.

"But the ratings are good."

"Have you seen the book?"

"No. But I can tell by your advertisers—"

"Well, you might not believe this, but for once Maurice is not worried about the ratings. He wants Lizette out. She's been doing cocaine."

Jill suppressed a sigh, a big, deep sigh. She had only wanted to find a lawyer for her husband. She had only wanted to come to New York early to escape the gloom at home. She had only wanted to dress up tonight to show Christopher she had not "lost" anything. She had not expected this news, or the whirlwind of emotions it set off in her mind.

And yes, her ego had told her that it was nice that he was looking at her, wanting her. But now to learn that what he really wanted was only a co-anchor . . .

She felt like a fool. "Christopher," she said, "I have a home and a husband. I have a business. I have no intention of relocating to the West Coast, or of forming a permanent career on *Good Night, USA*. I made that decision three years ago, and it has not changed."

"The show is moving to New York."

She tried to keep her surprise from showing on her face.

"We'll finish out December in L.A. with Lizette as best we can. January will be a hiatus—they'll build the new set then. When we return in February, it will be in the Big

Apple, and you will be beside me. It's the way I want it, Jill. It's how Maurice wants it."

"I just told you, I will not form a permanent career on *Good Night, USA*."

He leaned back in his chair. "Even if your husband goes to prison for child molestation?"

Jill did not remember getting up and leaving the restaurant. She did remember stumbling in her heels out onto the sidewalk. She did remember that it had started to rain, no, sleet. That it was cold. That she stood shivering until he hailed a cab. She did not want to go back indoors, where people might see her cry.

The next thing she remembered was Christopher helping her off with her dress, wrapping the Plaza robe around her, leaning down and kissing the hollow at her collarbone just below her shoulder.

Then he half-carried her out to the living room of her suite, where he set her down. He sat down next to her, where he cradled her face and her back as she cried.

If he'd had an erection, she would have let it slide into her. She would have done just about anything right then to feel warm and secure, safe and protected. But if he wanted sex, he did not let it show.

"How did you find out?" she asked when the numbness had faded enough that she was able to speak.

He stroked her hair. "Hugh Talbot, the Gay Head sheriff. He's always been a huge baseball fan—and a fan of mine, I guess. I hate to admit it, but Hugh has helped me keep track of your life these past few years." He chuckled a little. "I guess I wanted to be sure I knew if your life fell apart. If you would ever be ready to return to the real world."

"Oh, God," she moaned. It was a few minutes before

she could speak again. "How long?" she asked. "How long have you known?"

"From the day your husband was arrested. Actually, before he was arrested. Hugh called me right after Ashenbach left the station."

"Addie called me the same night," Jill said, trying to sort out the pieces.

"I saw my chance to get you back. I got on the phone with Maurice and told him about Lizette. I knew he'd freak. Did you know he had a son who died of a cocaine overdose?"

Jill shook her head as if she cared about Maurice Fischer or his dead son right then.

"Well, then I talked to Addie. She took care of the rest."

She closed her eyes and asked a question she did not want to ask. "Does . . . does Addie know about Ben?"

"No."

For that, Jill was grateful.

He smiled. "In case you declined the offer, I needed to use what I knew as leverage."

"Blackmail, you mean."

He was quiet for a moment. He stroked her hair again. "Jill, I cannot stand Lizette. I never could. All that time you thought I was fucking her, believe me, I was not. And now I want you back on our show. Where you belong."

He moved his hand to her neck, then ran it down her throat. Despite herself, Jill felt her breasts swell, her nipples grow firm. She wondered if he could see their outline through the terry robe. "Why did you sign the contract, Jill? Why did you agree to come back?"

She knew she should get up. She knew she should get up off the couch and ask him to leave. But his hand felt so warm and her heart ached so much. "Because I wanted to use Addie's connections to find Ben a good lawyer," she admitted.

"Then it seems we need each other," he said. "You need to save your husband. And I need *Good Night, USA.* I'm a washed-up baseball player with no family and no life. The show's all I have." His hand had stopped moving, but her heat had not abated.

"You never married," Jill said. "Was that my fault?"

He laughed. "Despite what the tabloids say, I do not take commitment lightly."

Sometime in the past three years, she'd stopped paying attention to the tabloids, for there no longer had been a need. "You could go back to sportscasting," she said.

"No. That would be like you returning to local street news."

"You could find someone other than me. A new face. No entanglements."

"You're a proven commodity. You'll give the show a big boost."

She wished he would move his hand again. She wished he would slide it inside the terry cloth and fondle her breast, squeeze her nipple, make her feel a woman's velvet heat again, remind her that there was life and love and ecstasy out there, and that she deserved it again. She arched her back a little in response to her growing need. "So now you only want me for my ratings," she said with an attempt at humor that rang oddly true.

His hand remained steady, it did not move. "That's all," he said, "I promise. I don't want to interfere in your personal life. Besides," he added, "I do care about you, Jill. I do want you to be happy."

She closed her eyes again, and her back relaxed. She wished she did not wish that he would interfere, that he would whisk her off on his white horse for good, that she could forget what it meant to love Ben and could return to the land of TV-make-believe and be quite happy there.

But she'd learned long ago that no man rode a white horse. And even if Christopher did, he would not whisk her away, because he only wanted her so his ratings would soar.

On her skin his hand now felt chilled. She slid from under his touch and slowly sat up, wondering why it seemed she now had so much more to lose than when she'd arrived.

"You promised you'd help paint and wallpaper the kitchen," Amy whined to Ben on Monday morning, when she called him at eleven and got him out of bed. He briefly wondered why he didn't just leave the answering machine on and pretend he wasn't home. But for some reason, leaving on an answering machine while one was in the next room seemed deceitful.

"I don't remember that I did," he told Amy truthfully. These days Ben found he forgot many things, like the date and the time and often his name.

"It's bad enough I had to order cable. Charlie never did anything to spruce up this place," Amy said. "Anyway, the new wallpaper I ordered is in. You've got nothing else to do, and Rita said she'd help. Are you reneging on the deal?"

He rubbed his beard growth, then looked down at his sweats. He couldn't be sure if he'd changed his clothes since Jill left days ago. Going to Amy's would mean he'd have to shower. And shave. And look human again, no matter how bad he felt.

"I don't know, honey," he said. "I haven't wallpapered in years. Besides," he added in what really wasn't a lie, "I planned to go Christmas shopping today."

"We're not doing it today. We're doing it Wednesday. Can I count on you, Ben? Please, please?"

Well, Wednesday was two days from now, forty-eight

hours. Maybe he'd feel up to it by then. Besides, Jill would be home at the end of the week, and sooner or later he'd have to buck up.

"Okay, you win. But only if Rita or her mother makes some food. I can't stand my own cooking another day."

"I'll cook!" Amy exclaimed, which was not the greatest culinary news.

Ben sighed and really wished he could drop the whole thing.

From doing a stint on a morning news show to being photographed at Rockefeller Center with its famous skaters and its festive tree, Jill had pretended to love this reunion for the good of the show.

By Wednesday she was ready to ask Addie for the favor. With Christopher's coaching, Jill had dreamed up a story that should seem plausible, as long as Addie didn't ask many questions.

They were having lunch at Tavern on the Green, because Addie felt that the more tourists who saw them together, the better. It was part of the limelight that Jill had once relished.

In the bright daylight of the garden room, though, Jill felt oddly self-conscious. She looked at Christopher for support: his unnerving wink made her feel a little bit naked.

She danced her fork through the salad of spring greens. "A friend of Amy's has himself in hot water," she said as nonchalantly as she could. "Would either of you know a decent lawyer?" She chewed a piece of lettuce and slowly swallowed.

"Seems to me you had a decent lawyer who got you out of your contract with me," Addie remarked, not lifting her eyes from the piece of bread that she slathered with butter. It amazed Jill that the woman had not died of overconsumption—or tactlessness. She was still as fat and brusque as ever, but now the brusqueness was more bothersome to Jill. Perhaps living back on the Vineyard had weaned her off barracudas, emotional and otherwise.

"What kind of a lawyer do you need?" Christopher asked, stepping up to the plate, the baseball-player-celebrity still pitching.

"Well," Jill replied, not daring to look at him for fear of revealing her anxiety, "a thirteen-year-old girl says he touched her in an 'inappropriate place.' He denies it."

"They all do," Addie said, gazing at the salmon in parchment that had just arrived.

Jill waited until the food was served before she continued. "Anyway," she added, "the girl claims he only touched her breast."

"He didn't rape her?" Christopher asked.

"He claims no. And there's no physical evidence that says otherwise."

Addie apparently wasn't interested. She dove into her meal.

"He needs a good criminal lawyer," Christopher said, glancing at Addie. "Don't you agree?"

The agent shrugged and took a huge forkful of garlic mashed potatoes. "Sounds like the kind of thing no one should get involved with."

"He's a friend of Amy's. And our whole family," Jill said. "And he lost both his parents in a car accident not long ago. He's got no one to go to bat for him." The "going to bat" term had come from Christopher. Jill hoped Addie didn't recognize the language.

"Aren't there any good attorneys on that island of yours?" the agent asked.

"Not who can help. Not with something this serious."

Addie swigged her wine as if it were water.

"Addie," Christopher said, "aren't you friends with Herb Bartlett?"

Jill tried not to show her surprise. Christopher had not

even hinted that Addie knew the famous Atlanta attorney who'd successfully defended a rock star on a murder-one charge. She wondered what other tricks her co-host had up his French-cuffed sleeves. She did not want to look at him. She was afraid he would wink again.

"I hardly think Herb would want to defend a nobody-kid for something he probably did."

Silence hung over the table. Jill looked at her plate.

"Well, I think Jill's doing us a favor by filling in for Lizette," her former co-anchor, lover, and fiancé said. "And I think a call to Herb Bartlett is the least we can do."

"Or?" Addie asked.

"Or *Good Night, USA* is history, Addie. Jill will pack up her Manhattan clothes and go back to her little island, and I will not break in a new anchor. It will be Jill, or I'll be gone."

Addie swigged more wine and moved her gaze from Christopher to Jill. "I hate it when I feel I've been had," she said.

"Jill is my best friend," Rita announced, as if it were news to anyone in the room: Hazel, Ben, and Amy. They had just polished off huge helpings of Hazel's beef stew.

Rita stood on a chair, guiding a plumb line so that Ben could hang up the next strip of prepasted wallpaper. She'd suggested that Jill would be a better assistant for Ben, but Amy explained that her mother was gone. Again.

So there stood Rita, lovely, pregnant Rita, substituting for her best friend, with her best friend's daughter holding one side of the chair and the husband, the other. Hazel sat at the table carefully reading today's newspaper in case the ink fell off before she got home.

"Jill's been my best friend since either one of us can remember, but for the life of me I don't understand why she keeps taking off."

"It's her job," Ben said flatly. Rita recognized that he was an unhappy man. He had lost a lot of money in the Menemsha fire, she knew; Jill was working to support them until the museum could turn a profit—and Sea Grove began paying its dues. She also knew that Ben Niles was not the kind of guy to take his wife's continued absences lightly. Not many on the island would.

Which was why Rita wanted to ask why he had closed the museum for the winter, but did not feel she should. Her curiosity could wait until Jill returned, assuming her best friend had time for her.

"When's she coming back?"

Neither Ben nor Amy answered.

"Is she in Los Angeles?" Hazel asked, her head bent closely to the paper. "It says here 'Jill McPhearson to host *Good Night, USA*.' "

Rita stopped what she was doing and looked down at Ben, who did not speak. "You must be reading that wrong, Mother."

"My eyesight is perfectly good," Hazel snipped. " 'Jill McPhearson to host *Good Night, USA*. An unidentified source recently reported that island native Jill Randall McPhearson will grace national television in February as her ex-fiancé's co-anchor on the popular newsmagazine, *Good Night, USA*.' "

Rita's gaze stayed on Ben. He shrugged. "Addie Becker must have planted that story to whet the audience's appetite. The truth is, we decided it would be a smart move for Jill's career."

Although he said "we," Rita wondered otherwise.

"She's in New York City right now," Ben continued, "doing prepublicity photos." He laughed a short, unenthusiastic laugh.

"What else does the article say?" Rita asked.

Hazel returned to the paper. "That's it."

"I hate this," Amy muttered. "All this publicity. It's going to surround her again. It's going to surround *us*."

"Well, don't worry about the Vineyard," Rita said. "Your mother has always been the island's sweetheart. Long before even you were aware, her face was front page news here."

"Yeah, well," Ben said, adjusting his Red Sox baseball cap, "maybe next time Addie will remember to tell them her name is Niles now."

"Oh, stop whining," Hazel said, turning the newspaper page, "all of you. Jill is a very talented girl. She works hard and deserves everything she gets."

Rita went back to the wall.

Amy turned to the table and measured, then cut another sheet of wallpaper. She handed it to Rita.

Ben said nothing more, as if he, too, knew that Hazel would have the last word, because she was the oldest, because that was how it worked.

"Besides," Hazel-of-the-last-word added, "things could be worse, Ben. You could end up like your friend Dave Ashenbach. Doesn't he live next door to your museum?"

Amy had just bent to get another roll of paper when Ben let go of his side of Rita's chair. The chair wobbled. Rita grabbed the counter, but slipped and landed on top of Amy, who cushioned her fall—luckily for Rita, painfully for Amy.

"Yeow!" Amy cried, as Ben shot across the kitchen and snapped the newspaper from Hazel's hands.

"What about Ashenbach?" he asked tightly, while Rita and Amy untangled themselves from each other and stood up to catch their breath.

"Up there," Hazel said, pointing to the open page. "In the top corner. It says his granddaughter found him yesterday, and that the guy is dead."

Chapter 16

The house smelled like fishermen because that's what the men were: Bruce Mallotti, Verge Benson, Frankie Paul. They had been Grandpa's friends: they'd worked with him on the boats for years, and they'd played cards with him in winter when there was nothing else to do.

They were fishermen whose fathers and grandfathers before them had been fishermen, too, or at least that's what Grandpa always said.

And like fishermen, they stuck together, which was why Mindy sat now in the living room of Bruce Mallotti's small cottage on Lobsterville Road. She wished everyone would stop talking in whispers, like she was a little girl.

"More cocoa, sweetie?" Mrs. Mallotti asked, which was weird. Well, not the cocoa part, but the fact that she called Mindy "sweetie" when she'd only seen her once or twice. Fishermen's families, after all, were not as close as fishermen.

Mindy shook her head.

Mrs. Mallotti smiled and patted Mindy's shoulder. She moved across the room and asked if Verge Benson or Frankie Paul would like another whiskey.

Yes, of course they would. It wasn't every day they lost one of their own, and at only sixty-one.

Mindy looked down into the remnants of her cocoa mug and realized she'd never known how old Grandpa was. Sixty-one seemed pretty old. But never knowing when somebody was going to die pretty much sucked.

Like yesterday, when she left for school, she'd never figured Grandpa would be dead by dinner.

Lifeless was a better word. She'd read that one time in a book. Yesterday when she'd come home from school, she'd seen Grandpa's feet sticking out from beside his pickup truck in the backyard. He didn't answer when she called to him; lately he'd seemed to be going deaf. So Mindy walked over to the truck.

That was when she learned that lifeless—*without life*—meant very still and kind of gray. Lifeless meant eyelids open and eyeballs staring upward at the sky, looking not scared or angry but blank. Lifeless meant hands that were sort of stiff, like someone had sprayed starch and tried to iron out the creases. Lifeless meant you didn't feel the brown oak leaves that had fallen on your jacket and pants and your face.

Now she glanced at her watch and wondered how soon it would be before she could say she was tired and sneaked off to bed. She liked the bed she had last night. It was small and tucked under an eave upstairs. Mrs. Mallotti had given her an afghan made of colored squares—a "Granny" afghan, she'd called it—and it was cozy, which was good, because Mindy couldn't seem to warm up and hadn't slept most of the night.

"The girl can stay with us until they find her," Mallotti said to the others.

Her, of course, was Mindy's mother. Little did they know that *Her* would most likely not be interested in coming to her daughter's rescue, any more than *Her* had cared a lot when Ben . . .

Mindy stared into the mug and wondered if Ben Niles knew. Then she wondered what would happen now; and if this court stuff would soon be over, without anyone ever knowing that she had told the lie.

Maybe it was over.

Ben fled from Amy and Rita and Rita's mother and raced back to the house. He grabbed the phone and started to dial before realizing he did not know Rick Fitzpatrick's number. He fumbled for the phone book. He dialed again.

"He's in court until this afternoon," the woman who answered said.

"Tell him I'll be in New York." He slammed down the phone.

As he grabbed the keys to the old Buick, a single fear tugged at his conscience: with Ashenbach dead, what would happen to Mindy? Would her long-lost mother return to the Vineyard to reclaim her?

It doesn't matter, he told himself over the lump in his stomach. *It's none of your business.*

Then he pushed himself out the door and turned his thoughts to the next flight, wondering when it would leave and how long it had been since he'd been off this damn island anyway.

Chapter 17

"It's over, honey," Ben said as he hugged his wife on the front steps of the Plaza Hotel. He'd been jumping up from the antique velvet sofa in the lobby to the brass and glass revolving doors and then sitting back down again—over and over—until finally the limo pulled up and she got out.

After her came the face that belonged to Mr. Edwards, and a fat woman in a big dress who he knew was Addie, even though they'd never been introduced.

He laughed, stepped away, and adjusted his cap. "Guess I should have said hello first."

Jill smiled. It has been so long since he'd seen her smile that he thought his heart would melt right there and pour out onto the entrance of the famous hotel which, the doorman had confided, Ivana Trump once had guarded from her perch across the street in Trump Tower and often telephoned to alert him to remove litter from the curb. It was information Ben could have lived without, but chatting with the doorman had been something to do while he'd been jumping from the sofa, waiting for this moment, waiting for that smile.

"Really?" she whispered.

Christopher sidestepped Jill. "This looks like a personal reunion, and I'm bushed, so I'll say good night."

Jill kept her eyes fixed on Ben. "What time tomorrow, Addie?"

"Five-forty-five," the agent replied. "I want the sunrise over the Hudson, with the skyline—and you—in the background."

Ben didn't think the sun rose on that side of the Hudson, but it didn't matter. He squeezed Jill's hand. "Come on, honey," he said, "I had them deliver a bottle of their best Chardonnay to the suite, and I'll bet it's well chilled by now."

Jill was stunned. Standing in the crowded elevator, with Ben's hand in hers, she tried to sort out what was happening.

Ben was not a child molester. It was over. It had been confirmed.

Of course, she'd known he was innocent all along.

The elevator door opened, and they got out. At room 204 he took her key and unlocked the door. Then he reached down and scooped her up. She squealed.

"Ben! What are you doing?"

He laughed his wonderful laugh, the one that made his gray eyes shine with mischief and love. He stepped into the suite and then kicked the door closed.

"I saw that in a movie once," he said, with a slow, seductive smile. "John Wayne, I think."

He carried her to the bedroom and gently placed her on the bed, her head on the pillow. He straightened her legs and took off her shoes: first from the right foot, then from the left.

She watched with great pleasure, her camel-hair coat still covering a chocolate wool dress.

He began to massage her toes, his strong fingers kneading one and then the next and then her entire foot from top to bottom, side to side.

She tingled all over. Yes, she thought, this was her Ben. Life would be right again. She slowly arched her back, wanting more, wanting it now.

He moved his hands up to her ankles, then her calves, kneading as he went. And when he reached under her skirt and touched her thighs, Jill thought she would go mad.

But his fingers did not rest on her. Instead, he hooked them around the waist of her pantyhose and carefully maneuvered them over her butt, down her legs, and off her feet.

And then he began again.

This time, however, as he massaged each toe, he bent and sucked them, too, one, then another, then another, encircling each with his warm, wet tongue.

He slid up higher, moving to her ankle, then to her calf, then to her thigh, his tongue sliding, gliding as it went, stopping off in hidden places.

And then he reached her in that place of mounting heat, that place grown damp and hungry. With his fingers, he moved aside her satin panties, then lowered his head, touching her with his mouth, his teeth, his tongue, gently licking at her little firm spot, then sucking it between his teeth and slowly biting down.

She moaned. She moaned again, because the air had left the room and time and pain had left her body and all sensation writhed with great pulsating fervor for his tongue that would not stop and her . . .

"Oh, God," she cried and grabbed his head, plunging his face into her heat, moving his head up and down as he nibbled and lapped and did not stop, thank God, he did not stop.

She moaned again.

He licked.

Again.

Again.

And then her body wilted into aching, throbbing oblivion, and tears spilled down her cheeks.

"Oh, God," she cried again, this time weakened, this time spent.

He did not leave, but rested his head against her thigh and tenderly wove his fingers through her damp hair.

"I love you so goddamn much," Ben whispered. "Do you know that?"

She could not answer; she could not speak. She merely moved her hand upon his head and removed his baseball cap.

When Jill awoke, it was dark. Ben was asleep beside her, one arm draped across her chest, his head tucked against her shoulder like a little boy in love. They were atop the blankets but covered by a satin quilt. Except for her panties and pantyhose, she was still dressed. She closed her eyes again and smiled, then moved her body closer to the man she so truly loved.

"Welcome home," he whispered in the dark.

She snuggled closer. "We're not home, darling. We're in New York."

"But you're back inside my heart again. Back home where you belong."

Jill smiled. She turned on her side and stroked his arm. "Tell me what happened. I want to know every detail."

He was silent for a moment. "Ashenbach's dead," he said matter-of-factly. "I never thought I'd see the day I wished anyone dead. But he is. Over-and-done-with dead."

Jill closed her eyes. "God," she said, "how did it happen?"

"Don't know. I guess his heart got tired of him being such a mean son of a bitch."

Moving her hand up to Ben's shoulder, Jill gently rubbed. "And?"

"And? And it's over. Without him to press charges, it's over. I'm pretty sure."

Her hand went still. "That's it?" she asked. "Did Rick say this means you're free?"

"He was in court. I haven't talked to him yet."

"So you're not really sure . . ."

He sighed. "Jesus, Jill. I thought you'd be excited."

She kissed his forehead. "I am, darling. I just hate to think you might be disappointed."

The telephone rang. Ben groaned. Jill did not move.

It rang again.

"Maybe it's Rick," he said.

She ducked, and Ben reached across her. He lifted the receiver.

His tightened face told her that the person on the other end was not his lawyer.

"She's busy right now," he said, then paused.

Jill frowned. She propped herself up on one elbow and watched her gray-eyed man.

"Yeah, okay, I'll be sure to tell her." His words were followed by a firm placement of the receiver in its cradle.

"That was your co-host," Ben said, sliding off the bed. "He said you don't have to be downstairs until nine in the morning. That you're not doing sunrise, you're doing F.A.O. Schwarz." He went into the bathroom.

Jill lay on the bed and wondered if she should tell him that Christopher knew, or if she should simply pray that if the two men were together, the subject would not come up.

Ben stuck his head from the doorway of the bathroom. "It's okay, honey," he said. "I promise I'm not jealous."

Guilt quickly washed through her, followed by another prayer that Ben would never learn that she'd come close to breaking her vows when she'd been so scared and so alone.

She closed her eyes again, grateful for her kind and loving husband, hopeful they could now put their lives back together again.

They could, if Ben was right and Ashenbach's curse—along with his body—was dead and buried and would not come back to haunt them.

During the night they made love again as if they needed to make up for these past weeks, when they'd slept apart more often than together. When the wake-up call came at seven-fifteen, Jill struggled to open her eyes, then keep them open.

Ben was no help. He reached across the huge bed and pulled her close to him, his warmth and his love enveloping her once again.

"I can't, you crazy man," she said. "I have to be downstairs at nine."

"One hour and forty-five minutes from now," he said as he buried his face in her neck.

She laughed. "It takes me that long to get ready. I don't exactly have an entourage to make me up and dress me, in case you didn't notice."

"Not like the old days, eh? Well, I'm sure your ex-fiancé won't notice."

She decided not to encourage any jealousy. "Well, Addie will notice if I'm ugly and if I'm five minutes late," she said, regretfully pulling herself from the bed. She was slipping into her silk robe just as a knock came on the door. She looked at Ben as if he might know who was at their door at this ungodly hour.

Ben shrugged. "Want me to get it?"

Jill smoothed her hair. "No," she replied. "Stay here where it's warm."

She went into the living room without shutting the bedroom door. The visitor was Addie, who seemed never to need sleep, surviving on sugar, caffeine, and lots of action.

"Sorry to stop by without phoning," the woman commented, "but I'm on my way to breakfast. I wanted you to know that Herb will be here at noon, but there won't be much time. He has to be in Chicago before dinner."

Jill pulled her robe together and looked at the agent. "Herb?" But she knew who it was the instant the word escaped, before she could close the door, before she could keep Ben from hearing.

Addie put her hand on her hip as if Jill were a dunce. "Herb Bartlett from Atlanta," she said. "Attorney at law."

Jill said good-bye and shut the door on Addie before Ben could bound out of bed, get red in the face, and ask what the hell was going on and why was an attorney en route.

But even when the door was closed, she did not want to turn around and see the look in his eyes as he lay on the bed that they'd just shared, where they'd made love with tenderness and with the bond of trust shared between husband and wife, the trust she had violated by having Addie contact Bartlett.

She did not want to turn around, but when Ben did not speak, she knew she must.

He was not in the bed, though. He was gone.

Slowly she moved back into the bedroom. He was standing at the window, looking out at Fifth Avenue as it yawned and stretched and began another day, as if the two people up in the Plaza suite were not about to have their marriage severed because the wife had been an insensitive, controlling ass, like those people she detested in the career of her choice.

"It was my problem," Ben said, his muscled back to her, wearing an old T-shirt from the Menemsha Blues store that had been silk-screened with a fish. "I thought we agreed it was my problem."

A chill from the air closed in on her. She wanted to lie, to say Herb Bartlett was coming for a different reason, for the contract, perhaps. But the man's name was as famous as F. Lee Bailey or Johnnie Cochran, and Ben would see through her. She shut her eyes. "I didn't tell Addie," she whispered. "I lied. I said that a boy on the Vineyard . . ." She didn't finish her sentence because she didn't know how.

"It doesn't matter," he said. "It doesn't matter because I don't need him anymore. Not Herb Bartlett or any other attorney. I don't need him because this is over."

Jill wished she felt as confident of that as he did.

"I'm willing to forget you did this, honey," he said, "because I know that you love me, and I know you only did it because you do."

She stood in place and started to shake. Then the tears fell from her eyes and ran down the front of her silk negligee. "I'm so sorry," she said.

"It doesn't matter," Ben said. Then he turned around, went to her, and gave her a forgiving hug. "It doesn't matter because it's over," he repeated.

"My grandfather's dead, so there's no one to pay you," Mindy said to Dr. Reynolds, who had come by the Mallotti house in the morning, as if no one had told her that her services would no longer be required.

"I know he died," the doctor said. "And I'm not here for the money. I came to see how you're doing."

Mindy scuffed her feet on the hard-packed dirt underneath the swing. She puffed out air and saw her breath, wishing the doctor would go away. "How'd you find me?"

The doctor leaned against the iron frame that was cemented into the ground and held the swing set, which must be really old because the Mallottis' kids had moved off-island years ago. "I went to your house yesterday afternoon. A policeman was there. He told me you were staying here with Mr. and Mrs. Mallotti."

Mindy pushed her swing back and pumped her legs. "Did they put yellow tape around the crime scene?" Had they tied one end to the garage and one end to the truck and made a circle around the oak trees with Grandpa dead inside? The question had plagued her ever since the cops made her leave.

"Your grandfather had a heart attack," the doctor replied. "There was no crime."

Mindy pumped her legs again. She hoped the cops had left a guard there, so the evidence wouldn't be disturbed, in case the autopsy showed he hadn't died of natural causes but from foul play. She had, after all, seen her share of *NYPD Blue,* though Grandpa had often remarked that a young girl shouldn't watch it.

"It must have been terrible to find him."

She wished the doctor hadn't mentioned that. It was bad enough that Mindy had to talk to her about *the afternoon in question,* the afternoon with Ben. Well, that was one thing, and this was another.

Without answering, she pushed off again and swung high in the air. Through the leafless trees, she could see Dutcher's Dock, where Grandpa had kept his boat. Maybe the boat would sit and rot there in the water, or maybe one of Grandpa's friends would take it. It would be sad to see it go somewhere else. It would be sad to see the back painted over where Grandpa had lettered "Melinda Anne," her name.

"I'll be there tomorrow," the doctor said, "at the funeral."

In midflight, Mindy shrugged.

"I wanted you to know. In case you need to talk to someone. In case you need a friend."

Mindy blinked against the breeze that had come up from the harbor. In summer there was no breeze, because the trees stopped it from coming. But in winter, when you didn't need it, there it was. Cold and raw and chilling.

The swing floated to a stop. Dr. Reynolds had her hand on the chain.

"Mindy," she said, "what about your mother? Has she been notified?"

Mindy wanted to take the doctor's hand off the chain. She wanted to swing again, to feel the cool November air on her face. She did not want to talk to this woman, now or ever again.

She sighed the way Grandpa had sighed when he was what he called "exasperated" with her. She gave a noncommittal shrug.

The doctor released her grip, and Mindy pushed off again.

"Have you talked with anyone from the police?" the doctor asked above the breeze. "Do you know what's going to happen next?"

Mindy knew the doctor was talking about *her*, about where she was going to go, on account of she was only ten. She pumped up high, then back again, then up. The doctor stood with her hands in her tweed coat pockets, sort of waiting for Mindy to speak again, like it was her turn, because the doctor had spoken last.

But Mindy was done talking. There was nothing left to say.

"We won't be needing your services after all," Ben said to Herb Bartlett when the attorney met them at lunchtime, downstairs in Palm Court. Thankfully the shots at F.A.O. Schwarz had not taken long, and they'd crossed the street to the Plaza in plenty of time. Christopher had whisked Addie into the Oak Room Bar to avoid interference.

"The guy who pressed charges is dead," Ben continued, "so the case will be dropped."

Bartlett had on a denim shirt and fringed leather jacket. Across the table, Jill studied the man, wondering if denim was legal attire for Atlanta. Then again, when one was as successful as Herb Bartlett, what one wore did not matter.

"What about the Commonwealth?" Bartlett asked. He had ordered a seafood salad and picked out the crab and the shrimp, dodging the vegetables like a man on a high-protein diet.

Ben laughed. "I don't think you understand, Mr. Bartlett. Thanks for your interest, but the man is dead."

"I thought the crime was committed against a young girl."

Ben lifted his fork to his fillet, then set it down before he took a bite. "It was," he replied. "But the man who pressed charges was the girl's grandfather. Now he's dead."

Glancing around the bright white, gold, and green room, Jill wondered how many others in the lunch crowd were beset with a problem as severe as this. Then her eyes caught herself in a huge mirror, where she saw anguish on her face, as if deep down she knew this was not going to be as easy as Ben had hoped. "Mr. Bartlett," she said, "we appreciate that you've flown here—"

Bartlett raised his hand. "Just so you know, the case may not be over. Addie has filled me in on the details. You should know that the Commonwealth of Massachusetts has the right to go forward, dead grandfather or not."

Ben pushed his chair back from the table. Jill took a bite of her Cobb salad, pretending to be nonchalant, the unaffected bystander at an accident scene.

"In Massachusetts the charge would be indecent assault and battery on a child under the age of fourteen," Bartlett continued in a soft southern drawl. "Those Yankee fathers take that very seriously. So seriously that if the accused is found guilty, it can mean seven years to life. And if there's no evidence, it's his word against the girl's. Of course," he continued, "deals can always be made. Plea bargains. A guilty plea avoids a trial. My guess is that it would result in supervised probation or house arrest. Your young man would be lucky, though. Although there's a register, Massachusetts doesn't publish the names of sex offenders on the Internet. At least not yet." He held out his hand and passed a card to Ben. "In case you need me after all, don't hesitate to call."

He took his napkin from his lap, set it on the table, and stood up. Then he mentioned something about a limo to the airport, and he was gone.

Ben looked at the card, then at his wife. "We won't need him, honey," he said, but his voice did not sound convincing, and Jill would have bet they were thinking the same thing.

Seven years to life.

His word against the girl's.

Jill plucked the card from Ben's hand and tucked it safely into her purse.

Chapter 18

She wore high white boots and a short white dress with fur around the hem. Her bleached blond hair was pinned up on her head, and her fingernails were painted blue and had silver glitter on the tips.

Mindy thought her mother looked like she belonged in a TV commercial for cool-refreshment-minty gum, not at a funeral, not at Grandpa's funeral.

But the truth was, Fern Alice Ashenbach had, as she said this morning, "not expected to be in attendance at a funeral," so she'd had no black dresses with her, down there in the islands where Mrs. Mallotti had tracked her from the itinerary in Grandpa's kitchen drawer.

Still, Mindy couldn't help but wonder why her mother didn't have something more appropriate to wear on the Vineyard, funeral or no funeral, fur-trimmed dresses being a long way from Black Dog sweatshirts. Maybe her mother and her dress belonged back in San Antonio, where she'd been born and raised. Maybe there she did not look out of place.

They walked down the short aisle of the little church in Chilmark. Mindy tried not to notice that people were staring at her mother and whispering to one another behind their hands.

The church was full: not because Grandpa had so many friends, but because he was a native islander and so was one of them. Zac Lambert and Terry Clarkson and, of course, the Mallottis and Verge Benson and Frankie Paul—they all were there, as if showing up proved that they had cheated death, that it wasn't them up front in that shiny wooden box.

The minister talked forever about a man he'd never met. Mindy mostly looked at her shoes, except when her mother took her hand and squeezed it. Then Mindy looked up to see her mother dab the corners of her eyes. Mindy could not imagine why her mother was crying. Her mother, the unemotional one. Her mother, Fern Alice Ashenbach— F.A.A., she used to love to say, adding she should have been an airline pilot instead of a yacht captain. It was a stupid joke, but it always made the men who heard it laugh.

Sitting on the hard pew, Mindy remembered the very different funeral of her father, Grandpa's son, F.A.A.'s not-so-devoted husband of eight years. Mindy had been six when he died, not so old, but not so young that she didn't remember the funeral or him.

That funeral had been small, just Grandpa and her mother and the minister and her. It wasn't in the church; it was in the cemetery, right over the hole that her father's coffin was later dropped into.

Grandpa had cried a lot.

"It's all your fault," Mindy had heard him tell her mother. "Your booze. Your boyfriends."

Her mother hadn't answered.

After that they'd gone back to the house. Mindy sat on the stool in the kitchen, looking at the big calendar where her father always crossed off each day as if he couldn't wait until the next one, as if today wasn't good enough and he wanted to eliminate it from the record of his life.

It had been while Mindy was sitting there after the funeral that her mother had emerged with a suitcase packed for one.

"I'll send you presents from every port," her mother said as she bent to kiss Mindy's cheek. "Grandpa will take good care of you. Behave for him, okay?"

Even then, even at six, Mindy knew her mother was giving up her duty and running off to a new life.

Now she was back, and they were at another funeral. Mindy felt an ache inside her belly and wondered what would happen to her this time when her mother left again.

Christopher agreed with Jill that it might not be over. Ben, however, was convinced that it was and had blissfully gone off to Christmas shop on Fifth Avenue while they did a final day of shooting in Central Park.

Jill cupped her hand around a thick mug of hot chocolate as the photographers and Addie set up another shot, this one on a small arched bridge over a pond, the shadow of the city framing the background, the sky dark and still and threatening snow.

"What are you going to do?" Christopher asked. It was a question she'd asked herself a hundred or so times since Bartlett had left, a thousand or so times since this had begun.

"I'm going home when we're finished tomorrow. I'm going to put together a reel to send Maurice to see if he might have some ideas for Vineyard Productions, based on the fact that once I've done *Good Night, USA,* the blackball will have been lifted. I'm going to concentrate on my work and on rebuilding my career in as small a way as necessary to maintain my Vineyard life."

He nodded as if he almost believed her. "What if the case isn't dropped?"

She sipped the hot chocolate, even though it was too hot. "Then I'm going to wait until the trial. It's all I can do."

"Will you call Bartlett?"

She shrugged.

"Will you call me?"

She looked away, off toward the pond. A thin glaze of ice coated the top like a fine layer of glass. She thought of Menemsha Pond back home, which was visible from the museum, Ben's dream gone dark.

"Why are you doing these things, Christopher? Is it really only for the good of the show?"

"No," he admitted. "It's because the worst day of my life was the day that you left me, and even if you won't be mine, I want to work with you. And I want you to be happy. Why can't you believe that?" He put his hands in his pockets and walked off toward Addie, leaving Jill standing, speechless, in the damp air.

"Neither one of them was my boyfriend," Amy told Rita as the two women ate Chinese food from white cardboard containers in the kitchen of Rita's house. The lo mein and spring rolls had been meant for Rita and Hazel, but at the last minute Rita's mother remembered she was supposed to play bingo at the church hall. Just then Amy had dropped by to ask if Rita would go to the apartment the next day and wait for the cable technician, because she had a hair appointment and it had taken so long for the cable guys to schedule the date that she didn't want to reschedule or she'd be waiting until June, and Charlie would be back long before then and she'd be gone anyway.

Rita had no houses to show or sell tomorrow, so she readily agreed, and asked Amy to stay and share dinner. She also wanted to know how Amy felt about the ponytail and the bald guy because she didn't know if Amy knew that they were gay, and she figured she might as well let her down gently.

"Neither one is my type. But I learned some things from them." Amy popped another spring roll into her mouth.

"Like what?"

"Like I thought maybe I'd like to get into video production. But what they showed me changed my mind. I'd go crazy sitting in a dark room at a computer every day. Computers are for geeks like my brother. I need people in my life."

Rita smiled. "Your mother hoped you'd fallen in love."

Amy wrinkled her nose. "With which one? Devon has a billion tattoos. Jimmy loves heavy metal. *Loud* heavy metal. Oh, and did I mention that they're gay?" Amy groaned. "Besides, when is my mother going to accept that not everyone wants the same things, that I don't want what she wants?"

Rita picked at her dinner. "When your mother was your age, she wanted nothing more than independence. I think having a family was the last thing on her mind."

A hurt look came into the girl's eyes.

"She surprised herself," Rita added quickly. "After Jeff and you were born, she wanted nothing more than to be a mother."

"That is utter bullshit, Rita," Jill's daughter replied. "You didn't even know my mother when we were born."

Rita scowled. "I *knew* her. I just wasn't around her."

"Well anyway," Amy said, "there is something that I want. But it's not video production and it's not a husband and kids. At least not yet."

"So what is it? And why the big secret?"

Throwing her napkin on the table, Amy sat back and laughed. "I want to run the tavern. I want my mother to buy it back from Charlie so we can have it in the family where it belongs. Then I want to run it the way my grandfather and his father did." Her eyebrows raised as if she'd surprised herself at what she'd just revealed.

"Well," Rita said, "what about Charlie?"

"Maybe he'll move to Florida permanently." She shook her head. "I don't know, Rita. All I know is that right now I don't want a man."

"Yeah, well, I once said I'd never have another, and look where it got me." She patted her belly that grumbled a little, as if displeased with the lo mein.

Amy stood up and walked to Rita's kitchen window. "It's hard to find a man to trust, isn't it, Rita?"

Rita sensed she was talking about Kyle. And Charlie. And every other man she'd known or heard of who had caused a woman heartache. Amy didn't have to say it, but somehow she'd deduced that Rita's baby was indeed Charlie's, and that the womanizing scoundrel had run off with someone else: Marge Bainey, liquor distributor unextraordinaire.

"You'll find your man someday," Rita said, "or not. In the meantime, my mother has always said we make our own misery. Which is probably the best way to think, because that way we can never feel like a victim. We can only blame ourselves."

"I don't feel like a victim," Amy replied.

"Me either. Actually what I feel like is crap. I don't think this baby is going to like Chinese food."

When Rita awoke at two-thirty in the morning, she was certain the cramps in her stomach were nothing more than gas. Or food poisoning.

She was always dead on with her instincts, and she hated being wrong, which was why she waited until five o'clock before going to the hospital. By then getting there seemed so imperative that she had to wake up Hazel to drive her.

Why she didn't call the ambulance was beyond her, because Hazel guiding the wheels of any vehicle more sophisticated than a shopping cart had to be more frightening than two paramedics and red lights ripping through the night sky.

Thankfully the hospital was not far from Edgartown. Unfortunately for Rita but fortunately for him, Doc Hastings could not be dragged there before dawn because he'd flown south for the winter.

"This is not food poisoning," said the young on-call female doctor whose name escaped Rita. "You nearly miscarried."

Miscarried. As in no longer with child. As in no second chance at motherhood. The word tasted as sour as the lo mein that had been in her stomach. But like a toothache that vanished once a dental appointment was made, Rita's cramps had ceased once Hazel ground the Toyota to a stop in the parking lot.

She squirmed a little on the high, hard exam table. "Are you sure?" she asked, not because she doubted the doctor's credentials, but because she'd never had a moment's discomfort when she was pregnant with Kyle, not even one. Of course, that was over twenty-five years ago.

"Yes." With a note to Rita's chart and a flick of the pen, the young doctor added, "I see you're due for your amnio and ultrasound. Have you scheduled them?"

Rita looked away. "I haven't had time."

"It's not a matter of time, Ms. Blair. It's for the good of the baby. To be sure nothing's wrong."

Grasping the front of her thin paper gown, Rita slid off the table. "The only thing wrong with this baby is a distaste for Chinese food."

The doctor raised her hand. "Please, Ms. Blair. Rita. At your age there are so many complications that could occur."

"And what would I do, doctor? Have an abortion?"

She peeled off the gown and climbed into her clothes, un-caring that the doctor still stood there, clipboard in hand. "I had one other child, doctor. He's dead. This one I'm not going to lose. No matter what." It was then that Rita realized the strength of her conviction: this was her baby, and she would raise it and protect it and take care of it, *no matter what.*

"Well, I certainly can't force you, but you must know it goes against—"

"Against protocol?" Rita asked with a smile as she buttoned her shirt.

"Well, yes. At least try to get as much rest as possible. And take your vitamins. And eat right."

Rita laughed. "Yes. Of course." She grabbed her purse. "It's not those crazy days of summer. So I'll do my best."

The doctor's eyes followed her out the door.

Rita returned to the waiting room, where a bleary-eyed Hazel sat. "Give me the keys, Mom," Rita said. "I'm okay now." No sense creating more trouble when there was enough in the world already.

Rita sat in Charlie/Amy's apartment, waiting for the ca-ble guy, flipping through baby magazines, and wondering what the deal was with her best friend, Jill, and why she was going to be on *Good Night, USA.*

Something clearly was up. Jill had not been the same since—since Rita could not remember when. Certainly not in the last few weeks.

Had she been wrong to think that Jill had it all? Maybe after Jill and Ben were married, the novelty had gone, the novelty of coming back to the Vineyard and settling down.

She sighed at this new evidence that commitment sucked. But there was nothing she could do to help her friend if she would not confide in her. Years ago that would have driven Rita crazy, but now she just accepted it. Accepted things, accepted life.

"Like you, little man," she said, patting her rounded tummy, "or little woman." She smiled. If she had the ultrasound, she'd know what to call the baby, this baby of hers, and hers alone. Maybe she'd do it next month or the month after, when it would be too late for anyone to tell her that her baby was not perfect and they should take it from her.

She would not let them.

Just as her thoughts were smiling over her baby, the doorbell rang. It was coming from the tavern, because the apartment had no entrance of its own. Rita sighed, pulled herself from the sofa, and made her way down-stairs to let the cable guy inside.

But instead of the cable guy, it was a man in uniform—a policeman, a cop from Aquinnah, if the cruiser parked in front belonged to him.

Rita opened the door. "Tavern's closed," she said. "We open again in spring." She realized she'd said "we" as if she would still be around Charlie, as if things would not have changed.

"I'm not here for lunch," the cop said. "I'm Hugh Talbot. Sheriff of Gay Head."

Rita knew the name. "Is something wrong?" she asked.

"I'm looking for Ben Niles. I've been by the house, but no one's home. A neighbor said his stepdaughter lives here. I thought she might know where to find him."

Rita figured it must have something to do with Menemsha House. God, she hoped it hadn't burned down again. The baby inside her kicked. "Maybe I can help you," she said. "I'm a close friend of the family."

The sheriff removed his cap. "Do you know where he is?"

"Is there a problem at Menemsha House?"

The sheriff scowled. "I just need to talk to him a minute."

Rita's defenses went on alert. "About what?"

The sheriff did not give her an answer but asked, "Do you expect to see him today?"

"I don't know. He's off-island."

The sheriff seemed to stiffen. "Off-island? Do you know where?"

Rita shifted her weight onto the other foot. "I don't know. Maybe you'd better ask him when he returns. What's this about, sheriff?"

"How long has he been gone?"

Rita shrugged. "A couple of days. Since Tuesday or Wednesday. The days all run together once the tourists have all gone." He did not laugh at her attempted joke.

"What about his wife? Is she around?"

"Jill? Actually, she's out of town on business. They might be together." Rita suspected Ben had taken off for New York, because where else would he go? But she'd always believed in protecting family and friends, even when—especially when—there might be trouble.

"Do you know when either of them will be back?"

Rita frowned. "No," she replied. "Ben didn't say. As for Jill, I haven't seen her since Thanksgiving."

The sheriff adjusted his belt, the one with the holster, the one with the gun. "If you see Ben, have him give me a call."

"Yeah," Rita replied. "Sure."

"And tell him it's important." He stuck his hat back on his head and moved with great deliberateness back to the black and white.

Rita fumbled in her sweatpants pocket and quickly found her car keys. Maybe Amy wouldn't mind waiting another day for cable if it meant helping Ben.

.　　.　　.

Rita didn't have a chance to tail the cruiser because Hugh Talbot was long gone by the time she made it out back and started up the old Toyota. But on a hunch, she headed toward Menemsha. God, she thought, crossing to South Water Street and heading out of town, maybe someone broke in to the museum, maybe damage was done, maybe lives were lost, as Kyle's had been.

With one eye on the road ahead and one in the rearview mirror, Rita gunned it. "Pedal to the metal," she said to no one, except maybe her baby, who was doing somersaults now, who seemed to always want a part of the action.

"Sorry, young female doctor," Rita said, "but 'rest' is out of the question. There are too many missions in my life."

She hunched forward on the seat and relished her adventure, so like the ones that she'd dragged Jill on when they were young.

She remembered the day they'd skipped school for the Chappaquiddick inquest. Rita had convinced Jill that this was a once-in-a-lifetime opportunity. They rode their bikes to the Dukes County Courthouse, and parked outside among the tourists and the media. There were no islanders gawking outside because islanders did not gawk, they were too reserved for that.

Rita and Jill had not gawked, but they'd peeked. And it was because of that adventure that Jill had decided to leave the island to become a big TV star. Funny thing, she had done it. And Rita had been left behind in so many, many ways.

But now they were on the same ground again, the Vineyard ground, whenever Jill happened to be in town. Her roots had firmly taken hold at last, and it was up to Rita to make sure things stayed copacetic.

At least, Rita convinced herself it was as she barreled

along toward Menemsha, which seemed to take forever to reach. Finally she made it to Beetlebung Corner, where she turned right at the crossroad.

When she saw the museum up ahead, Rita realized she'd not been here since Ben had broken ground again and she'd been there for support, for friendship, and for letting him know that this was all okay with her. That it would have been okay with Kyle, too—in fact, it would have been exactly what he wanted.

Now, seeing the museum fully restored atop the hill made her feel a little weak, and her heart raced a bit too fast.

Oh, Kyle, she said silently, and the tears began again, as if no time at all had passed, as if he'd just died last night. She banged her fist against the steering wheel. "Damn you, Rita Blair," she said, "stop it." Slowly the tears subsided. She pulled off to the roadside and wiped her eyes. That's when she realized that the museum had not burned down again, that it was standing there intact. And that's when she saw Hugh Talbot's cruiser come down the drive and head out onto the street.

Quickly, she turned her head so he would not see, hoping he would not recognize her red, red hair. Then she cursed herself for not removing the SurfSide Realty magnetic sign from the car door.

But when she looked back, Talbot was nowhere in sight.

She sat there for a moment, not knowing what to think. Perhaps her imagination had been running rampant on her again. Perhaps Hugh Talbot only wanted to ask Ben if he knew something about . . . nothing. Island cops, after all, often had far too much time on their uncallused hands off season.

Just as she decided to leave, a young girl came down the driveway of the house next to the museum. Rita remembered that next door lived Dave Ashenbach, the guy who had died, whose granddaughter had found him. "Must be her," Rita said, and watched with sadness as the little girl slowly walked away from what looked like an uninviting house.

Chapter 19

They were home. Ben cranked down his window and inhaled a deep breath of Vineyard air—a little breezy, a little salty, a little damp. He smiled as the old Buick lumbered from the parking lot of the Vineyard airport, where he'd left it. This time, however, he wasn't alone: his wonderful, beautiful wife sat beside him, and a heap of neat Christmas gifts—New York–bought Christmas gifts—were in the backseat: toys for the grandkids, pashminas for Amy and Jill, a Gucci bag for Carol Ann, and even a baby quilt for Rita's baby, not that she'd need it with all the booties Hazel was making.

But the gifts did not matter. What mattered to Ben was the renewed spirit in his heart. With his life stretched out before him once again, he was charged with energy, as if he'd gone to bed a leper and awakened with clear skin.

First, he would reopen the museum. Now that Ashenbach was dead, Ben had no idea what would become of Mindy—poor kid—but chances were she'd be taken from the island or at least from the house next door. That sure would make things easier.

Next, he'd put in a separate shop on the grounds,

where kids could learn to make lobster traps and fishing nets and other fun useful crafts. And in the spring, he'd plant a garden, where they'd grow corn and squash and pumpkins that they could harvest in the fall, as the Indians had done in John, Jr.'s school play.

The best part was, Ashenbach wouldn't be there to thwart the expansion.

He'd throw more effort into Sea Grove, too. Now that Charlie had up and gone, it was up to Rita and Ben to nail down those last two permits and get ready to break ground by tourist season. Six months would pass mighty quickly with so much to do.

As he reached the outskirts of town, he pulled over and stopped.

"What's wrong?" Jill asked.

He leaned across the seat and gave her one gigantic kiss. "I love you," he said when he was finished. "In case you didn't know."

She laughed and tugged down the visor of his hat. "You make me crazy," she said.

"I know. Shall we go home and make sweet love?"

"Later, okay? I want to stop by the studio first and check the mail."

He refused to let his good mood dissipate. "As madame wishes," he said, pulling back onto the road. "And I won't take it personally. In fact, I shall also check on Sea Grove, my investment properties. But be prepared," he said, "that later I will fuck madame's brains out."

She snatched off his cap and swatted him with it.

Rita sat across from Hazel, watching her mother knit baby booties: acrylic orange fingernails flicked in and out of soft white yarn and little plastic needles. She must have made five or six pairs already.

"You never did that for Kyle," Rita said.

"Never had the chance."

Oh, Rita thought, that was right. Rita had been off-island when Kyle was born, staying with Hazel's sister up in Worcester, hiding out in her illegitimate condition. She'd returned to the Vineyard when Kyle was four, but she had said he was three. Big for his age. Advanced. With White-Out and a copier, she'd doctored up his birth certificate and told everyone the sad, sad story about Kyle's father, a GI who'd she met in Worcester who had been killed in Vietnam.

Ah, she thought silently now as she listened to the click, click of the needles, those were the days. When people were either too dumb to learn the truth, or too busy to care once the gossip-mongers ceased.

Now, there was no such thing as gossip—there was nothing to hide. Everything and everyone was "out there," including single mothers and single grandmothers.

She—Rita Blair, for God's sake—was beginning to feel all cozy and maternal and about to suggest tea when the telephone rang.

She pushed aside a pile of magazines and reached across the maple end table that had seen much better days, though Rita could not remember when. "SurfSide Realty," she said with her most proper business voice. It was, after all, the middle of the morning and, who knew, maybe this was a client. Thankfully whoever it was could not see her in her pink chenille robe which, like the maple end table, had been purchased long ago.

She tied the long sash around her bulging middle.

"Rita?" the voice on the other end asked.

It was not a client. It was, speaking of babies, the unknowing father of her own. "Charlie," she said. "How hot is it in Boca?"

"Hotter than Dick's hatband," Charlie replied, using an old saying that always drove Rita crazy because it made absolutely no sense. "I just wanted to check up on you, see how you're doing."

Over the braided rug and across the room, Hazel put down the half-made booties. Rita turned from her and faced the window.

"Doing just fine, thanks," she replied, then waited for the next beat.

"Have you talked to Ben?"

"As in Niles?" she asked. "As in our partner who's married to the woman who once was my best friend? No. As a matter of fact, you're not the only one looking for him."

There was a pause. "Do you know where he is?"

"I think he's off-island. I think he's with Jill. I think she's in New York."

"Good," Charlie replied. "Because Hugh Talbot called, and I thought it was kind of strange. He didn't say why, but he was looking for Ben."

Rita scowled. "I saw the sheriff, too. He told me the same."

"It must be something out at Menemsha."

"That's what I thought, so I checked it out. The museum is fine."

"Well," Charlie said distantly, "good. I was afraid—"

"Yeah, well, no need. Everything's fine, I guess."

Another pause, and another breath drifted uncomfortably across the twelve hundred or so miles from his front door to hers.

"How the heck did Hugh find you way down there?" she asked.

"We serve together on a couple of island commissions. I left my number in a few places."

Leave it to good old, reliable Charlie not to skip town.

"What about Sea Grove?" he asked. "When do the next permits come up?"

Rita gave him the information she knew he already

had: that eight construction permits were doled out on the first Tuesday of each month. They had missed November and December, but Ben had sworn he'd be in line next month.

"Well, we could start without the last ones," Charlie was saying. It was a boring topic, and Rita really didn't care.

"Sure," she said. "Whatever."

"Okay then," Charlie said. "How's Hazel?"

Rita told him Hazel was fine, but did not mention booties. "And how's—what's her name?"

"Marge," Charlie said. "Marge is fine, too."

"Good," Rita said. "Well, thanks for the call. If I see Ben, I'll tell him you were checking up on him." She hung up before she could become more comfortable. Or more uncomfortable. On a whim she dialed Jill's number, hoping there would be an answer, hoping to talk to her wandering friend.

But the telephone on North Water Street rang four times, then voice mail kicked in. Rita did not leave a message.

Mindy hated it that her mother had made her move back into the house with her. It was not the same without Grandpa. The smell of fish had been replaced by a cloud of perfume and cigarette smoke, and the soft static of Grandpa's favorite two-way radio was now noisy bells and buzzers and people laughing and applauding on the television, on game shows mostly, people who wanted to be millionaires, though most never would.

But she didn't want to tell Dr. Reynolds, because her mother said she had a plan, and if Mindy rocked the boat, the state would put her in a foster home like the kids in school who no one liked. Not that anyone liked Mindy, but at least she wasn't an orphan.

Well, she still wasn't sure her mother *wanted* her, not as a kid to raise. But her mother did say it was most important for their future—for her *plan*—if Mindy kept seeing Dr. Reynolds, if nothing happened that would piss off the people at the court.

Mindy didn't really understand, but she decided it was best not to mention it to the doctor, who sat in Mindy's room now and smiled as if the fact that Mindy was "home" would make everything all better.

"How do you feel about having your mother home?" Dr. Reynolds asked.

"It's okay," Mindy replied. "She shops a lot." The money for all the clothes she bought was coming from the cash that Grandpa had always kept inside the kindling box for an emergency. Mindy did not think a "fashion crisis," as her mother called it, was an emergency, but Grandpa was gone and he would never know.

Besides, her mother said there would soon be a lot of money coming. As long as Mindy kept cooperating. As long as she didn't rock "the goddamn boat."

"You've had a lot of changes in your short life," the doctor went on. "Losing first your father and now your grandfather. And this awful incident with Mr. Niles."

She wished the woman wouldn't call him "Mr. Niles," as if Ben didn't have a first name. But instead of rocking the goddamn boat, Mindy said, "Yes."

The doctor gestured outside. "Have you seen him at all? Mr. Niles?"

Mindy shook her head. With all the people around her lately, she'd almost forgotten about him. "He wasn't at the funeral," she blurted out.

"Did you expect he'd be there?"

She shrugged. "No. I guess they never liked each other."

"Are you disappointed that he wasn't there?"

Mindy shrugged again. She did a lot of that with Dr.

Reynolds because it was easier than answering her stupid questions.

Dr. Reynolds leaned back in her chair. "Sometimes it doesn't seem that you're very angry at Mr. Niles," she said. "Are you?"

This time Mindy stopped herself from shrugging. She thought about it a minute, wondering how she was supposed to answer. It was the perfect time to tell Dr. Laura that Ben hadn't done anything, that Grandpa had made her say it way back in the beginning, that it was all a big, stupid mistake. It was a perfect time because, like the money in the kindling box, Grandpa would never know.

If she told Dr. Reynolds the truth, this would all be over. Ben could reopen Menemsha House, and everything would be like before.

Except that Grandpa was dead.

And her mother was here.

And she didn't have a clue what the hell would happen to her, because the boat would be rocked and she'd wind up an orphan. So she closed her eyes and bit her lip and said, "I hate Ben Niles now."

It was going to be a wonderful Christmas if it killed her, if she could pretend, like Ben, that all things were resolved, if she could spend time with Rita and act as if it didn't matter that Charlie did not know the baby was another Rollins; if she could act as if it were okay that Jeff was thousands of miles away, and Amy might as well be.

It was going to be wonderful, if she did not allow herself to think about Christopher.

Jill juggled her suitcases into the kitchen and dumped a pile of red velvet bows onto the counter at North Water Street. After she'd scanned the messages at the studio and rifled through the mail, Ben had brought her home, then gone to check on Sea Grove. As they drove from Oak

Bluffs to Edgartown, he reassured her that life would be much better now, if she could just relax. If she could just believe.

What he didn't seem to understand was that believing was the easy part; relaxing was what was tough. It didn't help that two dozen phone messages awaited her at home.

Three were for Amy—friends who had not yet learned that she'd "left home."

Three more were from subcontractors of Ben's; two were from Carol Ann.

One was from Christopher, announcing that fan mail was pouring in by the Santa sackful, now that the word was out.

Four calls were from Rita, whose last message said, "I can't seem to find you, so I don't know if you'll get this, but I want you and Ben to come to my Christmas party on the twenty-third. And I want you to bring those chicken things your mother used to make. Can you?"

Jill forced a tight smile at the red flashing light. Yes, this was going to be a wonderful Christmas. And no, it would not kill her.

Of the eleven messages that remained, two were not important, and nine were hang-ups. She feared that the hang-ups were harassment, from a person—or people—who knew about the accusation. Were nine hang-ups realistic to receive in one week? She'd never kept track before. She'd never needed to.

As she puzzled over the machine and its dark possibilities, the doorbell rang.

It was Hugh Talbot, the sheriff from Aquinnah. She recognized him from the tavern, when Ashenbach had punched Ben.

"I'm trying to find your husband," the sheriff said. "Is he at home?"

She shook her head. "We've been out of town. He's

gone to the development he's working on. Sea Grove. Out on Katama Road."

Hugh Talbot nodded. "I know where it is. Thank you, ma'am."

She closed the door behind him, leaned against it, and tried to decide whether she should unpack her things, adorn the house in red bows, or sit down on the floor and break down and cry.

Chapter 20

The land had cost a bloody fortune, but they would have been fools to pass it up. Twenty acres of small cedars and scrub oaks, a grassy meadow, a pine grove, even a babbling brook for Chrisake—a picture-perfect chunk of Vineyard land that stretched down to the sea.

They would have been fools, but Charlie, Rita, and Ben were not fools, at least, not about this. Nor did they intend to be greedy. Unlike the competition's bids, they were not planning to build four dozen tiny cottages with a quarter-million price tag each by virtue of the Edgartown mailing address. Sea Grove would hold only eight houses: eight beautifully constructed, discreetly distanced, elegant homes for folks who would appreciate the land and their good fortune to have such an exclusive place on such a special island.

He stood and surveyed the property that even in December was enticing. Its small wooden stakes and pink ribbon flags marked off the six two-acre building lots, leaving four acres for common area and two more lots for which they had not yet secured the permits.

Ben hadn't planned to become a real estate developer—

hell, neither had Charlie, neither had Rita—but when they heard what the competition had in mind, they could not allow it to happen. Now he needed to rediscover his enthusiasm for the project.

Closing his eyes, he took a deep breath, tasting the cool salt air and quietly reassuring himself that, yes, his nightmare was finally over. Just then, however, he heard his name called out. He opened his eyes and saw Sheriff Hugh Talbot moving toward him.

Ben quickly told himself that the sheriff must be there to inform him that all was well. He calmly thought about the irony that Hugh had come to this site to say that Ben's life could, at last, move forward, that he had a future after all.

"Sheriff Talbot," Ben said, his hand extended. "Can I interest you in a Sea Grove property?"

Talbot shook Ben's hand but did not look as if he were there to buy real estate. "I expect by now you've heard that Dave Ashenbach's dead," he said directly, without frills or hesitation.

Ben nodded, trying not to act as if the news had pleased him. If he did, he thought, he might be taken in for questioning for murder. A charge no more absurd than the one against him now.

"I've been trying to find you," Hugh continued. "No one knew where you went. No one at the tavern. Not your daughter."

He flinched. Hugh had gone to Carol Ann? Suddenly he felt a bit unsteady on his feet. He wished they were standing near a tree so he could brace himself. "I went to New York," he said. "To be with my wife."

The sheriff didn't nod or say "That's swell."

"He had a heart attack," he said.

Ben blinked.

"Ashenbach," the sheriff said. "He died of a heart attack. He'd had one last year, you know."

Yes, Ben remembered hearing that. He hoisted the waist of his jeans, which had grown too big in recent weeks. "How's Mindy?" Again he wondered if she'd be alone with nowhere to go and no one to care.

"She's the reason I'm here, Ben."

Ben waited another one of those long, slow-motion waits.

"If I were in your shoes, I'd figure now that Dave is dead, my troubles were over." The sheriff took off his hat and rubbed his finger along the brim. Ben's gaze followed the sheriff's hand. "Of course, that's not the case."

Ben blinked and looked up at Hugh. "What?" he asked, though he'd heard his words as clear as the cry of the gulls down on Sea Grove beach.

"The trial will go on as planned, April ninth," he said. *"The Commonwealth versus Benjamin Niles."*

For a minute, neither Ben nor Hugh said anything else. Then Hugh remarked, "I need to ask you not to leave the Vineyard until then," as casually as if he'd said have a nice day or could he have a light for his cigar.

A breeze came up off the water and iced its way through Ben's wool jacket. It felt like a blast of Canadian air had swooped inside his shirt.

Hugh put on his hat, tipped it to Ben, then turned and walked away.

Somewhere along the line, Ben had lost control of his life. Once again his every thought and action seemed to be determined by a ten-year-old, as if his past had no value and his future had no hope. The only thing that could change that was for the ten-year-old to say differently, to come forward and say he'd never touched her, never done a damn thing to her besides try to help.

All that had to happen was, Mindy had to tell the

truth. The odds of which, he figured, were zip, nada, not a rat's-ass chance in hell.

On the way back to the house, he went from stunned to scared to just plain pissed. By the time he marched into the kitchen, he knew there was only one thing left to do.

He found Jill's handbag in the kitchen. He rummaged through the rubble, then dumped out the contents. Soon he found what he needed.

"It's Ben Niles," Jill overheard her husband say into the telephone. "Jill McPhearson's husband. I need to speak with Attorney Bartlett as soon as possible."

She was in the living room hanging a wreath above the fireplace. She got down from the stepladder and moved to the doorway to listen.

"Yes, well, thanks," Ben said, but did not hang up.

Jill stood there, pruning shears in hand, wondering if she should make herself known. Apparently Hugh Talbot had not brought Ben good news; apparently the case would not be dropped, despite Dave Ashenbach's death. She tried to temper her disappointment with the fact that Ben was going on the offensive and calling Herb Bartlett, the man who could save him now.

"Bartlett?" Ben said. "Thanks for taking my call. There's been a change in the situation that my wife and I told you about. First of all, you were right. They're not going to drop this thing just because the old man's dead."

He paused.

Jill held her breath.

"And," he said, "there never was a boy. The molestation charge is against me. By a ten-year-old girl. My wife lied to you to protect me. I'm sure you understand."

She let out her breath and closed her eyes.

Ben spoke with the lawyer a few more minutes. When he hung up, he said, "I guess you heard."

"I heard," she confirmed.

"So," Ben said unperturbedly, as if he were about to relate tomorrow's weather prediction or the latest island gossip from Linda Jean's coffee shop in Oak Bluffs. "He said he'd take the case. He also said he'll come up after the holidays to meet with us." He took off his cap and looked down at the floor. "I can't go to Atlanta, of course, because I've been asked not to leave the island."

She leaned against the doorway, five or six feet from her husband, and knew she should go to him, put her arms around him, comfort him. But all she could do was lean against the doorway and wonder *Dear God, what next?*

"What if I told you I killed Grandpa?" Mindy asked Dr. Reynolds. They were sitting on the beach because it was an unusually warm day for mid-December, and because Mindy felt as if her mother were lurking around every corner in the house, trying to hear what Mindy was saying, doing, or even thinking. As if something that she said or did or thought would "rock the boat" and they'd be "out on the streets," as Fern put it.

"I've told you before," Dr. Laura said. "I'm not here to judge you, accuse you, or confront you. I am your doctor. Because of that, we have a kind of contract. Which means you can tell me anything, and I can't tell a soul. I can't tell your mother or the district attorney or even the judge. You're my patient; that's the law."

Mindy pulled off her sneakers, the ones with the flashing lights on the back. They were cool when Grandpa had bought them for her almost two years ago. They were old now and too tight, but he'd said they weren't worn out, so she'd had to keep them. Maybe her mother would buy her a new pair with Grandpa's emergency money.

"What makes you think you killed your grandfather?"

She took off her socks and wriggled her toes in the sand. It wasn't warm like in July or August.

"I figure he's dead on account of me. On account of all this stuff about the trial." She picked up a broken shell that the seagulls had picked clean, then threw it toward the surf that was small today and gentle in the receding tide. She did not say that maybe she should be the one who was dead, not Grandpa. She did not say maybe someone should kill her and get it over with.

Sometimes, though, she felt like that. She felt like Ben should kill her, that he should come and get her in the middle of the night, that he should sneak into her bedroom and cut her throat from ear to ear like she'd heard about on *Court TV*.

Or maybe he should grab her pillow and put it over her face with all his strength, until he'd smothered the life out of her. She tried that one night, putting her pillow over her face, so she could feel how it might feel. But it got hot under there and she started feeling funny in the head, so she'd ripped it off and decided to forget it.

"Well," the doctor said, "your grandfather was sick, Mindy. He had a heart attack."

Picking up a scallop shell, Mindy wondered if the scallop had died of heart disease or if it had been killed, then eaten by some rich tourist in a fancy restaurant. She wanted to ask the doctor what the hell did she know about heart disease anyway.

Dr. Reynolds reached over and traced a finger around the ruffled edges of the shell. "Do you understand that, Mindy? Do you understand it's not your fault he's gone?"

Mindy threw the shell out into the sea. She stood up, brushed off her feet, and picked up her shoes and socks. "How much longer do I have to talk to you?"

"Do you mean today or forever?"

"Forever. This is stupid. We just keep talking about the

same things." Well, Mindy knew that wasn't quite true, but she was tired of talking about Ben Niles and Grandpa and sex things and death. She'd rather talk about how Jennifer Tilley got her tongue pierced and she was only one grade ahead of Mindy in the sixth, or how the class had just found out that their teacher, Mrs. Galloway, was related to Lisa Andrews, the star of *Devonshire Place,* and was going to Los Angeles to see her over Christmas. Mindy would much rather talk about that stuff than all this other boring junk.

"The court wants me to keep seeing you at least until the trial."

"In April?"

"Yes. Maybe by then you will stop feeling guilty about your grandfather and allow yourself to grieve."

"I don't feel guilty."

"Then you don't really think you killed him?"

Mindy slung her shoes over her shoulder and said, "Of course I didn't kill him. I'm a little girl. How the hell could I have killed him?" She looked out across the water. "I don't want to talk to you anymore today. I'm going home." The doctor did not try to stop her, which, Mindy supposed, was part of their contract, too.

Chapter 21

At one point in her life, Jill had worked this hard: after her divorce from Richard, when she was trying to prove she could make it on her own, that Jill McPhearson was not just another single mother but a single *somebody,* a woman who would reach the top.

Then, of course, she'd met Christopher, and she was no longer single but coupled with a man, the heartthrob of the world, no less.

She'd walked away from him to be with Ben—another man, another opportunity to screw up things but good. But this time she was determined to separate her career from the chaos, to move on despite the sandbar on which their personal lives had gone aground.

All she needed was to keep focused on her priorities. All she needed was to do this one day at a time.

Nonstop news of audience excitement over the impending TV reunion obsessively fueled her drive. She only needed to work through the tough spots and prove herself once again. So today, the day of Rita's Christmas party, Jill had passed off the chicken-making to Amy and locked herself in the studio, sending out the last of her new demo reels to every independent broadcaster, including Maurice Fischer, RueCom king himself, the man who had placed his bets on *Good Night, USA* and had ended up a billionaire because of its success. The man who, perhaps, would someday see her worth.

She would have laughed out loud at her obvious arrogance except for the fact that this kind of persistence—*optimistic* persistence—had paid off for her before.

Glancing at her watch, she noticed she only had an hour before she was due at Rita's. Ben, of course, would not be going; he went nowhere since he'd met with Hugh, not even to his workshop or to the cliffs at Gay Head. He said he could not stand the thought of being seen, or being whispered about once he was out of earshot. As if those things did not bother Jill; as if she did not have to reckon with grocery shopping and buying gas and wondering if the person at the next aisle or the next pump . . . knew.

Ben was getting good at wrapping himself in a blanket of self-pity and sitting in the Adirondack chair on the porch. But Jill needed to do things, to move.

While Ben remained burrowed, it had become increasingly difficult for Jill to make excuses:

I'm sorry, Ben's not feeling well.

No, Ben made other plans.

Ben? Oh, gosh, I'm sure he'd love to, but he's working late tonight. Working on what, no one asked.

She sealed another videotape inside a bubble-packed bag. She had not yet decided what excuse she'd give Rita for Ben's absence tonight. She'd not yet decided what she'd say to Ben when he told her he was not going.

The phone rang. Jill tossed the last bag onto the chair and fumbled through a stack of paperwork until she located the receiver. "Vineyard Productions," she said boldly.

"Jill?"

"Hi, honey," she said automatically, out of habit.

"Rita's party is in an hour. Are you coming home to change?"

"I'm leaving in a minute," she said. "I have a few more things to do." She gazed around the messy office, grateful that she'd created so much busywork. She hoped there was enough to last until the trial—minus February, when she'd be gratefully away.

"Should I wear my red sweater?" he asked. "The one you gave me last year for Christmas?"

She pressed two fingers to her temple. "You're going?" she asked.

"Well, yes."

"I'm sorry, honey. It's just that lately—"

"I know. I've been a stick in the old cranberry bog. Well, it's Christmas. And if you look outside, it's snowing. And I figured that, no matter what, at least Ashenbach can't show up."

Jill knew the last remark was an attempt at humor, however misplaced.

"Well, I'm glad," she said. "Your red sweater will be perfect. And I'll wear my new red dress, the one I bought in New York."

"Good," he answered, though his voice sounded strained. "I'll see you shortly then?"

She closed her eyes and felt her heart slowly break for this strong, good, and kind man, who'd been brought to his knees by circumstance, who must be struggling for his sanity, and who was not receiving much support from his wife, who chose to work instead.

"Look at you two, the perfect couple," Hazel said, and without looking, Rita knew who had arrived. "Better late than never."

"Thank God for holidays," Rita said spinning to greet

them, "or I'd never see my gorgeous friend." And gorgeous Jill was. In a beautiful red dress trimmed with crimson sequins, the island's favorite celebrity looked dazzling. Ben, however, did not. He looked tired and gaunt and a little off-center.

He leaned down and gave Rita a kiss. "What about me?" he asked. "Am I gorgeous, too?"

"You are a handsome prince," Rita said. "And I haven't seen you in a hundred years. Have you gone into hibernation?"

Ben skipped the question and remarked how festive Rita looked in her red velvet tent dress. He handed her a gift that he said was for the baby.

"Amy brought the chicken a while ago," Rita said, hoping Ben's altered appearance was only her overactive imagination.

"We just took the first tray in to serve our other guests," Hazel said. "Come into the living room and join them."

The group moved into the small living room, which was crammed with people and a tree that she and her mother decorated in white and gold. Rita smiled. She liked it when her house was full of people, full of laughter.

Someone opened the door and let some air inside, and someone else had turned up the stereo and Perry Como could almost, not quite, be heard above the chatter.

"Punch?" she asked Jill and Ben.

"Sure," Jill replied.

"Maybe later," Ben said.

Why wasn't Ben drinking? she wondered. Maybe he was taking some kind of medication.

Cancer, she wondered again, then shuddered, because this was Christmas, and there should be no thought of that.

"Ben Niles doesn't look right," Hazel said when Rita returned to the kitchen for the punch.

Rita wished Hazel hadn't given credence to her imagination. "He's probably tired like the rest of us." No sense giving her mother something more to chew on.

"Never mind, I'll ask Amy." Hazel adjusted her light-up dangle earrings with the tiny jingle bells.

"Mother, please. This is Christmas." She poured a glass of punch for Jill and went back to the living room, just as Dick Bradley of Vineyard Haven's Mayfield House approached them.

"Not a Christmas party passes that I'm not grateful I moved here to the island," he said to Ben and Jill.

Rita handed Jill the punch as Ben nodded in agreement.

"You must meet one of my inn guests," Bradley continued. "Everyone, this is Laura Reynolds. Dr. Laura Reynolds."

Jill smiled, and Ben nodded again. Rita wondered how Bradley's new wife, Ginny, felt about the woman on her husband's arm. Then she told herself to stop acting like an island gossip.

"A doctor," Jill was saying. "Are you living on the island? We need all the good doctors we can find."

The pretty-but-plain girl in the long, dark green wool skirt replied, "I'm a pediatric psychiatrist, actually."

Bradley put his hand on Laura's shoulder just as Ginny appeared, with a confident stance and straight-arrow eye. She did not appear to be the jealous type.

"Laura lives in Boston," Ginny said. "She's here for a special case."

Jill said nothing; neither did Ben. In the awkward air that followed, Rita said, "Well, we all think we're pretty special cases on this godforsaken island."

Polite laughter followed. Then Rita moved to chat with other guests. Less than an hour later, Jill and Ben made their excuses, saying the snow was piling up outside and that they'd better go along.

Rita watched them go and knew she'd been right: something was wrong with the perfect couple, imagination or not.

They walked along South Water Street toward the center of Edgartown. Ben had jammed his hands into his pockets.

"Are you sure it's her?" Jill asked.

He closed his eyes and let himself feel the wet snow against his cheeks. "You heard what Bradley's wife said— she's here for a special case. She's a pediatric psychiatrist. How many *special cases* could there be here right now?"

Opening his eyes, he did not look at Jill, but kept his gaze steady on the street ahead. "The judge demanded that Mindy see a therapist three times a week."

Jill slipped her arm through his. They walked a while in silence, until South Water crossed Main Street and became North Water.

"Honey," she said into the darkness just before their house came into view, "I suppose there's a good chance you're right. But once Herb Bartlett gets here, things will be different. I know they will."

He leaned against her arm and wished he could cry. But his tears had vanished a long time ago, as if his pain had sucked them dry. "That's easy for you to say. In a few weeks you're going off to the bright lights and an old boyfriend who'd probably give just about anything to get you back into the sack."

She squeezed his arm. "And he doesn't have a prayer," she said, which eased his mind a little, because she hadn't said that until now. Beneath a lamppost, she stopped, and he stopped with her. She looked into his eyes. "I love you, do you know that? Do you really, really know that?"

And then his tears returned. From out of nowhere, on the damn street out in public, his eyes began to water. He stepped into her arms and pressed his cheek against hers, the snowflakes making little dots of wetness all around his tears.

"Come on," he whispered, "let's go home."

Arm in arm they walked another block or two. And though his tears had cleared, when they saw the house, it took Ben a minute to notice the woman standing at their front door. It did not take as long for the life to drain from his body again.

The woman looked no different than she had when Ben met her six—no, seven years ago. She'd been younger then—hell, they all had—but there were few flamboyant women on the Vineyard, and so she'd been quite memorable. The nonstop legs hadn't hurt, either.

And he remembered the rest. The thing he'd tried so hard to put behind him.

His stomach squeezed itself like an accordion. His chest grew heavy.

He stopped and stared at the woman on their front steps in the shadow of the falling snow, reflected by a brass lantern.

"Ben?" Jill asked. "It looks like we have company." She gestured to the front door. Ben would have turned and run but he was too damn tired and now too numb.

"Go around back," he ordered Jill. "Go around back and get into the house. I'll take care of this."

"Take care of what?"

Ben looked at his wife. Her hair was soft and snowflake dusted, and her eyes met his with the innocence of love.

She did not deserve this.

She did not deserve any of this.

His stomach curled, if stomachs could, as if the edges could fold up and roll into a pinwheel. A jelly roll. A slab of raw and boneless fish twirled quickly into sushi.

Jill looked to the woman, then back at her husband, confusion etched across her eyes. "Ben?" she asked. "What's going on?"

The corners of his mouth went dry. His tongue felt swollen. "Please, Jill, do as I ask."

She folded her arms and remained there, standing still. "Not until you tell me why."

The cords in his neck tensed. "Jill . . ." he began, then lost his voice as the woman left the front steps and headed toward them. "Go inside," he said quickly. "Now."

Jill looked at the woman, then back to Ben.

"It's Fern Ashenbach," he said. "It's Mindy's mother."

Jill should have known this was far from over, that that had been only an illusion, brought to life by Ben's hopes. She should have known because Herb Bartlett had been quite clear, and because Hugh Talbot had said as much.

But as she sat in the front room, peering out the lace draperies at her husband standing in the snow, talking with that woman, Mindy's mother, Jill suddenly wondered if it would ever truly be over. Even if Ben were vindicated, would the tension still be there between them, the underlying question mark as to what had really happened?

She had tried to make the question mark go away.

She had tried to take control by returning to her old life in order to find him a good attorney.

She had tried to keep herself so busy that she would not be bothered by it.

And yet the question mark persisted. Because she would never know the truth, because she had not been there, because, as Herb Bartlett so succinctly said, *it was her word against his.*

She blinked and strained to see what was going on in the dim light of the lantern.

The woman's hands were on her hips, her head tipped back in laughter that shot its way straight to Jill's wounded heart.

Ben didn't do it, she repeated to herself. *I know my husband, and I know he didn't do it.*

But if that were true, why did the question mark quickly surface whenever new doubt was created?

And why was Mindy's mother laughing?

She wished it were daytime and summertime and the windows were wide open. Instead, she tried to make sense out of the mouthing of their words, knowing that whatever they were discussing could change her life forever.

Her husband put his hands into his pockets, lowered his head, and scuffed his boots against the snow. If he was responding to her mouthing words, Jill could not decipher.

He lifted his head again and glanced toward the house.

And then Ben turned; his back went to the window. Perhaps he had seen her there.

She closed her eyes. Would she lose Ben because she was sitting in the window and he thought she should have been more trusting?

"Mom?" The voice behind her startled Jill. "What are you doing?"

She cleared her throat and quickly stood. Amy. God, why did she have to come now? "I didn't see you come in."

Her daughter entered the room, carrying the empty tray from the chicken she'd cooked for the party. She moved to the window and followed her mother's gaze.

"I drove in around back," she remarked. "Who's that?"

Jill stepped away. "No one," she said. "It's Fern Ashenbach." She went over to the rolltop desk, snapped on the lamp, and straightened the inkwell and the letter opener with the ivory scrimshaw handle that had belonged to her great-grandfather. "What are you doing here? Why aren't you at the party?"

"Rita was worried about the two of you. She thinks Ben might be sick." She set down the tray and kept her gaze fixed out the window.

"He's not sick," Jill said. "And stop staring. The woman is one of Ben's neighbors at the museum."

"Ashenbach? Didn't her husband just die?"

Jill opened the desktop and pulled a few bills from a pigeonhole compartment. She sorted through them as if she intended to sit right down and pay them, as if the drama being played out on her front steps did not presently exist. "It wasn't her husband who died," she said, her eyes on the envelopes, "it was her father-in-law."

Amy nodded and at last moved from the window and picked up the tray again. "Well, she dresses like a Forty-second Street whore."

Jill turned to her daughter. "Where on earth did you hear that expression?"

Just then an engine started. Jill spun back to the window and watched a pickup truck pull away, and saw Ben . . .

He opened the front door and came into the foyer. If "ashen" truly was a color, he'd become it. Maybe Rita had been right. Maybe he was sick, and he was going to die right there in the doorway, not unlike the way her father had dropped dead one sunny summer morning without warning, without reason.

Like all of life, she thought.

"Hey, Ben," Amy said, "that's some woman. A friend of yours?" She laughed a playful, teasing laugh.

Ben did not laugh back. "No one who matters," he replied, and his gaze told Jill that Fern Ashenbach's visit did matter quite a lot.

"I'm glad you're both here," Amy continued. "I was thinking tonight at the party that I really love it on the island. I love all the people here. If Charlie decides to stay in Florida and wants to sell the tavern, I really want to buy it. Wouldn't it be fun to have it come back into the family, Mom? I mean, college is not for everyone."

"Charlie's not gone for good yet," Ben commented, his voice still flat. He removed his cap and did not seem to notice that snow fell to the floor.

"Well, Rita thinks—"

"We'll talk about it later, okay?" Jill asked, her eyes still on her husband, doubt emblazoned on her face.

Amy looked from Jill to Ben, then back again. "Maybe I should come back another time," she said.

"Yes, honey," Jill replied, "that's a good idea."

"Some nights I lie awake and think that even after April has come and gone, this nightmare will never end," Jill said after Amy had gone and Ben had settled in the kitchen with a large mug of steaming coffee that he'd made in order to kill time so he could figure out how to tell his wife the things he had to say.

He wished he could simply say "I love you" and know that that would be enough.

"But the nightmare is far from over," his wife continued, "isn't it?"

If Ben still took sugar in his coffee he'd use this time to stir it slowly. He looked down onto the rich, dark liquid and was reminded of the story he'd heard of the scamming fortune teller who claimed to have ESP. A woman in a purple velvet turban had her client write his deepest secret on a small square of napkin. The fortune teller then took the napkin, passing it across the top of her cup of coffee, where her client didn't realize she could see his words clearly reflected in the liquid. She then revealed his deepest secret and—presto!—she'd found a new believer at fifty bucks a pop.

He stared into his cup now and wondered if a fortune lay there and, if so, could it save him now.

"Ben?"

He sighed. Because he could not stir his coffee, he put his hands onto his lap. "No," he said. "It's far from over."

Out in the hall, the grandfather's clock ticked, a symbol of all things sound and good, or at least dependable.

All things that he had always strived to be but now was not.

Jill attempted a laugh. "I actually had some hope that Fern Ashenbach had come to say Mindy changed her mind. That she said it was all a lie and that the charges would be dropped."

Ben stared back into his coffee. "I don't expect that's going to happen."

"But she's Mindy's mother! How can a mother allow her daughter to go through with this charade?"

"She doesn't think it's a charade, Jill." He could not tell his wife that this was the ticket Fern had been waiting for all her life. He could not tell Jill that Fern had just asked Ben for half a million dollars to get Mindy to "change her mind."

If he gave her the money, the Commonwealth could not prosecute: he'd be free.

Except that Fern would get away with blackmail.

And he didn't have half a million dollars.

"Ben?" Jill asked.

"She's not dropping the charge," he replied. He did not add that at least the gag order was on his side: if she tried to sell her story to the tabloids, she would go to jail. He'd warned her about that, not because he cared if she was incarcerated, but because he didn't want his face and Jill's at every checkout counter in the country.

The clock ticked again. And again.

He stood up and dragged his heavy body across the floor. He stared out the back door into the darkness, past the porch, out to the silhouette of the Chappaquiddick ferry that had seen its share of scandal, that was docked now, snow-covered on the pier, waiting for the next passengers who might not come tonight. He thought of Jill's career and wondered what would happen if—*when*—all the details leaked out.

"Maybe she wants money," Jill said. "Maybe we should pay her off."

He reminded himself that, unlike Fern, his wife was blessed with brains. She'd probably taken one look at Fern and known the woman's agenda. Well, part of it anyway.

"We can't do that, Jill. We're cash poor. Between restoring this house, building the museum and the studio, and putting up money for Sea Grove—most of yours is gone and all of mine."

"The money from *Good Night, USA* . . ."

Ben turned back to her. "Honey," he said slowly, "that's yours." He lowered his voice. "And Bartlett's too, I guess."

"I think they want me full time, Ben. I could agree to do the show for a year."

Heat rose in his cheeks. "No!" he said. "If you're away from me for a year, I might as well be in jail."

"I'll only be in New York. I could come home on weekends."

They were silent a moment.

"No," he said. "If we pay Fern, it will be blackmail. I won't let her get away with it." He went back to the table and sat down.

"If it meant you'd be free, I don't care what you call it."

The steam had left his coffee, the heat had left his

veins. "Don't you get it, Jill? Even if we had the money, even if we paid her off, I would not be vindicated. You'd never know the truth."

"I'd know the truth," she whispered. "I've known it all along."

He sighed heavily. "Jill," he said, "there's something you don't know."

He tried to force himself to look at her so she would see the truth that surely might show up somewhere in his eyes. "Fern is Mindy's mother," he said.

Jill scowled. "I know that."

"But what you don't know is that six or seven years ago," he continued, aching inside, "when Louise was really sick, I did a very dumb thing."

Keeping his eyes on Jill's was perhaps the hardest thing he'd ever done, yet for some reason, Ben felt compelled to do it. "I met Fern when I first scouted out the land to build Menemsha House. She was living with Ashenbach and her drunken husband."

Jill still said nothing, and he willed himself onward.

"We had an affair," he said. "Louise was sick and dying, and I committed adultery. I had sex with Fern Ashenbach. Not once, but many times."

Chapter 22

Looking out her window, Mindy thought about Santa Claus. As soon as the little kids on the island saw snow on the ground, they'd be convinced that he would come to the Vineyard, that he'd drive his sleigh, and presents would show up beneath their shiny Christmas trees, Barbies and jewelry kits and CDs of Ricky Martin and the Backstreet Boys.

Which, of course, was stupid.

"Put a white beard on Ben Niles this year," her mother said last night. "He's going to fund our future, as long as you don't rock the goddamn boat."

She'd said that at least a hundred times since Grandpa had dropped dead, but most times she'd been drunk, so Mindy wasn't sure how much it counted.

And the picture of Ben in a white beard seemed no more real than the guys who stood on street corners, ringing their small red bells.

Besides, there wasn't any Santa Claus, never had been, never would be.

She sat on her bed and hugged herself because there was no one else to hug, and she wished that she believed, wished that she'd ever, just once, believed.

· · ·

It was the dawn of Christmas Eve. A veil of snow was draped over the Gay Head cliffs; the air was still and calm, pausing, waiting, as if needing reassurance that all was well, the storm had passed.

But the storm inside Ben had not passed. So he'd driven there, because he had nowhere else to go.

He'd driven out long before dawn, when he'd known there would be no sleep for him that night. And now he sat within shouting distance of the rust-colored brick lighthouse where only months before he and Jill had married, where he'd vowed for the second time in his life to love and to cherish, in sickness and in health.

He had not kept his vows with Louise. He had loved her, but he had not honored her in sickness. He had cheated on her with a woman who was two decades younger and half as smart.

From deep inside his guilt, Ben had wanted to tell Louise, had wanted to absolve himself of his lustful crime.

"No." His friend Noepe had been adamant, right there upon the cliffs, so very long ago. "You are not a selfish man, Ben Niles. Do not be selfish now."

Ben pulled his plaid wool jacket tighter now, against the shiver of the wind that crept up off the water. On the horizon, light was breaking, the pale light of December's end, a silver wash that hinted of a cloudy sky, perhaps another touch of snow.

How he wished that Noepe were there, seated cross-legged atop the cliff, his long white ponytail caught in the breeze, his bronze skin burnished by the sun of many summers, the winds of many winters. His wizened eyes, Ben knew, would have been closed in silent prayer. Noepe was a tribal medicine man—a Wampanoag descendant who kept peace and kept tradition, and most likely kept his vows.

Not like Ben.

"Do not ask your wife's forgiveness," Noepe had said when, after three weeks of screwing Fern Ashenbach, Ben broke down and confessed his sin to his nonjudgmental friend. "Ask for forgiveness of yourself. You are the only one who can do that, Ben. But do not trouble your poor wife. She is in pain enough."

It had been long and difficult, but finally Ben had done it. He had explained—not excused—his behavior to himself as coming from the need to feel like a man again, an uncontrollable hormonal thrust from nursing his sick wife for so long (had it been a year? two?) and not having been able to love her fully, physically, in the way God had intended.

It was an explanation, however thin.

In time he had forgiven himself. He thought he'd also forgotten.

"Perhaps it's why you were so kind to Mindy," he could almost hear Noepe say, his words a whisper in the air. "Perhaps you felt her mother deserted both of you."

The raw air cut across his face now. A seagull's wail pierced the metallic sky.

Noepe would, of course, have been right. Because though it had been Ben who'd called it off, it had been Fern who'd up and gone, who'd abandoned her child and left him, too.

At the time, he'd been relieved.

Without Fern around, there was no concrete reminder of his deed. Without Fern around, he did not have to face the fact he had stooped to a loveless sexual relationship with a woman he would not want to be seen on the street with, a woman he had used.

She'd used him, too, or at least Noepe had suggested that.

"Her husband is a drunkard," his friend had said. "What kind of life do you believe she'd had with him?"

She had been the aggressor, the one who'd come on strong to Ben. Yet he had known the word *no*. He'd simply failed to use it, and he felt the blame was his own.

And now he could only sit on the cold, damp cliffs and picture the look on Jill's face yesterday, silently asking:

"How many more surprises, Ben? How much more will I be expected to understand?"

It was snowing again, and it was getting as icy as it was wet.

Despite the weather, Jill marched through the center of town as if she had a purpose, which she did not. Unless, of course, making a decision about whether to end your marriage could be considered purposeful.

Along the narrow streets, close to the snow-covered walks, the tall white houses stood, black-shuttered like her own house, where she'd been raised.

She walked another block or two, then turned right onto Main.

Shops lined both sides of the street. Some had closed for the season, and some were still open, though stock was sure to be limited to last-minute Christmas gift selections and stocking-stuffer items.

This was the first year she'd not made stockings for the kids. With Jeff in England, it seemed no longer to make sense. He'd not wanted to come home for the holidays, and as each week passed, Jill feared that soon he would consider England his home. England was where his father lived, good, bad, or in between. England was where the once-shy boy had made many friends—including Mick Daley, his roommate and best friend—none of whom cared that Jeff's mother was "who she was" because over there, no one knew her.

She passed the hardware store, the bookstore, and the jewelry store, with windows that were dressed in tinsel, evoking joy she did not feel. She heard the creak-creak of a hanging sign on which a plump strawberry ice cream cone was painted. It looked silly dangling there in the snow on Christmas Eve.

Silly, lonely, out of place, the way she felt now on the Vineyard, the way she'd thought she'd never feel again.

She snapped her yellow slicker over her thick wool turtleneck and pulled the hood up on her head. She thought of Christopher, who'd said Maurice had enjoyed his weekend there with them, and wondered how he would feel if the news of Ben leaked out, throwing his long-awaited heroine into the fierce cauldron of a morals scandal.

Would it really matter that it was about Ben and not her? Was she denying that Maurice would be consumed by rage?

And would Christopher defend her—or him?

With a mittened hand, she wiped the snow from her cheeks. This seemed like the kind of thing insane people did: walking in misery, letting their minds run to rambling things, catching their death of cold and not caring.

Fact: Ben had committed adultery.

Fact: Jill had not been the "wounded" party. It had been his other wife, Louise.

Still, she mused now as she passed the town hall then the whaling church, if he'd done it once, he could do it again.

"Circumstances were different," he'd said quietly last night.

Yes, yes, she knew that. He had not had sex for a long, long time. He was a man.

Child molestation.

Adultery.

Lies and cover-ups.

Where did one leave off and another start?

Who was the bigger fool here, Ben or her?

Was what she had "almost" done with Christopher any better than what he'd done with Fern?

But she hadn't done the deed. Something had stopped her, and it hadn't simply been Christopher's nonresponse. Something, some switch, had clicked off in her brain before it had been too late.

Not so with Ben. *Not once, but many times.*

She spat a flake of snow that had fallen on her lip. Then she cursed every man that God had ever made, especially those she'd known, especially those she'd loved or thought she had.

How would Rita have handled this? Too bad she couldn't tell her. But Jill wasn't free to have a confidante, not even her best friend who had known her forever, who had once known everything about her life and had loved her anyway.

But she couldn't tell Rita because Ben would be upset.

Ben. Whose life and problems apparently had become more important than her own, as if he mattered more than she did, as if her feelings did not count.

She swallowed down a great big lump. Then, at the next corner, she took a left.

"You walked?" Rita asked as she opened the door and hurried Jill inside. "Are you insane?"

"Nearly," Jill replied, noticing that Rita looked quite round and positively glowing in a red sweatshirt with a jeweled Christmas tree on the front. Jill might have told her she looked terrific if there weren't other things on her mind, or on what was left of it.

She stood in the living room of the ancient saltbox and breathed in the old, friendly warmth of the house she knew so well, which now stood in the weary yet still welcome light of Christmas decorations and postparty fatigue. "I thought you could use some help cleaning up. It was a wonderful party, Rita. We enjoyed it very much."

Rita took Jill's slicker and hung it on a string of pegs nailed up beside the staircase. "You left early," she said. "You missed Jesse Parker's reindeer imitation."

"From too much punch, no doubt."

Rita laughed. "He does that every year. God, it's crazy what we do to entertain ourselves off season."

Jill could not disagree. She followed Rita into the kitchen and was surprised to see that last night's disarray had vanished. "Where's the mess?" she asked.

Tossing a towel at Jill, Rita laughed. "Your daughter came back late to help. It was clean before I went to bed."

Yes, Amy would have done that. Amy had the caring spirit of Jill's father layered beneath the fire of her mother's soul.

"Where's your mother?" Jill dried her hair, her face, her neck.

"Believe it or not, she's at the senior center. She's playing Mrs. Claus at the Christmas party. She drove herself over and I haven't heard from the police, so I guess she made it without incident."

Jill set down the towel and tried not to wince when Rita said the word *police*.

"Sit," Rita instructed. "There's leftover chowder from last night. You look like you could use some."

The Formica table in this kitchen was where Jill had spent so many hours of her youth. Sitting there was a welcome, familiar thing to do, an unexpected comfort after learning that her husband, the accused child molester, was an adulterer as well. "It sounds as if Hazel's planning to stay on the Vineyard," she remarked.

"She'll never leave again. Not with the baby coming."

Jill watched her friend move around the kitchen, pulling crock bowls from the cabinet, ladling chowder, heaping oyster crackers on a plate, then tearing off paper towels to use as napkins because that was Rita, simply Rita. Jill wondered why she'd ever hesitated to share this pain with her. Because it had been Ben's request? Had that been good enough?

"It just goes to show you that life sometimes can be surprising," Rita said, setting a crock of soup and a spoon in front of Jill. "Take you, for example. Never in my wildest dreams would I have expected you'd show up at my door today. Let alone that you'd walk over in the snow." She set another crock across from Jill and sat down with the thud of unaccustomed extra weight. "Speaking of snow, I guess everyone made it home okay last night. Even Hattie Phillips. I swear that old woman gets feistier every year. She and my mother never got along, you know. But now that so many of their friends are dead, it's like she wants to be my mother's best friend. She brought the chocolate mint squares to the party. Did you try one? I probably shouldn't have, but I had two. Well, what the hell, I couldn't have the punch."

"I have something on my mind," Jill said, interrupting Rita's happy monologue. "I thought I could handle it myself, but I need to talk it out. I need to talk to you." She lowered her head. Two tears slid down her cheeks, then dropped onto her lap. "Oh, God, Rita," she cried, "what am I going to do?"

In a flash, Rita was by crouched by her side. Then Jill felt Rita's arm around her and Rita's "sssh-sssh, it's okay," whispered in her ear. And then Jill's tears flowed freely, perhaps more freely than she'd let them in many, many years.

Finally, she could speak. "It's Ben," she said.

Rita held Jill's hair a moment, then pressed her forehead to her friend's. Then she sighed, stood up, and returned to her seat. She propped her elbows on the table, as if prepared to listen, as if she were not surprised. Ben.

Men. Same thing. Same oil and water combination when mixed with women for too long.

"I found out he had an affair." Jill surprised herself that those were the words that popped out first. Not "He's been accused of child molestation." She did not say that, but rather, "He had an affair," as if, in the course of humankind, that was the more evil charge against him.

Rita put her hand out and rested it on Jill's. "Shit," she said. "They're all shit."

Jill nodded as if she'd known that all along.

"Who is it?" Rita asked. "How'd you find out?"

"He told me," Jill answered. "Only because she showed up at our door."

"Who?" Rita repeated, louder now, as if she were ready to tear the woman's eyes out, doing battle for her friend.

"Fern Ashenbach. She's blond. She wears boots with spike heels. And she's younger than us. Thirtysomething, maybe."

"Is she related to Dave Ashenbach? From Menemsha? He just died, you know."

"She was married to Ashenbach's son. He's dead, too."

"So now she has nothing better to do than screw around with your husband."

For the first time, Jill allowed herself to cringe. The words evoked an unwanted image of Ben, naked, hard, and wanting, mounting the long-legged, lusty being, kissing her mouth, sucking at her . . .

She squeezed her eyes shut and let out a moan. Now she knew why adultery seemed worse: it was because she could not imagine him doing that other thing, that other twisted, criminal thing. But she could imagine him with another woman; she could visualize the act.

Denial is the shock absorber of the soul, she'd once read.

If he was capable of one thing, could he not be capable of the other?

Do we ever really know anyone well enough to entrust them with our hearts, our souls, our lives?

"Honey," Rita's quiet voice said, as she patted Jill's hand, "he's not the first to do this. I know it's hard to hear, but it probably has more to do with his age and his ego and all that shit than with you."

Jill blinked. Rita had misunderstood. "Oh, it didn't happen now. Not while we've been married. It was when he was married before. To Louise."

Rita dropped her head. "Jesus Christ," she said, then lifted her eyes, grabbed a fistful of crackers, and crushed them into her chowder. "You had me worried for a minute. So he screwed around on his first wife. What's that got to do with you?"

"Louise was sick, Rita. She was dying."

Rita picked up her spoon and dove into her bowl. "Well, okay, so it was wrong. But at the risk of sounding ignorant, what does it have to do with you? How long ago was it?"

"Six years. Maybe seven."

"Jesus, Jill. So now what? She came to your front door looking for more? If that's the case, then you might have a right to be upset. No, cancel that. You only have a right to be upset if Ben said yes and he jumped into the sack with her."

Jill opened her mouth to say the rest, but the words took too long getting out. Rita spoke again.

"The trouble with you is you've had everything too easy all your life. I know it hasn't seemed that way to you, but God, Jill, you haven't had a whole lot of heartache, you know?"

She did not want to argue with that. Her first husband,

Richard, had had countless affairs, but Jill had looked the other way because once she'd stopped denying it, she was convinced he'd outgrow it, which of course he had not. But she could not explain this because she was far too tired, and because Rita might not understand, because Rita had never had a husband—her life had been more difficult than that.

And she could not explain that the second man she'd almost married had turned out to be a cad, willing to sell his soul—or hers—for ratings. And he still was.

And she could not explain the whole story about Ben.

Rita, after all, did not know what it meant to be committed to another, she had not been able to succumb to that, not one time in her life, not even with the man who loved her, Charlie Rollins.

Slowly she lifted her spoon and tried to smile. "You know something, Rita? You're right. I am an incorrigible brat."

Rita laughed. "I never said you were a brat. It's just that you've been luckier than most of us. There's nothing wrong with that."

Chapter 23

Ben took the long way back from Gay Head, through Chilmark to Vineyard Haven, then around the harbor to Oak Bluffs.

He knew he was procrastinating. But driving on a snowy day seemed preferable to going home, more appealing than facing Jill again and seeing the huge hurt in her eyes. Besides, the roads were mostly deserted because of the holiday.

Under "normal" circumstances, he'd have been at Carol Ann's. He'd be sitting at the table, drinking her strong coffee, watching her prepare Christmas dinner. He'd be listening to his grandkids, maybe helping them string popcorn or clumsily wrap presents. He'd be savoring their exuberance that Christmas Eve was finally there.

But he was not welcome at his daughter's—John had made that clear. And now, if Carol Ann had ever known that when her mother was alive . . .

He no longer wondered why men committed suicide, when the things they had done to the world, or the world had done to them, had squeezed around their airway and made it impossible to continue breathing the same air as those they'd loved and cheated on or hurt.

He could not believe Fern had come back.

At first, he'd been dumb enough to think that maybe it would help. Maybe she'd remember that Ben was not the sort of man who would do what Mindy claimed. Maybe she would tell that to the district attorney. Maybe that would get the charges dropped.

But she intended to do nothing of the sort.

Maybe he should simply knuckle under and pay her off. How much would she take once she learned that half a million was out of the question? He was wondering this as he automatically pulled into the driveway of his old house in Oak Bluffs—his house, Louise's house, the house where they'd raised Carol Ann.

He put the car in park and sat there, face to face with his workshop, where he'd built his plans for Menemsha House long into the wee hours of many nights. He saw the kitchen window where Louise had stood so many predictable years, making dinner, washing dishes, keeping their lives uncomplicated. As much as she'd loved their home, she'd loved her work as a teacher and the challenge of the classroom, too. She often shared the pride she'd felt when her students had responded to something they had learned.

She must have been a great teacher, Ben thought now, because she'd loved it so, because it seemed that every single child she'd ever taught had shown up at her funeral. They'd had to hold it in the open tabernacle because there hadn't been enough room in the church.

As the wipers streaked a path across his snowy windshield, he rested his face against the steering wheel and wondered if he'd been wrong to marry Jill. Maybe it hadn't been true love but merely another salve for his male ego, another Fern Ashenbach, this time with class, with grace, with smarts.

Who did he think he was, anyway? He certainly was no Paul Newman or Clint Eastwood. He was simply a small-town architect and builder who'd once tried to live a moral life, who'd once put together a successful business, then thrown it all away on dreams and his libido, not necessarily in that order.

And now he had little money and even less of his business. If he had to start again, he wasn't sure he'd make it. Or if he'd know where to start.

He looked back to the house and wished he'd never renovated it into a studio for Jill. He wished it was still the cozy place where he'd lived for years. He wished Louise were still there at the kitchen sink, when everything had been predictable and nothing ever hurt.

He sat there for an hour, before he put the pieces of his heart back into place, before he was able to face up to what he had to do.

"Jill?" Ben called up from the bottom of the stairs in the house on North Water Street. She wasn't in the sitting room or the kitchen, in the sewing room or the music room. He looked up the long staircase, now wrapped in pine boughs fastened with big red velvet bows. Was she taking a nap? Perhaps the night and day and the gloom of snow had helped her succumb to sleep. "Honey?"

She emerged from the doorway of their bedroom and stood at the top of the steep stairs, looking down. She was fully dressed; she did not say hello.

He pulled off his cap and smoothed his hair. "Honey, we need to talk," he said, and began to climb the stairs.

"No," she said, "I'm tired of talking."

He stopped on stair number five or six and held on to the mahogany banister. Okay, he thought. He couldn't say he blamed her.

"I want to make this easier on you," he said.

She shrugged and folded her arms. "Ben, you cannot

make this easier on me. It is not easy. It will not get easy until all of this is way behind us. If it ever is."

He looked down at his caramel-colored construction boots, which had seen little work of late. He wondered if she'd be more forgiving if she knew he'd been thinking about suicide. He moved two steps closer to his bride.

"Maybe you were right," he said. "Maybe we should tell the kids. If this were more out in the open . . ."

She did not respond. God, he wished that she'd respond.

He climbed two, then three more steps. He was almost to the top, yet still she hadn't moved. He wondered if this was some kind of psychological game in which she needed him to be the one to reach out, while she remained steadfast in her position. "I've been out to Gay Head," he said. "I've always done my best thinking there."

Jill stood up straighter. "Did you see your friend Fern?"

He took a breath, then let it out. "No, Jill. I did not see Fern. I went to the cliffs, and then I took the long way home." In the past, he had not had to explain himself or his every movement to her. He did not like the feeling.

"I went to Rita's," Jill said.

Something in her tone warned Ben that he was in trouble here, that whenever two women got together, the men ended up the losers. "Was she happy with the party?" he asked. "Did you tell her we enjoyed it?"

"Yes," she replied, but said it only once, so he guessed that was supposed to answer both his questions.

He now stood three steps below his wife, at eye level with her waist, the slender waist he loved to hold within his large, work-toughened hands.

"You and Rita talked about me," he said.

Her arms stayed folded. "I didn't tell her about Mindy. I can't bring myself to do that."

He needed to feel her arms around him, to feel her forgiveness, to feel her warmth. "Thank you," he said, but remained standing on the third step down.

For a moment, neither of them spoke. There was a time when that had felt comfortable, when Ben had known that he and Jill had passed the point where they needed to be always animated with one another, when quiet time between them still was filled with love. This, however, was not one of those times.

"What do we do next, Jill?" he said in the space and the air that hung between them. "I was thinking that maybe you'd want me to move back to the Oak Bluffs house. I can fix up a room upstairs. My workshop is still there. I can be out of the house when you need to be in the studio." He wished that she would jump right in and say, "No. No, Ben, that's not what I want."

Instead of saying anything, Jill turned and went into the bedroom. Ben climbed those last three stairs and followed. "It's not that I want to leave the house, Jill. It's not that I want to leave you . . ." Inside their bedroom, he noticed open suitcases on the bed.

If he'd eaten anything at all that day, it would have risen into his esophagus. Instead, only a thin, acidic bile came. "I'm going to England," Jill said. "I decided to go see my son."

Rita was thinking of how, just once, she'd love to meet a man who didn't turn out to be a bum. Then again, she supposed that that was an oxymoron, given the fact that most men had a penis and there must be some genetic link between stupidity and dicks.

It was Christmas morning, and though the snow had stopped and the sun was straining through the still-thick clouds, Rita was in the dumps. It could have been because she hadn't slept well, or because baby what's-his-

or-her-name was grinding against her innards most of the night, as if it already knew Santa was coming. Then again, maybe it was because from down the hall, Hazel's snores had been exceptionally loud.

It could have been a lot of things that kept Rita awake and troubled her now, as she stood at her kitchen window, gazing at a plump red cardinal that waited expectantly at the bird feeder that she hadn't yet filled.

But Rita knew that only one thing had sent her to the dumps. It was Ben Niles, and the grim reality that he'd turned out to be no better than the rest.

Though she'd tried to play it down to Jill to make her believe that it was no big deal, Rita knew differently. She knew that once illusions fell away, it was a long way to go back. She supposed it had some abstract thing to do with trust.

Above Hazel's snoring, the telephone suddenly rang. She glanced at it warily, as if a man were calling, as if it were one of *them*.

Then she decided it wouldn't be a man who mattered because she'd made damn sure none of them did.

It was not a man, it was a woman who wanted to list her house.

Rita perked up.

"I'm sorry to bother you on Christmas," the woman said. "But I've only just made the decision, and I don't want to change my mind. It's an old house, but it has a few acres."

Rita was not about to quibble with anyone about business, especially when the word *acres* was included. Acres on the Vineyard were like gold mines in them thar hills, whose commission could make a real estate person rich. And keep her from ever being dependent on a man.

"I'd like to put it on the market right away. How long do you think it will take to sell?"

"If you'd done this in September, it wouldn't take long

at all. If you wait until June, the price will automatically be higher."

The woman sighed. "It wasn't mine to sell in September, and I'm not going to wait until June. Do you want to list it or not?"

Rita recognized exasperation when she heard it. "Of course. When can I look at it?"

"Today."

She did not remind the woman that it was Christmas. "One o'clock?"

"Fine."

"Where are you?"

"Menemsha," the woman replied. "My name is Fern Ashenbach. The house is right next to the Menemsha House museum. Do you know the place?"

Hazel wanted to go with Rita, because Rita had made the mistake of telling her of Ben's "indiscretion," and now Hazel said she wanted to see for herself what kind of woman had lured the great Ben Niles away from his dying wife.

Besides, Hazel was intrigued that this woman had the audacity (a big word for her mother, reflective of cross-word puzzles in the paper), the *nerve*, to expect that Rita would come out on Christmas Day.

Hazel had however packed a basket of leftover party treats—mini-quiches and Amy's chicken things and the chocolate mint squares that Hattie Phillips had baked. Might as well be neighborly on this most neighborly of days.

Rita supposed that what Hazel really wanted was to ogle the woman, perhaps not without some envy, because perhaps she was not much more than Hazel—or for that matter, Rita—had been back in their days when they were young and sexy and went after any man, many men, single,

married, widowed, divorced, or anything, as long as they
breathed, as long as they had one of those godforsaken,
guaranteed-to-break-your-heart things dangling from their
loins.

Rita shivered as she steered the car toward Menemsha.
Hazel sat forward on the seat next to her, about to burst
from the excitement. When at last they arrived at the house,
Rita recalled the little girl she'd seen out there, the sad
child who'd found her grandfather dead. But she stopped
short of telling Hazel that she'd seen the girl: such news
might encourage Hazel to open her big mouth and ask
questions that were not her business. Hopefully, her
mother—with her basket of Red Riding Hood goodies
on her lap—would remember this adventure was, indeed,
for work, and not idle island gossip.

There was no doubt that Fern Ashenbach could lure a
man and lure him quickly.

She had the kind of legs Rita had prayed for when
she'd been a short chubby kid. She had curves that Rita
wished she still had beneath her blossoming belly. But
more than that, she had a presence, a confidence that se-
ductively suggested, "Hey, man, come to me, and I will
be your slave," which really meant that he would be
hers, not the other way around.

Plus she was a blonde, and everyone knew that they
had way more fun.

"I'm Rita Blair," Rita said. "This is my mother, Hazel."

Fern's "pleased to meet you" sounded sincere enough.
But it was hard to picture Ben with her, laden as she was
with cheap gold jewelry and decorated with black mas-
cara and bright green eye shadow. She was such a con-
trast to elegant, sophisticated Jill: she was much more
like Rita, with no smoothness on her edge.

Hazel handed her the basket, and the woman seemed impressed.

Then she escorted them through the rooms, which were quite old and needed fresh wallpaper and a few hundred gallons of paint. But Rita knew the place would sell in a heartbeat. The location was spectacular, and out-of-towners would quickly snap it up. Maybe some burned-out yuppies would convert it to a bed and breakfast, as if the island needed another one.

After the tour, Fern offered tea. "You're pregnant, huh?" she asked Rita. "When are you due?"

"April. Spring."

"Boy or girl?"

"I don't know yet. I've been too busy for the ultra-sound."

"Did you know my father-in-law?" Fern asked, as if she'd tired of baby talk. She took three cups down from the cabinet and wiped them with a paper towel.

Rita shot a glance to Hazel, a warning not to mention that they were friends with Ben, Ashenbach's longtime adversary. "I don't think we ever met," Rita said. "But of course, I knew his name. By the way, with all the real estaters on the island, why'd you call me?"

The enamel kettle whistled on the stove. "I saw your car the other day," Fern said. "On the street in front of the house. You have your name on the side."

"My mobile billboard," Rita said with a laugh. "I guess it was worth the eighty bucks." So far, Hazel was being quiet, and for that Rita was quite pleased.

"My daughter also told me she thought you were Ben Niles's friend."

Rita blinked, and Hazel coughed.

"Actually," Rita answered, "I'm friends with Ben's wife, Jill. We grew up together in Edgartown."

The woman poured hot water over the tea bags with what looked like angry gusto.

"I saw her the other day," Fern said, turning her back to them just long enough for Hazel to look at Rita and shake her head. "She's some kind of celebrity, isn't she?"

Rita wondered if Fern had been out of the country or just didn't own a television. But something cautioned her not to be sarcastic, and not to give too much away.

"She was a celebrity. In TV news. But she gave it up when she and Ben got married."

Fern turned and set two cups in front of them. "I think that's so pathetic, when a woman gives up her career for a man, don't you?"

Rita shrugged. "Depends on the career," she said. "Depends on the man."

Hazel drank her tea but did not say a single one of the twenty thousand things Rita knew she would say later, when they were safely in the car and out of earshot of the woman.

Fern laughed. "Well, I'm sure she's learned by now that it wasn't worth giving anything up. Especially for Ben." A serious look came across Fern's face. "I guess she didn't count on the scandal."

Rita scowled.

"What scandal?" Hazel asked, as if she couldn't keep her mouth shut another minute longer.

Fern smiled. "Well, surely everyone knows."

There was silence in the old, knotty pine kitchen. "No," Rita said, "everyone does not know."

Fern tossed back her hair and leveled her black-lined eyes first on Hazel, then on Rita. "Well, you could have asked my father-in-law, but he's dead. So I guess you'd better ask Ben." Then she cocked her head and sipped her tea and smirked like she'd won the lottery.

Mindy knew her mother was looking to start trouble.

After she heard her mother say those things, she left

the house, got on her bike, and pedaled down the snow-packed street toward West Basin Road as fast as she could pedal, as fast as she could get away from there, though she had no place else to go.

She knew her mother hadn't called Rita just because she saw Rita's car out in Menemsha. Since her mother had come back, she'd spent every day and night grilling Mindy about Ben, about his wife, about his life.

At one point Mindy almost told her the truth, that Grandpa had sort of made her say that Ben had touched her, that Grandpa had sort of made her tell the lie.

But just when Mindy was about to tell her mother, her mother said it was a good thing they were taking the son of a bitch to court because he would get what he deserved. And that they had to stick together because they were all each other had now, and that once they had some money, everything would be fine.

No matter how weird Fern Alice Ashenbach was, Mindy figured she was better than a foster home. She'd seen those kids in foster homes. They were the kids at the Christmas parties, who got the stupid gifts.

It grew more difficult to steer her bike, because the tires kept sticking in the snow. So Mindy got off and walked alongside, panting from exertion, wondering why Grandpa had to die and whether any of this would have happened if she hadn't told the lie.

Rita was determined to unearth what the hell was going on.

As quickly as she half-politely could, she "reminded" Hazel they had other "Christmas deliveries" to make, then left the house, not caring if Fern Ashenbach listed her house with Rita or not, not even sure that legally she could, because Ashenbach might have left it to the kid, and estate stuff took forever to settle. It had been her professional experience that people who wanted to sell post-haste were probably up to no good. And in Rita's book, calling her on Christmas Day constituted haste.

They climbed into the Toyota and barreled down the road, staying in the unplowed ruts that other cars had carved.

"This is absurd," she said to Hazel. "What kind of scandal could involve Ben? I wouldn't think that adultery—especially from years ago—was exactly newsworthy today."

"How well do you know him?" Hazel asked.

Rita blinked, then looked sharply at her mother, then to the road again. It was Hazel who didn't really know Ben—she'd left the island long before Jill had returned and met and married him. "He's kind and generous and an upstanding guy. He's my business partner. And for God's sake, Mother, he's married to Jill."

"So that means he can't have any secrets?"

If her mother didn't sound so genuinely doubtful, Rita might have been pissed. She shook her head. "No way. Not Ben."

Her mother shrugged, as if it were no skin off her false teeth. "I'm sure Jill felt the same until she learned about Fern Ashenbach."

As Rita turned the corner, she saw the kid walking beside her bike, trudging along as if she had a fire to get to and without her the whole island would burn down.

Rita steered the car into a small snowbank and slammed on the brakes. She quickly jumped out, banging her belly on the steering wheel. She slipped on the snow. "Shit," she muttered, grasping the sideview mirror and pulling herself up.

"Rita Mae, be careful!" Hazel hissed.

Rita caught what was left of her breath, apologized to the baby, and then shouted "Hey, kid!" at the little girl who was back on her bike now and trying to escape at snow-impeded speed. "Stop! I have to talk to you about your house!" The kid kept struggling to pedal. "I have to ask you about your grandfather!"

The kid slowed to a halt, a hundred or so feet ahead of Rita. She stopped but did not turn around.

Rita bent sideways and pressed her hand against the gas pain in her side. "Could you come here, kid? I'm pregnant. I can't run up there."

The little girl turned and looked back at Rita but made no move to return.

"Please," Rita said. "I know you're friends with Ben Niles. I need to know what's going on. Do you know about some sort of scandal that maybe had to do with Ben and your grandfather?"

At first the little girl did not move. Then she hoisted herself back on the seat, set her feet squarely on the pedals, and pushed off down the road, heading toward that fire, wherever the hell it was.

Chapter 24

Ben rang the doorbell at Carol Ann's and hoisted a sack of presents, like Santa fresh off the sleigh.

"Dad," Carol Ann said in surprise. "What are you doing here?"

"It's Christmas," he replied. "In case you forgot."

"Well, of course not. But I thought you and Jill were in New York."

He looked past his daughter to John. "Why would you think that?"

His daughter turned to her husband. "Honey, I thought you said my father and Jill were going to the city."

Ben stepped inside the house, as if he did not know that John had lied again. "Well, pretend I did go, and now I'm wishing you a Merry Christmas in person instead of on the phone."

The kids ran in from the other room. "Poppa!" Emily squealed. She hugged his leg while John, Jr. seemed more interested in the sack.

Carol Ann ushered him into the living room, with a reluctant John close behind. Ben did not dare look at his son-in-law—he was too inclined to kill him, or at least to try.

They sat on the wooden-armed, plaid-cushioned couches and opened presents. Ben lied (what the hell, he figured, everything else was out of whack, so he might as well lie, too) and said Jill had gone off to England because Jeff was homesick. "She decided to surprise him for Christmas," he said, wondering if John lied to Carol Ann without guilt or remorse.

Carol Ann and John gave him a framed black-and-white drawing of Menemsha House. He winced and thanked his daughter, who undoubtedly had had it commissioned without the knowledge of her husband. The kids gave him new mittens, "just like theirs" that Mrs. Bowen made, Mrs. Bowen being a widowed lady who'd once tried to woo a widowed Ben with casseroles and small talk.

They seemed to like their gifts, though John did not have much to say. Ben reminded himself he'd come there for his daughter and the kids. But when Carol Ann offered to heat up leftovers from the early dinner they'd had, the tension between Ben and John became more tense, the silence more silent.

"Thanks, honey," Ben said, "but I want to get home for Jill's phone call." Carol Ann accepted that, apparently without realizing that it was too late in England for anyone to be calling. He chalked it up to holiday exhaustion.

"Oh, Dad," she said instead, "I forgot to ask. Did Hugh Talbot ever reach you?"

Ben was standing by the back door between his daughter and his son-in-law.

"Hugh?" he asked, as if he could not recall the name.

"You know," Carol Ann replied, "Hugh Talbot. The sheriff at Gay Head."

"Oh," Ben said. "Him." He'd forgotten that Hugh had gone to Carol Ann when Ben was in New York.

"I'm sure he must have seen Hugh by now," John said, nearly shoving Ben toward the door. "I think it was something about Menemsha, wasn't it, Ben?"

He felt ridiculous and turned to the back door, his black-and-white framed drawing tucked under one arm. "Sure," he said with a shrug. "I guess. I don't remember, so it must not have been important."

"No," John said, "I'm sure it wasn't."

But as Ben said good-bye and slipped out the door, he did not miss the quizzical look on Carol Ann's face, a look so like Louise's that nothing much escaped.

Jill sat on a bench in the international terminal at Logan Airport, sad and numb from a sleepless night in a nearby hotel and a long, dull day of waiting for the evening flight to London.

Not long ago, she could simply have telephoned the Four Seasons in downtown Boston, and they would have made a suite available even on such short notice, because the name Jill McPhearson meant something in this town—hell, her face had been on half a dozen billboards on Route 128 alone.

The name Jill McPhearson had meant something, but the name Jill Niles did not, so she'd checked into a small dark room that matched her mood and tried to bring some order to her mind.

Rita had said the fact that Ben had screwed around with Fern Ashenbach did not matter because it was ancient history and did not involve Jill.

Would Rita have felt the same if she'd known about Mindy Ashenbach? Or if she'd known about the question mark that lingered in Jill's mind, the one that asked how well we can know one another and how much we should trust?

A cacophony of strangers hurried through the huge hall beneath the canopy of flags of many nations, bound for destinations far from Boston. Brassy, life-size angels glittered with blinding lights; yards and yards of inexpensive plastic garland were draped from up above. She found the decorations as irritating as the incessant drone of Christmas carols, the Muzak of Noel.

Deciding to go to England had been one of two smart things she'd done. She would stay there for five weeks, then fly to New York and return at least temporarily to her old life as Jill McPhearson, co-host to Mr. Edwards. She did not know how she would feel by then, or if she would go back to Ben, but today it did not matter. What mattered today was her sanity and her children, the only people she could truly trust.

She'd tried to phone Ben this morning, to at least say Merry Christmas, to thank him for the lovely blue pashmina he must have packed inside her bag while she'd been calling Amy to say good-bye.

She'd tried to phone him, but he'd been out.

Maybe he'd been with Fern Ashenbach.

A chill crawled through her. She dropped her gaze to the floor.

"Mom?"

Jill picked up her head. On her weakened body, she managed to stand up, then wrapped her arms around her daughter and hugged her with all the strength she had left.

"Mom, are you okay?"

Jill pulled back and looked at Amy, her beautiful, little-bit-crazy daughter with the burgundy hair. "I am now, honey," she said, pushing a strand of runaway burgundy from Amy's forehead. "Did you check your bags?"

It had been the other smart thing that she'd done. Right after she'd tried calling Ben this morning, Jill had called her daughter again. She'd told her to make her way to Boston, that they were going on a family holiday and were going to have some fun.

Chapter 25

Richard McPhearson was at Gatwick, on the other side of the glass, waiting for Jill and Amy to pass through immigration. At first Jill didn't recognize him. When Amy shouted, "Hey, Dad!" it took a moment for Jill's eyes to light on the face she'd once known so well.

A handsome man returned their daughter's wave. He did not look like Richard: he had a neatly trimmed beard sprinkled abundantly with gray, and he wore a bulky navy turtleneck, a wool jacket and jeans. It had been many years since she'd seen him, since their last in-person rift. During that time he'd apparently shed his proper, stuffy image for one that was more human and more hip.

She stood off to the side and waited for Amy to break from her father's huge embrace. "I wondered when I'd see you again," he said and at first Jill thought he meant her.

"I've been busy, Dad," Amy replied, slipping her arm through his and looking around the vast arched ceiling of the terminal. "I love living on the Vineyard, but it's great to be back. You look smashing."

Jill quickly reminded herself not to judge the relationship her children had with their father. She must encourage it, not judge it. But right now she hadn't slept all night and not much the night before.

"Jill," Richard noted, as if suddenly recognizing her as well. He did not take her hand or kiss her cheek, for which she was grateful. Instead he took her carry-on from her and began leading the way. "You look wonderful," he said.

"And you," she replied. "Silver hair becomes you." She had not meant it to sound sarcastic, but Amy rolled her eyes.

"Mom," she said, "no fights, okay?"

Jill smiled. Of course there would be no fights, because she was no longer married to this man, and he could no longer hurt her, no matter how many women he chose to sleep with. "Where's Jeff?" she asked.

"He and Mick are trying to make their flat presentable. I suppose that means getting rid of beer bottles and pizza boxes and girls."

Jill did not know why she was surprised. Her son had been in college two years, after all. His roommate would finish this year: surely they would have normal, healthy lives.

But Jeff? Quiet, introverted Jeff?

"I'll drive you to Oxford," Richard was saying, "so you won't have to take the train. I'll take my favorite girl and her mom for eggs and bangers before they settle out there in the country." He winked at Amy and gave her another one-armed hug.

Jill stepped back to walk behind them, Dad and daughter.

"How long are you staying?" Dad asked.

Mom did not respond that they'd be here until February, unless her new husband was cleared before then of assault and battery of a child under the age of fourteen. Instead she said, "For a while," and let it go at that.

•　　　•　　　•

Ben wandered through the quiet rooms of the house on North Water Street in the middle of the goddamn day, trying to figure out where to put himself and what to do and how much longer this day or the next would—could—last.

He'd thought about going to bed, but if he took a nap now, he'd set himself up to pace half the goddamn night.

So he wandered, stepping over dried pine needles, straightening sad red bows, while the hollow clomping of his work boots on the hardwood floors reminded him that this time the house felt different, that Jill was simply not off at work but off—well, gone, perhaps for good.

He couldn't blame her. What woman in her right mind would have stuck around even this long? It was bad enough what Ashenbach had made Mindy do. But dear God, now Fern? He almost wished he had the guts to call Jill in England and tell her not to bother coming home at all.

How many more surprises? the look on her face had asked. Well, he couldn't quite be sure.

He balled his fist and slammed it against the hallway doorjamb, the solid, hard oak doorjamb that he had painfully restored, hand-carving the turns and grooves to replicate the authenticity of the past.

Back when he was a respected craftsman. Back before anyone would have thought that he was a child molester and an adulterer to boot.

"Shit," he cried, his knuckles quickly reddening. He straightened out his fingers. Pain shot up his arm. "Shit," he said again, then worked to catch his breath. "Shit."

At least the pain had taken the edge off the emptiness in his gut, the deadened air, and his indecision about what to do next. He went into the kitchen, cracked some ice, and pressed it against his knuckles, hoping he hadn't done any real damage, wondering where in hell he'd found the anger to do that in the first place.

Just then he heard footsteps cross the porch, followed by a determined knock on the back screen door.

He figured he might as well see who it was. After all, how much worse could things get?

"Common sense—and, believe it or not, my mother—told me to mind my own damn business," Rita said, stepping into the kitchen and eyeing the ice on the back of his hand, "but as you may know, I've never had much sense, common or otherwise." She shoved her hands into the deep pockets of her street-length quilted parka. "Where's Jill?"

Ben moved to the sink and dropped the paper towel with the ice cubes. "She's not home," he said.

Rita nodded, and Ben got the feeling she knew more than she was saying. "Does she know that Fern Ashenbach is trying to make trouble?"

Leave it to Rita to come right out and say what was on her mind. "She can try if she wants," he replied, holding his throbbing hand. "I can't stop her." He didn't ask Rita what she knew or how she found out. Any second now, she'd blurt it all out.

Rita went to the counter and plunked herself down, uninvited, on a stool. "Is this so-called scandal about the affair you had with her?"

Scandal? He laughed because it was safer than crying. He laughed because Rita's no-nonsense approach to life was so refreshing after the spoken and unspoken stress between him and Jill these past weeks.

"Want some tea, Rita? I'd offer you a drink, but I suppose—"

"Tea's fine," she said. She rubbed her belly, and the image made him smile. It was nice that she was going to have a baby. That way she wouldn't have to go through the rest of her life without a child, without Kyle.

"Nice party the other night," he said, making tea as if it were just another day, as if everything were fine.

"Thanks."

He dug out tea bags. "Have you heard from Charlie?" He wasn't sure if he should mention him, what with the baby and everything.

"He called to say Hugh Talbot was looking for you."

Ben set the kettle on the stove and ignited the gas jet beneath. Christ, had Hugh checked with everyone? His knuckles throbbed, and now his head did, too. "Speaking of scandal," he said, "I didn't know you knew Fern." He kept his back to Rita.

"I didn't. But Jill told me you'd screwed around with her. Then Fern called and asked me to list the house out in Menemsha. She said she saw my car—and my sign—the day I drove out there after Hugh Talbot came looking for you at the tavern. Anyway, I don't exactly believe in coincidence. I think Fern found out I'm Jill's friend, and yours. I think that's why she wants me to list the house."

Ah. So that was what Rita knew and that was how she found out. "Do you think Fern is trying to get to me?"

"You tell me. But it seems like a lot of folderol for something that happened years ago."

The kettle whistled. With mechanical precision, Ben poured water into two mugs where he'd already dropped the tea bags.

"What else did she tell you?" he asked.

"Not much. That her father-in-law knew about the two of you."

"What else?"

"That's all. What else is there?"

He bobbed the tea bag up and down inside the mug. He slunk down on the stool across the breakfast bar from Rita. Then he propped his elbows on the counter and dropped his face into them. Suddenly he was so tired.

"Jill's not here because she left me," he said through his closed hands. "She left me, and she's gone to England."

Rita squeezed tea from the bag and set down the spoon. Ben thought he could hear her breathing, or maybe that was him.

"I knew she was upset about you and Fern," Rita said in a quiet voice, respectful of his pain, "but I tried to tell her Fern was no threat to her. That it wasn't as if she caught the two of you in bed."

Ben pushed out a puff of air and dropped his hands into his lap. He looked at Rita through aching, tired eyes. "That's not the only problem," Ben said. "Fern's trying to blackmail me."

Rita had class enough and smarts enough not to press him for more. But as the world closed in around Ben, he had to share the load.

"Rita," he said slowly, afraid to look into her eyes, "how good are you at keeping secrets?"

When Ben was finished telling her, Rita tried to close her mouth, although she wanted very much to gulp.

"Does Charlie know?"

He shook his head. "No one but Jill and my son-in-law. Not even Carol Ann. I tried to tell Charlie one night, but he was busy, and now he's gone."

She watched him take a sip of tea and wondered if he felt relieved now, if his burden had been lifted, now that he'd told someone besides his wife, who had too much at stake to be objective. She wished she hadn't blown off Jill's troubles as petty jealousy.

She studied Ben's drooping shoulders, his pale, gaunt face. This, she supposed, explained it all: the weight loss, the excuses not to socialize. Rita was no shrink, but she would have bet that Ben had not done it. He looked like a man who was caught in a trap not of his making. "Have you talked to Mindy?"

He shook his head. "I tried, at the Thanksgiving school play. She screamed. It made the paper."

Rita had a vague recollection about a story Hazel had read to her. "Why not try again? There's no restraining order against you, is there? Aren't they only for people you live with?"

He shook his head. "Legal or not, my attorney has advised me not to go near her."

"If it were me, I'd want to face my accuser."

"She's just a child, Rita. I don't want to scare her. For some reason, she's been scared enough."

That answered it for Rita. Whether it was the words he spoke or the way his voice cracked when he spoke them, Rita knew then that Ben positively could not have done this. He was too kind and too good. "Who's your lawyer?"

"A fellow named Bartlett. From Atlanta."

"Atlanta? For chrissake, Ben, where'd you get him?"

"Addie Becker knows him. She's Jill's old agent."

Rita thought a moment. "So that explains why she was willing to do *Good Night, USA* and team up with those jerks again."

Ben took a sip of tea. "Yep. That explains it."

Rita looked into her mug as if the tea leaves held the answer. "I'm not going to ask if you did it, Ben, because I know better."

"I did have sex with Fern Ashenbach years ago. But I did not touch Mindy. I would never touch a child."

"I know," Rita said. "But it looks like you're getting in deeper shit each day. What are we going to do about it?"

"We?"

"Well, the way I see it, your wife is on the lam in England, and your best friend is sucking up the sunshine in Florida. Your daughter doesn't know, so that leaves me. Rita Blair. At your service."

"I'd kiss you, Rita darling, but I can't afford the gossip."

Chapter 26

Richard wanted to take them to lunch at a perfect little tavern he knew of right there in Oxford. Jeff and Mick would be in class, it would just be the three of them.

Thankfully, Amy begged off—jet lag had attacked, and she and her mother needed sleep. So at noon Oxford time, six A.M. on the Vineyard, they'd let themselves into Jeff's apartment with the key the boys had hidden under the front stoop. They stepped past neatly stacked disarray, found a note with instructions to make themselves at home, and fell into sofabeds that had been clumsily made up.

They'd slept until midnight, then had tea and scones with Jeff, and finally had a chance to meet his roommate, Mick from the Lake District, who didn't seem to mind Jeff's penchant for the computer or that he put empty cereal boxes back in the cabinet. *"Cupboard,"* Mick corrected, and Amy laughed.

They caught up on the events of the months since they'd been together—what they hadn't covered by e-mail—then returned to bed and slept until dawn. Richard phoned shortly thereafter: he had stayed in town, and was determined to take them all to lunch today, jet lag or not.

Jill decided she was awake enough to handle it. He arrived at one o'clock with a copious bouquet of flowers for "his favorite girl," Amy. Jill said she'd put them in water and retreated to the kitchen. She emptied a milk bottle that smelled as if it had been there since last month, and parked the flowers in it. Standing in Jeff's kitchen, she listened to the voices in the other room: her children's mixed with Mick's and Richard's, her ex-husband's voice still rich with that disarming British accent that had spelled trouble when she'd first met him so long ago.

She'd been a news reporter on the streets of Boston then. He'd been in the States in the brokerage business. As a sideline, he'd dealt in antiquities. He'd been robbed in his hotel, but he'd single-handedly caught the thief who'd been absconding with a million pounds worth of rare coins. Jill had covered the story, and that had somehow led to dinner. The remaining history seemed now as ancient as those coins. A few years later, Jill realized that the trait she'd mistaken for bravery was really an overinflated ego that could not tolerate defeat.

How many more misjudgments about men would she make before her life was over?

None, if you don't let them get too close, she thought. Such a warning could have come from Rita.

But this was not the time or place to start thinking about the Vineyard. There were too few opportunities these days, weeks, and years to have her children both together as a family, plus Richard, plus Mick.

A family, of which Ben might or might not still be part.

Determined to make this visit an improvement over life back home, Jill poured water into the bottle and returned, vase in hand, to the living room. She looked at Richard and smiled. "I'm starving. How far is it to the restaurant?"

They walked down a narrow alley that Jill doubted anyone could have found unless they knew it was there.

"I thought this place might remind you of the tavern you always talked about," Richard said, "the place your family owned."

Amy jumped in and said how cool the 1802 was, and that her goal was to own it again one day. Jill pondered Richard's comment that she'd "always" talked about the tavern. Had she done that? In that moment she remembered that not once, in the eight years that they were married, had her parents ever met him, had he ever gone to the island. It had been as if she could not afford to let her two worlds—the present and the past—come together, merge as one. It had been as if she'd been afraid to interrupt her dream.

The alley suddenly opened to a garden, where remnants of a flower-filled autumn were now trimmed to winter's lifeless remains. Like her garden back home. Home—that place she refused to think about.

To the right was a small stone building. A low, narrow doorway welcomed them inside.

"Watch your head," Richard warned as they made their way through a bar area, where low beams stretched across the ceiling. It was most difficult for Jeff and Mick, who each stood over six feet. "This place was built in the fourteen hundreds," Richard continued above the din of afternoon pint-drinkers who decorated the bar. "People were shorter then."

They ducked to the back and climbed a few stone stairs. "Find a table," their leader said, "I'll go order."

There was one free table, actually half a table, as the other half was taken by some serious Oxford-looking types with philosophy on their minds. Jeff squeezed between the table and the wall, and Amy went next, sandwiched between the boys. That left Jill to share close quarters with her ex-husband, the father of her children.

The small room reminded her of her own college days—carefree, indulgent, loud. It was packed with people, and the air was filled with laughter and jolly-goodness so indicative of Europeans at feeding time, even the English, who had not exactly been known for fine cuisine until recently.

The fine cuisine Richard offered was fish and chips and shepherd's pie. He set overflowing baskets on the uncovered wooden table, then returned to fetch beer. Jill wanted to comment on his hostmanship, but knew it would come out sarcastic and upset the kids. Instead of saying anything, she shoved a french fry into her mouth.

The beers were large and slopped over the rims. Richard set them down and set himself beside the woman he'd once said he loved.

"What do you think?" he asked. "Isn't this great?"

"I didn't know it was here, Dad," Jeff said.

Amy pushed her beer over to Mick. "Too strong," she said. Mick smiled appreciatively, and Amy smiled back. Jill suspected that the spark that flashed between them was only her imagination.

She cleared her throat. "It's a wonderful place."

"I'll bet I could get some ideas here," Amy said. "For authenticity. Old English stuff."

Jill smiled and settled back to be the listener, not the speaker, to savor the camaraderie of the busy, laughing people at their table and all around them and know that none of them—not one—had heard anything about Ben. There was no possibility that after they left, the others would gab about them or call their phone number and hang up. Until now she had not known how much those possibilities had nagged her, and how much energy it had consumed to pretend it didn't matter.

"So how's married life, Jill?" her ex-husband asked. She chewed a piece of fried fish, pretending to have a mouthful, when in reality she was trying to figure out how to answer.

She faked a swallow. "Fine," she said, and took a swig of beer.

Richard laughed. "Well, I guess some of us do it better than others. I'm divorcing Becky."

She nodded with slight amusement. She'd thought his wife's name was Brenda. Maybe that had been the previous one.

"I'm never going to get married," Amy announced. "That way I'll never have to get divorced."

Jill and Richard looked at each other, then at Amy. Jill wanted to say something to Richard about the great example he was setting for their children, but decided she wasn't one to talk.

"My parents are still married," Mick contributed. "Thirty years this summer."

It reminded Jill of the freelancer from Providence. She wondered if it were possible that the divorce rate wasn't nearly what she'd thought, and if, in reality, she—and Richard—were among the few people left in existence who couldn't seem to get it right.

Suddenly the room grew warm; the noise around them grew louder. She took another sip of beer and wondered how soon lunch could end and she could get out into the fresh air.

Rita told Ben she'd stay out of it.

They'd talked until way past dark, when Rita said she'd better get home or Hazel would be frantic. She tried to get it through his thick, balding head that by not sharing this with others, he was selling his friends and family short. "Secrets suck," she said.

He'd nodded and pointed to her belly. "Don't they, though."

She'd said, "Touché," and felt like the pot calling the kettle a lousy shade of black.

But women handle secrets much better than men, she reasoned. Except, apparently, for Jill, whose response had been to run away even though Ben needed her—her support and her love.

The next morning when Rita tried to call Jill, all she got was the machine. Even in England, her friend could be elusive.

So now, as Rita took off in the Toyota, again headed up-island for Menemsha, she knew that fixing this might be solely up to her.

Sure, she'd said she'd stay out of it.

But, well, she was Rita, after all.

She decided to befriend Fern Ashenbach. Maybe that would allow her to get close to Mindy and carve a pathway to the truth.

As the old car rumbled up-island, Rita felt good to have a mission, like a sleuth in a detective story, a private eye. But when she turned into the driveway at the Ashenbach three acres, she thought it sad that Jill wasn't here to share this. It was the kind of escapade they would have relished when they were kids.

Fern greeted Rita in a fancy bathrobe, waving her fingernails into the wind. "Manicure," she explained. "Not quite dry."

Rita hoped it was dry enough for Fern to sign the contract for the listing. She had planned to check with probate first, to see who really owned this house, but decided it could wait: a signed contract warranted reason for being there, and right now being there was all that she needed.

"Hap was supposed to come up this weekend from

Barbados, but he took a charter to Cuba instead." She blew on her nails. "Hap is my boyfriend."

Rita wondered if Hap knew about the "scandal" and was in on the blackmail attempt.

"Ever been to Cuba?" Fern asked.

"No," Rita replied, and did not ask if Hap was going to come back on a raft. She followed Fern into the kitchen and took a seat at the table across from a collection of polish bottles and removers and little pieces of cotton.

"Are you going to marry him?" Rita asked.

Fern laughed. "Who knows?"

"Well, I think being married is even scarier than being a single parent."

"No shit," Fern agreed. "So you're not married. Is this your first baby?"

"My first one died. So this will be my one and only."

Fern plunged her fingers into two water glasses that were filled with chunks of ice. "Mindy's my one and only."

Rita pretended that she and Mindy had been properly introduced. "I have this lousy feeling that raising a kid isn't as easy as it used to be. It's like the world is different, you know?"

Pulling her fingers from the glasses, Fern examined them closely. "Kids are a pain in the ass," she said with perfect clarity. "Well," she added, as if realizing she'd sounded harsh, "sometimes they're okay. But they're kind of like dogs. I mean, your life changes, but theirs doesn't. Know what I mean?"

No, Rita did not know. She had never considered Kyle a pain in the anything. It was obvious why the little girl on the roadside had seemed so forlorn. "Well, Fern," she said quietly, then plunged in, the way Fern had plunged her fingernails into the ice, "I guess nothing's ever perfect, and things change all the time. How does your daughter feel about leaving the Vineyard? I assume that's what you'll do."

"Right now she thinks I have to sell the house because her grandfather left some debts, that it's the only way we can survive."

Excited that Fern was taking her into her confidence, Rita knew she must go slowly so she wouldn't seem suspiciously eager. She must be concerned, but not nosy.

"Dave Ashenbach worked hard all his life," Rita said, not knowing if it was true or not, but knowing that few fishermen had it easy. "It's hard to believe he didn't have any money."

"Not enough for Hap and me to buy our boat. When my father-in-law kicked the bucket, I realized that this could be my chance to finally make it. Shit, you can't imagine how degrading it is to always work for rich people."

Rita tried to look sympathetic.

"I deserve to be the one living on a boat. A sixty-footer at least. No more schlepping for those rich slobs. Hap and I decided we're even going to dock in a slip right next to them. If they're lucky, maybe we'll invite them over for cocktails."

Then Fern stood and plucked a pen from the counter. "Did you bring the contract?"

Rita swiftly opened her bag, her heart beating softly at this piece of news: *Fern and her boyfriend wanted a yacht.* Even with Vineyard house prices, even with three acres, Fern would need to amass all the money that she could. And Ben was an easy, ready-made target.

Sliding over the contracts, Rita asked nonchalantly, "What about your daughter? Will she live on the boat, too?"

"Who knows?" Fern scanned the papers, then signed them. "But believe me, I'm going to do whatever it takes. I've been gypped long enough."

And then Rita felt dread. Dread for Ben, for the child—and for Jill, who needed to get her ass back here, the sooner the better.

Ben was glad he'd told Rita. There was a certain kind of solace in unburdening the soul. He had not felt it since Noepe died. He did not know if Rita believed him, but she was an objective person, with nothing at stake. He supposed this was why shrinks did so well—their lives would not be uprooted and destroyed by anyone's confession.

He wished he could tell Carol Ann. Was Rita right—was he selling his friends and family short? Jill had implied the same thing. But neither woman could know the shame that just the thought of child molestation evoked inside a man, the accusation that he was capable of violating the most sacred trust of innocence.

The very thought made him want to vomit.

He ran a square of sandpaper across a two-by-four and wondered what the hell he'd thought about before this happened, before it consumed every waking moment of his days and many nights.

The doorbell rang upstairs. Ben put down his work and climbed the winding cellar steps. But even before he reached the door, he knew who was on the other side by the silhouette that played upon the frosted glass. His elation, however, quickly dissipated when he saw the look upon Carol Ann's face.

In one short second, he knew that she knew.

"Dad," his daughter said when he opened the door, "we have to talk."

Yes, they did.

Carol Ann had heard it at the town hall where she worked.

"Too bad about your father," one of the local cops had whispered. "It's hard to believe a guy his age would, well, you know, touch a kid."

So much for the gag order.

She didn't cry while she related it, didn't even flinch. But Ben recognized the stonelike quality to her voice as anger. It was the way he always sounded when he was so pissed that he could shout. Or scream. Or ram his fist at a doorjamb as he'd done last night.

"I didn't even go home and tell John," she said. "I called him and told him to pick up the kids. I said there was something urgent I had to do, and that I'd see him later."

"It doesn't matter," Ben said, "John already knows."

They had moved into the music room; she was sitting on the settee, he on the high-backed wing chair facing her.

Pink rose in her cheeks. "How long has he known?"

Ben sighed. "Since the beginning of October. That's when it started. Your husband bailed me out."

For a moment neither said anything. Then Carol Ann said, "Is this why he's always made sure we're too busy to see you? Why he said the kids couldn't go to Sturbridge. . . ." Her words trailed off, then she said, "Is this why he said you and Jill wouldn't be home on Christmas? Oh, God, Dad. Please tell me none of this is happening."

He rose from the wing chair and crossed the room to her. He was not going to avoid touching her—she was his daughter, for chrissake. He sat down next to her and took her hands in his. "John was trying to protect you, Carol Ann," he said. No matter how pissed off he was at John, he wasn't going to cause trouble between them.

She stared at him a moment and did not blink. "I want to know what happened."

He did not pause a heartbeat. "Mindy Ashenbach accused me of touching her breast. But even if she had a breast—which she does not as yet—I wouldn't go near it. I hope you know that."

"Of course I know that, Dad."

She didn't have to say anything more. She only had to look at him, her gray eyes reflecting his, with Louise's gentle, caring face, the face that he knew, no matter what, would always love him, would always stand behind him. That history of *family*, those years of struggle and survival and sharing to the depths, had built a strong foundation layered with trust. It was the innate trust that he and Jill could never have, no matter how much they loved each other.

A trembling started inside his shoulders as he held the soft hands of his lovely, trusting daughter. Then it quivered in his back and traveled down his arms and up inside his head. And there on the antique settee, Ben broke down and cried.

Carol Ann brought Ben a shot of the single malt, neat, the way he liked it in the best of times, the worst of times.

As he touched the warm, golden liquid to his lips, it almost seemed amusing the way his life had suddenly been transformed and women were flocking to his aid. Well, Rita and Carol Ann did not exactly constitute a flock, but their support mattered. Would Jill think he deserved it? He also wondered if Carol Ann's trust would be uprooted when she learned everything.

"So Fern is trying to blackmail you? Please, Dad. Why don't you just tell the police?"

He had not wanted to tell the police because he hadn't even told his wife. He had told Rita and now he had told Carol Ann, but he had not told Jill about the blackmail attempt for a half million dollars. As it was, Jill already wanted to pay Fern off and let her get away with it.

"I need to let my lawyer take care of it. I didn't want to screw things up more than they already are." He moved back to the wing chair where he was more comfortable, and to gain distance to tell her what was coming next. "Besides," he said, "there's something that could complicate the situation."

"What?"

He took another swallow. This was the most difficult part: telling a daughter that her father had cheated on her mother. While her mother had still been living. While her mother was in the slow process of dying. He wondered if Carol Ann would feel he'd cheated on her, too, on their family, and if his sin might be too great for her to pardon.

She returned to the settee and folded her hands, ever the lady.

Swigging from the shot glass again, he realized it was empty. He started to set it on the roll top desk, then decided to keep it in his hand, a mini crutch, a glass accomplice.

He took a deep breath. "Jill went to England."

"I know. You told us that on Christmas."

"Amy's with her, too. I couldn't go, of course. I've been asked not to leave the island."

Tiny little frown lines stretched across Carol Ann's forehead. "This is ridiculous, Dad."

He rolled the shot glass in his hand. "Jill didn't want me there anyway. She's run out of patience. I guess that's the most tactful way to say it."

"Good grief, Dad. She's your wife!"

"Well, honey, there's more—"

"There's nothing, Dad." She stood up and moved to the fireplace, gesturing with her hands, wringing them together. "How can she desert you?"

"She was justified, honey."

"Justified? How much are you supposed to take? First

Mindy and her ridiculous charge, then Fern Ashenbach and *blackmail,* for God's sake, and now Jill . . ."

Ben set down the glass, stood up, and went to her. He put his hand on her elbow. He lightly touched the folds of her shirt as they curved over her elbow, then he closed his eyes. "The problem with Fern goes much deeper than blackmail," he said, praying the words would be right. "Something happened a long time ago, and it's going to kill me to tell you. But I can't let you find out another way. Not like you found out about Mindy."

Carol Ann turned around. Ben opened his eyes, and she looked squarely into them.

He patted her elbow, shook his head, and walked to the window. "I had an affair, Carol Ann. With Fern."

There was silence a moment.

"When?"

Silence again. Then he blinked. "When your mother was sick." His words were so faint, she might not have heard them, but the quiet that followed told him that she had.

From the window, Ben could see Mrs. Warner, the old woman across the street, supervise young Teddy Lyons cleaning up the last of the driveway snow—sprucing up her property for New Year's Eve, no doubt, when her children and grandchildren would gather and be a family like he once had. At the foot of Mrs. Warner's white picket fence, a tangle of bittersweet still clung way past autumn, showing off its still-vibrant red-orange berries. Bittersweet, like life itself.

"Dad," Carol Ann said softly, "I'm sorry to do this, but I'll have to get back to you. It's going to take me some time to understand what you've said."

He stayed standing at the window, not looking back. Carol Ann left the room, walked down the hall, and let herself out.

When he heard the door latch, he gritted his teeth. Then the boil rolled inside him once again, the heated, angry agitation of losing control, of being at life's mercy. He turned from the window, fueled by fervor, marched into the hall, and called Herb Bartlett.

He reached a secretary.

"Tell him I want to know when he's coming to the Vineyard," he said in a raised, exasperated voice.

"I'm sorry," the secretary replied, "but Attorney Bartlett is vacationing in Barcelona. I'll have him phone you when he returns."

Ben slammed down the receiver, wondering why the whole damn world had gone to Europe, when they were needed here.

"I'm sorry Rita, but my mother doesn't want to talk to you," Amy said, when Rita finally got through to England on the twenty thousandth try.

"Amy," Rita said firmly, "put her on the phone."

"Can't, even if I wanted to. She's out with my father."

"Sorry kid, I don't believe it."

"Believe it. She had a fight with Ben, but she won't say about what. Did she tell you about it?"

Rita thought a moment. "Not really. But even if they had a fight, why won't she talk to me?"

"Who knows. She won't talk to anyone about it."

Oh God, Rita thought, Jill was being such a fool.

She said good-bye to Amy and sat at her kitchen table. As she listened to the click-click of knitting needles from the other room, she contemplated what she should do next, and whether she could accomplish it without calling the one person in the world who could and would help her out.

Chapter 27

 When Jeff had been accepted at Oxford, Jill had assumed it was one college, the place she'd read about in Chaucer, the foundation of some of England's greatest scholars, priests, and kings. But it was actually dozens of colleges and halls that constituted "The University City of Oxford." None of these institutions was actually called "Oxford"—they had names like The Queen's College, Manchester College, Trinity, St. John's, University, Hertford, and on and on.

New College, according to alumni, was the most beautiful, with its six-centuries-old, pale stone buildings. In its sprawling gardens, through its archway, lay a respite for meditation, for gathering harmony of thought.

Jill walked through the gardens and hoped that Jeff was able to harmonize more of his thoughts there than she was capable of doing. The initial relief she'd felt at being away from Ben and the Vineyard had dissipated and left a painful hole somewhere in her heart.

It didn't help that Richard was hovering, taking them to dinner, a performance at Exeter, an exhibition at the museum. He hadn't returned to London but kept calling this "family time." Jeff and Amy and Mick had begun to dodge his invitations and take off together in other directions. She suspected that Richard's real motive had little to do with "family time," and more to do with distracting himself from his new-found loneliness. She wondered if he would try to get her into bed.

In a way, she was flattered. At forty-six, being pursued by a male, even an ex-husband, was good for the ego, especially hers, especially now.

Not that she would consider it. Unlike her ex and apparently current husbands, she was not ready to jump into bed with someone simply because that might solve all her problems.

Well, there were those needy moments with Christopher in New York. . . .

But that was different, wasn't it? And she hadn't gone through with it.

She clenched her jaw and told herself to forget it, that she was beating herself up about that incident far more than necessary. She was hardly sexually promiscuous, after all. She was not like Richard, who most likely had not changed. No one really, truly changed, she believed. Which was why she'd decided that leaving Ben was what she had to do.

She ambled through the gardens, looking up at the majestic buildings, marveling at the beveled window glass, trying to distract herself, when a voice across the courtyard called out.

"Jill! Hey!"

Oh, God, it was Richard again. He looked exceptionally debonair today, with his faded jeans and a cashmere turtleneck and a matching deerskin jacket that looked as if it had stepped off a mannequin in Harrod's best window.

Reluctantly, she waved.

He caught up to her.

"I must return to London tonight," he said apologetically.

Though she should have been glad, part of her felt disappointed. "Well, thank you for everything, Richard. These past days have been fun."

They walked together along the walkway, falling into stride as two people with a past. "This is quite a place, isn't it?" he asked, scanning the grounds.

"You can almost feel the history," Jill replied.

"And it's curious that it's so close to London."

At first she didn't get what he was saying, didn't "pick up what he was laying down," as Jeff would have said.

"Catch the train with me to London," he said. "I know a great little restaurant in Covent Garden that serves a fabulous duck. You'd enjoy it, Jill. Just the two of us. What do you say?"

Oh. A romantic train trip into the city, a late dinner, maybe a stroll through Piccadilly and Trafalgar Square. London would be wonderful, but it would probably include overnight. And there was little question as to what would happen next. She looked down at the plain gold band that encircled not only her finger but her other world, the world that she'd left. "This is so strange. I feel like you've been courting me. In fact, you weren't this attentive when you did," she said.

He smiled magnetically.

"I'm a married woman, Richard."

"I didn't think you were planning to stay married," he said. "At least, that's not what Amy said."

She stumbled on the footpath but thankfully righted herself before he had the chance to help. "What exactly did she tell you?" *What exactly did Amy know?*

"That you and your new hubby haven't been getting along. That she thinks this trip is to give you time to think. A separation leading to—well, you know."

Her breath grew shallow, and that familiar pain returned to her heart. "Well, thanks for the concern. But if anything were wrong with my marriage, it's really no one's business."

"Our kids included?"

She turned her face from Richard and gazed off toward one of the seminar rooms, where a dozen or so students sat at a huge round table. One of them might become a world leader, a renowned physician, a gifted peacemaker. It made her problems seem quite insignificant.

She wondered if Ben would like being here. She decided that he would, that he would marvel at the architecture and at the growth of young minds. He would not wear a deerskin coat, but it would not matter. Not to her. Not to his wife.

She realized she was thinking of him again, that she had slid back into feeling he was a part of her. How long would it take her to detach? Would she be able to stop loving Ben after the divorce?

"If you'd like to take me anywhere, Richard, I'd like to cross the street to the Bodleian Library. It may not be London, but it's the best I can do."

In another second, Rita was going to throw up. She was sure she'd lost her mind, to be sitting on an airplane somewhere over the Atlantic.

She loosened the seat belt across her blossomed belly. Closing her eyes and trying to breathe, she reminded herself that she was there because she had to be, because she could coax Jill to come home only if she showed up in person.

But Rita hadn't had a passport. One did not need one for a trip across Vineyard Sound once or twice a year, the less often the better because Rita had a history of motion sickness on anything that rocked or flew.

She hadn't forgotten that when she'd phoned Charlie down in Florida and begged him to find a way to get her one in a hurry, so she could save Jill's marriage and maybe Ben's life as well. She didn't go into details, and Charlie hadn't asked. Good old trusting Charlie.

And he had come through.

She'd had a photo taken at the carousel pavilion over in Oak Bluffs, in one of those booths with a black curtain that spat out your pictures on a strip. She brought it to the travel agent where Charlie said to go. Twenty-four hours later, a courier showed up at her door, passport in one hand, a British Airways ticket in the other. Charlie had even arranged for a car to meet her at the airport and drive her out to Oxford.

Hazel thought she was nuts, but Rita pointed to the dozen or so booties and reminded her that the apple didn't fall . . . and all that.

So now Rita was trying not to throw up, wondering if she'd become a masochist for the sake of her best friend. And if her attempt to drag Jill back was even going to work.

They were laughing on the way back to Jeff's apartment, Jill and Jeff, Amy and Mick. They'd been telling Mick about Addie Becker, and Jeff had done an imitation of her that he'd perfected back when the woman had been a daily presence in their lives.

"I can't believe you're going back to work with them," Jeff said, and Jill's laughter slowly subsided.

"Think of it as a means to an end," she said. "A door opening for my new career."

Jeff shrugged, and they turned the corner onto the street where he lived.

Amy put up her umbrella, though today it hadn't rained. "Have it your way," she mocked beneath it, twirling the handle as if it were a movie prop. "And I'll have it mine." Mick laughed, but then, he laughed a lot when he was with Amy. It warmed Jill to think her daughter had that effect: to bring laughter into life, to share joy.

She also hoped that Amy's lightheartedness indicated that she was headed toward acceptance of *Good Night, USA.*

"Oh, no," Jeff interrupted her thoughts. "A vagrant on my step."

Her eyes moved to Jeff's front door stoop where a woman sat slumped. But it was not a vagrant. It was Rita.

"Rita!" Jill shrieked. "What the hell are you—" She helped her best friend to her feet, then saw how pale she looked. "Rita, are you okay?"

"No," Rita moaned. "I'm sick as shit. And I'm not altogether sure, but I'm either in labor or in the middle of a miscarriage."

Rita did not have a miscarriage. She experienced "premature labor," according to the doctor, who stood on one side of the hospital bed now, while Jill was on the other.

"We've done an ultrasound," he said, "and it appears that everything is fine. But you must take it easy. Both for yourself and for the twins."

Glancing from the doctor, Rita looked at Jill, then back again. "What?" she asked.

"You must take it easy. Flying all night without sleep is not healthy for you or for your babies."

Rita frowned. "That's the second time you've mentioned something in the plural form."

"Surely you know you are having twins."

Rita looked at Jill again, who had broken into a big fat grin. "No, I did not know."

"This was your first ultrasound? Didn't you have one with the amniocentesis?"

"I didn't have either. I've been too busy."

The doctor looked puzzled. "Well, then, let me be the first to congratulate you."

She did not dare look at Jill again. "Thanks. Now when can I get out of here?"

"I'd like to keep you overnight."

"Fine. I could use the rest."

He left quickly.

"Well?" Jill asked, sitting down on the side of the bed. "This changes things, doesn't it?"

"Changes what?" Rita asked, as if she didn't know.

"It's time, Rita. You have to tell Charlie now. You're going to have twins. *His* twins."

She turned her head on the pillow away from her best friend. "I can't."

"Rita, don't be a jerk. You get seasick on a forty-five-minute trip across Vineyard Sound, but you flew all the way across the ocean because you wanted to haul me back to the man who loves me and who I love. Isn't that why you're here? Well, this is no different. Charlie loves you. And whether or not you know it, you love him. Own up to it, for once in your life."

"I can't," she said. "It wouldn't work."

"Why? Because you're afraid of a commitment? That's not fair to those babies, Rita."

"It's not because of commitment, Jill. It's because I don't trust him. I don't trust any man."

Jill laughed. "Excuse me, but that's my line."

"No," Rita said into the pillow. She wished that Jill would leave. The ache in her stomach had moved to her chest. "Maybe you'd better go," she said. "Come back tomorrow. We can talk then." Maybe by tomorrow, she would have had time to think. Maybe by then she wouldn't feel so—vulnerable.

Twins?

Twice blessed?

Her?

"Why did you come, Rita?" Jill persisted.

From the corridor came hospital sounds: footsteps on tile, low-talking voices, a couple of dings from the call button of someone in more distress than Rita.

Jill's voice grew low. "He told you, didn't he? Ben told you. About Mindy."

"Yes."

A few more footsteps passed, and another call button dinged.

"I don't think he did it," Jill said. "Most days I don't think he did. But he's not fighting it. Sometimes I think this is harder on me than on him."

"That's because he was there, Jill. He knows he didn't do it." She shook her head. "And so do I. I know what happens to a kid. I don't think it happened to Mindy. Call it a gut feeling. But I'm speaking from experience."

"Make sense, Rita."

The room in the hospital—in *hospital,* the Brits called it, without the *the*—grew eerily quiet as if even people in the hallway waited for an answer. Rita closed her eyes. She could almost taste the bleach that had been used to launder the pillowcase. "When we were kids," she said, "there was a man named Mr. Blanchette. Remember him?"

"The one who read the girlie magazines in the corner store?"

"Yes."

"What about him?"

"One summer when Hazel rented out our house, we bunked in with Blanchette and his wife and their two sons and three dogs."

"And?"

She felt Jill's hand against her back, as if her friend knew what was coming next. "And I slept on the porch, and the bastard used to come out to my cot at night and feel me up." There. She'd said it fast to get it done. For the first time ever, she had said it.

"Rita . . ."

"He never raped me. But he touched me, Jill. He touched my breasts and my butt, and he ran his fingers between my legs."

"Oh, God."

"And he jerked off across my sheets."

Jill was quiet for a moment. "Did you ever tell your mother?"

"I was too afraid. We needed to stay somewhere. We needed to rent the house so we could survive. I was afraid if I told Hazel, we'd have nowhere to live."

Rita felt the weight of Jill's long body lie gently down beside her, then her arm on her shoulder.

"That's why I doubt that anything happened," she said. "Even today, I'll bet most kids are too scared to tell."

"I'm not sure I agree," Jill answered. "Today I think most kids are aware. They know it isn't their fault."

Rita shook her head. "I know when a kid's lying, Jill. I built my life on a lie. Besides, awareness or not, truth or lies, I think when it comes to hurting a kid, everyone is scared. Hell, I'm still scared after almost forty fucking years."

Jill tucked her head against her hair. "Oh, God, Rita," she said. "My poor, poor Rita."

They lay still like that for a long, long time until Rita fell asleep, her pillowcase damp with tears.

Jill shivered a little as she stepped into the cab an hour or so later, after Rita had drifted off to sleep. She gave the driver the address of Jeff's apartment, settled back against the seat, and began to think about secrets. Damn, god-forsaken secrets.

It was not the first time Jill had learned how damaging secrets were to a family, to a life, to many other lives. Her mother's secrets had caused Jill to leave the Vineyard, and always to struggle to be "someone" because her mother's seeming indifference at home made her feel unwanted there. Her own insecurities, brought on by those secrets, had affected her kids, had shaped and skewed and probably screwed up their lives.

It had been because of Rita's secret that Kyle had not known his father, that his father had not known him. It had been because of Rita's secret that Rita herself had been cheated out of love, cheated out of a better life.

And now it was because of Ben's secret that Jill had run off to England and huddled her children together, not to protect them but to protect herself from the pain bottled up inside her, from the sense she'd been betrayed.

Looking out the window, she knew how wrong she'd been. If she'd told her children, perhaps they could have gotten through this mess together. After all, her children were not children anymore: They were adults with sound judgment and level minds. It had only been because of Ben—because of his fear and of his shame—that Jill had not told them yet, that she'd been racing in small circles, trying to keep things glued together, living behind a mask.

As the driver pulled to Jeff's front door, Jill knew the time had come to stop living the facade.

It was morning in England but the middle of the night in Florida, which did not stop Rita from picking up the phone on the bedside table and dialing the number in area code five-six-one.

She had to do it, after all, before she chickened out.

Thankfully Charlie, not Marge, picked up the phone.

"Charlie, it's me, Rita," she said. Her eyes were closed, as if that would make this easier.

"Hey," he said groggily but not unhappily, "did you make it? Where are you?"

"Yes, I made it."

"What happened? Is Jill there?"

"Well, yes, of course she's here. Well, not here, exactly. She's here in England, but not here with me right now."

Charlie chuckled. "I have no idea what you're saying."

Rita sighed. "She's safe and sound at Jeff's apartment. As for me, I'm safe and sound, too. But I'm not at the apartment, I'm in the hospital. Excuse me, that's *in hospital*."

There was a pause, then he said, "Wait a minute, let me sit up."

She guessed that he sat up.

"What happened? You're okay?"

"I'm just peachy, Charlie. But there's something I need to tell you."

She paused.

"I'm pregnant," she said.

The time between the dialogue grew further spaced apart.

"Yes," he said, "you told me."

She opened her eyes and looked around the room. It was interesting that hospital rooms looked the same here and in the States, as if there was an international hospital consultant who'd specialized in wall-mount TV stands, plastic bedpans, and disposable, gripper-bottom slippers.

"I didn't tell you everything."

Running her fingers alongside of the metal bed table, Rita wondered if the consultant specified one global manufacturer, the Microsoft of hospital bed tables. She wondered why the company had not been split up.

"It's mine, isn't it?" Charlie asked.

"Well," she said, holding out her hand and examining her fingernails, "actually, yes."

There was another pause, a pregnant one, Rita thought with a small smile.

"Rita," he said. "Rita."

His voice choked up as if he were going to cry.

"Jesus Christ, Charlie, don't go crying on me. This doesn't mean I'm going to marry you or anything."

He did not answer, then he said, "Rita, I don't give a shit if you marry me. I love you. I always have. You don't have to marry me, but I hope we can be a family."

"You'd better lower your voice. I'm not sure Miss Margie would be pleased to hear what you just said." When she said "Margie," a damn lump showed up inside her throat. She tried, unsuccessfully, to swallow it away.

"Marge isn't here," he said.

She wanted to respond, but she did not know what to say. She did not know if he meant she wasn't there, as in she wasn't in the room with him, or wasn't in the state of Florida.

"She went back to the Cape," he said.

"Oh," Rita replied. So. She wasn't in the state.

"It wasn't working, Rita."

"When did she leave?" Rita asked.

"A couple of weeks after we came down."

"So you've been there—alone? Through the holidays?"

He laughed. "You rented my apartment!"

"Bull. You could have come back!"

"I needed to think."

"About what?"

"About my life. I was looking for some answers. Now, I think I have them. You don't have to marry me if you don't want to, but can't we be a family? You, me, the baby—"

"Excuse me, that would be babies."

"What?"

"Babies. There are two of them."

That pause returned. Then, "What?"

"Stop repeating yourself. I said babies. Two. Twins."

"OhmyGod," he said without pausing this time.

She played with the corner of the sheet a bit. It was clean and white and stiff from starch. In another second she was going to cry. "Is that okay?" she asked. "Are you happy we're going to have twins?"

"OhmyGod," he said again. "Rita, I love you so much."

The tears began. "Me, too," she said, "I love you so much, too."

"Lunch," Jill announced as she walked into Rita's room, carrying a tray. "Steak and kidney pie."

Rita plumped her pillow. "You're going to make me puke if it's the last thing you do."

"Never." She set down the tray and whipped the plastic dome off a plate, atop which rested a bowl of thick clam chowder and a dish of what looked suspiciously like blueberry buckle. "I did some cooking this morning," Jill said. "We have to keep up your strength."

If she'd had to get sick, this had turned out to be as good a place as any. "Bless you," Rita said, fluffing her red-gray, matted curls. "Pardon my appearance, but my stylist and makeup woman haven't arrived as yet."

"There's still hope. Amy will be here shortly."

Rita laughed and gestured to the edge of the bed. "Sit down and watch me eat. I need to watch you gloat when I tell you I told Charlie."

If Jill's mouth dropped further open, she'd have to scrape it from the floor.

"You did what?"

"I said sit down. Before you fall down."

Jill sat down, and Rita told her, and Jill gave her a hug. "It will be good," Jill said. "Whatever happens, it will be good." Her grin was sardonic, as if she were mocking herself. "I have to believe that now. Because I've done something, too."

"Oh, no," Rita groaned. "What?"

Jill patted Rita's knee and looked off toward the window, her mouth set in a grin. "Last night when I went back to Jeff's, I was determined to face the music, to tell the kids about Ben. I was upset about it, though. And I was anxious.

"Then when I walked through the door, something happened that made me realize life can be beautiful."

Nibbling on the blueberry buckle, Rita watched Jill's grin grow wider.

"When I walked through the door," Jill continued, turning her gaze back to her friend, "Amy was there with Jeff's roommate, Mick. They were standing in the doorway into the kitchen, and Mick was kissing her. And she seemed to be liking it."

Rita dropped her spoon. "No shit."

"So you see? Nothing stays the same."

"No shit," Rita repeated.

"Then I asked if Mick would excuse us, and I called Jeff from his room. Then I sat down my two kids and told them everything."

"No shit" seemed to be all Rita could say.

"No more secrets, Little Red. The cat's out of this weary bag."

Rita picked up her spoon again. "How did the kids react?"

"Amy wants to 'wring Mindy's twerpy neck'—that's a quote. Jeff, of course, was not so animated. But he did look at me and say that no matter what problems he's had—and is trying to work out—about Ben and me, he does not believe Ben is capable of anything of the sort."

Rita took a spoonful of the chowder. It tasted wonderfully like home. "So now Charlie knows about me and the kids know about Ben and so do I. And Amy let a boy kiss her and did not run away. So what's next?"

"Next," Jill said with a big, deep breath, "next we go home. I've thought a lot about this, and I know I need to forgive Ben. I found out for myself how easy it would be to turn to someone for physical solace when you're in emotional pain." She cleared her throat. "So you and I will go home. Amy asked if she can stay here a little while. In England with Jeff. And Mick."

"And you said yes?"

Jill smiled.

"No shit," she said again.

"So you and I will leave my daughter here and go home as soon as you're able. Then I do my stint in February— hopefully the only ramification of which will be a career boost. And enough money to pay Ben's attorney. After that, we sit and wait until the trial."

Rita nodded but did not say that Jill could do all the waiting she wanted, but Rita had no intention of sitting around. Not when, surely, there was something she could do.

Chapter 28

 Mindy wondered where she and her mother were going to go and if they'd live in a house or an apartment and if they'd be on an island or on land. She looked at the real estate brochure that Rita Blair had brought and studied the picture of Grandpa's house—*her* house—on the cover. Then she shoved it under her bed and wished that red-headed woman would stop meddling in their lives.

"Hi," Rita had said this morning when Mindy was outside cleaning the snow off Grandpa's old rowboat as if he'd be using it today. "Is everything okay?"

Mindy had not known how to answer, so she'd just said, "Sure." Then she told Rita that Fern had gone into town, so if she wanted to tell her anything, she'd better save her breath.

Rita dug into her purse and pulled out the brochure. "Hot off the press," she said, and pushed it toward Mindy, who took it the way people take a summons they've been handed. She'd seen that on *Law & Order*, too.

She looked down at the cover and saw the picture of the house. She felt that awful tremble in her belly. Then she sucked in her lower lip so she wouldn't start to cry.

Rita smiled. "Can you keep a secret?" she asked. "Can I tell you something you promise you won't tell your mother?"

Mindy shrugged.

Rita smiled some more. "I think I have a buyer for your house."

Hauling a tarp up from the ground, Mindy smoothed it across the top of the boat. "Oh," she said.

"We'll keep our fingers crossed, but the buyer knows the property. He's coming by tomorrow to check it out. That will be good, won't it? To sell your house?"

Mindy shrugged. "I've got to go inside now."

"Mindy?" Rita had called after her. "I know Ben Niles."

She stopped dead in the tracks she made with her light-up sneakers, which her mother hadn't yet replaced. "I know you do," she said, staring straight ahead. "You brought fudge to the museum."

She felt Rita move up close behind her. "That's right, I did. Ben's wife is a friend of mine. And I don't think he's a bad person, do you?"

Mindy looked away. "I'm not going to talk to you about any of this stuff," she said. "I'm not allowed to. It's the law."

Rita nodded. "Sure. That's okay. But just remember, if you ever want to talk, I'm Ben's friend, too. And he's very worried about you." The woman turned and started walking toward the Toyota.

Then, not knowing why, Mindy heard herself call out, "Ritablair?" The name came out as one word, letters strung together.

Rita turned around.

"Is he okay?" she asked. "Is Ben okay?"

"Sure," Rita replied with a shrug that matched her own.

Mindy watched the woman leave, then went inside the

house and up into her room where she sat and wondered if sometime between now and April she could be dead like Grandpa, or at least if she could run away.

This time they did not make up by making love.

Instead, they walked on the beach, said little but touched often, hand in hand, arm in arm, fingers touching lips and eyes and cheeks.

There was little to be said except I'm sorry, which she said to him and he to her.

Then they held hands again and walked along the water, past the pilings and the pier, past the lighthouse and around the harbor, escorted only by the gulls and a forgiving winter sky.

Charlie flew up to Logan from Florida, so Rita wouldn't have to drive back to the ferry alone, in case there was a snowstorm, in case she didn't feel well. So after Jill had set off in her car, Rita climbed in next to Charlie. The expectant father then carefully headed south toward Woods Hole. He never, not once, went over the speed limit, as if two yellow baby-on-board signs were already flopping in the back window of her car.

Along the way, he convinced Rita that she should let him stay with Hazel and her (in the downstairs den, of course), in case Rita needed him in the middle of the night.

All of which helped prove to her (not that she really needed proof) that she could count on Charlie, that he'd be there no matter what.

She therefore did not hesitate to lure him into her scheme, and loyal Charlie, the father of her children, did not question why she wanted him to pretend to be interested in the Ashenbach property. And he did not say it was odd that Rita was trying to befriend a little girl, or suggest that Rita was using him as a ruse to get to spend more time with the girl.

"Do you like babies?" she asked Mindy now, while Charlie talked with Fern about the septic system, about which Fern probably knew squat. "I'm going to have twins."

"My friend Suzanne has a twin brother," Mindy said to Rita, who stood inside her bedroom, pretending to examine the ceiling for any parts that might indicate a leaky roof. "Well, she's not a friend, really. Just a kid in school."

Rita walked over to a group of stuffed animals lined up on Mindy's shelf. "I like your stuffed animals. I never had stuffed animals. I had a doll, though. Peggy, I called her. She had dark hair, and her eyes opened and closed, her knees and elbows bent." Rita laughed. "When I was a kid, that was the best you could expect. Today dolls talk to you."

"I don't like dolls," Mindy replied.

Rita turned and looked back at Mindy. "No? Wow. I don't know what I would've have done without Peggy. She was my best friend. I told her everything."

"I thought Ben's wife was your best friend."

Well, Rita hadn't expected that. She smiled, watching the little girl who was a step ahead of her. "I mean Peggy was *bester* than my best friend. She never thought anything I said or did was dumb. It was like having a big sister."

"Oh," Mindy said. She walked to the window away from Rita's line of sight. "I had a doll. Raggedy Ann. I threw her out."

"How come?"

Mindy laughed and turned back around. "Because I'm ten!"

"Well, I'm older than that, and I still have Peggy. She sits on my dresser now, and she still helps me with my problems." It was true, her doll did sit on the dresser, but she'd become a dust collector, hardly a confessor. But Mindy wouldn't know that. "It helps to have someone to talk to sometimes. Not a friend and not your mother." Rita shrugged. "Well, I gotta go see if Charlie's going to buy this place."

"What are you doing, Rita?" Charlie asked after they'd left the Ashenbach place and he was driving back toward Edgartown.

"Why, Charlie Rollins, whatever are you asking?"

He shook his head. "You're up to something. Ordinarily I wouldn't care—I'd do anything you asked, you know that. I have. I helped you get the passport so you could go rescue Jill. I never asked for an explanation, not once. But this woman started grilling me about Ben. I didn't like the things she asked. Like how much I think he's worth."

Rita shifted on the seat. The baby, one or both, whacked her in the side. "I can only say that while you were in Florida, a lot happened." She thought for a moment. "Actually, it started before you left, but I didn't know it."

"Such as?"

"Such as I'm not the one who should be telling you."

"Jesus, Rita, I'm the father of your unborn children."

She turned her head toward him. "That has nothing to do with this."

He smiled. "Tell me, Rita. I want to know."

She sighed and looked back toward the sea that hugged the narrow strip of road. "At the beginning of October, Mindy Ashenbach told her grandfather that Ben had touched her. Dave Ashenbach had Ben arrested. The trial is in April, and in the meantime, I'm trying to make friends with Mindy so she'll recant her story and tell the truth. And before you ask how I'm qualified to do that, I'll tell you that when I was a kid, a man molested me. Several times. He never raped me, but he might as well have. It was old Blanchette at the corner store, remember him? Anyway, I figure if I can win Mindy's trust, she'll 'fess up before it's too late. Oh, and in the meantime, another wrinkle popped up. Apparently Ben and Fern Ashenbach had a thing a few years back. She's trying to blackmail him out of half a million dollars. She says if Ben antes up, she'll have Mindy say she lied." She moved her hip the other way, to ward off another kick. "For obvious reasons, few people know. We're trying to keep it that way."

The ocean looked calm for January, and the sun sparkled off the water almost as if it were spring. Thankfully, it was not, for the progress Rita was making with Mindy was definitely slow going. And on top of that, there was the babies' room to do.

"I'd say you were joking," Charlie finally said, "but I've known you long enough to know when you are and when you're not."

Rita nodded.

"I can't believe this, though. It all sounds preposterous."

"It is," she said. "It's also very real."

Ben and Jill did not hear from Herb Bartlett until the end of January, the week before Jill left for New York for her February coming-out party. They had telephoned the attorney five times in between—Jill three times, Ben twice. She wanted to ask Addie what the hell was going on, but Addie would tell her to hold her horses, that men like Herb Bartlett worked on their own time, in their own way. Besides, Addie did not know the real reason they needed Bartlett: she still thought they needed him for the island boy accused of molesting the island girl.

So it came as a surprise on a Tuesday evening when someone knocked at the front door and it turned out to be the fringed-leather-jacketed attorney, a briefcase in his hand, a young female assistant at his side.

"There wasn't time to phone," Bartlett said, making his way into the living room before he'd been invited. He sat down in the wing chair, and his straight dark-haired assistant, in a gray pin-striped suit, made herself at home across from him.

Jill glanced down at the heavy cowboy boots on her great-grandmother's braided rug. "May I take your coats?" she asked.

Bartlett shook his head. "We'll just be a minute."

Ben had moved into the room and was standing next to Jill.

She sat down and introduced herself and Ben to the assistant.

"Are there any new developments?" the attorney asked.

"No," Ben said. "Except I went to the co-op the other day and Bill Harrington looked at me oddly, and I think that he might know. Then again, I think pretty much everyone knows, not that they'd say it to my face, not on this blessed island."

Bartlett clicked open his briefcase and withdrew some papers. "You'd better get used to that," he said in a matter-of-fact voice, "because the girl's mother has been in touch with my office."

Jill looked from Bartlett to Ben, who was motionless by the fireplace.

"What?" he asked.

The attorney perched half-glasses on his nose and peered at the papers. The assistant sat mute. "Fern Alice Ashenbach," he said, and Jill tried to quell the chill that crawled through her veins at the mention of the name. "Attorney Fitzpatrick notified the court that I had joined your defense team. The court, in turn, notified Ms. Ashenbach." He sifted through the papers.

Ben leaned against the fireplace.

"Why did he do that?" Jill asked, because Ben was saying nothing.

"Courtesy," Bartlett said, "and the law." The attorney cleared his throat. "Ms. Ashenbach called to say that if you were trying to intimidate her by bringing in a 'high-priced lawyer,' then you'd better think twice. She said she knows Ms. McPhearson is going to be back on TV soon, and how would everyone like it if the news about what Ben did was on the front page of the *National Exposé*. She said she'd even send them pictures of her daughter, that she really didn't mind, because someone was going to pay for her story. If not Ben, then someone else."

His soft, easy Atlanta-speak helped mask the threat in those words and the horror of it all.

"That's blackmail," Jill said, the cords in her neck tightening. "She can't blackmail us. She'll go to jail."

The attorney shook his head. "She can't go to the tabloids, either. I reminded her of the gag order. I told her she'd be the one in jail."

Ben let out a breath as if he'd been holding it.

"So she asked for a 'settlement.' In other words, if we pay her, she'll have her daughter change her story."

Closing his eyes, Ben said, "She already tried. I already said no."

Jill looked at her husband. "She asked you for money?"

"Half a million dollars," he replied. "Even if we had that kind of money, the price of freedom is too high."

Jill was too stunned to know how to reply.

Bartlett retrieved another paper from his pin-striped assistant. "There's more," he said.

Jill held her breath, braced for the other proverbial shoe to thud to the floor.

"Even though right now she can't sell her story or get

you to 'settle,' the woman apparently is determined to make a big score. She said she knows her 'rights.' And that after the criminal trial, she'll file a civil suit. She thinks she'll get her money that way, because of all the attention it will draw because of Jill's celebrity."

"A civil suit?" Ben asked, and Jill was glad, because she could only hear the words "Jill's celebrity" echo like a death sentence somewhere in her mind.

"Yes. At which time, I have to caution you, there will most likely be no gag order, because she, Fern Ashenbach, will sue you, Ben Niles, for pain and suffering brought on by what she claims you did to her daughter and by the humiliation of the trial." He laced his words with sarcasm and mockery toward the woman who claimed she had rights.

"And no matter what happens at the trial, the whole world will know," Jill stated.

Bartlett nodded, and in Ben's face, Jill saw that pale anguish return. She closed her eyes a moment, then stood up and left the room.

Chapter 29

There was no sense calling Addie, who would probably lash out with hot-headed anger. Not that telling Christopher would be any easier, but Jill thought he might handle it better, with fewer threats and less intimidation.

She went upstairs and called him and left a message on his voice mail. Twenty minutes later, just as she heard Herb Bartlett and his assistant downstairs saying good-bye, Christopher called.

"I'm en route to New York," he said. "Good-bye, L.A."

Jill drew in a shallow breath. "You're en route, as in for good?"

"Yep. I'm in an airplane as we speak. Thirty-some-odd thousand feet over somewhere. The Rockies, maybe. I don't know. It's dark."

"It's dark here, too."

He laughed. "Did you call to tell me that?"

She twirled the cord around her finger. "No. I called to say I'm backing out of the contract. I won't be doing *Good Night, USA*."

He paused a second, then laughed again. "Have you been drinking?"

"This is serious, Christopher. You know about the situation with Ben. Well, now the girl's mother has said she will file a civil suit. There will be no gag order against it, so chances are she'll also sell her story to the tabloids. She thinks she can get away with it, because it will cause a huge scandal because"—she choked on her next words— "because of who I am. If I—we—are just getting back into the spotlight together, the world will jump on it. It will kill the show, and you'll go down as well."

"How much does she want? Whatever it is, I'm sure Addie will pay."

"No, I don't want Addie involved."

"Then I'll pay her, goddammit. This affects my future, too."

She wanted to say it was his own fault. She wanted to remind him that he was the one who'd stayed in touch with Hugh, as if he had possessed her even when she'd married someone else. She wanted to say it was his own fault because she needed so badly to blame someone else.

She stared down at the deacon's bench and remembered the day Ben sat there, the day he told her the news. "I'm out, Christopher. It means Ben and I will no longer be able to afford Herb Bartlett, but we'll work something out. As for the show, I should have known better. I should have left well enough alone."

"Addie will sue you."

"I'm sure she will. But let her know that my house is in my kids' names and Ben's is in his daughter's. There's nothing else she can touch. She's already taken it all."

In the silence, she could hear the gentle hum of the jet engines.

"Are you sure?" he asked.

"I cannot do this to my family," she said. "And I will not do this to my husband. If I weren't who I am, no one would care. By being in the public eye—by returning to the public eye—I can't have a real life, with its flaws and its hurdles. I've forgotten what a miserable place fame creates."

He did not say anything for a minute. "Why do you still want to be with me, Christopher? Can't you see I belong where I am?"

"You belong with me, Jill." He laughed. "You're the first woman who ever walked out on me, did you know that?"

She did not. "But why did you help us get Bartlett? I thought you wanted Ben to be found innocent. You said you wanted me to be happy."

He laughed again. Oh God, he laughed.

"I thought you'd need to know you had the best man on your side. But even Bartlett can't help your husband. He's not innocent, Jill. Wake up and accept that Ben is as guilty as sin. He's a child molester, for chrissake. Get your head out of the clouds."

He clicked off without saying good-bye. Jill held the receiver, the dial tone droning in her ear. Then she looked up to see Ben standing in the door.

"Bartlett's gone," he said.

Jill nodded.

"We don't need him," Ben added.

She nodded again.

"I told him to take the next ferry back to Atlanta."

She broke into a smile. "What the hell are we going to do?"

He approached the bed and flopped down on it. "We're going to be glad that we agree on something. It's time to end the bullshit, honey. Tomorrow I'm going to find Mindy. And I'm going to talk to her."

In the morning, Ben drove out to Menemsha with determination firing his gut. He had no intention of turning this into a confrontation; he only wanted to talk to her.

He only wanted to let her know that this had gotten out of hand. It was Sunday morning, so hopefully Mindy would be home. Unless, of course, Fern had taken up church-going.

He spotted the sign for the turnoff to the cliffs of Gay Head. Noepe would approve of what he was doing: taking charge, taking the risk to be right.

On the way, he'd stopped at Dippin' Donuts for a coffee and a honey-dipped cruller. He'd also bought a dozen doughnut holes to take to Carol Ann's—he might as well stop by there later and give them the resounding news that all hell was going to break loose, or was not. Either way, Ben thought as he drove along State Road, chewing on his cruller and realizing it had been months since food tasted so good, it didn't matter anymore. He and Jill were on the same team now, and they'd get through this on their own.

Or so he thought until he rounded the corner, pulled up to the driveway, and saw the FOR SALE sign.

SurfSide Realty.

Rita Blair.

He stopped the Buick, took off his baseball cap, scratched what was left of his hair, and wondered what the hell was going on. Then he tossed the remnants of his cruller out the window for the gulls, backed up, and made a U-turn. Before he talked to Mindy, before he talked to anyone, he needed to find Rita. And find out why she hadn't stayed the hell out of it, as they had agreed.

It was a leisurely Sunday brunch, with eggs Benedict and waffles with last season's blueberries and fresh whipped cream. The whipped cream had been Hazel's idea. Charlie pleaded for his waistline, but Hazel said it was too late for that, that he was over forty and had already broken one too many rules.

OFF SEASON / 319

They laughed at that and were still laughing when the back doorbell rang. Rita waddled off to see who was interrupting their gourmet Sunday meal.

She wished it had been someone, anyone, other than Ben Niles.

"Rita," he said. That was it, nothing more.

She stood in the doorway, half-shutting the door right in his face. "Now's not a good time, Ben."

He smiled. "No, I think it is."

She closed the door behind her and stepped out onto the steps.

"Why did you put Ashenbach's house on the market? I thought you were going to stay out of it."

"Ben, please. I'm working on something. Charlie's helping. Trust me, okay?"

He wanted to say something flippant like "the last guy who said that to me had me arrested," but the look on Rita's face said this was not the time or the place.

"I'll call you later," she added.

He began to leave, and Rita went inside. But just before she shut the door, and Ben turned around to ask her when she'd call, tonight or tomorrow or next fucking week, he saw Mindy right there at Rita's kitchen table, and sitting next to her was none other than Fern herself.

"After all this, I can't believe Rita has turned against us," Jill said, trying to console Ben, who'd arrived home with anger in his eyes and desolation on his face.

"What's she thinking?" he asked. "Doesn't she know this isn't a game?"

"She knows, honey, she knows." Even while she was fixing tea, Jill wondered why she thought a cup of tea solved everything. "If they're at Rita's for breakfast, she has something on her mind."

He muttered something incoherent about how they

hadn't spoken since Rita and Jill had been back from England, because they'd wanted to give Rita and Charlie time alone, and wasn't that a kick in the ass that they hadn't been alone at all but in the company of the "other side."

"Take off your jacket," Jill said. "Sit down."

He did as he was told, with no resistance.

"I phoned Rick Fitzpatrick," Jill said. "I told him you fired Bartlett. He said he'd stop by later to talk about what we should do next."

Ben dropped his face into his hands. "I feel like I've been betrayed."

"Rita hasn't betrayed us, Ben. We don't know yet what's going on." She fumbled in the pantry, looking for those muffins they'd had yesterday, trying once again to feed that emptiness with calories and fat, wondering if it was beginning again—his isolation, her annoyance, a subsequent urge for her to run.

"I was going to go to Carol Ann's. I was going to warn them that all hell might break loose. I wonder if it already has and someone forgot to tell me."

She plunked a plate of muffins on the table and sat down across from him. "Nothing has broken loose, Ben."

He shook his head. "I can't take it anymore, Jill. I'm going to ask Rick if I should take the plea."

"Plead guilty?" she asked.

"It will be easier. Cleaner. It will get it over with."

She shot up from the stool as if fired from a cannon. "That is the most ridiculous thing I've ever heard," she said. "You will not plead guilty! Not unless I'm dead and buried and not here to stop you from self-destruction. You didn't do anything, Ben! Maybe you made a mistake in judgment, by spending time with her alone. Maybe you made a mistake years ago, when you slept with her unbalanced mother. Or maybe Mindy would have done this anyway because she had a vindictive grandfather who hated everything about you. But as long as I'm alive, you will admit to no such thing, because you are *not guilty*."

She stood still, trying to catch her breath. Ben was staring at her. Then he smiled, stood up, and went to her. He slipped his arms around her. "You're right," he said, "I'm not guilty."

Then he led her from the kitchen and up the stairs, where they, at last, made love.

They stayed in bed and were still there later in the day, when the doorbell rang. Knowing it might be Rick, but hoping it would be Rita with an explanation, Jill insisted on going down to greet their guest.

She might have put on something other than gray sweats and socks if she'd known the guest was Addie Becker.

The first thing Addie did was hold up the first two fingers of both hands. "I come in peace," the agent said. Aside from the shock of seeing her at the door, Jill was startled by how tired the woman appeared: the hair under her angora hat was limp and uncoiffed, her pink cheeks were puffed with water weight, and worry lines streaked across her forehead. "Please, Jill," she said. "It's freezing out."

"I talked to Christopher last night. I have nothing else to say."

"Well, I do."

Jill supposed it was futile, so she let the woman in. Addie swept off her long wool cape and hung it on a peg beside the door, as if she came here every day. She tugged at the high throat of her turtleneck trapeze dress. "Tea would be nice," she said. "Herbal, if you have it." She eyed the wing chair, then the settee, then opted for the wing chair.

"I'll get it," Ben said from the doorway.

Jill sat down.

"Shall we wait for your husband?" Addie asked. "Or does he already know that you're overreacting?"

Jill smiled. "I'm not overreacting, Addie. You don't know the whole story."

"Yes, I do. Christopher told me. Not that he had to. I knew all along that your little story about the teenage boy was crap."

Jill folded her hands and tried not to grimace at the woman who seemed to always know it all. "How did you find out?"

"I have my ways. Besides, I'm smarter than you are. At least, about some things. For example, firing Herb Bartlett was a fairly stupid thing to do."

"We didn't have any choice. The child's mother has threatened a civil suit, which will no doubt come out in the tabloids. She has threatened to use my celebrity to blackmail us. So you see, there would be no *Good Night, USA,* with or without Jill McPhearson. Without the show, we won't have money to pay Herb. Not to mention that when Maurice Fischer got wind of this scandal, he'd cry 'morals clause' anyway."

Ben arrived without the tea. He leaned against the doorway.

Addie picked a piece of lint from her large breast that strained against her dress. "Maurice already knows," she said. "He wants you anyway. Besides, someone once said, 'It doesn't matter what they say about you, as long as they are talking.' I don't know who the hell said it, but they must have been in television."

Jill was stunned. "But he got rid of Lizette. Surely this charge is more controversial than doing drugs."

The one thing Jill had not expected was for Addie to

laugh out loud. "I thought by now you'd have grown up, Jill. I thought by now you'd have realized that television is not about talent. And it's certainly not about morals. It's about one thing, and one thing only: *ratings*. The fact is, your reunion with Christopher will bring in huge numbers in the February book. A little scandal? Well, Maurice is willing to take the chance."

"This isn't so little, Addie. A child is involved."

Addie turned to Ben. "Did you do it?"

"Of course not," he replied.

"Then pay her off."

"We can't. We won't."

She sighed. "Well, if it's money you need, you've got it." She turned back to Jill. "How much did it cost you to get out of our contract?"

Jill blinked, but did not look at Ben, because she'd never told him the full amount. "Over four hundred thousand," she said.

Ben's gasp was gratefully small.

"Well, that was three years ago, and it's worth nearly six now. You were my family, Jill. When you left, I was angry. I wanted to make you hurt. So I took your money. But I invested it for you. Because I always hoped someday you'd come back."

The whistle on the teakettle blew. Jill looked at Ben, and Addie stood up. "Forget the tea," she said. "The money is yours to pay off that woman. If you don't want to do it, then I suggest you use a chunk of it to rehire Herb Bartlett. Either way, *any* way, it's yours. Think about it. In the meantime, I'll be at the Charlotte Inn. Herb is still there, but we're leaving tomorrow at noon. With or without you, there's a show that will go on."

She moved into the hall, swept on her cape, and departed as quickly as she had come.

• • •

"My God, Jill, I had no idea she took you for so much money."

"It looks like she didn't. This is incredible."

They had moved back into the kitchen; she again made tea, because tea could fix everything, including shock and disbelief.

"She's not even using it as leverage to get you to reconsider doing the show."

At first it surprised Jill that Ben thought Addie would be so ruthless. Then again, what else should he think? All Jill had ever done was tell Ben what an ogre she was, a horrible, pushy woman. She'd never once told him how Addie had taken a chance on Jill, how she'd groomed her and paraded her and made sure she was the best she could be, network quality, just as Jill once wanted.

But, no, Ben's opinion of Addie Becker had been formed around the words *witch* and *bitch,* which hadn't been fair.

"Three years ago," Jill said, "I was so angry at her. She was only concerned about what she was losing. She wasn't excited for me that at last I'd found peace and love."

Ben sipped his tea; he made no comment.

"If I take the money, I'd feel like I have to go through with the show."

Ben smiled. "Maybe she's counting on that."

"Would it be so bad?" she asked. "Would you feel as if I were deserting you at your neediest hour?"

"That depends. You'd be gone for Valentine's Day. Are you going to let Mr. Celebrity buy you dinner that night?"

"Not if you send me roses," she said. "Big fat red ones. Three dozen."

"Three dozen?" He whistled. "Looks like you really need to get that money back."

She laughed, marveling at the way Ben could find

lightness in a tense situation. It had been a long time since she'd felt that; it was almost as if the rush of new love was returning.

"If it's all the same to you, I don't want to pay off Fern Ashenbach," she said. "I'd rather use it for Herb Bartlett."

"Well, I can't argue with that. Besides, we may need him even more if Rita's changed sides."

It was something Jill did not want to consider. And yet it was nearly dark now, and Rita still hadn't phoned.

"The bottom line is," he interrupted her thoughts, "it's your money. Your choice."

"No, Ben, it's *our* choice. Just as the decision to go on *Good Night, USA* should have been our choice. I'm still not very good at this business of sharing. I had to make so many decisions alone, struggling as a single mother for so many years."

He leaned forward on his stool and looked into her eyes. "Take your time," he said. "I've got the rest of my life."

Fern Ashenbach looked like she needed a break, or so Rita told her after brunch, when Hazel was in the other room showing Mindy how to knit booties and Charlie had walked down to the tavern to check on the heating system because the Vineyard was being attacked by an unusual deep freeze. And because Amy was still in England.

Rita had handed Fern a dish from the dishpan and hoped she'd finished whining about how cold it had become, and that it was much warmer in the islands where she usually was this time of year.

"I just had an idea," Rita said, which was a lie, because she'd had it yesterday, and it was the reason she'd invited Fern and Mindy there today.

"Charlie has signed the papers for your house, so now there's that infernal waiting period for inspections and title searches and all that. Why don't you use the time to take off for the islands? Go see your friends. Have a little fun."

Fern wiped the dish with the terry towel hand-painted with ducks. "I can't leave right now. Too much to do."

"That's just it!" Rita said. "There's nothing for you to do. It's only red tape now. Red tape and a few weeks. Six to eight, as a rule."

"Six to eight?" Fern groaned and took another dish. "God, the Caribbean season will practically be over by then."

She said "Caribbean" with the emphasis on "Car-ib-be-an," not on "Ca-rib-e-an" like people with class. Rita scrubbed the eggs Benedict pan. "Exactly," she said. "So take advantage of it now."

With thoughtful precision, Fern wiped the plate, making small circles on the front, then on the back, her blue neon fingernails flicking, making this domestic chore seem tedious for a queen such as her.

"Well, it's a good idea, but I can't. There's so much crap in that house, it'll take me a year to clean it out, let alone six to eight weeks."

Rita did not say that it did not matter, because Charlie had not bought the house, but had signed dummy papers in order to string Fern along and create a reason for them to become friends. Rita could not tell the truth so instead she said, "Oh, God, Fern, no one cleans out houses anymore. They have people who do that. They hold estate sales to sell what you don't want, then they take a cut and you're rid of all the headaches. Besides, it's probably a bunch of musty old junk. How long did old Ashenbach live there?"

Fern laughed. "A hundred years? Who knows. I think there's a cellar, but I've never been down in it."

"Yuck," Rita said, snapping off her rubber gloves and draping them over the faucet. "I know a million people who can help out with this stuff. You can take off for a couple of weeks, then I'll call one when you get back. It's perfect."

She shook her head. "Not exactly. I've got a kid in the other room who no longer has a grandfather to stay with." She laughed. "And believe me, if I go to the islands, one thing I don't need is a kid tagging along."

Rita hated that Fern acted as if Mindy were an obstacle in her life. For all the craziness in which Hazel had raised Rita, Rita had never once felt unloved. Which could be why she'd never had to make up stories to get attention.

She dried her hands and did not dare ask Fern what she intended to do with the "kid" once the house was sold and the trial was over. "Well, I could use some help around here," Rita said softly.

It took Fern a minute, but finally she got it. "What?"

Rita shrugged. "I'm almost seven months pregnant and fatter than a cow. There are things to do around here that I can't manage myself. My mother's too old, and Charlie is a man. Need I say more?" She plunked a bowl of leftover blueberries into the refrigerator.

"Doing what?" Fern asked. "Like laundry and dusting?"

"Sure." She tried to act not overly pushy, as if she could take or leave Mindy.

"For a couple of weeks?"

"As long as you like. I'm sure it wouldn't be a problem for her to take the school bus from here. We're a little cramped, but Charlie could fix up the den for her bedroom." Which, on account of the twins coming, meant Charlie would have to move into her room.

"Well, hell, honey," Fern said, tossing the dish towel down on the table, "you might just have yourself a deal."

She whooped. "Aruba here I come!" She headed into the living room. "Melinda!" she shrieked. "How would you like to stay with these nice people a spell?"

Rita leaned against the sink, folded her arms, and wondered what Charlie Rollins was going to think about sleeping in her bed.

Chapter 30

Ben had kissed Jill good-bye and sent her off to New York with confidence that she would return—to what he did not know, but she would return, nonetheless.

In the meantime, he got on with his life.

On the first Tuesday of February, he awoke before dawn and headed to the town hall to stand in line for one of the two building permits that they needed for Sea Grove.

If he got one permit now, and one in March, they would be ready to start building about the time the spring thaw was ready to let them.

He had not heard from Rita, nor spoken with Charlie. But Jill advised him to forget it, to trust that both of them knew what they were doing and would reemerge when they were ready. She had also reminded him that at least Charlie and Rita were finally together, as if that excused it all.

Which was partly why Ben trudged through the early morning now, so that Rita and Charlie wouldn't have to be bothered.

He was also trying to keep himself busy, to stay positive, focused on the future, as if there were no chance he'd be seeing the future from behind bars. April, of course, was only weeks away now.

As Ben turned down the next street, he could see that the line at the town hall had already formed, like a line at a convenience store when the Megabucks jackpot reached heady heights. He sighed, glad he had all his paperwork in order, hoping he'd be lucky enough to receive one of the coveted permits on this crisp February morning.

He stepped into line behind a tall, wide-shouldered man he recognized from town meetings but whose name he couldn't recall. The man turned around.

"Morning," he said, his chilly breath crystallizing in the air.

"Morning," Ben responded.

The man turned back and faced the building, his New England salutation over and done. Ben leaned back on his heels and glanced at his watch. In only minutes, a few others had lined up behind him.

They stood and waited. Every so often someone greeted someone else; every so often a few words were exchanged. But all were there on business—this was not a social event.

Dawn arrived slowly, and a great tiredness seemed to crawl through the crowd. One after another, they sat down on blankets that they'd spread on the ground. When the big man in front of Ben sat down, Ben idly scanned the line up ahead.

Then he did a double-take, not once but twice.

He squinted; he blinked.

Half a dozen people in front of him, wrapped in a plaid wool blanket, was a red-headed woman who looked very pregnant. Next to her was Charlie. And standing between them, laughing and smiling, holding a tube in which were undoubtedly the building plans for Sea Grove—the plans he'd drawn up—was Mindy Ashenbach.

· · ·

Ben didn't get the permit. He didn't stick around long enough.

Instead, he steamed all the way home, muttering obscenities about trust and friendship and wasn't it nice that Rita and Charlie had taken Ben's accuser into their fold.

His accuser: A ten-year-old, obviously highly manipulative *little girl*.

Had Mindy convinced Rita and Charlie that he'd touched her breast, the way she'd convinced her grandfather and police and the court?

Storming into the house, he slammed the door behind him and let out a scream that could have been heard up in Boston if the wind had been coming up off Nantucket. Then he stomped down the hall to the phone, picked up the receiver, and placed a call to the Plaza to *Ms*. Niles's suite.

"I know, honey, I woke you. I'm sorry." He paced as far as he could until the phone cord pulled him back. Then he paced in the other direction, into the kitchen and back again.

"That's okay," Jill mumbled. "What's wrong?"

"Nothing. No one, anyway. Everyone's fine. Except for me." He told her of the trio he'd just seen at the town hall. "I'm furious, Jill. What the hell's going on? What are they trying to do—put me away for life?"

"Ben, honey, calm down. Rita and Charlie can't put you away for life."

"That's not how it feels."

"Well, think about it. Intellectually."

"I can't. I'm too pissed."

"I'd offer to call Rita, but I think it would be a mistake." Her voice was clearer now, as if she were fully awake.

"No. I'll call her. I'm sorry for waking you."

"Don't be sorry, Ben. I can understand why you're upset."

He stopped pacing and closed his eyes. "I just don't get it, Jill. The last thing Rita said to me was 'trust me.' How can I do that?"

Jill was quiet a moment, then she said, "Well, she's never let either one of us down, Ben. Maybe we both need to remember that."

She was right. Damn, she was right.

"Yeah. I guess. Hey, how was your night? I saw the show. You were beautiful. Did Edwards try to attack you?"

"Yes. But I told him you'd string him up by the caps on his front teeth."

He laughed a small laugh, but a laugh, nonetheless.

"Everything's fine here, honey," she said. "Now make yourself some coffee and try to relax. Why don't you work on the plans for the netting shed today?"

"Thanks for the effort, but stop trying to distract me," he said. "I'll figure this out. I'll call Rita right now and get it over with."

"No, Ben," Jill said firmly. "Let it go. I've known her forever, and if there's one thing I've learned, it's to give her space. She'll come around in her own time, on her own terms." She paused for a second, then added, "As most of us do."

Rita didn't have any real video games, but she had this cool thing called Pac-Man that you plugged into the TV and made it eat up the screen. Well, not really, but it was better than nothing. Rita also had some old videos from the 1970s, way before Mindy was born, when people dressed funny and wore their hair long and straight, even boys.

Rita's mother, Hazel, was nice, too. She helped Mindy learn how to make a knit and a purl and said she reminded her of Rita Mae when Rita Mae was a girl.

At night, over dinner, Charlie told real funny stories about old island fishermen and how they hid treasures in the secret room at the tavern. One time they even brought her there so she could see the tavern for herself.

And every night Rita tucked her in bed, kissed her forehead, and said "Sweet dreams." Nobody had ever done that before, and at first it felt stupid, but now she kind of liked it. She wondered if this was how real families lived.

"Are you happy here, Mindy?" Dr. Reynolds asked in mid-February, when she'd been at Rita's for two weeks.

"It's better than home," she told the doctor as they walked toward the lighthouse.

"In what way?"

"Lots of ways. Rita's a good cook."

"What about Charlie?"

Mindy rolled her eyes. She hoped the doctor wasn't trying to talk about sex again. "He makes me laugh. And Hazel thinks that soon I'll be able to make a pair of booties myself. Rita will need lots because she's having two babies." She sat down on the edge of the walkway that led to the lighthouse. The air was crisp, but the sun was shining. She shielded her eyes against the sharp glare off the water. "My mother's in Caracas."

"Venezuela?" The doctor crouched beside her and picked up a shell.

"Yeah. She met some friends in Aruba, and they took someone's yacht over there."

"Do you think she'll be home soon?"

"No," Mindy replied, lowering her head and scuffing her feet in the sand. "I don't care."

The doctor was quiet, then asked, "This is a beautiful shell, isn't it?"

She was surprised the doctor didn't say something else about her mother. She usually liked it when Mindy talked about her. Mindy glanced at the fanned white shell. "Scallop shell," she announced, because she knew all of them.

"In a way, it's sad," the doctor said. "If it weren't for the scallop, this beautiful shell wouldn't exist. But the rest of us in the world rarely get to see it until the scallop is gone, until the shell is left alone on the beach."

"Wampum," Mindy said.

"What?"

"Wampum. It's the purple and white pieces of clamshells the Indians once used for money. Ben used to say the shell was real valuable, not when it was all together, but when it was in parts. Except to the clam."

"Ben Niles?"

"Well. Yes."

Dr. Reynolds set the shell back down on the sand. "Do you miss him?" she asked. "He was your friend."

Mindy shrugged. She lowered her eyes to the small low-tide wave that licked the piling at the end of the pier. "He'll never speak to me again," she said. "It doesn't matter. My mother will come back and get me, and I'll be gone away soon."

"Is that what you want?"

She didn't reply.

"When will you go?"

"My mother said not until our affairs are in order, so I'm not sure what that means. By the end of the school year, I guess."

"By then Mr. Niles might be in jail."

That ripply feeling came into her stomach. "My mother said he won't go to jail. But she said once he's convicted, she's going to sue him, and we'll get the cash she deserves for everything he's done."

"What's he done, Mindy?"

She shrugged again. "I don't know," she said. "Nothing."

"Do you think it's time to tell someone that?"

Mindy didn't answer. She simply stood up, brushed the sand from herself, and said it was time to go home.

Rita stood at the kitchen sink, where she hadn't spent this much time since Kyle was alive.

She would have thought it would make her nuts: her mother in the other room knitting booties as if Rita were having octuplets not twins; Charlie fussing out in the garage, building birdhouses, for God's sake, happy as a clam because he now had a garage to mess around in. He also had a woman to sleep with—she had a feeling he was happy as a clam about that, too.

And now, cutting across the backyard were Mindy and Dr. Reynolds. Mindy was sort of skipping, as if she were happy to be home, back at this domestic palace, where the very pregnant woman who stood at the sink must have completely lost her undomesticated mind. The woman who had once connived to get as close to Mindy as she could hadn't counted on becoming so damn attached to her, hadn't counted on caring so damn much.

Rita shook her head and opened the back door to let Mindy inside.

"Hot chocolate on the stove," she said.

Closing the door behind the girl, Rita went outside to walk Dr. Reynolds to her old Volvo.

"How's it going?" she asked the doctor.

"Fine."

"Is Mindy okay? Is she happy here?"

The doctor smiled. "She's fine."

They reached the car, and the doctor opened the door. Rita put her hand on the window to stop her. "Wait. There's something I need to ask you."

The doctor waited. Rita put her hands in the large pouch-pocket at the front of her sweatshirt. "I know you can't tell me anything about Mindy's . . . well, about her state of mind. Nothing important, anyway. But I'm only using my instinct here when I say I'm trying to be the poor kid's friend. See, I think this whole trial thing is a big fat lie, and I think Ben Niles didn't do anything, but I think Mindy's in too deep and too scared to say otherwise. It seems to me that if she has some kind of stability, maybe she'll tell the truth as it really happened." She shrugged. "Hell, the way I figure it, even if I'm wrong, at least Mindy will know someone cares about her."

The doctor, of course, would not say anything concrete. But she did wink at Rita and say, "Keep doing what you're doing. Just please don't disappoint her."

Rita wasn't a hundred percent sure what the woman meant, but she figured that was her way of saying she was on the right track.

Jill had no idea how she was able to stay on track, how she could tune out what was really going on in her mind and sit next to that ass she'd almost married every night on the set—the coveted, long-awaited *network* set—and act as if she were the most together woman on planet Earth, seated next to the most together man.

She had no idea how she'd sobbed all afternoon on Valentine's Day when Ben's three dozen red roses arrived, yet managed to smile and look clear-eyed by evening.

Nor did she know how she went to bed every evening in her Plaza suite and did not die from the loneliness of the empty other side of the bed. She tried not to obsess about what she would do if this was what would happen night after night for months and then years if Ben were convicted, if Ben went to jail.

Jill could have gone home on weekends—Ben, of course, could not leave the island to come here—but there were stories to plan and mail to weed through and she'd decided it was better to stay and get through it, all of it.

She had no idea how she did it, but Addie said it was because she was a pro, that Addie had known it all along, even if Jill herself had not.

And though Jill hated to admit it, it was great to be back to work, real work, not freelance stringer stuff that made her feel as if she'd been demoted back to her apprentice-reporter days. Surprisingly, her fan mail was arriving in much greater abundance that Christopher's—a fact Addie cheered as if the letters had been written to her, even though Christopher had been her client long before Jill had been. But Addie told her she'd always known he was an overblown jerk.

"I wonder how many people would write if they knew about Ben," Jill said, sifting through the latest mailbag, when the month of February had almost finished its cold, lonely penance, when the only heat in New York came from the fired-up ratings, and when the only warmth in Jill's heart came from knowing that soon she'd be home. For better or for worse.

"That reminds me," Addie said. "Have you talked with your husband today?"

"Not yet. He usually calls after lunch. Why?"

Addie just smiled.

On the morning of the fourth day of the last week that Jill was gone, Rick Fitzpatrick called Ben. Ben had been killing time repainting the sewing room, because he was close to jumping out of his skin, an old saying he'd never fully understood until these recent months.

"Hey, Rick," he said, grateful for the interruption.

"Bartlett called," the attorney said quickly. "They've come up with something you might be interested in."

Ben said a quick prayer but steeled himself against disappointment.

"There's a technique he wants to try that's been used a

few times. He'll have to get the judge to approve it, but he wants to take Mindy back to the scene of the alleged crime."

Ben loved the way Rick said "alleged," as if always conscious he was speaking with the defendant, his paying client. "What good will that do?"

"The attorneys will go. And the judge. And the jury. Mindy will have to reenact exactly what happened."

Ben wasn't sure what he thought about that.

"It's a great idea, Ben. It will really put her to the test."

"Jesus, Rick, she's just a kid."

"Do I have to remind you your life is in her hands?"

"But I thought she wouldn't have to even show up at the trial. I thought that was what her video deposition was all about."

"I thought so, too, but I was wrong. Bartlett said that by going to a jury trial, we have the right to cross-examine her."

So Mindy was going to take the stand. It did not escape Ben that Rick had not known that, but Bartlett had. One point for the high price tag, he supposed.

He sighed. "Does she know?"

"I have no idea." Rick paused, as if he were unsure what to say next, as if he had not expected Ben to be quite so . . . underwhelmed. "These are positive things for your case, Ben. It's good news."

"Oh," Ben replied. But as he envisioned Mindy sitting in a witness chair, he felt sorry for her, whether anyone liked it or not.

"There's something else," Rick added. "Bartlett is going to bring in experts who will testify that Mindy clearly was not traumatized."

"How do they know? They've never met her."

"They've seen her deposition."

"Oh" was all he could say again.

"Ben?" Rick asked. "I know Herb Bartlett can spin

circles around me in the courtroom, but I need to know that you're okay with all of this."

"No," Ben laughed, "I'm not okay with any of it. But I don't have a lot of choice."

Rick paused, then said, "I'm not an expert like Bartlett, but I've done some homework." He sighed. "A guy I spoke with in the Midwest went to jail for two years because he insisted on going to trial and refused to take a plea."

"Because he was innocent?"

"It looks that way. It was one of those nasty divorce cases. No evidence. His word against hers."

The words reverberated in Ben's mind. "But he's out now," he said, "and he survived."

"Yeah," Rick said, "but he said it wasn't worth two years to stand on principle."

Ben scraped a bit of paint that had dried on his hand.

"Another man—this one in Florida—was given life. No penetration. No physical evidence. No previous complaints." He did not have to add that it was his word against the girl's.

"Why are you telling me this, Rick?"

"Because I want to be sure you understand what you may be up against. If you plead guilty, at the worst you will get house arrest."

Ben nodded. "I know that. And I also know I didn't do anything, and I'm not going to say I did. But thanks for the news," he said, then added, "I guess." He said good-bye and went back to the sewing room, promising himself that if the phone rang again, he was not going to answer it because he'd had all the good news he could take for one day.

Chapter 31

The night of Jill's final appearance on *Good Night, USA,* Maurice Fischer waited in the wings like a groupie in awe, not a media mogul in charge. As the credits rolled and the lights criss-crossed the set, he looked as if he were about to dance onto the stage and toss flower bouquets at the anchor desk.

Instead, he ignored Christopher, gave Jill a two thumbs-up, and invited her to supper at his penthouse uptown. A thanks-for-the-good-work party, she deduced.

As Jill stood at the wall of windows overlooking the treetops of Central Park and gazed at the imposing Manhattan skyline to the south, she wondered what it must be like to wake up each morning and have this for a view, fifty-three flights above the rest of the world. Perhaps when one reached these heights, both physical and spiritual, one simply did not notice the little people below.

"On a clear night you can see the Vineyard from here," Maurice said, handing Jill a flute of Cristal.

"Oh, yes," Jill replied. "I think I can see my husband. He's doing the laundry."

Maurice raised his glass in a toast. "To laundry and other necessities of life," he said.

Jill smiled and took a sip.

"Speaking of necessities," he said, "you know the importance of ratings. Last week's ratings for *Good Night, USA* blew every other show—network and otherwise—out of the time slot."

Yes, Jill nodded. She knew.

"It's because of you, Jill," Maurice continued. Then he smiled. "I want more of the same, and you can deliver."

She lowered her eyes to her champagne and lightly turned the glass, gently swirling its contents. "I'm glad you were pleased," she said.

"Pleased, yes. And as I said, I want more."

She smiled. "I heard you. But I've fulfilled my commitment. The month of February. Sweeps."

He raised an old eyebrow. "God, woman, aren't we paying you enough?"

"What are you talking about, Maurice? Do you want me to sign for the duration?"

"You could do worse for your career."

"I'm sure. But I live on the Vineyard."

"It's not as if I'm asking you to commute from L.A. We're in New York now. Permanently."

She knew, of course that nothing in television was permanent.

"I don't want to commute from New York, either."

He raised his glass once again. "Thirty thousand," he said.

In spite of herself, Jill blinked. "What?"

"Thirty thousand a week. Thirty-nine weeks a year. That comes to a little less than one point two million."

She stopped herself from reminding him that *Good Night, USA* was only an entertainment show wrapped up as a news magazine. That it was not network news and not even prime time, but early fringe, stuck in the seven-to-eight time slot of reruns of reruns and bell-clanging game shows. "That's a lot of money, Maurice."

"You're worth it."

She moved from his aura and turned back to the window. Her mother, Florence Randall, had been born here in the city, to wealth and prominence, but she had married a tavern owner who lived on the Vineyard. Florence had sacrificed her socialite's position for the man she loved—and she had lived out her days in misery on an island, cut off from the world.

But of course, Jill was not Florence, and for one point two million a year, she could practically buy a damn airplane and a damn pilot and fly back and forth whenever she wanted.

If that's what she wanted. If Ben would agree.

Ben.

"What about my husband?" she asked, her eyes still fixed on the view. "I may be worth nothing if this scandal breaks. If he is convicted."

"If he is convicted, we'll deal with it then."

She sipped her champagne and thought of her options. One point two million a year was certainly more attractive than the unknown. But was *Good Night, USA* what she really wanted? To sit next to Christopher every weeknight from now until the show was canceled because, sooner or later, they all were? And was the veiled entertainment really where her work, her passion lay?

She closed her eyes and knew the answers to all three questions.

"No," she said. She turned back to Maurice. "I appreciate the offer, Maurice, honestly I do. And as important as my home is to me, so is the work I do every day. *Good Night, USA* is not really me. It's frilly and glamorous. I want something more meaningful."

Just then a waiter appeared and announced that their supper was being served in the dining room.

Maurice finished his champagne and held out his arm

to Jill. "Well, I have from the squash soup through the tiramisu to change your mind."

The food was delicious, but her mind went unchanged. It was too close to April to make such a life-altering move.

Ben wondered if they were all going to hold their breaths until spring. Jill returned home and spent only a little time at her studio and more at home, helping him redecorate the sewing room, then move on to the kitchen. Carol Ann came by two or three nights a week, which increased to four or five as April drew nearer. Amy and Jeff called from England; Amy assured Jill she'd be back in time for the trial, and in time for tourist season. Even Addie Becker checked in regularly to see if all was okay, if there were any new developments.

He was glad for their support, grateful that they cared, but he would have been happier if they'd stop talking in whispers, even to him, as if someone had died—which, as yet, he had not.

The mystery, of course, was what had happened to Rita and Charlie. He knew he should call them or go over there. But Jill kept reminding him that trust was important to Rita. He wondered—but did not ask—if it was simply easier for Jill not to have to see Rita, and if she secretly regretted confiding to her about Fern in the first place.

"What about Sea Grove?" he'd complained one night well into March. "Rita and Charlie are my business partners, remember? We're supposed to break ground soon. I don't even know if they got the last of the permits."

Against the renowned island stubbornness he'd developed over the years as if he'd actually been born there, Jill had effectively shushed him.

So he waited. And he trusted. And on the last day of

March, nine days before trial, Rita Blair showed up at their door at eight-thirty at night.

She looked like she was having quadruplets, not twins, and she was about to have them right there on the steps.

"Ben?" she asked. Jill was out shopping; but it was better this way, just Rita and him. "I only have a minute. May I come in?"

They went into the music room, where he'd been sitting in front of a fire, because though it was nearly April, it was damp and chilly in the house.

He supposed he should offer her something, coffee or tea, but he did not.

"Sorry I didn't get back to you sooner," Rita said, awkwardly placing herself on a chair.

Ben warmed his hands by the fire and wondered if he should help her sit down and if she'd be able to get up again.

"Yeah," he said, "I kind of wondered what happened."

She looked around. "Is Jill home?"

He shook his head.

"Oh. Well." She lifted her chin. "Hey, I saw her on *Good Night, USA.*"

Ben supposed Rita already knew Jill had done it for the money, so they could hire Herb Bartlett to defend him against the little girl whom Rita had befriended.

"How's Charlie?" he asked.

"Fine."

"And your mother?"

"Hazel's fine, too."

He picked up the poker and stuck it into the fireplace. A couple of sparks ignited into small orange flames. "What about you?" he asked. "You doin' okay?"

She didn't answer right away, then sighed. "I have some bad news," she said.

"Oh," he said. "Well."

She started to play with the buttons of her jacket.

Fidgeting was the word for what she was doing. For some reason he remembered a grammar school teacher, God only knew how long ago, telling him to stop fidgeting and pay attention in class. "Benjamin Niles! Stop fidgeting!" he could still hear her shriek. He wondered if any of Rita's teachers had said the same thing to her.

"I didn't tell you what I've been doing because I didn't think you'd approve."

"Spending time with Mindy Ashenbach?"

She hesitated only a second, caught off guard. "Ben, you yourself said Mindy's an unhappy child. The way I figure it is, kids are unhappy if they don't receive love. Well, I've got plenty of that to go around right now, what with these hormones and all."

If she was trying to make a joke, he was too tired to laugh.

"Anyway, I figured if she got some much-needed love and a lot of attention, maybe she'd end up telling the truth. Maybe I could find some goodness beneath her frightened exterior, and she'd realize that what she'd done—what she was doing—was wrong. So I befriended Fern Ashenbach. Then I convinced her to take off for the islands. Mindy has been living with Charlie and me since the beginning of February. And Hazel, too. So far, though, Mindy hasn't admitted anything."

Ben sat down. "Why do I sense a *but* coming?"

Rita tried to sit forward as if to make a point, but her big belly stopped her and she slid back again. "But I thought she was going to. The other day, she asked me how long it was until the trial. It's the first time she acknowledged that I must know about it."

Tenting his fingers, Ben looked at the firelight glinting off his wedding band. Jill had said *trust her,* and so he was trying. "So what's the bad news?"

"Originally Fern was going to be gone a couple of weeks. Then she ended up in Caracas. Anyway, she came back this morning. She thinks I sold Ashenbach's house to Charlie, which I only did to get close to her." Rita waved her hand as if that didn't matter. "She said she needs the house closing soon because she's running out of money. That's when she told me about the trial. About Mindy's accusation. About how she tried to get you to pay; about how you refused even though she'd slept with you in your 'hour of need,' was how she put it."

Ben stood up then and put another log on the fire, so he wouldn't become sick. "None of this is news to either one of us, Rita."

"You're right," she agreed. "But there's more. She said she needs the money from the house to tide her over until the civil trial."

Ben sighed. "So she's going to go through with it."

"She's desperate for money, Ben. She's sure she'll win the civil suit because she's convinced there will be a conviction in the criminal trial."

Picking up the poker, he attacked the flames. "Did she mention that she's going to the tabloids? That with the civil trial, she's finagling a way to bypass the gag order and sell her daughter's story—her daughter's lie—to the *National Exposé*? And what makes her so all-fired sure they'll convict me? I thought she knew Herb Bartlett was my attorney."

A thin line of sweat formed on Rita's brow. "She's sure there will be a conviction because she's going to take the stand." Rita stared into the fire and took a long breath. "She's going to tell the court that this wasn't the first time you touched Mindy. She's going to say that when you and she were lovers, when Mindy was three, she caught you touching her then."

The world seemed to stop, seemed to stand still in that motionless, weightless, timeless space he remembered from the night he was arrested.

He set the poker back in its stand. He covered his eyes

with his hand. He wondered why it was that he hadn't yet died.

"Now," Rita said, struggling to get up again, "I hate to give you bad news and run, but apparently it's time for me to get to the hospital. Can you give me a lift?"

It was eerily like the night Kyle had died. Ben had left Jill a note and she met them at the hospital, then Charlie did, too, and the three of them stood, waiting for nature to do as it needed. This time they should have been happy. But Ben was still in shock, and Jill sensed something was wrong, and Charlie was too nervous, so none of them shared the excitement that there should have been.

Nor had Jill shared these last weeks of Rita's pregnancy and for that Jill felt sad and a little bit guilty. Then she reminded herself that what counted was that she and Rita always—always—had been there for each other when it truly mattered—like the night Kyle died, like when Jill fled to England, like . . . now.

So Jill and Rita and Ben and Charlie didn't speak much, but they waited together, Jill holding one of Rita's hands, Charlie holding the other.

At just past midnight, their sorrow lifted, their moods escalated in an instant: two healthy, screaming babies arrived, a boy and a girl, both with red hair, and, Rita proclaimed, both looking exactly like Kyle. Her Kyle. Their Kyle.

Ben and Jill hugged her and hugged Charlie and shared tears of raw, pent-up emotion. Then they left the hospital before Hazel could get there with Mindy, for all they knew.

As soon as they got home, Ben told Jill of Rita's visit, and what Fern said she planned to do.

Jill bolted toward the door. Ben grabbed her arm.

"Stop!" he pleaded. "Please, honey. Stop."

But she could not, because until that moment Jill had never known what rage was, not pure, primal, hateful rage.

She ripped her arm away from Ben and stormed outside to her car. Without looking right, left or behind, she peeled out onto North Water Street, punched down on the accelerator, and lit out for Menemsha.

She banged on Fern Ashenbach's front door with both fists. The glass shook but did not break, though she kept banging until the door was opened, not by Fern but by her daughter.

Jill caught her breath: the child stood there in her pajamas and old, bedraggled slippers. Then she remembered why she'd come.

"I want to see your mother," Jill managed to say.

"Who is it?" came a voice from behind the child. The sound of the shrill voice sent sharp anger down Jill's spine.

Mindy had the sense to leave and go upstairs. She did, however, leave the front door open.

Jill stepped inside.

And then Fern Ashenbach was there, her hair askew, a snarl on her face, a stink coming from her body that smelled an awful lot like gin. Jill stepped back.

"You won't get away with this," Jill screamed. "You won't get away with destroying my husband."

Fern laughed. "Hello to you, too."

Jill planted her hands on her hips. "You won't get away with it, Fern. No one will believe you. Too many people know Ben. Too many people know him better."

Fern leaned forward, inches from Jill's face. "Excuse me, Miss America, but your husband molested a little girl. Why the hell are you protecting him?"

"*My husband did nothing of the sort*. And if he did—as we've learned you're going to say—do such a thing years ago too, then why the hell did you abandon her? Why the hell did you allow her to be raised by her grandfather, who lived next door to where Ben was going to work? Why, if you were so all-fired concerned about Mindy's welfare, didn't you do something about it then and not years later, when you just happen to need money?"

Fern raised her arm and threw a closed-fisted punch that led with a grotesque imitation diamond jutting from her finger.

Jill's hand flew to her face. The sting was unbelievable. The blood that gushed was even greater.

"Get out of here, bitch, before I kill you!" Fern demanded.

Just as Jill reached in to grab Fern's hair, a hand came up from behind her. "*All right, ladies,*" a man's voice said. "*That's enough.*"

Jill was escorted from the property and driven to the hospital by none other than Hugh Talbot, who had a nerve as far as she was concerned.

"You told Christopher," she accused him in the cruiser. "You broke the judge's gag order and called Christopher. You should go to jail."

He shook his head. "I told your friend before the judge issued any order. Even before Ben was arrested. It was a mistake. I was wrong."

Jill clutched a cloth against her face, which did not want to stop bleeding.

"I'm sorry, Ms. Niles," Hugh said as they arrived at the emergency room.

She was stitched up and had a chance to peek in on Rita once again, then called Ben to come and get her. It was Ben, of course, who'd called Talbot and warned him that Jill was headed for Menemsha. It was Ben who made certain Talbot ruined all her fun.

Rita shrieked when Jill walked in, a bandage from the corner of her eye down to her lip.

Then she said she was sorry she'd missed the show-down, and offered Jill a baby to hold to help ease her pain.

For another hour, Jill and Rita sat together, each holding one of Rita's babies, friends trusting friends.

Chapter 32

 The morning of April the ninth was sunny and cool and more like early June than the end of winter, not like a day that could start the end of all things good in Ben's life.

It was too nice a day to spend in court waiting to be humiliated in front of the world.

In the small courtroom that appeared to have been filled with furniture from a secondhand shop, Ben was proud that his wife was a symbol of beauty—inside and out. Under other circumstances, he might have chastised himself for thinking such a shallow thought, but she was wearing the pashmina wrap that he'd bought in New York—and the black and blue badge of courage, from her eye to her lip.

From the table where he sat—flanked by Rick and Herb Bartlett—he turned around and smiled at her. Amy was beside her with Jeff and Jeff's roommate Mick, who had just graduated from Oxford and was holding Amy's hand.

And God, there was Carol Ann. And John. Jesus, his son-in-law had come. Apparently a "closed proceeding" did not exempt family.

Or Sheriff Hugh Talbot, who sat on the opposite side.

Earlier Ben had seen the beefy D.A. along with Mister Rogers, the cardigan-clad man who perhaps was there, like Rick, as the island representative, deferring to the seasoned pros.

He did not let his eyes drift to the table where Mindy sat, undoubtedly accompanied by Fern, the concerned mother who'd been away for two months.

The judge arrived with little fanfare.

Ben shifted on the hard wooden chair, and the proceedings began.

The reading of the charges.

"How does the defendant plead?"

"Not guilty, your honor."

One motion accepted. One motion denied. Ben tried to pretend that he was watching television, that this was fiction, not fact, and that the life involved was not his own.

"Before we call the defendant to the stand, the defense has a special request." Herb Bartlett was on his feet, wearing a modest suit, as if he knew not to wear his city-slicker, big-shot Atlanta clothes in a courtroom on the Vineyard.

He asked the judge if Mindy could be brought to the scene to reenact what had happened.

Highly unusual, the judge called the request.

Herb soft-shoed his words, citing this case and that. It had been proven, he explained, that even after only a short period of time, a child—or adult, for that matter—who weaves a story becomes able to not only believe the story, but to embellish it with new memory they unknowingly created.

The judge listened. Then, under the objection of the prosecution, she allowed Bartlett's special request.

They went during the lunch break.

· · ·

Mindy did not want to get out of the truck.

She sat on the worn seat of Grandpa's old pickup and looked at Menemsha House. It looked different close-up than from her bedroom window; it seemed smaller, lonelier, not quite as scary.

Had it been that long since Grandpa had grumbled at the old yellow school buses that rumbled up and down the hill? The buses that carried laughing schoolkids to and from the fun at the museum Ben made for them?

Had it been because of her that Grandpa's grumbling had stopped? And the children's laughter, too?

She tried not to think about it, but the memories came back, Kodak moments floating in her brain, of tying straw brooms and pegboarding floors and being in charge of making sure the kids swept up when they were done, being in charge because Ben said he needed her because she was so smart and because he could trust her more than the others, even the boys.

She was too far away to be able to read the sign on the door. But Mindy knew it must read "Closed Until Further Notice."

Was there a line underneath that said, "If you want to know why, ask Mindy Ashenbach"?

"Melinda," her mother said from outside now, where she'd walked around to the passenger door, "you have to come outside."

She stared past her mother, who did not seem unhappy to be on center stage, as Grandpa would have called it.

And then Mindy saw Ben, who stood with his head down like he was examining the ants on the ground. Next to him was his beautiful wife who wore a beautiful blue shawl. Did Ben have a lump in his stomach, as she did? Did his beautiful wife have one, too?

Did they too notice that nobody was talking?

Then Fern spoke up.

"She won't get out of the goddamn truck," her mother told everyone.

Mindy felt that too-familiar tremble begin in her belly. She sucked it in; she held it back.

Her mother yanked open the passenger door. Mindy stared at her and wished her mother were dead. Or at least on some other island.

"Mindy?" It was the judge's voice. The judge was crossing the lawn, headed for the truck.

Mindy closed her eyes and wished that instead of her mother, it was she who was dead. Or that she'd never been born in the first place.

For Ben, it was chilling to stand on top of the hill overlooking the bay, on the lawn of the place where he had once had a dream, back when he believed in dreams.

They had moved up to the back porch. The onlookers—the family—were relegated to the driveway.

He handed the bailiff the key to the door, which had not been opened in months.

And then Mindy was in his line of sight, and he could not look away. Fern had dressed her in a dress, for God's sake, a pink dress that made her look like she was going to a kids' birthday party, kids who were much younger than ten. Or eleven, if that's how old Mindy was now.

To Fern, maybe this was a party.

"I went into the office, behind the big room where the kids learned to make pegboarded floors."

The sound of Mindy's small voice startled him. He tried hard to swallow, but he could not.

They went inside.

His lungs filled with dust—carpenters' dust, dust-in-the-air dust. He tried to clear his throat.

They moved into the office behind the big room. He looked up to the transom where it had all happened, where Mindy had jumped down on him in her childish game. He closed his eyes. He wanted to cry.

"What happened once you were in here?" the judge asked her now.

"Well," she said, "well."

Why was she stuttering?

He opened his eyes. When he blinked, she was looking right at him.

She folded her arms around her waist. She lowered her eyes to the floor.

"Mindy?" the judge asked. "Do you remember what you said on your video deposition?"

He wanted Herb to leap forward and shout "Leading the witness!" But they weren't in the courtroom, so maybe it was different.

Then Mindy began to cry. Her body quivered in that slow-motion motion that Ben knew so well. She bit her lip, but the quivering did not stop. Then the tears flowed down her young cheeks, onto her dress, onto the dust on the floor.

She ran from the room, out the front door, and raced down the hill.

Ben found her at the Gay Head cliffs. She'd fled to her house, grabbed her bike, and must have pedaled like hell to get out of sight.

But there she sat, her pink dress all dirty, her knees pulled up, her hands clasped around them. She was looking out to the sea. And despite the sun, she was shivering.

He watched her a moment. He thought of Noepe and prayed that his old friend would help him out once again, that he would give him a few words of wisdom to help this child in pain. Then he crossed the cliff and sat down next to her.

"I see one that looks like a canoe," he said, following her gaze past the clay cliffs and up to the puffy white clouds in the sky over Cuttyhunk. "Birchbark, I think."

She sniffed a little. She hugged herself tighter. "It's probably worthless," her small voice replied with a crack. "But maybe we should buy it, then set up a souvenir shop and sell it with other junk to the tourists." She lowered her head. Her tears fell again.

"I miss my grandpa," she said quietly. "It's because of him, you know. Well, it wasn't his fault, really. It just sort of happened."

And then she told Ben the story of how it all happened, how she was angry, how she made a mistake and told her grandfather what she thought he wanted to hear, how she never meant it to go this far but that once it had started she did not know how to stop it, especially when Grandpa died and her mother showed up and told her not to rock the boat to their future.

When she was finished Mindy said, "I'm sorry."

He had not interrupted her because he was too choked up to speak. But now, as he looked at the frail child, clothed in a dress that didn't at all suit her, Ben felt nothing but compassion. "Child molestation is a terrible thing. Do you understand that, Mindy?"

She nodded.

"And it happens too often. And it makes people scared."

She nodded again. "I guess I'm lucky," she said, "that it didn't happen to me."

Ben put his arm around her. She hesitated at first, then moved closer beside him.

Epilogue

Charlie opened the tavern, and they had a damn party.

Amy was there, organizing everyone, Hazel included, who claimed she was most upset that she'd not been told of the arrest or the charges or the trial, but what the hell, a party was a party. Amy announced that she was home for good, that she absolutely intended—someday—to buy the tavern from Charlie, and that, by the way, Mick would be sticking around. Jeff moaned that he'd have to find another roommate and that Mick would hate living on an island. Then Mick reminded him that he'd done that all his life.

Carol Ann and John came as well, and they brought the kids, who had no idea why they were there except they wanted to see the two red-headed babies who, it was promised, would show up.

Addie Becker was there, along with that bigwig, Maurice Fischer. Christopher, thank God, was nowhere to be seen.

Hugh Talbot came with some egg on his face, but it faded when he was reassured that if he'd never called Christopher, who'd called Jill, who'd called Addie, who'd called Herb Bartlett, well, maybe they never would have gotten to the bottom of what really had happened.

Bartlett, of course, made an appearance, as did Rick Fitzpatrick, who didn't seem to mind that the hotshot lawyer had saved the day, as long as the truth had come out, as long as Ben was free.

Fern was not there. After Ben brought Mindy back to Menemsha House, Mindy had told the judge it had all been one big mistake that she'd never meant to happen. Fern became exasperated and announced she was leaving the Vineyard and said Rita and Charlie could take care of the kid if they wanted, they'd done such a good job. She'd even tried to straighten the ruffle on Mindy's dress.

"I guess I'm not much of a mother," she said.

Mindy had kissed her on the cheek and said Fern was like a scallop and that Mindy was the beautiful shell that the scallop had to leave behind.

Fern didn't look like she'd understood, but she seemed grateful Mindy had said it.

After the trial and before the party, Fern called Rita and asked her to forward the money from the sale of the house to her in Caracas. That's when Rita told her there had been no sale, but that when there was, Dave Ashenbach's will had left everything in trust to Mindy, so she wouldn't see a dime. In charge of the trust was Bruce Mallotti, one of Ashenbach's own.

There were others at the party, too: Hattie Phillips and Jesse Parker; Dick Bradley and his wife, Ginny, from Vineyard Haven; and all of the fishermen who'd worked with Dave Ashenbach. They'd known all along about the pending trial, they'd heard gossip last fall, but they'd had the Yankee decorum to not stand in judgment, though Hattie admitted they'd "known damn well Ben wouldn't do that."

Ben was on his second beer that was sliding down nicely. He was thinking of Louise, his once-beloved, who would have been proud he'd stood his ground, and proud that his new wife had had the guts to defend him at all costs. He figured she'd also be pleased that he'd decided to buy Ashenbach's house to use for his add-ons to Menemsha. Until Sea Grove was a reality, he'd have to rent the property. Bruce Mallotti agreed with those conditions and agreed that the money would be placed in Mindy's trust fund.

He smiled and set the bottle down, as Jill approached him. Addie and Maurice trailed close behind.

"Honey," she said, kissing his cheek, "I've got good news for a change."

He looked from Jill to Addie to Fischer, then back to his wife. "Oh, no," he said. "I have the feeling I'm going to lose you again."

Jill laughed. "Two days a week? Do you think you can stand it?"

He listened and waited because he'd gotten so good at it.

"Maurice has offered me what's called a franchise. A twice-a-week segment on the evening news."

"Network?" Ben asked, because that was the one word he'd learned from Jill that had any clout.

"Yes, of course."

He took another drink of beer. "Tell me more."

Maurice stepped forward. "Apparently your wife does not like 'fluff' pieces, as she calls them. So she'll get news. A regular segment about heroes. Something our country needs more of every day."

"I said I'd only do it if the heroes were kids," Jill said, her eyes dancing. "And of course, if you agree."

"What about Edwards?"

"He'll be doing a sports show. Different days, different times."

He took her hand. "Then I think this is wonderful."

"That I'll be away from you two nights a week?"

"Hey," he said with a shrug, "it'll keep the fires burning, don't you think?" He had long since given up on the idea that she'd want to be there every night, with a pot of clam chowder on the stove and a fire in the grate.

"It would be fun if you came," Rita said to Mindy as she bundled the twins and set them in the carriage. "Ben would like it, I'm sure."

Mindy shrugged.

"His grandkids will be there."

"They're little."

"Hey!" Rita said with a laugh. "You were little once, too." She adjusted the blanket under little Olivia's chin, then made sure that Oliver, beside her, was tucked in as well.

"Is Dr. Reynolds going to be there?" Mindy asked.

"I don't think so. But she's agreed to stay on the island for a while, so you'll still get to see her. If you want."

"Yeah," Mindy nodded, "I like her okay."

Rita smiled. "That reminds me," she said, "I bought something for you."

Mindy looked surprised. "It isn't my birthday."

Rita shrugged and walked to the closet in the living room. "Don't need a birthday to get a present around here," she said, and pulled out a box that was wrapped in paper with big red and yellow and purple flowers. A pouf of curly purple ribbon was perched on the top. She handed the box to Mindy.

"For me?" Mindy repeated.

"Yeah, special for you. Now hurry up. We don't want to be late. It's not every day Charlie Rollins throws a party."

Mindy stopped before opening it and looked square at Rita. "You ought to marry him, you know. He's really nice."

"Yeah, well, one thing at a time. But if you can keep a secret, I've decided I'm going to marry him this summer. And you can be a bridesmaid."

The little girl's smile grew wide. Then she took off the ribbon and tore off the paper. Inside, looking up at her, was a beautiful red-headed Raggedy Ann.

Rita folded her arms and felt a rush of warmth. She figured it was Kyle, saying she'd done good.

About the Author

A native New Englander, Jean Stone loves doing the research for her novels set on Cape Cod and the Islands. While working on *Off Season,* she was marooned on Martha's Vineyard by a hurricane; a later trip to Nantucket had her stranded by a coastal snowstorm. Undaunted, her next book (her ninth) will also take place on the Vineyard. She lives in western Massachusetts.